VOLUME TWO
The Ozark Mountains Historical Fiction Series

THE
MIGHTY CEDAR

A FRIEND LOVETH
AT ALL TIMES

JOANN KLUSMEYER

innovo
PUBLISHING

Published by Innovo Publishing, LLC
www.innovopublishing.com
1-888-546-2111

Providing Full-Service Publishing Services for Christian Authors, Artists &
Ministries: Books, eBooks, Audiobooks, Music, Screenplays, Film & Curricula

**THE OZARK MOUNTAINS
HISTORICAL FICTION SERIES
FOR ADULTS**

VOLUME 2

**THE MIGHTY CEDAR
&
A FRIEND LOVETH AT ALL TIMES:**
An Anthology of Southern Historical Fiction

ISBN: 978-1-61314-697-2

Cover Design & Interior Layout: Innovo Publishing, LLC

Printed in the United States of America
U.S. Printing History
First Edition: 2021

Has God called you to create a Christian book, ebook, audiobook, music album,
screenplay, film, or curricula? If so, visit the ChristianPublishingPortal.com to learn
how to accomplish your calling with excellence. Learn to do everything yourself, or
hire trusted Christian Experts from our Marketplace to help.

CONTENTS

The old man was on his deathbed after a long and productive life, and his aged wife sat in vigil beside his bed. Her own life had been spent in service to her husband, to others, and, when God insisted, to Him. She had one request as she neared the end of her life, and that request was not for something for herself. It was for her granddaughter. THE MIGHTY CEDAR shares the hopes, dreams, and final acceptance of a young girl who follows and sustains her husband through a long life of service while he follows his own calling. The trip leads to another state and another culture, but wherever he went, she would go, and his God was also her God, for as long as there was breath.

Marybeth became entangled in her best friend's life, seeing no way to free herself and be loosed from a promise that attached itself to her like a bandage to a wound. She struggled to make sense of life by picking up the burden left by a friend, and the duty caused by the problem blinded her to the answer.

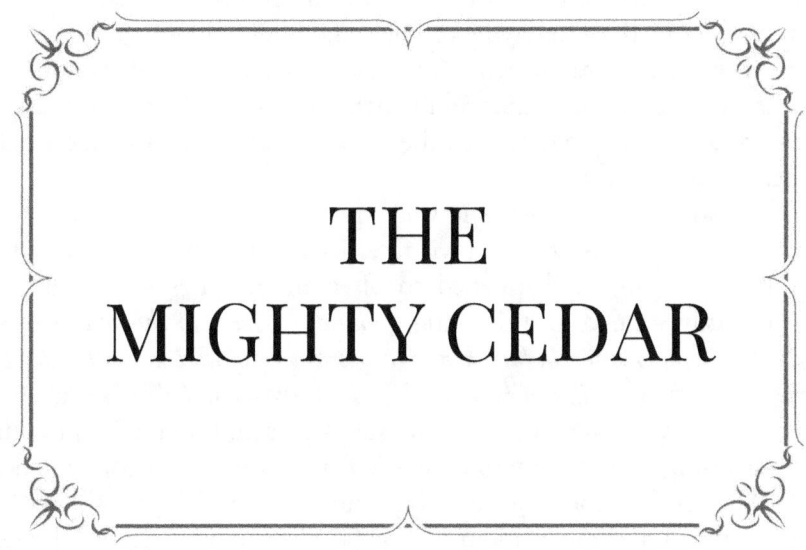

THE MIGHTY CEDAR

1

The old man on the bed groaned and shifted slightly on his bed in the dark room. The woman, though herself half asleep, responded in a reflex which had been perfected through the many years by his side.

"Marion? Are you all right, Marion?"

When she received no response, she arose and lighted the kerosene lamp beside the bed. Its light made shadows that deepened the creases and hollows of his face, giving his pale features a golden glow.

She placed a hand on his forehead. Not that she expected to learn anything about his condition from this touch, but it seemed the thing to do. It was what she had always done, and there was comfort for them both in this simple act. It was his need and her instant response. It said, "I'm here with you," and that act was its own comfort, be the malady a fever, or chills or just a bad day.

Yes, it was necessary to place her hand on his forehead.

The man did not acknowledge the hand. It had been a part of his life for nigh onto seventy years. To him, it had always meant that he was not alone, and if he was not alone, it meant that she was with him, and he had access to her strength as well as his own, and therefore, together, they had enough strength to go on.

The groan sounded again... actually, not a groan but a low moan. A cool cloth might give him ease. The kitchen was dark, and her own unsteadiness precluded the carrying of the oil lamp with her, so she lit the stub of a candle that was laying on the stand beside the lamp.

The match flared its flame and released its puff of sulfur odor. The candlewick caught the flame and the paraffin odor of the candle masked the sulfur of the match. She blew the flame from the matchstick she held in her wrinkled hand.

As she left the room, she walked by the tall mirror on the wall and caught a glimpse of her own face, its wrinkles highlighted in the candlelight. Again, as happened so often in her later years, she was momentarily startled into thinking, *How did I get into this old woman's body? I remember smooth, fair skin, dark curling hair, and steady footsteps. I remember them so well, but how did I get into this wrinkled old body?*

It was not stated as a concern, just a passing thought. A puzzling and surprising thought, but of no particular importance or consequence.

She set the candle on the table, and in its feeble light, she took a clean cloth from a drawer and moistened it in a pan of water. She did not really need the light of the candle at all. After more than sixty years of habit, she could have performed this duty with her eyes closed.

She brought the candle and the damp cloth back to the man's bedside. After blowing out the candle, she began to stroke the fevered forehead with the cool cloth. At her touch, the strained facial muscles relaxed.

"Esther?"

"I'm here, Marion."

"Let's take a walk up to the top of the bluff and watch the sunrise."

A game. A word game they had developed between them when the ability to climb to the top of the bluff was a thing of the past, but the memory of the sunrise was still vivid. He must be better to want to enter the little game.

"Sure, Marion. Just let me go change my slippers."

She waited. There was no responding remark, only another moan and a spell of erratic breathing. Her attention was caught by the sound. His words had been just a reflex, she decided, and she continued to stroke his head and to talk with the only other Presence in the room.

"I got'a thank You, Lord, for lettin' me stay here to tend to 'im in his last days. It was the one thing I felt confident You'd give me. I was always there when he needed someone. 'Member when I promised before You that I'd be doin' that?" She hesitated to add, 'till death do us part'.

She left the bedside to pull her comfortable old rocker nearer to him. The chair was not far away, but the weight of it took her strength and made her knees shaky. She sat down gratefully.

"Shouldn't be too much longer, Lord. Time and again, back through the past years, I thought it'd be me bein' the one first to go, but You pulled me through every ailment. Not wantin' to tell You Your business, Lord, but quick as he's gone, I'm ready to go. But it's whatever You want, and You know that, Lord."

She rocked back and forth as she looked at the black square of window behind the sheer curtain ruffles. No moon at all tonight. "Yea, though I walk through the valley," she quoted to herself to bring a bit of comfort. Her eyes were too dim to read, but the words from the Good Book committed to memory years ago had never failed her.

There had been many valleys along the way. She knew in her heart that this one would be the last one for her to walk beside her husband. "I appreciate You lettin' me be here, Lord. If I wasn't here, the takin' care'a him would fall on that precious little Jane Ann, and her with that new baby and all. She'd do it, though. For her granddad, she'd do whatever she could, but it's for me to do, and I thank You for leaving me here to do it."

Jane Ann, such a sweet child she was. She was around a lot when she was a tiny girl, and then other things came into her life. But here she was, back again, with that wonderful husband of hers, and she was helping him pastor the little church in River Bend.

It was the same little church that she and Marion had dreamed of and built and together had shepherded for more than twenty five years. They were years that had rolled past so quickly.

The old eyes closed, and the head eased onto the pillow on the back of the rocker, the pillow that was shaped to the exact size of her head. It was a pillow to dream on and relive old memories.

The years evaporated and the wrinkled skin disappeared. Her small, sturdy legs were smooth, and the tight curls bounced on her head. She slid from her bed in the cool, sod house located on the plains of Kansas, and when her tiny feet hit the thick, braided rug beside her bed, she leaped and bounded out the door, leaving it swinging on its leather hinges. Her exuberance propelled her into the golden Kansas sunshine.

"Come on, Esther. Let's go pick the flowers," came the voice of Louis, her brother just three years older than she. Her favorite brother, he was, and out of the ten of her mother's children, it was to him she felt the closest.

Together they ran, barefoot, across the rolling, grassy knolls to pick the morning's offering of wine-cup blossoms from the crawling green vine. The small, reddish-purple flower bowls of the plant petals glistened freshly in the morning sun.

With hands full of the fresh flowers, they raced back to the soddy to put them in the cracked cup that was set aside for that purpose.

The plains of Kansas were exciting and different from the woodlands of eastern Missouri, where she had been born. The train ride had brought them part of the way to the homestead claim in Kansas, and the covered wagon had finished the trip. It had all happened only months ago... at least not more than a year.

The happy scene played itself through her mind as she sat in the darkness, rocking quietly in the log cabin in central Arkansas. The little settlement called River Bend had been her home for a half a century. The tiny town was nestled among the hills within the sound of the noisy Tuscalara River, sometimes murmuring, often roaring, on its way to the Mississippi.

The scenes of childhood in her mind were still vivid, and she could even feel the coolness of the early morning soil against her small feet, though the sun would soon heat the baked earth to a searing hardness.

The family soddy in Kansas had been large, as soddies go, but still the beds had touched each other in their closeness, and from her own bed, crowded with sisters, she could thrust an exploring toe and touch the wood box beside the stove.

Their few changes of clothing were strung on the lines across the bed, and the doll she shared with her sisters hung on the wall by the cord around its neck. So many things she remembered.

She remembered happiness. There were inconveniences, to be sure, but she chose not to think of them.

Except sometimes. There were the driving rainstorms, dagger raindrops sheeting across the plains that caused water to flow into the sod house, creating a mud hole underfoot. Thick braided rugs were put into the mud to make a place, though soggy wet, where one could stand when absolutely necessary. Children spent rainy days on the bed, playing with their few toys or with string games on their fingers or re-reading the few books.

Overhead, a ceiling of tacked cheesecloth had been attached to keep spiders and other insects from dropping onto the bed or into the soup kettle. The ceiling of cheesecloth was washed when the sun came out and then put back. The rugs were also put outside as soon as the rain stopped. In this treeless prairie, the drying rack was a massive pile of deer antlers on which the clothing was spread. Or it might be a heap of tumbleweeds, having rotted themselves off at the base and been blown by the wind into mountains, coming to lodge against any solid structure.

She knew there was not precious wood to burn to cook the meals but that "hay cats", made of the prairie grass, tightly twisted, would supplement the buffalo chips that she and her brother gathered. She knew these things, but they did not worry her from inside her protected cocoon of childhood. Her mother took care of difficulties, as mothers do. All that Esther could remember of that period was the fun.

Kansas was a lot different from the land that surrounded her present cabin. Here, there were mountains, tall trees, bluffs, and wide, swift streams of water. There were vines that grew across the paths and small animals that hid in the bushes. So different.

In Kansas, her older brothers took the gun and a bag of shot and came back with rabbits or maybe a deer. Here, the rabbits came into the garden and ate your lettuce, and the deer nibbled the blossoms off the yard shrubs. So very different.

They had spent less than two years in the soddy. By then, her father had earned enough money by working for others to build a house out of wood for his family. The new house was a lot dryer, but it wasn't as warm when the Kansas snowstorms came.

Back then, neighbors settled around them. Neighbors with children… and then there was a school. It was a wonderful school with books and a blackboard, slates and chalk, and songs to be sung in the mornings. Games were played in the schoolyard. Life was wonderful, free and open.

And there were churches. Her father, a licensed minister, held services in the church. Such a wonderful life!

The old man on the bed beside her seemed to be resting peacefully, and Esther knew she should lie down and save her strength. Perhaps she'd get a little sleep… but she was reluctant. Journeys into the past brought comfort, and the pictures in her mind were as clear as when they were seen through her still-young eyes.

She remembered her friend from school and church. A good friend, whose name was Desta. Desta also came from a large family, as did nearly everyone. Esther let her mind wander with pleasure through the remembered fun the girls had that summer she spent at Desta's house. There had been such a lot of work!

The friend's family owned a large field of wheat, and Desta's brothers worked hard in the fields. The wheat ripened all at once, and many "hands" were hired to help with the reaping, and Esther and Desta helped to prepare the meals. Platters of eggs, sheets of biscuits, and skillets of gravy were set on the harvest table. There were stacks of fried chicken at every meal. There was potato salad, and potatoes fried with sweet onions, and green cabbages and squashes were steamed and fruit pies were baked.

Looking back now, she smiled. She probably should have looked closer at Desta's oldest brother, because he was certainly looking at her. His shyness, however, kept him from speaking to her, and all she saw of him was when he came in, hungry and hot, to eat his meals and then return to the fields.

"Yea, though I walk through the valley." Esther had not known that after that sunny mountaintop of a summer, she would walk through her first dark valley. Her friend Desta was well and happy one month and was in the church graveyard the next month. Quick and deadly came the diseases.

Years before, she had lost a brother and a sister in infancy, but the death of her friend was her first long, dark valley, and the Lord had been with her, just as He had promised.

It was several years later that Desta's oldest brother, Marion, found her again. By then, the family had proved out the homestead in western Kansas, sold it, and had moved to the big city of Topeka. Marion found her there and was still too shy to ask permission to court her. What he could not bear to say to her face, he had managed to write in a letter. They were married in the church at Topeka, Kansas.

A small smile formed on her lips. She had never liked his name and had commented to Desta on the strangeness of it. Desta had explained. It seemed that, being the first grandson on both sides, he was named after his two grandfathers. There was Allen Alexander Gilbert on his mother's side, and Francis Marion Francisco on his father's side. It seemed that Francis Marion was the name of a revolutionary war officer nicknamed "The Swamp Fox." Without doubt, he was a brave soldier, but should his name be carried by the family through the next five generations? It seemed so.

Esther had thought how nice it would be if they had thought of the "Allen" grandfather first, but she was glad they had not chosen "Francis". His family had dropped the first part of their last name three generations ago, and he was given the name of Marion Allen Sisco.

Somehow, Marion rose above the strangeness of his name. He had always been handy with tools. Broken things got mended, buildings were built, wobbly chairs became solid and wagon wheels stayed firmly attached to wagon axels.

He went to work for a company that made wagons. Good, solid strong wagons, and he made good salary. Plenty to live on. It could have been a good life.

"Oh, I'm sorry, Lord. I didn't mean it to sound critical of what I know now to be Your plan. Wouldn't want You to hold against me these ramblin' thoughts. I'll be seein' You before too long, and I want everything to be straight between You and me."

"Esther?"

The bony hand slid toward her over the patchwork quilt that her own fingers had pieced so many years ago. His fingers groped toward hers, though he did not open his eyes. She clasped his hand.

He sighed deeply. "Esther, you're gonna hafta come along with me. I'll not be able to be comin' back to you."

He don't know what he's saying, she told herself and hurriedly assured him, "Don't you worry yourself none, Marion. I'll be comin' right along behind you, like I always did." She stroked the gnarled fingers. If he could hear her, which she doubted, she hoped he would be comforted through whatever it was that was making him uneasy.

It had been the truth. She had always come right along behind. Not that she was always willing, but she had promised him and she had promised God, and she had kept her promise to both of them.

She did, however, have words to say about it. "But, Marion, we're doin' so good here. Earnin' a good pay like you are, we can buy us a house in no time." She had quit talking, though, when she saw the young husband was hearing none of what she said.

That copy of delinquent property tax listing he had brought home from the courthouse had totally occupied his mind.

"See here? There's eighty acres. How long would it take to save up for eighty acres'a Kansas soil? This here is for sale for the unpaid taxes, and we can buy it now."

She had countered weakly, "But we live here, and you're doin' so good. Do you have to have land to farm on? Couldn't we live here in town with our friends and everyone?"

He looked at her as though she had asked if he really had to have breath to breathe. Physical pain had clutched her chest. She just couldn't leave Kansas. The city was settling so fast. Her family, the church, everything. Surely he'd change his mind when he realized what they would be giving up.

"We can buy this right now," he had continued. "I can make us a new wagon and get an extra team, and we can make the trip down there."

She remembered the stinging tears that had sprung up in her eyes. She had been unable to respond and had left the room. He didn't notice, so absorbed he was with the listing.

Arkansas! Why would anyone want to go to a place like Arkansas? Esther's heart sunk. Her Marion was a patient man, but he was also a stubborn man, and when he started on a task, nothing could turn him aside. She had finally decided that patience and stubbornness were first cousins! He stayed with a job until it was finished. That was a good thing, and it was also a bad thing. Esther knew at that moment, as sure as the sun passed overhead, she would be going to Arkansas.

She heard his voice in the other room. He didn't realize she had gone away. He said to the walls, "Now, eighty acres, that'd be a good-sized farm for one man with the help of a son or two." His head, crowned with a mop of thick black hair, nodded in complete agreement with himself.

Esther walked away from the neat little house on a neat street in the civilized town of Topeka, Kansas. She could look around her and almost believe that nothing was going to happen. That her world was still intact. That life would go on as usual, and nothing was going to tear it apart.

But she knew. Deep inside her, she knew.

"But, Lord, why?" she argued uselessly. A voice within her promised, "I lead you in the path of righteousness for My name's sake," and she had answered, "You win, Lord, when You put it that way."

So from then on, after that short walk to the end of the block and back, she did not struggle. She did, however, remember Gideon and the way he had tested the Lord with the fleece. When he wasn't sure God knew what He was asking of him, or perhaps when he doubted his own understanding, Gideon requested the wool he left outside to be wet with dew and the grass to be dry. God had honored his test with sopping wet wool. If it was all right for Gideon to do that, then she could do it, too. Couldn't she?

When she entered the house, he was still studying the property description, not aware that she had returned, nor that she had even gone. He was also not aware of the torment within her.

He continued, "Trip like that'd be hard on wheels. Could make a place on the underside of the wagon to take along a spare. Yep, I could do that."

It was time for the test. Esther took a deep breath and questioned, "How much of the furniture can we take in the wagon after we get the pump organ loaded?"

"Pump organ? Hmmmm."

Esther held her breath. Without the pump organ, she did not intend to go. It had cost too much and had taken too long to get, and she would not go without it. She needed the organ. Her fingers needed the feel of the cool, ivory keys, and her soul needed the sound of the notes. Marion could understand that. She waited, her heart pounding.

"It'll be easy," he announced, and her heart sank. She should have known, with his ability to solve problems, this one would be swept away as inconsequential.

"It'll be easy. We'll just take two wagons. I'll drive one, and you can drive the other one, and we can take everything we own. Of course, we could never leave your pump organ behind. Likely there'd be a chance to sell the other wagon once we get there."

Esther knew then, as Gideon of old must have known, that she would hesitate no longer. God had spoken, and she would go.

During the weeks that followed, she stored sights and feelings within her mind, visits with her family, activities at church and around town, but woven through it all, she made plans. This would go, and that would stay. She knew the final decision on every household item would be hers, and she would be ready.

The Arkansas property had a house and a barn, so the paper said. She wondered, absently, why property of such value had been abandoned, but she said nothing. What would it accomplish, and what would it change? But a house was a house, and she owned nothing that she did not need; in the end therefore, everything must go.

Two months on the road. At least, that was what she'd prepare for. There would be the daily living during those weeks, and that would be her concern. It was what a woman did.

When it was told to the woman what must be done, then it was up to her to see that it got done as comfortably as possible. Food when they were hungry, clean clothes, protection from the elements... these things would be up to her.

So she took two sheets of paper. The organ and everything that would not be needed during the trip could be solidly packed into one wagon. Food, clothing, bedding, plus all the tools needed for repair of the wagons, provisions for the horses (four of them?), and what else? She left the sheets of paper on the table, so she could add to them as she remembered things.

Marion whistled in his tuneless way as he went happily about his preparation. His money had been paid for the property, and his heart was already on his eighty-acre Arkansas farm. In time, the new wagons, clad in fresh paint, stood in the yard.

Like Noah of old, with the unfinished ark in his yard for years, Marion's wagons filled the tiny yard of the neat little house in Topeka, Kansas, for the next weeks.

Being a wagon builder by trade, Marion was in his element. The best (absolutely the best) and strongest wheels were solidly attached to the axle-tree, and the pins and bolts were oiled and tightened to a turn.

Esther measured, arranged and rearranged, drawing the outline of each piece as it would be placed in the wagon. The two sheets of paper became many more. She washed and set aside the older quilts destined to wrap the pump organ to protect it from the oilskin covering and the guy-ropes that would stabilize it. She packed her music, several hymnals and the embroidered scarf she always kept on the organ. She arranged them in a box and set it aside. These would go on the wagon first.

Seeking settled weather, they decided on late spring. After the April rains and before the July heat. May was a good month, and perhaps there would be time for late crops to be planted on the new land. At least something to get them through the first winter. How cold would it be in Arkansas?

The old woman on the rocker drew her shawl more closely around her shoulders at the thought of that first winter and all the other winters she had spent in River Bend. Blizzards on the Kansas plains were fast and furious, but here, the winters in the valley produced a damp and penetrating cold that seemed to seep inside each joint, stealing its warmth and moisture, leaving chills and creaky sounds in knees and necks. They were part of winter.

She looked anxiously toward the dark squares of the windows as though she could see the approach of fall and then the winter cold to follow. This could be the first winter she would spend alone in the cabin.

The light of the lamp shone on the old man. His pale lids were closed, and a dark shadow of beard outlined his chin and jaw. He was resting, and rest was what he needed.

Esther's memory of those last weeks in Kansas was vague and sketchy. Somehow, the wagons were loaded, and the families came to say goodbye. Tears were shed, fond words were spoken and small gifts of food or some usable item were pressed upon them.

Esther drove the first wagon, pulled by a matched set of bay mares. The new, metal-rimmed wheels ground into the gravel of the street, and the glistening animals turned and faced into the rising sun. She adjusted her sunbonnet and waved again to those she left behind, but she did not turn back.

To turn and look back would be to start the tears, and it was too late for them. But then, it had always been too late for the tears, because there was never a time that this trip would not happen. She had tested God, and He had honored her test. She looked at the expensive Swiss pendant watch her older sister had given her and saw the time was exactly 9:00.

Marion's voice yelling a forceful "Giddap" told her that her husband was now on the road behind her. She was alone with her thoughts. Her first wedding anniversary would be celebrated on the road, somewhere in Arkansas. Marion had not mentioned it and probably had given it no thought. There was something else that had not been mentioned, and he knew nothing of it. It had been her secret.

A smile played at the corner of her mouth, even now, for after more than sixty years, she remembered how she had felt. She had sat alone on the bouncing buckboard, but she was not alone. She had not told Marion, because he didn't need another thing to be concerned with, and it would have changed nothing, anyway.

Many babies had been born in Arkansas, and hers would be just one more. And, truth to be told, it was far easier for her to make the trip with the baby within her where it was, rather than lying in a basket beside her.

2

Now they were finally on the road. As Esther directed the horses toward Missouri, the sun climbed warmly overhead, and with the passage of miles, her annoyance began to evaporate. Her petty concerns and worries were melting and easing out of her mind. Though the Lord had insisted on "leading her in the paths" where she preferred not to go, He was also "restoring her soul." It would be all right. She knew it would be.

They had stopped in the shade of one of Kansas' few trees to eat the sandwiches and fruit they had brought for their lunch. They drank from the tepid water in the fruit jar and were on the way again.

According to their plan, at late afternoon, they would begin to look for a farmhouse to make their night camp nearby. Water was not always available on the plains unless a farm was close by.

The Daltons, just fifteen miles outside of Topeka, welcomed them like beloved relatives, insisting they join the family for supper. Their horses were turned into the pasture, and the evening was spent talking and singing, but morning saw them on the road. They had fresh water in the fruit jars, hot biscuits and freshly boiled eggs in their lunch baskets... and many good wishes in their ears.

Esther's pendant watch told her it was now 5:30 am and a half an hour before daylight. It would be a long, hot Kansas day. By noon, she was sweaty and flushed, and there were no trees in sight under which to rest while they ate. They sat on the dusty ground in the scant shade of the wagon while the horses stood in the traces and switched flies.

After he ate, Marion extracted the limber wooden ribs that converted the wagon to the silhouette of the Conestoga. The ends were inserted in their cleats and bent overhead to create the framework. An oilskin tarpaulin was stretched over all. It was still hot, but the cover provided welcome shade.

Marion called a halt in mid-afternoon and attached his horses to the rear corners of her wagon, joining her in the shade of her canopy. Now they could ride together.

"Tell me, Marion, what is it gonna be like? Talk to me about how it'll be."

She knew she was not being fair. Shy Marion would have preferred to attempt to fly rather than to spin the kind of talk she wanted to hear, but he tried.

"Well, the weather, it likely won't be too different. Got two good teams here, if somethin' don't happen to any of 'em. Got two good wagons and likely could sell one. There's sure to be a demand for a good, solid wagon." He paused, watching the sleek, sweaty rumps of the bays, plodding their steady steps ahead of him.

She was relentless. "Tell me about the people. How big is the town, did the paper say? Will they like us?"

"People are people, down inside themselves. Out'a the whole town, there'll be some that likes us. Likely some that don't. We'll just stay out'a the way of them people."

"Will you plant wheat?"

"Likely so, that bein' what I know best. There'll be other grains and local crops. Just hafta learn about 'em when we get there."

The late afternoon heat became oppressive, even though it was only the middle of May. The air was heavy and still. Shreds of cirrus clouds decorated the sky overhead, but the western horizon behind them was darkening. The late afternoon sun disappeared into the blackness of the cloudbank, and a dusky darkness spread over the prairie. A storm was coming, and spring storms came quickly.

Marion searched the horizon for protection, and there was none. He stopped the wagons and drew them up side by side. The horses were tied securely on the downwind side of the wagons.

While Esther watched, Marion rechecked the double layer of the oilskin tarp covering the organ, testing the tautness of the knots tied to the wagon cleats. All was solid.

Then the first, huge drops, forerunners of the storm, began to plunk and plop on the rounded top of the tarpaulin over her head. Like a drum roll, the tapping of the drops increased into a deafening staccato as he climbed in beside her. His shirt was wet, and the mop of black hair was plastered to his forehead as rivulets of water poured down his face. It had been necessary to take care of the horses first, then himself. It was the way of her husband.

From the traveling provisions, she had already selected a dry shirt, knowing he would be wet, and she held it ready for him to put on as soon as he wiped the water from his eyes. For a little while, he would be more comfortable, and it was something she could do for him. It was the way of women.

Fiery bolts of lightning split the sky, momentarily lighting the interior of the wagon only to plunge it into darkness again. Gusts of wind flung themselves against the canvas, rocking the wagon furiously.

It was a time for holding tightly to each other in the safe darkness while the storm raged overhead. In their closeness, it was a time for confidences, and she knew she would never be able to wait any longer. Besides, he had a right to know.

"It's so good to be here where it's safe and dry. So good for all three of us."

"Three of us?"

"Well, one of us is very, very young and won't remember it, but he should be born in Arkansas on your new land."

"Esther! Are you sure?"

"How could I not be sure?"

"But how do you feel?"

"I feel wonderful. We wanted children, and we will have 'em."

The storm raged on for more than two hours, but the waterproof canvas held. A legitimate darkness had fallen by the time the storm passed. The fury of the wind was gone now, and it was now possible to light the kerosene lantern to see to peel the rest of the boiled eggs and unwrap the buttered biscuits.

Esther ate the bread and the eggs and drank the water, and she thought, *What I really want is beans. I want tender, brown beans, simmered slowly in ham and served hot in thick, fragrant broth.*

That was what she really wanted, but she may as well have desired a piece of the moon for all the good it would do her. Slow-cooking beans on a campfire did not lend themselves well to a moving wagon.

It was four days later, after entering the scrubby tree growths in Missouri, that she was able to satisfy that craving. The weather was hot and dry, and they had started so early, it seemed only fair to stop early. A river was handy, and a small mountain provided the shelter of a shallow cave.

Marion set up the tripod and built a fire as Esther washed the beans and the ham hocks purchased in the last town. The horses were staked in the tall, tender spring grass.

It was ten o'clock that night, long after dark, before the beans were tender and an hour later before they were thick-brothed and full-flavored.

Esther knew she would never forget that night. At midnight, they sat at the mouth of the shallow cave and ate bowls of beans by the flickering light of the coal oil lantern. The sounds were of running water, night insects and the movement of horses, the snorting of their noses as they cropped the grass.

It had been a magical night. As she fell asleep on the ground, the words surrounded her, "I will fear no evil, for Thou art with me."

And now, as she remembered that night, more than sixty years ago, she knew that no beans had ever tasted so good as those. Her wrinkled face, even now, formed into a small smile as she remembered Marion's surprise at being served beans for breakfast instead of the skillet-baked biscuits, but he had said nothing as he ate them. That was the way of Marion.

Later that day, they reached the road that would turn south, and it would take them into Arkansas. The first hills were small, rounded ones, and the graveled roads made their uneventful way up one side and down the other.

Then, the next day, the hills became steeper, and the roads jogged to the east or the west to skirt around them. Finally, there came the wider, higher, steeper mountains that could not be gone around.

The team of grays hitched to the second wagon pulled and struggled with the weight of the pump organ. As they climbed the hills, Marion walked beside the wagon, carrying a flat-edged chock of wood to "scotch" the wheel as an additional brake, so the horses could catch their breath for the next lunge forward.

Then, finally, it became necessary to attach the tongue of the second wagon to the rear of the first wagon and drive the teams together to share the weight. Esther, from her seat in the front wagon, learned to shout encouragement to the team to ease them past the rough places, and she learned to handle the wheel brake as they topped the hill to slow the pace down into the next valley.

Traveling days became shorter to spare the horses, and there was often time to shoot small game for the evening meal or to pull a mud turtle or two from the many small streams that ran between the mountains.

The activity and the mountain air made them hungry all the time, and the tripod that held the kettle and the grill for the iron skillet were well used.

Outside the town of Fayetteville, they camped over for a whole day to rest the horses and, to a lesser degree, themselves. Marion went into the town to replenish the supply of grain for the hard-working animals and came back with a small bag of chocolate bonbons. Esther had eaten bonbons many times after that, but none had tasted so good as those she ate that day.

After Fayetteville, there was nothing but hills, and they were always either going up or coming down, and both were a severe strain on the horses. They had been seventeen days on the road.

Already, life on the road had begun to play tricks with her mind, and Esther felt that she had been traveling for years and would likely be doing so the rest of her life. In the evenings, she sorted, repacked and rearranged the content of the wagon. She washed clothes in the streams and hung them from convenient low limbs on the trees to dry. She shook the dust of the road from the bedding and cooked something to be eaten cold for lunch the next day.

Her tiny world moved along each day, a separate universe wrapped around herself, her husband and their new person and around the wagons and the animals. Her contentment reminded her that "the Lord was the shepherd," and she "would not want." What else was there to want for that she did not have?

There were the mountains to think about, and they were all around her. The horses struggled up the ruggedness of the tree-lined roads with their weary plodding, only to descend the precarious slopes, fighting the downpull of the weight of the wagons. Esther leaned her weight into wheel brakes.

When Marion called to her, she lowered the bar, which forced itself against the wheel, causing it to slow. Behind her, he manned the brake on the second wagon. There were those terrifying times, however, that Marion wanted her to leave the wagon and walk, and he ran beside the team with the chock block.

He was tensely ready to fling the block in front of the wagon wheel in the event the downpull of the wagon threatened to overrun the horses. There was always the danger of a horse tripping or of a hoof landing on a rolling rock. He had explained to her that, in the event of a runaway, the loss of the horses and wagons did not compare to the loss of herself, and she must walk clearly and safely behind.

They were two days south of Fayetteville, and she walked a lot.

Then there were the times that the road seemed to have been hacked from the edge of a mountain, with the terrain seeming to go straight up on the right hand and straight down on the left.

In these places, the road was hardly wider than the wagon wheels and would have required expert maneuvering to get past each other, if they met an oncoming traveler. But they never met another wagon, and they never met another person. Early on a morning, they could see small plumes of smoke dotting about the trees on the mountains. Cabins, certainly.

A week south of Fayetteville they descended an extra long, totally exhausting mountain and saw ahead of them a long, green valley. Trees had been cleared back from the road, and a few houses were visible.

A small, crystal-clear stream ran the length of the valley, murmuring and chuckling as it flowed over and around the rocks in the stream bed. They had crossed many nameless streams and brooks, but this one had a name. A small, hand-painted sign proclaimed it to be Pigeon Creek.

They saw people. Fresh-washed clothes hung on a clothesline, and plowing was done in the fields beside the road. Children laughed and squealed in their play, and the dogs barked at a pair of strange wagons traveling the gravel road in front of their masters' homes. Strange, foreign-smelling wagons and horses. Esther's heart leaped within her at the sight of a town. It was not Topeka, but it was a town.

There was a store selling supplies. Bushels of oats, dried beans, leather for repair of harnesses and kerosene for lamps… all were available at the store that was built against the mountain from smooth, water-washed native stone.

The store had flour, cornmeal and sugar. It had molasses, pocket knives and safety pins. It was a town indeed, and it had a name. It was most appropriately called Mountainburg.

They stayed in Mountainburg for two days, resting and talking with those who gathered around the wagon, eager for any news brought to them from any other place. Too soon, it was time to go. It caused Esther a physical pain to leave this valley. Why could not their land have been here? Why, Lord? But God did not answer her pleading question.

Restocked and refortified, they started up the switchback road leading out of Mountainburg Valley. The road would have been almost too steep for humans on foot if it had gone straight up the mountain, hence the sign that warned of "hairpin curves".

The track of rutted red clay climbed, gradually at first, along the foot of the mountain, then twisted in a "sheep-nose curve" and gradually climbed the other way. Back and forth up the mountain it zigzagged in a way that made the distance at least four times as long, but at least it was possible to climb it. How many more of these would there be? Later, she was glad she had not known.

The road angled east with its destination to be Little Rock, the capitol of Arkansas. Esther noticed the humidity of the valleys, so heavy after the dry winds of Kansas. Just the act of breathing seemed to tire her. Marion said it was likely because of the extra passenger she carried, but she wasn't sure. One thing she knew: it wasn't Kansas anymore.

A thought had nibbled at her mind for days. "Marion, lookin' at the land we're passin' through, are you thinkin' there'll be a place flat enough to grow wheat?"

There followed a full two minutes of silence, telling her that Marion had, indeed, considered the same possibility. "Likely not," he finally agreed, "and that'd not be the only thing against growin' wheat. There's a moisture in the air that'd be enough to cause smut or mold in the wheat ears. Could be, though, that this is just the wet time of the year."

"Possibly, but remember we've not been rained on at all since that storm the second day out."

He nodded and was silent. What else was there to say, and talking took energy. Twice, that morning, they had unloaded the first wagon, lashing the tongue of the second wagon to the axle of the first to pull the load up a hill of frightening steepness.

Esther had waited at the top of the hill while Marion went back for the unloaded items. She was glad of the rest and took a short nap under the bed of the wagon that carried her pump organ.

They did not stop in Little Rock but headed on toward Jacksonville, twenty-five miles away. It was then that they first crossed the last river, but they would recross it several times before they reached their destination.

A rusty metal bridge spanned the wide, swift-running Tuscalara River. Esther stared down at it, fascinated by its size and cloudiness, strange after the many clear, sparkling streams they had crossed.

Marion followed her gaze. "If we had us a flat boat or barge, we could likely go the rest of the way on the water," he commented.

She turned to stare at him. "Is this... really...?"

"One and the same!" Marion's grin told her he was eager to get to his land, and the river provided a moving, tangible thread, drawing him onward.

Esther shivered involuntarily. She had made a world around herself and him, the wagons, horses and the road. Just as she had made a world around the little house in Topeka. She resented the approaching town of River Bend, steadily becoming closer, pushing itself into her space.

Marion had no conception of this space she had created. "Yessirree, this river is the one that goes through River Bend. Couldn't hardly be two of the same name, so this'd hafta be it. A mite bigger than I expected, and the water moves a sight faster here than it does in Kansas." He strained to look down into the water. "I'd figure there'd be catfish a'plenty down there, longer'n my arm. If we had time, I'd wet a hook and see. I could do with a good mess of mudcat."

When Esther made no encouraging response, he concluded, "Well, if there's mudcat in there, there'll be some in River Bend. They'll be just as good when we get there."

More mountains. Late on the second day after passing through Little Rock, they reached the top of an exceptionally long mountain. It had been a steady climb since noon, with considerable time spent resting the horses, but now they were on the top. The sun was low in the sky behind them as they looked into the long valley.

There was the river again, threading its silver path between the hills, reflecting blue from the afternoon sky. The last rays of the sun caught the rooftops of a town of considerable size. The buildings were stretched along beside the river and divided by tree-lined streets paved in sun-dried brick. The east side of the river arose sharply into the sky in a massive, blue-topped mountain. The lower part of the mountain was a mosaic of green from the various species of trees, dotted with specks and patches of white and pink. It was a year later before she learned that the white and pink had been dogwood and wild peach blossoms.

The blend of bright and muted colors of the town resembled a quilt spread out for her inspection. A soft breeze wafted away the day's heat and humidity, and she thought, *It's good to be here.* She would have liked to spend the night on the hilltop, but already, he was moving the horses onto the road again, so she said nothing. They needed to use the daylight, and the slope into town would be light travel for the horses after the long pull uphill. Darkness caught them at the edge of the city of Jacksonville.

Several times during that night, Esther was startled awake to the strange sounds of human activity. After weeks of quiet woodlands, animal sounds and the wind in the trees, the noises of the city seemed alien and fearful.

Tomorrow would be spent restocking provisions (for who could guess what would be available in River Bend?), and early the next day, they would travel the remaining twelve miles that would take them to their new home.

Jacksonville was interesting. There was an animal auction, a small hospital with four doctors available, several churches and a livery stable. Judging from the view from the mountaintop, a lot of people lived here, too. Now that it was daylight, the size and activity of the town tended to reassure rather than frighten her.

At the south edge of town, near the road that would take them to River Bend, there was a large, shady meadow, apparently meant for the use of out-of-town shoppers. Horses and mules drawing wagons and buggies, as well as a number of saddle horses, were tied in the shady grove. It seemed to be a good place to spend the night. The river that had been a ribbon of silver when viewed from the mountaintop became a wide, cloudy, whispering thing, and it flowed within yards of their campsite. It was a restless night full of strange sounds, and Esther was glad for the morning to come.

The road to River Bend was a narrow, one-track trail. Meeting a wagon meant both must leave the road with one wheel, giving room for the axles to clear. Not that they met many wagons.

The river and the road stretched companionably together as they traveled east. Small brooks and streams cascaded out of the mountain to be forded.

The road was in such bad repair that they made very poor time. There were rocks and potholes to be avoided and fallen limbs to be removed, but finally they reached the looked-for fork in the road. This fork was the landmark they needed, because it meant their land was very near.

At the fork, a hand-painted sign had been affixed to a tree directly ahead. One arrow pointed to the right to the town of Piney, and the other arrow pointed to the river and River Bend. Because of the dense trees, they were not able to see the bridge until they were beside it.

Yes, it really was a bridge. Maybe. It consisted of boards lashed together and attached to cables. The cables were bolted to large trees on either side of the river. This flimsy web spanned the wide and rolling river, with only another cable as a hand railing.

Marion halted the wagons and walked out onto the bridge, stroking his chin thoughtfully. He stomped on the bridge, rattling the boards and causing the whole thing to sway on its suspending cables.

"Believe you might be able to get yours across," he finally told Esther. "The other'n is gonna take some thought."

Esther looked at the river and shook her head. "I can't take that wagon over that water." She felt her eyes fill with tears of discouragement and exhaustion. "I can't do it, Marion. I'll walk across and wait for you on the other side."

She took a few hesitant steps onto the bridge, then squared her shoulders and marched bravely forward, looking neither to the right or the left, unresponsive to the rattle of the boards under her feet. She climbed to the flat surface of a large rock that gave a clear view of the bridge, and she sat down.

She felt herself totally apart from the problem and unrelated to the man and the two loaded wagons. Her capacity for worry and problem-solving had reached overload, and she felt only the solid surface beneath her and the absence of movement that had been her life for weeks. She sighed and looked out across the water.

Marion wordlessly climbed onto the buckboard of the first wagon and urged the horses forward. They hesitated as they felt the unsteadiness underfoot, but he was insistent, and they moved on a little farther, staring at the water beneath them with rolled-back eyes and flattened ears.

What if the horses decided to bolt? The flimsy bridge would never hold a galloping team.

Her non-involvement suddenly melted, and she sat bolt upright. Words came softly into her frantic mind: "I will fear no evil, for Thou art with me."

"Do you see this evil, Lord? Where are You?"

Marion's steady voice talked to the horses, reassuring, wheedling, caressing, urging them on. Foot by foot, they came. The sway of the bridge as they reached the center of the river was truly frightening, though she herself was safely on the bank. How must it feel to the horses... and to him?

His soothing voice and skillful hand brought them on, inch by inch, and when the first horse stepped onto the bank, Esther realized she was dizzy from holding her breath. She sighed a long sigh of relief and thankfulness. *Thank you, Lord.*

But that was only part of it. Marion walked back across the bridge and began to unload the second wagon of everything except the organ. He crawled under the wagon for a considerable length of time, then crawled back out and loosed the horses. She saw him step onto the bridge, leading a horse with each hand, walking backward away from the wagon and the pump organ. She gasped involuntarily. *He's leaving it behind!* Did she bring the organ this far, only to finally lose it?

The horses reached the center of the bridge, walking calmly and sedately behind their trusted owner. When they were about two thirds of the way across, the wagon began to magically creep forward. He left the horses on the bridge and went back to the wagon, straightening the tongue just little, and then came back to the horses.

With slow steps they continued, and the wagon crawled unsteadily onto the swinging bridge. As the horses stepped off the bridge onto the bank, the wagon was in the center of the bridge over the rushing water. He loosed the horses and let them graze while he took his pulley from the first wagon. Using a small tree as an anchor, he inched the wagon forward with the new, strong rope he had bought in Jacksonville.

Esther was dizzy again, so she consciously forced herself to breathe. The bridge did not sway but held steady beneath him and still as the wagon continued its slow way to the bank.

He loaded boxes from the first wagon into the second, piling everything loosely around the organ, then he hitched the steady team of grays to the empty first wagon and returned for the rest of the load.

By the time everything was across the river, the sun had sunk below the top of the mountains. The matched bay mares were again attached to their wagon, and Marion was consulting the tattered map.

"Follow me," he called to her. "It can't be very far now."

Esther forced herself to ease down from the rock and walk woodenly to the second wagon. With no urging from her, the bays followed the wagon that was disappearing down the lane in front of them.

Massive maple trees intertwined their branches overhead, and squirrels raced up and down the trunks. Where a patch of sunlight hit the ground, flowers sprang up, heavy with blossoms and swaying with visiting butterflies. Pent-up weariness began to settle around her. Almost there. After weeks on the road, she would sleep inside a house tonight. On the floor, most likely, but under a civilized roof.

A sense of responsibility settled on her. *Food*, she thought. They had eaten nothing since breakfast in Jacksonville. What did she have that she could fix quickly, and where would it now be, after the reloading at the river? Her mind refused to settle on a solid thought but hovered vaguely just out of reach.

Now the road had left the grove of maples and was following alongside a sheer wall of rock, extending vertically thirty or more feet into the air. It was like a giant stair step rising up, just a few feet to the left of the road. Sprigs of grass and flowering vines rooted themselves into the stonewall crevasses, decorating the gray face of the rock with bits of color.

The sun had gone down, and dusk was falling fast. She saw a point of light appear in the wagon before her. He had lighted the lantern.

A short distance farther on, the light stopped. Could he be there? Could this actually be the end of the eternal road? The bays plodded steadily on, pulling their wagon alongside the first one and stopping without direction from her.

He helped her down from the wagon, steadying her above her cramped and shaky legs, and together they went toward the house. Maybe it was a house. The door hung awkwardly from one rotted-leather hinge, and the gaping windows held no glass at all.

"Careful, the floor looks bad," he warned, as a rotted board creaked under his own foot. In the distance, a horse whinnied and the four animals attached to the wagons answered enthusiastically. An owl hooted and flapped noisily away.

A look overhead revealed portions of gray sky through the rotting and crumbled shingles. They looked around them in silence. No one would sleep in this house any time soon.

A human voice sounded in the distance. "Hello, the house?"

A pair of lanterns bobbed along together, visible from the paneless window, and a voice called again, "Hello?"

Esther stood in the door of the crumbling house, knowing she was in the midst of a dream and would soon wake up. Marion had called "Hello!" through the window frames in the direction of the bobbing lights.

Strange humans were invading her world. No, this was not her world. She had nothing to do with this crumbling house. She gazed up to reassure herself, and two shining dots of fire looked down at her, turning this way and that. Then she saw another pair of fiery dots. Her eyes adjusted to the dimness, and she saw that the fiery dots were lantern's reflection in the eyes of two enormous rats, longer than her arm.

"Marion!" she screamed, pointing to the rats, and she continued to scream at the top of her voice. She thought, *I'll scream as loud as I can and I'll wake myself up from this dream. I've done it before.* So she screamed and screamed.

Even now, sixty years later, she could remember how she had tried to scream herself awake. Gooseflesh now arose on her wrinkled arms as she remembered her terror. Even though she knew now that her rats were only a pair of harmless possums who had taken over the abandoned cabin, the bumps on her arms refused to go down. That last day on the road had been another "valley of the shadow."

The darkness of that valley was still vivid now, years later, and she stirred, flexing her tired shoulders and settling again into the comfort of the rocker. The old man's breathing was faint but steady. All was well.

Esther remembered how she had thought the people with the lanterns were a part of the horrible dream. A young, feminine voice had answered Marion's response.

"We're neighbors here. Harley heard your horses, and we come down to see if someone got lost. My name's Beatrice. Did you folks get strayed off the main road?"

Without waiting for an answer, the young man took up the conversation. "You folks gonna have trouble gettin' back on the road, dark comin' on, like it is. You better think on pullin' on up the road a piece to our house. This here'd not be a good place to camp."

Esther kept looking at the rats as they clung to the rotting rafters. No reason to bother with answering these people. They were not there, and she'd wake up any time now.

She heard her husband say, "Much obliged. My wife here, she's gettin' too tired. We need to get where we can fix somethin' to eat."

The woman, actually just a girl, laughed a clear, happy laugh. "No need to be thinkin' on food. We just this minute got up from the table, and we got all kinds of food left. Harley, if you'll bring 'em on over, I'll run on ahead and get somethin' heated up."

With that, one of the lanterns bobbed away in the direction it had come. Esther was helped back into the wagon, and Marion climbed in beside her, and the young man brought along the other wagon.

Esther would never forget that meal. Savory potatoes cooked with ham and onions. Tiny garden peas, swimming in butter, and crisp radishes and onions. Spicy peach cobbler topped with cream. Fluffy biscuits baked in a stove, not in a skillet over a campfire.

That was the first time she had seen Beatrice Nelson, the woman who would become her lifelong friend. The Lord taketh away, and then He giveth back. Her school friend, Desta, was gone, but here was Beatrice.

Thinking back, she grinned, realizing that she herself might be the only person in the entire town who knew that Beatrice's first name was not Granny. For the last thirty years, at least, she was Granny Nelson, friend and confidant to the whole town.

That night, the Nelsons had climbed to their sleeping loft, giving their soft featherbed to the travelers. Sometime in the night, Esther had realized she was not dreaming and that they had reached their destination. For good or bad, this was it.

3

If Marion had been disappointed, he had never let it be known. Handling problems was something he did best, and there were problems aplenty.

The house was a total loss, not even good enough to repair. The barn, however, was in much better shape. It had a central feed room with a solid floor that was at least fourteen feet wide by more than twenty feet long. Lean-to stalls came in from either side for housing of the animals.

"Esther, we got no choice but to move into the barn and be grateful it's good enough."

"It's fine, Marion. Can you bring in the organ? Think this floor'll be strong enough?"

"Been thinkin' about that. I could brace the corner, and we'd move it right up next to the wall. Harley and me, we'll box this in, and then we'll not be havin' the animals look in on us."

The eighty acres they had bought, sight unseen, was also a painful surprise. About five acres of it were on the valley floor, flat and level, and that's where the house and barn were. The vertical stone bluff cut them off from the rest of the land. Harley helped Marion step it off.

His own property adjoined them on one side, and he knew where the other survey markers were. From the top edge of the bluff, the land arose gradually, then steeply up the side of the hill.

Harley tried to help. "Ain't so bad, really. Just limits a body on the choices of what to do with it. 'Course, this valley floor, it makes a good kitchen garden. You'd have to take out a few trees, but you'd be needin' the lumber from 'em for when we start in on your new house."

Gardens came before houses, so they lived in the barn until fall. The maples they had cut down to make the garden were skinned of bark and fitted together into a cabin, twelve by twenty.

That cabin had since been built onto in all directions, but it was in that first room that she now sat and rocked. She looked around the room at the logs, smooth as satin with their patina of years of wear and careful cleaning and regular oiling. They were now the color and smoothness of pulled taffy candy.

There were about twenty families within a half-mile radius. An old man named Jenkins operated a store of sorts, stocking staples such as flour, salt, lard, harnesses and cow feed. He usually had jars for canning, piles of oilskin tarpaulins, and sometimes dried or smoked meat.

He had a young son who helped him. When he died, the son took over. The young people of the town now call the son "Old Man Jenkins." The years have their price. The Markhams from down the road sent their son to Little Rock to a special school, and he came back and opened a pharmacy. Things got better, but it took time.

Marion put in a crop of corn and managed to make food for the livestock and cornmeal to cook with. The first year was hard. She missed her family, and she missed her church. If it had not been for Bea, how could she ever have made it?

Bea had been there when little Daniel ("Dee" they had called him while he was a baby) came yelling and kicking into the world on New Year's Day.

"It's gonna be a good day," Bea had told her. "We have a new baby and blackeye peas for dinner. Figured you wouldn't be up and around, painin' like you were, so I cooked up enough for us all. We'll come on down here and eat with you and Marion."

"That sounds good, but what does blackeye peas have to do with being a good day?"

"You don't know that?" Bea had demanded incredulously. "Don't they know nothin' out there in Kansas? That sayin' started back after the war between the states. The south, hard-put like they was, had trouble makin' it at first. If it hadn't been for them peas, folks would'a starved.

"Them peas seem to have a special strength, like eatin' meat. Seemed like it was thought that if a body could reach the first day of the year still havin' peas to eat, happen he'd be able to make it on till spring. A chunk of fat meat to flavor 'em all up, and a pone'a cornbread alongside, you'd know you was lucky. And bein' lucky on the first day of the year, that'd mean luck'd be going on all year.

"Likely don't mean nothin', but Harley and me, we don't take no chances. We eat them peas, and you're gonna eat 'em, too. I'll go get 'em and call the fellows in."

The "lucky" blackeye peas were accompanied by thick, brown sausages, pumpkin pie sweetened with persimmon sugar, and a huge skillet of crusty, brown cornbread. Also, there were chewy molasses cookies.

"Had me a hankerin' for them cookies. Seems like I crave that taste." Bea took advantage of being "in a family way" to indulge herself in whatever she happened to like. No way a body could fault her for that.

Marion had bought a cow from the neighbors down the road, and it had been due to come fresh momentarily. It happened on that same New Year's Day. And, thinking back, Esther nodded her silver-crowned head. Yes, that next year had been a good year.

Marion Sisco had begun to make a name for himself as a good, honest, hardworking man, straight in all his dealings. The Siscos and the Nelsons began having weekly prayer meetings in their cabins, inviting those neighbors who would come. Then others requested to have the meeting in their homes, and there were six regular families, sometimes more, and the cabins became exceedingly crowded. It created such a wonderful problem. They now needed to think on building a regular church.

Marion began to talk to everyone in the town about the church. He prayed long hours, and he spoke at the prayer meetings. Two of the men offered logs off their land; another offered himself and his son to cut the logs and help skin bark. It was a beginning.

4

Marion's farm proved somewhat less than he had hoped for. He had given up the idea of raising wheat before he even reached it. Just getting the horses into the field was a tussle until he bought an armload of dynamite and blasted a cut in the rock wall. It was still difficult, but it was then at least possible.

He built a shed on the upper part of the land and left the horses there most of the time. Early the next spring, he had four baby colts from his mares. Well, if he couldn't grow wheat, he'd grow something else. He added a brood sow and a goat. He had always liked animals.

He soon realized he did not need two strong teams for his own use and found himself loaning them out a lot. And the colts were growing up, needing to be broken. It was time for life to take a new turn.

That was when he remembered the well-set-up livery stable in Jacksonville. They had horses for sale and for rent. They had wagons, buggies and harnesses. They had extra stalls to board animals. River Bend had nothing like that. Marion had a total of eight horses and colts. He had two good wagons, and his capable hands knew all there was to know about the construction of wagons and buggies.

"Esther, how'd you like us to open up a livery stable on Main Street? I'm thinkin' it'd bring in cash money, and I can see the farm ain't never gonna do that."

By the time the garden was laid by in the fall, he had arranged to buy a five-acre lot facing Main Street, and he built the stable. Its sign advertised, "Animal Feed for Sale" and "Horses boarded and Sold". It also made a place to store the logs being saved for the new church.

With his team of strong grays and his solid wagon, he hauled logs for the church out of impossible places, over bluffs and across rivers. He hauled from wherever the donated logs grew.

Harley Nelson was always there, running alongside with the chock block to slap below a wagon wheel if the horses seemed to falter. Every log was hauled up from a valley or down from a mountain peak, and Harley's chock block was there to "scotch" the load, which made the hauling possible.

Bea's first baby did not draw its first breath. The beautiful little girl lay on the pink pad in the tiny pine box. There were several graves in one corner of the Fields' land, down off the end of Main Street, and a small hole was dug for this tiny box.

Friends gathered and stood about with wet eyes as Marion Sisco opened his Bible. The shyness he had fought all his life descended upon him, and his knees seemed to turn to water. His tongue was too thick to form words. The assembled group waited in respectful silence.

Finally he breathed deeply and squared his shoulders. Harley had "scotched" for him all spring, and he could, with God's help, do this little thing for a friend, and he began to speak words over the grave of Harley's child.

Esther, knowing him so well, watched the struggle and finally the release. His words came clearly and easily from his years of study. The grave was closed, and they took Harley and Bea home in their wagon.

Her own little Dee, in his healthy noisiness, squealed and cooed, and his dimpled hand patted Esther's face. Bea watched the little boy in silence, holding her pain within her. Losses must be born, and she was bearing her first great loss. It was her walk through "the valley". She could cry, and she could turn within herself, but nothing could ease the pain. When someone you loved was laid away, a part of yourself went along, and that was the way of it. So Esther could only honor Bea's bravery and go on with her own life.

Remembering it all, Esther's eyes were wet as she rocked gently back and forth and clasped her wrinkled hands together. Yes, Bea was the friend to have when things went bad. Many people could laugh with you when you laughed, but as it had turned out, Beatrice Nelson was the one to cry with those who cried.

River Bend had suffered many losses since that day, and Granny Nelson, as she was now respectfully called, knew her place. In times of loss, others brought food and laid out the deceased. Others patted shoulders and murmured, "Poor dear". There were many who could do that.

But later, when the crowd thinned, when everyone went away to their homes, families and chores, it became time for Beatrice Nelson. She had suffered so many losses that they held no surprises, and she knew the depth of pain to be endured.

She stayed the night with the family, saving them the necessity of being alone with their deceased one. She told of her own losses and the pain she had felt. She cried with the family over their loss. A loss was not to be hurried through, and tears were not meant to be held back. The Good Book had said to "cry with those who cry," and this was the mission of Esther's friend, Bea.

Even now, in her advanced age, Beatrice Nelson went, with the help of her two canes, to minister to every family in the time of their loss. Esther had been rocking with her eyes closed, tears oozing from under the thin lids, thinking of her friend.

She thought of the old man on the bed. Her own next "valley of the shadow" was just ahead. Marion would be leaving her. If not tonight, it would certainly be soon. Harley had gone four years ago. Marion would follow, and those two fast friends would be together again. Then Beatrice would come to her. They would sit together, and they would cry for this, their life's greatest loss, as she had cried with Bea. Yes, Bea would be here when she was needed.

Esther opened her eyes and looked at Marion, lying on the featherbed. The light quilt rose and fell with his shallow breath. She closed her eyes again and sighed. Her time had not yet come. He still lived. Her crying would come later.

5

It was not all bad. A lot of it was good. Beatrice had a healthy girl the next year and had followed with two boys. After her own little Dee, Esther had Ellena, and two years later came baby Catherine.

Her young Daniel had moved to Jacksonville, as many did, seeking more opportunities. He had died two years ago.

Ellena had three rollicking sons, and, as it had turned out, she got little Jane Ann, as well.

Later in life, her baby, Catherine, had finally given birth. Precious little Jane Ann had been a joy to all and was spending a few summer weeks with her and her granddad when the house fire took away her parents. The loss of a daughter was painful, and her only comfort was that Jane Ann had been in River Bend and had not been taken with them.

Ellena was happy to take Jane Ann to raise and to send to school, but summer had belonged to Esther and Granddad and to River Bend.

It was so wonderful how the Good Lord worked things out. And now there was the grownup Jane Ann, living in Jacksonville, and she met that wonderful husband. It was hard to think of anyone being good enough for her granddaughter, but if there was such a one, it would have to be that young Joe.

The Good Book promised "goodness and mercy to follow, all the days of her life," and she knew that was why the Good Lord had spoken to Jane Ann's husband about becoming a preacher.

And then, wonder of wonders, he had come to River Bend, bringing her precious Jane Ann along, and Esther was able to see her often. And that new little one of Jane Ann's! She was such a sweetheart, looking so much like Catherine.

Ellena was gone, now, and her boys were scattered, taking care of their own lives, but Jane Ann was here, helping her husband take care of the little church.

Her mind drifted back to the first days in River Bend.

Esther's own little Daniel had been such a live wire! Never still a minute, and he could hardly keep his feet on the ground. He stood alone at seven months and walked at nine months, and he had climbed everything before him for the next ten years.

To the tip-tops of the maples he'd shinny, clinging to the thin, limber branches, swaying back and forth, terrifying her. He climbed up the smooth face of the rock wall, hanging on by his toes and fingertips. Everything was a challenge. The wild grapes that filled the trees made tempting, ropelike vines to climb and swing from.

Esther now shook her head from side to side, willing the painful memory to pass her by, but it was not to be. Thinking of Daniel meant she must think of the frightful tumble. A little past four years old, he had been. He would dash up the dynamited cut in the rock face and race recklessly along the sheer edge of the bluff. No words or threats from her could seem to stop him.

A vine hung near the edge of the rock, and Daniel, in his exuberance, grabbed the vine, yelling, "Mommy, look at me!"

In her mind's eye she could still see the tiny body as it lifted off the rock and swung out over the edge of the bluff, small feet kicking joyfully. Esther had watched, helplessly, as the vine unraveled its upper tentacles, separating itself from the tree. The tiny form of her son glided overhead, trailing the long length of leafy vine. He landed in a scrub bush, the vine settling in a heap over him. Then silence! Horrible, terrifying silence!

She lifted him from the bush and saw he was still breathing. She began to scream, and Bea came running. As soon as she saw Bea, she yelled, "Get Harley to hitch up the buggy! I got'a go to Jacksonville!"

Harley came running, then turned back to his house. In seconds, it seemed, he was back. He was astride his fastest saddle horse.

"This is faster than the buggy. I'll get him to Marion."

Esther had crumbled into a sobbing heap, and Bea had been there.

It was several hours later that Marion had come in from the livery stable and sat down wearily.

"Where is he?" Esther had demanded.

"Where is who?"

"Little Daniel! He got hurt! Didn't Harley come by the livery?"

Marion shook his head. "I been gone. Took a horse up the road. What's wrong with Daniel?"

"Fell off the bluff and busted in his face. Maybe he's blind. Blood was everywhere. I was gonna take him in the buggy, but Harley said the saddle horse'd be faster, and he'd find you. Where is he?"

Marion was already on his way out. In minutes the buggy was ready to go. It was a three-hour trip, at best, but Harley would have made it in less than two hours on horseback.

Hard thoughts had to be considered. If his son was still alive, or if he wasn't, the buggy would be needed to bring him back. Wherever he was, Harley would stay with him until someone came. "Toss in a couple'a quilts, will you, Esther, and I'll be back soon as I can."

Then he was gone, and Esther wandered about, unable to settle into anything or to control her thoughts. How could he possibly be alive?

Surely the flour had helped some. It must have been reflex action, and she did not remember thinking of it, but when she saw the rivers of scarlet blood running down the little face and neck, she knew it had to be stopped. She had scooped handfuls of the flour from the bin and pressed it against his face. At least, at the time Harley had ridden out of the yard, the blood was not flowing. Neither was little Daniel moving or crying. She knew this was another "valley of the shadow of death." *Where are You, Lord? You said You'd be here. I can't feel You.*

Bea brought her little girl and the baby, three months old, and spent the night. The Good Book said to "Cry with those who cry," and they had done a lot of it that night.

It was daybreak when Harley opened the door without knocking. He sat down wearily in the nearest chair. Looking up at the two wordless, expectant faces before him, he had said, "He's still alive."

Esther could breathe again. "Where is he?"

"When I couldn't find Marion, knowin' there wasn't no time to lose, I went on in. Got 'im in the hospital, and two of them doctors, they started to work on 'im. Two hours later, another doctor come in and started to help. They was past midnight, they said, pullin' out little slivers'a bone where his nose got smashed into his head. They got it where they thought he could breathe all right and took stitches to hold it in place. He got a cut over his eye that they sewed up, and one arm was broke. It was about three this mornin', and Marion told me to go on home, so you'd know how things was. He's stayin' and'll be in when he can."

Harley leaned forward, placing his elbows on his knees and his face in his hands. "Dear Lord, it was frightenin'. But them doctors, they know'd what to do."

In a small voice, Esther dared to ask, "Did you see him? How does he look?"

Harley hesitated, as if choosing his words carefully. "Well, there'll be a scar, well as you'd expect, but, Esther, he's got a face now, and he didn't when they started. I'm glad to tell you, his face looked good to me."

He stood up wearily. "'Spect I'll be gettin' at the chores, and then go on down to the livery. The animals down there gonna be needin' things done."

As he went out the door, he turned to Esther. "The Lord was good to you. 'Spect you know that."

The Lord had always been in the valley with her. She just hadn't seen Him at first.

Four days later, Marion came in with little Daniel. His first words were, "Mommy! Look at me!" He had pointed to the wide, white bandage covering the bridge of his nose and one eye. His father carried him gently into the house and put him in a chair.

"Doctor said we was to hold him down, sort'a, and not let him get bumped. Could mess up everything, and they couldn't fix it no more." Esther nodded. That was better than she had expected. Daniel could walk, and he could talk. He was alive.

She amused her son for a while, then went to the kitchen to prepare food. When she looked back where she had left him, the chair was empty. She ran out of the cabin, and her eyes automatically lifted to the rock face. There was her baby, racing along the edge of the rock, slapping his hands on his sides to make the sound of a galloping horse. "Giddap! Giddap!" he yelled joyfully.

Esther had looked up into the sky. "You see what's goin' on, Lord? You sent me down that child, now I got'a have Your help or he ain't gonna grow up to be a man."

God must have taken her up on the challenge. About three years later, Daniel raced by on a bucking, half-broke colt, yelling, "Mommy! Look at me!" The colt had promptly shed him into the same scrubby bush, but by age ten, he helped his dad break colts, and by twelve, he did it alone. He stayed at home and helped his dad for several years, then moved into Jacksonville where there was more going on.

It could be that Daniel could have lived a few years longer if he had taken better care of himself. However, no one could say he did not enjoy the life he had.

6

The rock bluff caused Bea a little trouble as well. When her Susie was just over two and played with Ellena, the little girls had crept away, unnoticed. Esther and Bea had been in the midst of canning beans and had joined forces for company.

Ellena had come in the cabin and patted her mother on the knee. "Mommy, c'mere."

"What do you want, Ellena?"

"C'mere. Oozie."

"Where is Oozie, I mean Suzie? Where is she?"

"C'mere."

It was not like Ellena to insist this way. They followed her outside and halfway to Bea's house, where Ellena pointed up.

There, on the side of the rock face, hung Suzie by her dress tail, caught on a gnarled bush growing from a crevasse.

Bea's eyes were wide and startled. *Dear Merciful God, where had those girls been?* Bea scrambled up the dynamited path and Esther followed, carrying a light rope from the shed. While Bea talked soothingly to the little girl, Esther set a noose in the rope and lowered it.

Suzie kept pushing it away at first, but finally allowed herself to be lassoed and pulled to the top of the bluff, kicking and yelling. She was somewhat scratched and had bad rope burns under her arms but was otherwise unhurt.

The men had immediately built a fence around the base of the cut, with a locking gate. It had not deterred her son, but the girls were held below. For a few years.

After Suzie had been cleaned up and the girls had been put down for a nap, Bea had confided in her.

"They's an awful sayin' here in the mountains. Didn't feel right sayin' it to you, when it was Daniel that was hurt. But now my Suzie could'a got herself killed, and I'll say to you what it is."

Esther paused, her hands full of unsnapped beans. "What is it?"

"They got a sayin' when a woman's plannin' her family. They say however many you want, you got'a add another one, 'cause you're sure to lose one over the edge of the mountain. It's awful to say, but it can happen. That's what we almost did."

They sighed and continued to snap the beans in silence for a while. Finally, they had the courage to discuss what they would be fixing for their respective suppers.

Ellena had married a local boy, but they had moved to Jacksonville for better employment. Little Catherine had followed her sister's path. At least, they had each other until the house fire had taken Catherine.

Jane Ann had been seven and was visiting grandparents for the summer. No one knew what had started the fire, but when discovered, it had already been too late.

And then there was the funeral. When a pine box is placed in view in the living room and then taken to the church for the services, it is a horrible, painful thing. But when there is no pine box on which to focus the tears, it is infinitely worse.

Esther's heart was a gaping wound, continuing to bleed and unable to be bound together. She could not even go to the churchyard cemetery and grieve, because there was no grave.

She was like a bird flying over the ocean, knowing there was no place to put her foot to rest. Where there is death, there needs to be a grave.

Beatrice was there. Weeds grew in her garden, and dust bunnies took up residence under the bed, but Bea did not leave her alone. Bea had talked with her about Catherine and about the things she remembered from when she was small, about things the three girls had done together. Bea had helped her bind up her broken heart.

It was another "valley of the shadow of death," and where was God that time? Just where was He, anyway? She had demanded an answer of Bea. She let her anger rise up in her throat, bitter and burning.

"No way to know the all of it, Esther, but God was there. Else why would He have let you keep your little Jane Ann?"

Jane Ann had been spared. *Yes, Lord, You were there. I'm sorry I doubted You. I keep thinking I know more than You do. I loved my Catherine, but I reckon You loved her more, but I thank You for leaving Jane Ann.*

When her tears came again, they were cleansing tears, and they washed away the bitterness and anger, then finally they removed the sorrow and loneliness.

Jane Ann was such a comfort, now that she was grown up and lived nearby. Every few days, without fail, she came to sit and talk. Busy as she was, she saved time for her old grandparents. *Thank you, Lord.*

7

Thinking back, baby Catherine seemed tied in, somehow, with the new church. Possibly because the baby was still nursing when she and Bea had taken lunches to the men working on the building. Daniel was six, and Ellena was three. Such a long time to be saving up for the day they could have a place to worship!

The Fields family, living right at the end of Main Street, owned the property that was being used as a cemetery. They wanted to deed that land, with additional land for the church building, over to the church. It took a trip to Jacksonville to get it done, legal and proper.

Of course, going to Jacksonville was not the scary trip it was when they had first crossed the river. Her Marion, with his ability to fix problems, had strengthened and tightened the cables, anchoring them to massive rocks instead of trees, and the bridge clattered not nearly so much as it had and was not washed away at every high water.

When the land deeded to the church had been made legal, it seemed that the road in front it needed a name. It consisted of a curved extension off Main Street, cutting across the Fields' property, through the grove of ancient maples and finally reaching the sheer rock face, following it as far as there were people to travel on it. Eventually, it disappeared into thickets of oak, persimmon and tangled vines.

Someone said it could be part of Main Street; others thought of Maple Street. Even River Street was suggested. Over the adult voices came Dee's little-boy voice.

"Bein' that a church was fixin' to be built, a body'd think it'd be called Church Street."

They had taken a vote to make it official, but there had been no one against it. The church was the first building on the street, so it was given the address of Number One.

Money was scarce, and the church was made totally from native material, labor, sweat and time stolen from days already too short to get everything done. It seemed that the people had a mind to work and had pulled together.

The original building was twenty by forty with a split-log floor and walls of smooth, peeled maple, cured and oiled and trimmed to fit tightly without clay chinking.

Their small hoard of hard money was saved for plate glass windows and "sawmill" boards for the benches. Marion made these, one by one, at the livery stable, planing them smooth and coating them with clear shellac. They were beautiful.

The men had made shingles at their homes, in spare minutes, and they brought them on a designated day, shingling the entire roof before sundown. The benches were brought from the livery and placed in the building.

The women brought food, and a picnic was held in the yard to celebrate the completion of the building. Children played games in the grove of trees that would later be used to tie the horses and mules that had brought the buggies and wagons.

At the end of the picnic, after the games and when all the talking was done, the people gathered into the church and settled themselves on the new benches.

Marion had taken his Bible to give him courage and had stood before the people. "We've finished the building now. You've done so well and sacrificed so much, but now we have it, and we can hold up our heads as we look for a pastor. It'll not take long to put up a cabin for 'im to live in, and we'll start on it soon. Meanwhile, we'll be prayin' and askin' God for the right person. The one to lead us in our worship of Himself."

He had dismissed them with prayer, and they had gone to their homes. They promised to spend time waiting on God in prayer.

For weeks after the dedication of the church, Esther could hear her husband's voice as he knelt on the stones at the top of the rock face. After the evening meal and when the chores were done, he would disappear into the mountain, often not returning until midnight or later. Esther was always restless until he would finally come in and go to bed.

One night, as she could hear his voice as usual, another Voice came to her. "Do you really love Me?"

She was startled. "Is that you, Lord?"

Again the question, "Do you love Me? How much do you love Me?"

When it was repeated over the next few days, it became worrisome. She couldn't seem to find a way to confide in her husband or in Bea. But there it was. "How much do you love Me?"

She went about her duties, heavy with dread. What could it mean? "Is it one of the children, Lord? Are You fixin' to take one of them? Please don't take my child, Lord!"

But there it was, continually with her. "Is this a valley, Lord? If it is, I don't feel You're with me."

"Esther, what would you give Me? Abraham offered me his son, and I counted it unto him for righteousness."

"My child, Lord? No. I can't." But the heaviness was more than she could bear, and she finally answered the voice.

"Yes, Lord. Whatever I have that You want, it's Yours. Yes, Lord, take what You will." With that, a quiet peace swept over her.

Then she asked, "When, Lord?"

And the answer came. "Next Sunday. What I want is your organ for My house. I bore it up in My hand as it crossed the river, so it could be placed in My house."

"My organ? My lovely, beautiful organ that was a gift from my husband?" She sighed, long and slow. "Yes, Lord, You may have my pump organ. Your house needs it worse than mine."

8

The old man on the bed shuffled restlessly, turning his head from side to side. "Esther? Are you comin'?" He murmured with a muffled voice, and she could hardly understand his words.

"I'm here, Marion. I'm comin'. I'm right behind you."

His voice mumbled on. "Try on keepin' up, Esther. Can't be lettin' you fall behind."

"I won't, Marion. You just rest now." She patted the large, bony, once-capable hand, and he settled down quietly again.

Esther glanced at the clock. It was two in the morning. She had so recently been pulled from her deep thought that she glanced toward the wall, where she had kept the organ. No matter what she had put there, it always seemed wrong. Only the organ had looked right.

The thought passed through her mind, as it had many times over the years. The organ had always belonged to God. It must have, because He kept it in tune. Occasionally a wondering tinker would come through the town, and they would ask him to check it, but it never needed tuning or repair.

After a month of mountainside prayer, Esther had asked Marion, "You any closer to knowin' what to do about a preacher?" He had continued to act as leader in the Bible reading and prayer, but she knew the matter was hard on his mind.

"I find myself in a puzzle over gettin' a preacher. I'd like to be talkin' to you about it, but it all sounds so strange, I can't see the sense of it yet. I'll have to be waitin' till the Good Lord sees His way clear to make things plainer. Seems like He may be thinkin' I'm smarter than I think I am. Likely things'll be gettin' clearer, soon."

Esther had understood and was content to let things stand. She did, however, tell him that she wanted to put her organ in the church.

Marion was startled. "You sure about that? You thought about this a lot and know that's what you want?"

Esther nodded. "God told me He wanted it, and I can see He needs it worse'n me. He said he wanted it in the church by next Sunday."

Her husband had nodded understandingly. "Harley and me, we'll get it down there."

Esther was proud of herself that she allowed the organ to leave her house without shedding tears. A gift must be cheerfully given. That was expected.

The organ was a perfect fit for the church platform, like a sparkling gem set in a gold ring. As her feet worked the pump, her fingers seemed to take on a life of their own. "When the Roll is called up Yonder," "In the Sweet Bye and Bye," and "Lift me Up Above the Shadows, Plant my Feet on Higher Ground"... these hymns and others filled the church with their sound, accompanied by the organ she had given to God.

A sense of peace and completeness swept over her, a feeling that she had unwittingly been an important part of something big.

The meeting that day was a strange one. For the last couple of weeks, Marion had been preoccupied and seemingly lost in thought most of the time. He had passed over opportunities to confide in her, so Esther had tried to put it from her mind. When he could talk with her, he would, and until then, there was nothing she could do.

The group of worshipers sang song after song, feeling exhilarated with the sound of the organ accompaniment. Then came time for the Bible reading.

Marion had sighed and started to stand when Harley Nelson moved out in front of him.

"Beggin' the pardon of my friend, Brother Sisco, here, and of all you good folks, but there's a thing to be talked about, and this morning seems as good a time as could be."

There were nods of agreement and smiles of encouragement all along the shiny new benches. Harley hesitated, as though reluctant to continue, but finally began to speak again.

"We been prayin', all of us, along with our work on this here buildin' we put up. Knowin' it was God's house, and that He'd be the One to direct us, we been waitin' on Him. Figure it might be the time to move on, seemin' like there's a way openin' up.

"Now I'm not the one wantin' to say what's on my mind. It'd be known to all of you folks that Brother Sisco, here, him and me, we've been good friends, mostly like brothers. Us bein' neighbors, we found ourselves in position to do for one another like brothers would likely be.

"There was the time the storm started the fire on the mountain above us and swept down with no warnin', wipin' out most of my livestock. All of his was saved from the fire, and with no second thought, he divided with me, takin' no payment.

"All you fellows know about this, and that makes it harder for me to say what's on my mind. But it's got'a be said, or I ain't gonna get me no relief from the misery that's come on me."

Harley hesitated, looking around at the small congregation. His eyes pled for help, but he drew a breath to continue.

A voice came from the back of the church, "Wait up there, Brother Harley. 'Afore you go on, let me say a word or two that'll likely ease your mind a bit, happen I been where you are."

All eyes turned to Olen Jenkins at the back of the church. He went on. "We all been prayin' and lookin' up to the Good Lord to send us down a preacher, and not realizin' He done answered our prayers, and us too blind to see it. Would that be your line o'thought, Brother Harley?"

Before Olen Jenkins could continue, Elliot Simms stood and took the floor. "Yeah, and that's our problem, bein' too blind to see what's been set down here in our midst. We been thinkin' we need us a preacher sent in here from somewhere else, and the Good Lord done took care of that, years ago, way before we ever had sense enough to ask. What are we doin' askin' the Good Lord for a preacher when we got Brother Marion right here in our town?"

The tension that had been building now reached a climax with Brother Simms' words. Marion had bowed his head into his hands and fought to control his profound relief and abject fear.

Harley Nelson kept control of the pulpit, his face wreathed in smiles. "Can't say how much of a relief it is to me, havin' all you fellows get the same message from the Good Lord. Bein' a friend of Brother Marion made it a heavy burden for me to be passin' on, knowin' the work to be throwed on him, studyin' for the license and all."

Robert Stone stood and was given the floor. "Don't see no reason for change from what we got, whilst he's doin' the studyin'. If he's got things got'a be done, then it'd be up to us to see his family got fed and took care of. I, for one, aim to bring a tenth part of my crops, from hay to green beans, just like it says in the Scriptures. How many of you fellows gonna stand alongside of me?"

A chorus of "ayes" had sounded. Still, Marion sat bowed forward with his face in his hands. Knowing his shyness, Esther's heart bled for him, but she also knew, at last, what had been weighing him down over the last weeks. At least it was now out in the open and could be dealt with.

When Marion finally stood behind the pulpit, he was unable to speak at all, which made the men of the church all the more determined to call him as their pastor.

9

The clock on the cabin wall proclaimed the time to be two thirty in the morning. Esther leaned forward and clasped the hand lying motionless on the quilt.

Yes, sirree, that was an exciting and terrifying time for herself and for him. There was the study course required for a minister's license to preach. Strange thing that God had not chosen to call someone with a license already. It was all right, though, and the study course had finally been completed in the minutes and hours stolen from what always seemed to be important. Esther's own schedule had been changed even more.

Gone were the lazy days of companionship with Bea, and here before her were the days of visitation. She and Marion had systematically called on every household in the valley and all of those on the hillside that they knew about.

It was necessary that Esther go with him, because there was no way to know whether the man of the house would be at home when they called. It would be unseemly for the pastor to call alone on a household with the man away. They could not afford to create even a hint of a scandal, no matter how false it would be. Then there were the visits she had made by herself. It was on these visits that she learned something of great importance.

Esther, herself, secure in the easy friendship of Bea, had no idea of the isolation and loneliness of the women on the small mountain farms, seeing no one to talk with from one day's end to the next.

Of course, the church services helped, and after dismissal, the women were reluctant to round up their family and leave with the need for talk and idea exchange not met. It became a worry, nagging painfully at Esther's thoughts.

Sure, a farm woman could lay down her work for one day and visit another, but would the person she visited be expecting her? And even if that was so, the visit would be one on one, and something much bigger was needed. Nothing seemed to come to mind. Bea, herself, presented the obvious solution.

"Esther, I got somethin' to ask. You know I got me these quilts needin' to be quilted up, me with these youngens growin' up. I figure quiltin' to be about the loneliest of jobs a woman finds herself up against. We could set up a day, and you could come over and work on mine with me, then we'd go do up yours. Workin' that needle seems to be made for workin' the mouth. That be satisfactory to you?"

It was, and it gave birth to the Tuesday Sewing Circle. It was held every Tuesday, unless there was a funeral on that day requiring the use of the church. In that event, the Tuesday Sewing Circle was held on Thursday.

Every lady of the community was invited. If she couldn't make it, for whatever reason, there was always next week. It was a day to work their schedule around, to enjoy refreshments together, to visit as a group, and to have a purpose to it. The first meeting set the conditions.

All quilts would be quilted on a first-come basis. You just added your name to the list, and when they reached your name, your quilt was worked. You could pay for this service at the rate of 50 cents a quilt, paid to the church treasury (actually used to buy the tea served to the ladies), or you could bring the church a half-cord of stove wood for winter heating, or you could do the janitorial work at the church building for two weeks. This last method of payment was a popular option.

It was while they were quilting the first quilt that Maggie Raleigh made an interesting suggestion.

"I been thinkin' of funerals held here in town and the ones gonna be held here at the church. You know, them summer funerals, and even the spring and fall ones, they got bunches of flowers to set out to cheer up the family. But them winter funerals, they got nothin' but gloom and dullness. It don't seem right, somehow, bein' a person has no say in when the Good Lord pleases to call 'im on."

Nods of understanding passed around the circle of women. Skillful hands wielding their needles paused over the quilt, as the matter was considered. It would seem that a problem that had been brought out clear, the way had Maggie put it, would have an answer somewhere.

"So I was thinkin'," Maggie went on, "Out'a that last cotton crop, I spun up a lot of really fine thread, got it all ready, and I got the dye to color it up. I was thinkin' if we had a cover, crocheted with roses, violets and lilies, and all kinds of flowers, made to stand up stiff when they was starched, we could lay it over the box."

She looked around at the nods of agreement and then continued, "Them flowers standin' up stiff, like they would, that'd be almost like havin' real flowers, and it seems like it'd be a comfort to the family."

There was a collective release of breath as each of the ladies pictured the blanket of flowers and the way it would cover the bare wood of the casket.

Maggie continued, "But they's one problem in my idea. I got me these four youngens, and the one to come," and she patted her bulging abdomen, "and the time left over to do what I want ain't as much as it used to be."

More nods of agreement passed among the women. Several were in the same condition.

"So I was thinkin," Maggie continued, "when I get that thread dyed up and dried, if each of us was to take some and crochet up their favorite kind of flower, usin' bits of time between doin' other things, it'd be like a flowerbed, planted and tended by all of us. The thing is, though, that I'd like to do it all myself, but likely it'd be needed to cover my own box 'afore I got through with it, long as it'd take me."

Voices buzzed excitedly as each woman began to describe what she would contribute.

Then Elsie Jenkins offered, "When you all get them flowers done and brought in, I can take some boughten green thread from the store and put 'em all together in the blanket, if that'd be all right with all of you. We can get that thread down at the store, cause we'd be needin' so much green. That'a'way we'd not be usin' up all of Maggie's thread. I got some time, likely more'n some of you, me with that one boy of mine. It'd give me a real pleasure to do the green part."

In due time, the casket cover was finished. Spring and summer flowers of every description, permanently fashioned from thread, stood up brightly from the green background. Starch and skillful fingers had shaped the bright colors of the petals in three dimensions, creating a thick and alive-like appearance.

Maggie's old grandmother did not make it to her 100th year of life, and the second week of December, she escaped the penetrating cold of the valley by being called up to be with the Good Lord. Maggie's idea of a brilliant casket cover was first used to cover the pine box bed of her beloved Granny. The other ladies thought it most appropriate.

Then there was the livery stable. Esther remembered the pain it caused her husband to realize he would have to sell it. It would have been good if young Daniel had been interested in that direction and given them a reason to hold it for him, but it was not to be. His restlessness was already evident.

Marion had finally set a price, but the scarcity of money in the valley had kept it from being sold. Then, after Harley lost another cotton crop to the insects, he and Marion had a meeting for serious discussion. Their talk involved another problem Esther had seen looming before them.

With her children being toddlers, she had not thought of a schoolroom. But now her oldest was about to turn eight, and a schoolhouse and a teacher were nowhere in sight. Esther had taken time from her busy day to teach her son his letters and numbers, but now the girls were coming along as well.

Also, in a number of the families, the parents themselves had no schooling, and then there were Bea's children, and a lot of others in the town had missed schooling. There had to be a school.

It was finally decided that the five acres on which the livery was built would be divided down the middle and a road cut through to the rear of the property. Marion would retain half the property for the purpose of a schoolhouse.

The livery would be operated by Marion and Harley as partners, with most of the work being done by Harley. So Harley became the new manager of the livery, and he painted a bright sign for the front of the building. "River Bend Livery Stable," it said.

With the raising of that sign, the livery became the unofficial location for exchange of ideas among the men of the town. That became the place where notices were posted, where news was passed on, and where lonely men found companionship.

In short, it became the male counterpart of the Tuesday Sewing Circle. It had been Harley who built the whittler's bench to make on-site loafing more comfortable and convenient.

Harley, friendly and outgoing, knew the livery must become a gathering place to be successful, and the business began to expand rapidly. It became the place to meet, much more so than it had under the management of the shy and more solitary Marion. Busy men with a little time on their hands began to gravitate to the stable, hopeful of relieving the tedium of their lives in a few minutes of conversation with an equal.

One day, they had a good topic going.

"You fellows see anything of that bum, the one livin' over the other side of the river?"

"You mean that old ragged man? Reckon if he's really a bum?"

"Well, he don't do no work, does he?"

"I don't know nothin' about him. I never been over there."

"Well, I was close. That cabin he put up, that's about the littlest kind of a cabin I ever seen."

"How big, would you estimate?"

By this time, the conversation included at least six of the customers and whittlers.

"Didn't have my measurin' with me, but I'd judge it to be likely eight feet square."

"Well, now, an eight-foot log to be lifted overhead, that'd be right smart of a load for one man. Didn't see he had no help on it, did you?"

"Reckon not. Shore looked little, though, no bigger'n an outhouse. Wouldn't be room enough in there to yell at the cat 'thout gettin' fur in your mouth."

"He got 'im a cat, did you say?"

"If he ain't, I could give him one. I had twenty-six, last count. I got 'em out there raisin' their own mice for feedin' their youngens, bein' careful they don't run out."

This bit of humor brought a round of chuckles.

"Don't see much of the bum in town."

"I saw 'im over to Jenkins' store, buyin' cornmeal and salt."

"Wonder what he uses for money?"

"Nickels and dimes. Same as us."

"Aw, you know what I mean. He's got him no occupation to make money. You don't see 'im sellin' nothin'."

"No. But ya got'a agree, he don't go 'round askin' for handouts."

"That's a fact. Did see him wet a hook in the river, though. Eats a lot'a fish, I'd say."

"Nothin' bad to say about that. Been hungry for a mess of fish, myself, but seems I ain't got down to the river to get 'em."

"Might be a good life that bum's got. Eatin', fishin' and layin' 'round of a hot afternoon."

"Wonder what he does all the time, and where at he came from?"

"No knowin'. Just that one day he was here, and that cabin was up. Feel confident he didn't bother to buy that land."

"Who owns it?"

"Never did rightly know. The riverbed had it for a spell, then it shifted course. 'Speck whoever it is that has it may not know it or care for him bein' there if they did."

"Hope he ain't no escaped criminal. We got youngens runnin' loose all over town."

"He don't seem to notice 'em, over much."

"Hey, you fellows havin' any trouble with the borers in your corn? I'm figurin' this to be a bad year."

So the conversation drifted from the solitary man in the cabin across the river to the condition of the crops, present and future.

Esther recalled conversations about the strange man who seemed to have come from nowhere and who had no connection with the town, but it was of no concern to her. She had much bigger problems.

The ladies of the Tuesday Sewing Circle had decided that a Christmas party for the children would be in order. They wanted it to be a program put on by the children, a party with coffee and cookies for the whole church and a big, brightly decorated Christmas tree. That part of it they could handle with no problem.

They (especially Esther) had also wanted gifts to be on the tree for the children, but that was certainly out of the question, because of the lack of money. They even realized, with the other things they had to do, there would be no time even to make the toys.

Finally they decided to go on with what they could do, and possibly next year would be a better year.

Young children who came with their mothers to the quilting were put to work making colored paper chains and stringing red berries. The stickery burrs from the sweet gum tree and the thistle bush were dyed in bright colors. Maggie Raleigh found time to crochet a yellow star and starch it, board-stiff, for the top of the tree.

As the time drew near, the discussion of edible treats was begun.

Bea Nelson was first with her offering. "I'd be glad to make up a batch of molasses cookies. We'd need those."

"I got pecans and walnuts a'plenty. How'd it be to bring nut candy?"

"And roasted peanuts? We had us a good crop this year. I been makin' a lot of peanut butter. My youngens seem to have such a taste for it, and it's easy and quick to fill 'em up."

"If we was to serve coffee, we got'a buy it. Tea, we could furnish for ourselves if we used peppermint to flavor it up, Christmas-like."

"I like that peppermint tea, myself. Seems to go good with cookies."

"I like tea, too, but somethin' about coffee seems to go with a party."

"Likely we could have both, givin' folks a choice. How'd that be, Esther?"

Esther had found herself the unofficial clearing house for ideas and also the arbitrator of discussions. Just another thing that went with being the wife of the pastor, she guessed.

Elsie Jenkins reminded them the store could arrange the coffee at a lower price, being that it was for the church, so the decision was to spend their accumulated money on coffee and serve it as far as it went, then finish out with local tea.

Then Esther asked, "What about ideas for the children's program?"

Faces turned toward her, and if there was an idea in the group, they were bent on keeping it a secret. So on her visitation trips for the next several days, she gave her attention to the problem.

Songs were good, and they should be the basis for the program. Some scenery, somehow, and perhaps two or three of the children would like a solo recitation or Bible verse. And there'd need to be parts that could be added on the spot, if extra children came.

None must be left out. Also, there was the necessary practice. It was a lot to try to put together, but if she didn't do it, who would?

The first part of December was plagued with severe weather. One of the sudden freezeups, common to the area, happened on a Sunday when she had counted on a good practice period.

Rain had poured down, totally soaking every surface, then the north wind came blasting down the valley, and within minutes every twig on every tree and every flat surface underfoot was layered with clear ice. Buggy wheels refused to turn, and it was not safe to have animals on hard surfaces, for the danger of slipping down. Only those residents who could walk (or slide) to the building were able to come.

She and Marion had walked, pulling the children on a sled. They practiced the songs with those who were there, and she went home, deep in the pit of discouragement.

On the Tuesday before Christmas, the ice suddenly melted, as was also common, and the ladies were anxious for a day out. The Christmas tree had been brought in and put on its stand. While they ate cookies and drank their tea, they decorated the tree. Maggie's stiffly starched yellow star was placed on top, where it shone brightly. A good start.

Fluffy, white popcorn strings, red berry strings and bright paper chains were draped along the branches. Blue and yellow stickery balls were thickly hung, giving shape and depth to the creation. A multitude of gingerbread children suffered the indignity of having their heads pierced by a needle but were rewarded by becoming part of the decoration on the tree.

Things began to look better. If only there had been a way to have at least a small gift for each child, it would have been perfect. But there would be plenty of goodies to eat, and every child would be given cookies and nuts to take home. That would be as good as a gift... surely...? Wouldn't it?

The weather in southern Arkansas is as unpredictable as a tailless kite in a March wind. A blizzard can be followed by weather almost shirt-sleeve warm, and that was what happened on the Sunday they were planning to celebrate the birth of Baby Jesus.

Marion had read the Christmas story in his deep, expressive voice. Esther had gone to the organ to play the music. The children had been herded into a small room at the front of the church near the door, partly because their curiosity was eating painfully at their manners.

The tree had been wrapped in a large bedsheet to create an anticipation and surprise (and also to keep small hands away from the gingerbread children hanging temptingly from its branches), and it was working too well. The best of the children could not keep their eyes off the cloth-wrapped object, and the worst and the bravest kept slipping away to peek under the drape.

So they were all put in the small front room, and they were now sorting out their stage props as Esther began to play the songs.

The first of the children were permitted out the door, carrying pasteboard pictures of biblical houses, such as would be seen in Bethlehem. On cue, they began to sing "O Little Town of Bethlehem" as they marched to the platform to stand in a row, creating a "town."

The next song was "It Came upon a Midnight Clear," and three little girls wrapped in white sheets with a yellow paper star pasted to their foreheads stepped daintily down the aisle. These angels stood outside the "Little Town of Bethlehem."

Parents watched with pride and wonder as their own offspring appeared. The "angels" stood carefully apart from the town. Suzie Nelson put her thumb in her mouth and looked out the window of the "house" she held. She did not want to risk being part of the strange things she saw going on.

The little white "house" second from the end became weary with it all and sat down on the floor. The "house" on the end tried to pull him to his feet, but slipped and fell on top.

The blue "house" with many cut out windows, which was the inn, kept poking his nose through each of the windows, one by one. A pink "house" stuck out his tongue through a window and so convulsed the neighborhood with laughter that Esther was forced to leave the organ and regroup the entire village.

Cassie Raleigh, one of the three angels, decided she would rather be a house. She exchanged her forehead star with the nearest "house" and became part of Bethlehem, still wrapped in her angel bed sheet.

The robe-less angel happily took her place with Suzie Nelson and Lizzie Tucker, whereupon Lizzie took exception to the switch and shoved the unrobed angel to the floor, where she was collected and comforted by her mother.

It was at this point that the church door opened and the "bum" from the other side of the river came in and sat down in the back row. Heads turned and glances were exchanged, but the program went on.

Esther began to play "Away in the Manger," and Josie Markham came walking sedately down the aisle carrying a cardboard box "manger" containing a rag doll wrapped in a white blanket. She set the box in Bethlehem, just as she had been instructed to do, and turned to take her place behind the town.

Her careful walk and dainty feet were more than the "inn" could stand, and he thrust out one foot, sending Josie sprawling forward on her face.

Josie was a trooper. There were no tears, and vengeance came swift and sure. While the audience held its collective breath, little Josie carefully stood and rearranged her new Christmas dress that had been made special for the occasion.

She looked at the "inn" and doubled up her small fist. She shot a well-deserved right jab to the ear of the "inn" and sedately took her assigned place.

For the last number, Esther had chosen "When Shepherds Watched Their Flocks by Night." As the music began, three boys whom she knew for sure would be there came up the aisle. They were dressed in their father's shirts for robes. The sleeves were rolled up, and on their heads they wore tea towels as their "shepherd hats." Jamie Raleigh's tea towel was embroidered with the words, "Monday is a Happy Washday."

With the shepherds came a flock of "sheep," their number to correspond with the number of children who did not have another part. Also, this covered any unexpected children, as plenty of paper "sheep ears" had been provided. The shepherds carried realistic-looking shepherd crooks, and they used them freely to punish any straying "sheep" in their flock.

In due time, they reached "Bethlehem" and settled down on the floor, as they had practiced.

The "inn" was still rubbing his ringing ear, and Josie surveyed the congregation with a small smile of satisfaction.

The main sponsors of the program were Esther, who missed most of the entertainment by being at the organ (except for regrouping the town of Bethlehem), and Bea, who missed it all, seeing only the finished product, as she had been confined to the little room at the front by the door.

The program was well received, and the ovation was painful to the ears and hard on the hands, so ringing was the applause.

Already the fragrance of the coffee and tea, being heated on the potbelly stove, had filled the church. Trays of cookies, candy and cake were set on the coloring table borrowed from the children's classroom.

The suspense of the children was now a tangible thing, and their curiosity was acute. It was decided that they could wait no longer, and all the children were made to sit down.

Esther was apprehensive. Would the tree really look as wonderful as they had thought it did? Would the children, who had helped decorate it, still have a happy surprise?

Together, Esther and Bea unfastened the pins and drew the drape aside. A collective "Ahh" of appreciation arose. Esther breathed a sigh of relief and dared to turn and look at the tree.

The colors of the popcorn, berries and gingerbread cookies glowed just as warmly as they had when they were put on, but there was something else. She and Bea stared in open-mouthed amazement and wonder.

Every limb of the tree was laden with small, brightly painted birds and animals, carefully and skillfully carved from wood. Birds with brilliant, widely spread wings! Cows with white spots! Fat pigs! Chickens! A whole barnyard flock of them!

There were tiny wagons and sleds in red and blue, and horses with flying manes and tails. There were goats with tiny horns and many dogs and cats. There seemed to be hundreds of them, weighing down the limbs. In among the animals, there were tiny baby dolls with painted faces, smiling at the world.

Esther remembered that she had looked at Bea with a question in her mind, and Bea had shrugged and nodded.

As Esther began to untie the tiny objects from the limbs, Bea lined up the children along the aisle. As they passed by her, Esther selected an appropriate toy for each child, making sure the little girls got the dolls. Over and over the line of children passed by her and were given another toy until each child had seven different things.

Their eyes were sparkling with wonder with each new gift. Esther told herself, I *know this isn't happening, and I'll wake up in a minute. I'm dreaming this just because I wanted presents so badly.*

The dream had lasted, though, and finally, full of cookies and candy and clutching a bag of goodies and a handful of toys, the children were gone. Esther remembered how she and Bea had finally looked at each other and had wept in each other's arms at the sheer wonder of it all.

Even today, Esther might have believed it was a dream, except that she still had one of the baby dolls, one that had been given to her Catherine. It would be a good thing to give to Jane Ann's little girl when she was bigger.

There were many in the town who could not believe that Esther and Bea had not privately arranged the surprise. But how would they possibly have had the time, even if they had the ability to do such intricate carving? And certainly there had not been money to buy them.

And there was something else.

Marion commented later that he had looked for the old man to make him welcome, but when the party started, he had slipped out. Some thought it just as well. A tattered, unsociable stranger could hardly add much to the festivities.

There was talk about the old man, though. The men on the whittler's bench at the livery discussed it thoroughly, and this was reported to the Tuesday Sewing Circle by the wives.

"A body'd think he'd put on better clothes to come in the Lord's house. I could see his long-handles through the hole in the knee of his trousers."

"Could be he didn't have no better ones."

"Didn't speak to a soul, did he? You'd think he'd want to share the coffee and cookies, but no, he just up and left, givin' nobody a chance to invite him."

"Reckon he had things to do?"

"Now what things would a bum have to do, tell me that?"

"I say we need to keep an eye on him. Our youngens are runnin' loose around town, and we don't want nothin' to happen."

"What could happen?"

"Well, if he was a criminal that got loose, they could be killed, or maybe somethin' else. Ain't no way to know."

Over the period of a couple of weeks, they discussed the old man, time and again, and then along about the last of January, a cold snap brought in another freeze up.

"You know, I ain't seen no smoke out'a the bum's chimney during this cold spell. Reckon he's got no wood?"

"A body'd freeze in this weather, havin' no wood."

"Been thinkin' it'd be a good thing to go check on 'im."

"Well, he's been kind'a stand-offish."

"That wouldn't keep 'im from gettin' cold, or maybe he's took down sick."

"Or died."

"I figure to go on over there and see. Harley, you want'a come?"

"I'm a little tied up here," Harley told them. "You could ask Marion. If the man's sick, likely he'd want a visit from the preacher."

So they had gone. Marion and three of the men struggled through the underbrush, climbed rocks and ducked limbs. There was no road, and hardly a path. Goodness only knows how he came and went, and no wonder his clothes were in tatters.

When they came in sight of the cabin, the preacher called out, "Hello, the house!" as a proper warning that people were approaching. It was a good way to avoid possibly facing a shotgun. Most times, the call brought someone from the house to the door to greet the visitors.

His call brought no one. They went up to the house, and when he reached up his hand to knock, the door had swung back on its hinges, which was strange, as there was practically no wind. There was no sound within.

The men stepped back to let the preacher enter first, as was his due. Inside they saw the bed, just a wide shelf against the wall, but there was no bedding. There were several smaller shelves on the wall, but all were bare.

In the corner was absolutely the tiniest stove imaginable. Not a bite of food, prepared or unprepared, or utensil for cooking, or one thread of garment was there. There was no sign that the cabin had been occupied within the last year. That is, except for one thing.

On the cabin floor, near the window, lay a small pile of whittling chips. Setting on the windowsill was the carving of a small dog and a cat, complete but unpainted. Beside them was a bird with exquisite wings, painted in shiny blues and greens, with a tiny yellow beak and yellow feet.

The men had looked at each other in meaningful silence. Marion had picked up the three carved objects and put them in his pocket. He had showed them to Esther before he put them in a small box and took them to the church.

Likely they were still there in the storeroom and would probably stay there. They seemed to belong, somehow.

Later that evening, Marion had read to her the verse in the Good Book about being kind to strangers, because some people had entertained angels without knowing it. That old man surely didn't look like an angel to her, but how did she know what an angel looked like? Likely not like a little girl wrapped in a bed sheet with a yellow star pasted on her head.

10

There was a damp chill in the dark room where Esther sat and rocked. She really should get into the bed where it was warmer, but instead, she just sat, alone with her memories and the old man who was deep in uneasy sleep in the bed.

"Lord, I wasn't too happy about comin' here and leavin' Kansas, but You had ways to make it up to me." Esther grinned as she remembered.

"Now, Lord, there's times I felt like You was just usin' me to get your pump organ down here and wantin' me to think it was all my own idea. That's all right, Lord. It all worked out fine."

Marion had found himself having to study far into the night, reading by lamplight, to pass the study course for a minister's license. He had questions to answer and sermons to write down the outline of, and it was harder than any school Esther had ever heard of, but he had made it. And there was the proof of it hanging on the wall. She glanced up at the diploma. It said Marion A. Sisco was now qualified to preach. Esther remembered the humor of it all.

"It must'a seemed like a joke to You, Lord, them givin' our Marion permission to preach after You done told him to, and it was Your word he was preachin' anyway!"

What was even stranger, though, was the way she became a schoolteacher, and she didn't have the piece of paper telling her she could.

In the deal Marion and Harvey made over the livery stable, a piece of land the size of two acres was set aside for a school. The fellows at the livery had gotten together a "work day," and the twenty by twenty-four foot building had gone up in the yard before sundown. The desks took a little longer. Marion had made them here at the house.

After the thing Marion had gotten into (helping to put up the church, then being the preacher), it should have been a lesson to Esther. She was the force behind getting the school building and then found herself there doing the teaching.

Every month she had written to the people in Jacksonville, telling them how badly a teacher was needed, but no one came. Likely, they thought seventeen children in a tiny river town were not important enough to be concerned about. But one of those children was hers, and though the girls were not old enough yet, one had to start somewhere.

There were no books, pencils or paper. She hoarded pieces of cardboard boxes and printed words on them. It wasn't enough. They needed chalk and slates, at a bare minimum, and a big board for the teacher to use. It was Bea's idea, once more, that provided the necessary supplies.

"Way I see it, Esther," Bea had said, "my Suzie won't be there for two more years, but it's got'a be done. We got us a new litter'a pigs out there in the pen, and I'd hand one over for whatever it'll bring, if it'd do you any good."

The animal auction! Of course! The Jacksonville Auction House was well known for counties around, and it operated two days a week. If everyone in town had one animal they could spare, well, maybe....

It had taken a sight of convincing to make Marion see the practicality of it. Actually, what had finally convinced him was that she said she would quit trying to teach the school unless she got something to teach with. She said she'd just bring her Daniel home and have a class of one.

A day was set, and a notice was posted in the livery and in Mr. Jenkins' store. Those interested in supplying the school could bring an animal, any animal, and be at the livery at five-thirty in the morning of the designated day. Those who were willing could bring a wagon and help to haul the animals into the auction.

Esther offered to drive one of the wagons (now that her husband had made the swinging bridge safe to cross), and he could take the other one. Likely there'd be at least two other wagons.

Before daylight, they began to gather around the grounds of the livery stable. Marion had a newly-broke pony attached to the back of his wagon, as his contribution. Two more horses were added. Pigs were the favorite and numbered 28. There were three goats and two young kids. Three beef calves, a Shanghai rooster and two hens in a crate. There were three beagle pups and four kittens to round out the menagerie.

The pigs were graded by size and divided between three of the wagons, and everything else, other than the calves and horses, were put in the fourth wagon.

The horses and calves were tied at the back of the wagons. Actually, the trip could have been made with three wagons, but the festivities of the day had become infectious, and a number of people decided to come along to enjoy the holiday and do a bit of shopping in the city.

The Evans' wagon was first in line, then Esther, with her son and two other small boys (the girls had been left at home with Bea). Behind her was Clyde Barker, the town blacksmith, and bringing up the rear was Marion, his wagon leading the three sale horses.

Even now, Esther grinned to think what a picture they must have made as they entered Jacksonville and followed the river road to the auction arena.

That was long ago. The auction house is no longer an arena but is now a large, covered pavilion with chutes and loading ramps. Her young Daniel had been part of its management until just months before his death. Likely this very trip had a lot to do with his decision to make his living there.

But back to the trip.

Her Daniel, along with Davie Evans and Leon Barker, climbed in and out of the slow-moving wagon, playing games of skill and bravery. Often they abandoned the wagon to run along beside the caravan, inventing games and making up the rules as they went along.

It was good that she had packed an enormous food basket, because three boys, she knew, were going to be very hungry.

At the auction, they registered their stock, took their number and settled down to wait their turn. It was a beautiful day, and the auctioneer was in full voice.

The first of their animals, a dapple gray mare, came into the ring. The auctioneer read a note and then looked around at the assembled group.

"This here next lot of animals has been donated to the River Bend private school for the purpose of havin' money for slates and chalk. Don't recollect we ever had anything like that before.

"So now we got us a gray mare, strong and healthy, lot'a good years left in 'er. Gonna start 'er in at a dollar. Who'll give a dollar, gi' a dollar, gi' a dollar? Need me a dollar for a young gray mare. Gotcha, there mister. Got me a dollar, got a dollar, got a dollar, who'll gi' me two? Got me a two, got a two, now I wanna three. Three'll gi' me three, gi' me three. Got me a three, now I wanna four...."

The bidding rose to eight dollars and stalled. "Got me a eight, gotta eight, gotta eight. You gonna give a nine? No? Then I got'a let this here fine horse go for eight silver dollars to the fellow in the black hat with the feather. Next!"

He looked around at the colt, frisking between the handlers. "Got a fresh-broke colt, here. Bring 'im on down, boys. Look at the shine on that animal! Gonna start him at five silver dollars. Got'a fi', got'a fi', got'a fi', gonna have a six. I got'a 'fi, and a six, I got'a fi' need a six. I got'a six. Rather have a seven, come a seven, come a seven. Come on, fellows, let's have a seven."

A voice from the crowd shouted, "I got'a ten."

The auctioneer shifted to the higher number. "Got'a ten, come-a ten, come -a ten. Who'll raise it up for this frisky colt?"

Bidding died out at fifteen dollars, a wonderful price, but then, he had been a beautiful colt, and it had cost Marion extreme physical pain to let it go. The price it brought made the giving of it more bearable.

The same person bid on and bought all the goats for fourteen dollars. A very good price for goats. *Thank you, Lord.* The calves, somewhat gaunt and droopy from their twelve-mile trip, brought two dollars each. The pigs averaged out fifty cents to a dollar, and then the crate containing the Shanghi rooster and two hens was brought in by the handlers.

Esther was standing with Maddie Benson, the contributor of the fowls, and she asked Maddie, "Thought your Bert was wantin' to switch over to Shanghais, 'cause'a the way they looked."

Maddie chuckled. "That was his thought, them Shanghais bein' so big and colorful, but they got a habit he don't like. Our old roosters, them Domineckers, they start crowin' at four o'clock, time a fellow was gettin' out'a the bed, but that Shanghai, he took to crowin' at midnight, just to get one up on the Domineckers. Kept up his infernal crowin' till daylight, wakin' up the other stock. By three o'clock everything on the place is settin' it up, baaain', bawlin', bleatin', cacklin' and whinnyin'. It was either bring 'em on over here to the sale or have Shanghai stew. The youngens set up a howl, not wantin' 'im to be ate, so here he is."

The bidding cleared three dollars. "Got a three, got a three, ya' gonna gi' me more? No? Well, it's a'goin', goin', and gone to the young fellow by the gate. Bring on the next thing."

The beagle pups went fast at fifty cents each, and last was the box containing the four kittens.

The auctioneer looked into the box and looked up, grinning. "Aw, fellers, you pullin' some kind of a joke on me? You know there ain't nobody gonna pay money for no cats. Cats is somethin' a body's lucky to find a place to give away. Get these varmints on out'a here and stop wastin' my time."

Someone passed a note to the handler, who passed it to the auctioneer, who curbed his impatience long enough to read it. Then he grinned. "Gonna take back most'a them mean words I said. These here is special cats."

He took one from the box and held it high. The kitten had a muted stripe of gray and grayish yellow and a head decorated with pointed ears. The crowd was pindrop quiet and the kitten looked out at the sea of faces and spat, vehemently.

"This here little old kitty had herself a bobcat daddy. I figure you all know what that means. A body lucky enough to get this little thing to stick around their house and catch snakes and mice, they ain't gonna be bothered with havin' kittens all the time. A tabby ma and a bobcat daddy, that means a neuter litter. Now who wants a good housecat, not makin' a litter every year?"

A chuckle rippled through the crowd and the bidding started. The kittens went to four separate places at a dollar each. The group from River Bend cheered with enthusiasm and left the arena.

The parents began to look for their children, scattered about in the grove playing games. All were easily accounted for except for Daniel, Davie and Leon. Why was Esther not surprised? Very few things about her son were routine.

The three sets of parents circled the arena and called, then widened their circle, their voices bordering on panic. As they worked their way outward, the river became closer and closer.

Then they heard Davie's father's whooping call, signifying that he had found them, and everyone hurried to the sound of the call. There were Davie and Leon, standing on the sloping back of the swiftly moving river, under a tree with wide-spreading limbs.

"Where's Daniel?"

The boys pointed to a limb of the tree that extended out over the river. There sat Daniel, looking up and down the river, watching the water and the boat traffic. One slip of the foot and he would be swept downstream instantly.

"Wait, Daniel," his father had called nervously. "Don't move."

"Sure, Pa."

From the wagon, Marion took a light rope and knotted it into a lasso, flinging it toward the boy. "Now catch onto it, son."

"How come?"

"Because I told you to. Now grab onto it."

Daniel let a few throws go by that Esther was sure he could have caught. Between throws, he grinned and looked around. How often did he have this much attention all to himself?

Then his father, in his special, stern, "I mean it," voice, demanded, "Daniel, you grab a'holt onto that rope."

He did.

"Now put that over your head and pull it tight up under your arms."

Daniel squirmed around, finally standing up on the limb. "You mean I got'a get inside the loop?"

"Yes, that's what I mean."

"Why don't I just come on down?"

"DO AS I SAID!"

"Sure, Pa."

The boy put the loop over his head and squirmed his arms up, swaying precariously on the oak limb. Finally it was in position, and he called back, "What you want now, Pa?"

"Get yourself on down from there, and be careful."

Daniel stood up on the limb, as solid and steady as if he had been one of the twigs growing from the limb. He walked sedately along the limb toward the trunk of the tree. Those on the bank were too tense to breathe.

Then, just as he reached the edge of the river, he reached up and caught a smaller limb, did a quick "skin the cat" between his arms and swung to the next higher limb. Using that limb as a springboard, he leaped toward the bank of the river.

A gasp escaped the onlookers as the body of the little boy left the limb and flew into space. From the angle of trajectory, he would have landed squarely on the grassy bank, but he had not calculated the rope around his chest. It caught him short, and he now swung down from the limb, no more than five feet above the raging water.

"Pa!" he yelled indignantly, swinging at the end of the rope.

The concerned minds on the bank sized up the situation. To release the tension on the rope would lower him into the water. The bark of the tree caused too much friction to pull him back up. He was barely too far out to reach.

"Ouch, Pa. This here rope's tryin' to squeeze the breath out'a me."

His son's pain, however deserved, spurred his decision, and Marion tied himself to the other end of the rope, instructing the men to hang onto it.

Clumsily, the man had climbed the tree and, with shaking, uncertain feet, had worked his way out onto the limb and hauled his son up beside him. To his credit, though, he knew when he was beaten.

With a tug and a jerk, the rope was loosened and slipped off over Daniel's head.

"All right, son, scat on out of this tree."

Joyfully the boy skittered down the limb near the trunk and crouched, taking aim. Like a squirrel from a walnut tree, he sailed out over the water, landing on his feet on the bank.

The onlookers sighed a collective sigh then watched, to the humiliating end, as their pastor worked his shaky way back to the riverbank. No one had the heart to scold the boy or sympathize with the man. They walked away in silence and boarded the wagons.

At the edge of the city, they tied three of the wagons in the grove, and they all boarded the other one to go spend their profits.

The unofficial school had seventeen students, but there would be at least twenty-five next years. It was finally foresightedly decided they would purchase 50 slates, as this would allow for extras and for exhibition work to be displayed.

Two large teacher's boards, 2 feet by 3 feet, were bought to attach to the wall. Three cases of chalk and seven erasers were added. It was decided that each student would bring something from home to clean his own slate. Everyone could afford a soft cloth of some kind.

From the bookstore, they selected "Numbers for Children," "Spelling Book No. 1 and No. 2," and five story books to be used as readers. Everyone voted that the day, all in all, had been a success beyond expectation.

Daniel, Davie and Leon climbed into the wagon, and Esther pulled her team into the road behind the Evans' wagon, still deep in thought. That day's success made other avenues possible.

No doubt it would have been easier to have had some training in teaching methods, but she remembered many things her own teacher had done and had been successful.

How hard could it be? And anyway, in a few weeks or months, someone from Jacksonville would send out a teacher. It was their responsibility, after all. Wasn't it?

Her thoughts continued. Riding behind the horses in the slow-moving wagon was the ideal place to plan. She would put Nellie, Ira, Callie and Alf, the oldest ones, on the back row. They had some training, and being older, they would likely progress more rapidly. There were several children just younger, maybe she'd put Caroline Forte with them.

That would make up the advanced class. Then next would be Daniel, Davie and Leon. They would be a class all by themselves, but she couldn't let them sit together. It would be too dangerous and disruptive.

The rest of the children were young, either five or barely six, and they'd need to be on the front row so she could help them more. However, Josie Markham could likely recite with the three boys. She was tough and could hold her own as well as being very quick and bright.

The obliging sun of the autumn afternoon warmed her shoulders and the back of her head, making her drowsy. The sounds of the earlier trip, the excited calling back and forth, were now quieted.

Quiet? Sounds!

An alarm went off in her head. Where were the boys? In a panic, she turned to look behind her, hoping to see them playing quietly near the end gate. Not to be! She had not heard from them in miles. They were gone! Then she looked down.

There, in the bed of the wagon, lay the boys. David and Leon lay on their sides, each curled into a comfortable ball, pillowing his heads in his arms. Her son was flat on his back, legs spread. In his hand was a half-eaten biscuit from the lunch basket. All were sound asleep, and she sighed with relief. Disaster averted by a nap.

Her thoughts drifted back to the schoolroom. More storybooks would be nice. When the new teacher came, she was sure to bring books with her.

Remembering back, Esther could still feel the tension and frustration at having too little time for anything. The usual rule that a teacher must be unmarried seemed to have merit. How did one keep food cooked, clothing in repair and be a decent mother?

The usual winter chores of spinning cotton and wool, making soap and candles, dip-dying the thread for clothing, and the eternal knitting of socks and caps took second place, sometimes third place, with lessons to plan and the disputes of seventeen children to settle.

It would be temporary, of course, and she could handle it. She would have to. There was no one else. Though, if she had known it would be two years before a teacher came, discouragement might have made her give up. Better she had not known.

A few incidents made her smile. There was when Kenny Lacey, barely five and shy, became so unnerved by recitation that his bladder failed him. Regularly. Finally she solved the problem by sending Kenny to the outhouse behind the school just minutes before recitation.

It worked! Kenny grew up to be a fine man, and his children were friends of Jane Ann.

Then there was the day of Nellie Bascom's trials. Nellie was going on eleven and was in charge of the donkey and cart which brought herself and her two brothers down out of the mountains each day.

Along the way she would pick up Marilou Manford and two of the Mathers' children. At the foot of the hill, just beyond Wild Turkey Creek, she usually collected tiny Lola Ramey. That made a cartful.

Now, Wild Turkey Creek was not named after wild turkeys. It was named that because it gushed suddenly out of the ground near a good spot for hunting turkeys, themselves not nearly as wild as the creek. The wildness of the creek came about because of the dozens of small streams and brooks that contributed their load of water just as it cascaded out of the mountain, swelling it to the limit of its banks.

It seemed that rain falling anywhere on Five Mile Hill or Red Rock Mountain swelled the tributaries and consequently also Wild Turkey Creek, sending it roaring over the rocks at the foot of the hill.

After one particularly bad storm, Nellie checked the river and deemed it unsafe to take the cart through the water. Being responsible for six younger children made her cautious.

She unhitched the donkey from the cart, tying the cart securely to a tree. Then she attached a line to the donkey's neck and set her oldest brother, almost seven, on the donkey with five-year-old Lola in front of him, instructing him to take her across and come back. That done, he took the youngest Mather boy, also five, and came back.

The decision not to use the cart proved to be a wise one, because the icy cold water reached the lower stomach of the donkey, and the children were forced to hold their feet wide to keep them dry.

After this trip, Nellie told her brother to stay on the other side, and she pulled on the line, drawing the now irritated donkey back to her. Next, she sent Marilou and the other Mathers boy, yelling for her brother to come back on the donkey and get their youngest brother, barely five. Which he did.

It took a lot of verbal and physical persuasion to get the donkey across the creek once more, but finally only Nellie herself was left on the far side. She had considered taking her youngest brother with her as she crossed, but the donkey was a small one, and she weighed somewhat more than the older brother. And the donkey was becoming very unhappy.

Nellie climbed aboard the donkey and urged him into the stream. He snorted and blew and tossed his head in angry frustration as he walked into the water.

In exact midstream, the donkey sat down, sliding Nellie off his back into the icy water. At the sound of the gasp from Nellie and the excited squeals from the opposite bank, the donkey nickered with gleeful satisfaction and continued to sit in the cold water.

Nellie righted herself and fought against the current to lead the donkey, but he refused to budge. The yells and squeals from the bank had now reached a roar. Nellie tugged and pulled and, at one point, lost her footing entirely. She came up out of the water, spitting and sputtering and shaking from the cold.

Now, Nellie was a responsible child, and though she could have taken herself from the frigid water, she knew she could not leave the animal where it was.

Still securely holding the lead line, she approached the sitting donkey from the rear, straddled him, and grabbed one long ear in each hand. With the skill of her capable ten years, Nellie tied the donkey's ears into a knot, causing him to fling his head this way and that and bare his yellow teeth, trying to nip her. To get a better footing, he stood up, and Nellie beat a staccato on his ribs with her feet.

It was then that the donkey decided to cross the river, snorting and shaking his head to loosen his ears. He stepped out of the water, dripping and shaking, but Nellie stuck to his back like a burr under a saddle, riding him the last quarter of a mile, with her six-person cheering section dancing around her in circles.

The drenched girl tied the donkey to the downwind side of the schoolhouse and marched into the classroom, holding her head high. Her hair hung in drippy strings, and her clothing was plastered to her shivering body.

Esther had been frightened that Nellie would be sick, being cold and wet for so long, but one thing for sure: she would have to get her out of the wet clothes.

Esther took Nellie to the cloakroom, calling Callie, Dolly, Josie and Miriam to come with her.

"Girls," she told them, "take stock of what you got on. We're fixin' to share with Nellie till her clothes get dry."

The best prepared was Callie, wearing two pettislips. She began to strip down to that layer to donate her outer garment. Dolly was wearing a flannel pettislip, good and warm, so she shed her drawers and offered them. Josie handed over a camisole and sweater.

Esther, herself, had worn a rectangular wool shawl that she wrapped snuggly around Callie, whose dress had been part of the offering to Nellie.

Nellie's shoes squdged water when she stepped, so they were set on a rack above the potbelly stove to dry. Her small feet were red and bruised, but obviously no child had extra shoes to offer.

Esther had stood, biting her lip, trying to decide what to do about the feet when Nellie's brother held up his hand.

"Miz Sisco? You know what? My feet are big as Nellie's, and I got warm socks. You thinkin' she ought'a wear my shoes?"

Problem solved. "Why, yes, Jimmie. I'd say she ought'a be wearin' your shoes."

Classes were held that day with the strong aroma of wet wool and leather, but by the end of the day, the clothes were dry. The children had told her later that the donkey had decided to carry them back to the cart with no untoward incident.

Little Nellie grew up nicely and raised her own family of eleven children wisely and capably. She was living just down the road, enjoying a new grandchild. The town had been full of girls like Nellie who, if there was a problem, they simply tackled it, solved it and went on.

What else was one to do?

11

The old man on the bed was quiet and breathing softly. The old woman's dreams continued.

It had been a few weeks after the trip to the auction that young Daniel went about for a day or two seemingly preoccupied. These moments were rare and a time to be appreciated by the whole family.

The eight-year-old had spent a lot of time in the woods above the rock face. On occasion, Esther could hear the sounds of hacking and hammering, also cheerful whistling.

This was almost too good to be believed, and at one point, Esther had sent Ellena to see what he was doing. He was playing in the trees, Ellena had said, and generally Ellena could be counted onto be a faithful reporter.

Trying to teach at the school had made Saturdays so valuable as a work day that Esther had put her son from her mind and had gone about her work.

Young Daniel, himself, had been acting on the grain of an idea picked up on the day of the auction. The only reason he involved Ellena was that he needed a little help.

The five-foot-long poles he had axed from the saplings above the rock face had been lashed together with short pieces of rope and bits of leather. He had twelve of them securely attached together and decided it was time to test his creation.

He pulled the toy sled into position, but the unwieldy logs were difficult to load. In return for getting to ride on the loaded sled, Ellena agreed to pull the sled up under the log raft when her brother lifted it.

Comparing notes later, no one thought anything about a little boy pulling his little sister down the road on the metal runner.

The next thing Esther knew, Ellena had burst into the house, tears streaming down her flushed face, screaming, "Daniel! Gone! Round and round in the river! Hurry!"

Esther had wondered, later, how the whole town knew about every catastrophe so quickly. How did they always know to drop everything and run to the aid of the distressed?

The bank of the river was crowded, trying to make sense of Ellena's five-year-old terror. She pointed to the sled beside the water, then out to the fast-moving center of the river.

"Dee got on the poles, and they went round and round. He said I had to wait and help him load the poles, and he'd pull me home. He went down the river."

"Under the water?"

With a shake of her head, she screamed, "NO! NO! Down the river that way," and she pointed in the direction of the current.

A glance down the river revealed only water. Marion and several of the men began to rush in the direction of Ellena's pointing finger. One man hurried for a rope and would meet them farther downstream. The women stood silently as blood drained from their faces from fear. A raft small enough to fit on the child's sled would be no match for the murky, rolling water, and the girl had said he went "round and round." And now he was gone. What hope could there be? At top speed, the men could not outrun the current.

No one noticed Harley Nelson as he turned away, jumped on his paint filly, and galloped back toward town. At the livery stable, he snatched up a long rope from its peg and galloped toward the swinging bridge.

The road, actually not much more than a trail that climbed up over Rock Mountain, was steep and rough, with many small, roundish rocks, dangerous under a horse's hoof. Harley headed the filly up the hill, gouging the good-natured animal unmercifully in her ribs, not sparing her when she began to heave to get her breath.

Man and horse took the two-mile hill without a pause for breath. They raced through the pine grove at the top of the hill and headed recklessly down the other side. The little horse scrambled for footing among the rolling rocks as the downhill trail twisted and turned.

Back across the mountain in River Bend, a frantic crowd followed the riverbank, jumping over vines, beating their way through bushes and splashing through tributary streams flowing into the river.

A thread of hope, the merest thread, pulled them on. The raft could have lodged in a sand bank. It could have run against a tree root. But he could have fallen off. The raft could have broken up. Don't think about that. Maybe a low limb was there... maybe... maybe... And the men ran on, panting through the brush of the river bank.

The little town was not called River Bend for no reason. The river that tore down the valley, through Jacksonville, on down through Dogwood Valley, circled toward River Bend. The foot of Rock Mountain and its piles of lava stone in the direct path of the river turned the water aside, forcing it to circle the base of the mountain.

As the water followed the mountain, it doubled back on itself. From the top of Rock Mountain, from the branches of the pine grove at its peak, it was possible to see the river on the right hand and on the left. As it raced past River Bend, it circled the mountain and cut down through the center of the even tinier town of Piney.

Harley Nelson, on his favorite little filly, herself lathered and heaving dangerously, cleared the last downhill curve of Rock Mountain and leveled out on the trail toward the river. While he rode, he had fashioned a noose in the rope on the outside chance that he had an opportunity to throw it. The free end he looped over the saddle horn.

He could see the shiny surface of the river ahead, and he kept his eyes glued to the water as the horse found its way through the brush and vines.

The only part of the river he could see was downstream from Piney, and Harley prayed he wouldn't see anything there. But that was not to be. With a sinking heart, he saw a tiny pole raft bobbing riderless in the current, twisting and turning as it went.

The horse ran on, past a few houses and onto the road, much easier to negotiate than the trail. Ahead was the swinging bridge, hanging low over the water.

The horse galloped fearlessly onto the rattling boards of the bridge. Harley could hardly see the tiny raft as it followed a bend in the river.

The crunch of a splintering board forced him to draw the horse to a sudden stop.... then he saw the leg. A small leg, it was, swinging wildly beneath the bridge.

Harley leaped off the horse and ran to the leg. Leaning over, he looked under the bridge and found the little boy, clinging with white knuckles to the under cable, his feet barely touching the water.

"Uncle Harley! Help me out!" demanded the terrified boy.

But how? Surely the boy would not be able to hold on more than mere seconds. Leaning down, the trembling man eased over the edge of the bridge, holding himself to the bridge by his bended knees. This put him with his back to the boy, but he could finally reach the flailing leg.

"Hang on, son! Don't let go!"

"I can't, Uncle Harley!"

"You have to!"

With a sudden flip, Harley drew himself back on the bridge, circled his waist with the rope, and passed it over the cable used as a handrail. Back down again on the bent knees he went, he himself was now attached solidly.

He grabbed the flailing leg seconds before Daniel's fingers gave out, and the little boy swung down, head first, into the water, being held by his foot.

"Climb up! Come on, son! Climb up your leg!"

Daniel heaved himself up from the water and caught his own knee, then reached higher and caught Harley's shirt collar. This let Harley move his grip to the boy's waist.

He shouted, "Son, climb up the rope!" and Daniel climbed, his excellent balance serving him well.

On the swinging bridge, man and boy stood looking at each other, fully realizing what had almost happened. The boy turned his gaze to the roiling, twisting water of the river and drew in a long breath, then turned back to his neighbor and friend.

"I was a'gettin' scared, Uncle Harley," he said with great sincerity.

"That's all right, son. I was a'gettin' that way, myself."

All of the action happened in seconds, and when man and boy were sitting safely on the boards of the bridge, the filly still heaved, hanging her head and drooling.

Harley jumped to his feet and began to rub the horse on her neck and sides, talking to and encouraging her. The boy rubbed her from the other side. Finally the animal's ragged breath began to smooth out, and her head began to rise. Harley was encouraged. Maybe she'd make it. It was cruel to treat a horse the way he'd treated her, and he was lucky she was still on her feet. There'd be a long rest ahead for her, once they got her home.

"Daniel, I 'speck you and me gonna have a long walk home, don't you think? This ole horse'll be lucky to get herself back up the hill."

"That's all right, Uncle Harley. It ain't far."

It had been somewhat after dark before the man, boy and the footsore horse came walking down Rock Mountain and across the bridge into River Bend.

It had been only minutes earlier that the men of the town had returned, sad and sorrowful, with empty hands. They had followed the river until dusk had begun to settle and, knowing they could do nothing in the dark, had returned.

Here in the cold, dark room, Esther's old and wrinkled face was wet with tears, just from the memory. For a couple of hours, she had known what it was like to lose a child. Her heart had seemed to melt and drain out from her body.

During the excitement, no one had thought to question where Harley was. Even Bea had not given particular thought to it, because he so often worked late.

Up Church Street in the dark came the exhausted horse, the wrung-out man and the tired little boy. The daring rescue had been the talk of the town for weeks. Once more, Esther and Marion had been indebted to Harley for the life of their son.

From that day forward, Esther could readily empathize with a parent for the loss of a child. Death of a child seemed, somehow, to be an indecent thing. One could expect to bury an older parent, but a child was intended to live on after one's own death. Wasn't it?

So there was Daniel, and she had been too busy smothering him with hugs and kisses to scold or discipline him. The boy was who he was and could not be anyone else. He had his own internal driving force that seemingly must be obeyed. He was a person who squeezed life from every second, up until that day he had died, just lying down for a nap. He went to sleep and didn't wake up. So typical of her son.

Then, a few years later, he had felt he had to leave the little town, and it seemed right, somehow, for him to leave the quiet little town and look for the action. He was over thirty when he married a lovely young widow with two girls.

It had proved to be a good move on his part, because his many years of marriage failed to produce a child of his own. His stepdaughters were lovely girls, but they had never belonged to Esther. They had their own grandparents, so it was not expected.

Even Ellena's boys, though they spent time at River Bend, were never really hers either, and they were quick to go their own way. It was natural for them to do what they wanted to. But Jane Ann was hers. She loved her parents but begged to stay the summers in River Bend. *Thank You, Lord, for precious little Jane Ann and the time You gave us with her.*

12

Esther was so old now, and she had lived in River Bend for so many years, it was sometimes difficult to remember how it had been those first years after leaving Kansas.

There had been days, sometimes weeks, that the loneliness for Kansas bore down on her like a weighty, palpable beast, sapping her strength and energy. With all her heart, she wanted her husband to go back.

She missed the place of her childhood. She missed the freedom of the rolling plains, the baking heat of the summers, the sunflowers that grew higher than a house, and even the winter storms that settled in, white and cold for weeks at a time.

Arkansas even had trouble producing a decent snowstorm. Drizzly rain, penetrating cold and the sudden freezeup that layered every surface with a shell of clear ice. Two days later, the sun shone, and the ice was gone without a trace. Crows would be racing through the trees, green shoots of grass would appear in a protected place, and an occasional doe a with her fawn strolled through the woodland as though there had never been a winter.

The north wind would come barreling past Five Mile Hill, scraping over field and farm, yanking clothing off the clothesline and tossing birds about the sky. Then by evening, a mildness would set in, and little girls would be spreading their "dresser scarves" over the stone furniture of their playhouses and tending their dolls with the care they would someday lavish on their human children. Little boys were complaining that there was no wind to fill their kites. That was the way of Arkansas. Exasperating but never boring.

Summers were hot, but clouds drifted about, and moisture arose from the river, creating humidity that made her feel lazy. But then a frisky breeze came from the south, and the humidity turned into a refreshing coolness, encouraging fun and raising energy.

She had prayed that her husband would get restless and long for his fields of wheat... for his flat farmland, as far as the eye could see... for the flowing, golden heads of ripening grain. If he did get restless, Esther had never noticed it. With determination, he grew where he had been planted, and if it seemed his seed had blown far, that did not seem to be his worry. His attention was centered on his God... and there was nothing that she, Esther, could do about that.

And the years went by.

As each child was born, another tenuous tie was formed with River Bend, but those ties did not bind up her loneliness for her home. She was often as one suspended, her feet firmly planted in the Arkansas town and her hopes still on the plains of Kansas.

Building the church, that was another tie, but it was also one that could have been broken. She would miss Bea, but she knew in her heart that she would go back to Kansas if she had the chance.

But then came the tie that was impossible to break. On that memorable day when God spoke directly to several men from the church, men who had been praying for an answer, the unbreakable tie was made. God told these men that her husband was His choice as a shepherd of the flock, relieving him from having to tell them himself. It was on that day that the final, unbreakable tie bound her to this place.

Those ties that she herself had arranged, such as the children, were still in her power. The tie that came from God, that one could not be broken. She would not set herself up against God's will. From that day forward, Esther had cast aside any thought of ever seeing Kansas again.

But God was merciful. Her new duties at the church went a long way toward filling her life. So many of her present memories were centered there. Even more memories than the childhood ones of her beloved Kansas.

There were such memories as Thelma. The six-year-old girl walked a mile and a half out of the woods to attend school. She was a clinging child, eager to please, asking nothing of anyone and blending herself into any circumstance. That is, until she felt brave enough to ask the ultimate favor.

"Miz Sisco?"

"Yes, Thelma?"

"I wanna ask you somethin', Miz Sisco." She had stood looking up at Esther with her eyes of forget-me-not blue from a face spattered with tan freckles. Her hands were clasped behind her, but the motion of her arms betrayed the fact that she was wringing and twisting her hanky, in anticipation of her request.

"What did you want to ask, Thelma?"

"Well, I said to my mama, could I say this to you, and she said to me, it couldn't hurt none. I could ask if I wanted to." Her eyes tried to speak as her voice failed her. She caught her lower lip in her teeth and sighed, lowering her head.

Esther sought to help this shy, timid child get her words out. "It's all right, Thelma. What's it about?"

"You."

"Me?"

"Yeah, Miz Sisco. You and the organ at the church house."

"Really? What about the organ?"

"I wanna learn to play songs on it."

Hmmmmm. What could she do now, in the face of this eager anticipation? How could she tell this child it would be impossible to fulfill her request?

Brutal bluntness would be the kindest in the end. "Thelma, it takes a long time to learn to play songs."

"That's all right. I don't mind. I'm not very old, and I got lots'a time."

"Well, there's another thing. You have to be able to practice at home. You don't have an organ at your house, do you?"

The blue eyes danced with excitement, and Thelma had run to her school desk and brought a board to show Esther. It was about fifteen inches long and eight inches wide. It was drawn like a keyboard, almost exactly to scale, and identical to the shape of the keys on the organ.

"Where did you get this?"

"We made it. My daddy, he scraped it smooth like the organ keys, and my ma, she helped me make the lines. Then we made them black keys out'a pasteboard and stuck 'em on. If you'd be having' time to show me somethin' once, then I'd learn it like I learn my spellin', and then when you had more time to be tellin' me another thing, I'd learn that."

Dear Lord, what do I do with faith like this?

So time was made on her crowded Saturday for Thelma. She told her the names of the notes and how they sounded, and the little girl hummed the tone as she punched the key. The wonder of it all made her tiny shoulders shiver with excitement.

After the lesson, she skipped away, happily humming the tones she had just heard. Then it was about Wednesday of the following week that Thelma had again brought her "keyboard" to school. At recess, she begged Esther to listen as she pressed her wooden keys, humming the tone as she touched them.

Once she made a mistake, her tone not matching her finger, and she scolded herself. "No, Thelma, that ain't right. You got'a do better!"

Then she started from the beginning, humming and touching the keys again, finally getting it right. She looked up and smiled widely, displaying twinkling eyes, dimples, freckles and a space where a tooth had been lost.

That had been enough to convince Esther. So every Friday, Thelma walked with her to the church for her lesson after school. At first, only fifteen minutes were spared, but later it was much longer, as Thelma progressed rapidly.

A year later, she began leaving the church building for Thelma to lock up, so she could have more time to practice. When Thelma learned a hymn all the way through, she was permitted to play it for the church to sing along (but only on Wednesday night prayer service, at first).

Then they worked on another song.

Five years later, Thelma was doing much of the playing, and of recent years, she was considered the official organist. It was a good thing, too, because Esther's wrinkled and gnarled hands no longer had the skill.

Thelma herself was getting on in years, and very soon the music would be played by the young lady who had moved into town from St. Louis. She had a good, light hand and had even taught music, she'd heard Bea say. Esther didn't hear much news herself since she hadn't been able to go to the Sewing Circle.

Another thing that happened at the church was the thing with the baby.

A family came through town in the midweek, parking their wagon down by the river. They did a little fishing, not seeming to be in a hurry to move on. Marion had gone down to visit and see if they needed any help and to invite them to the church services.

They were polite and thanked him, though they weren't sure how long they'd stay, and they'd be pleased to attend church while they were here. "Thank you, preacher."

Marion had let it go at that. No need to try to help folks that didn't need no help. They stuck around till Saturday, cooking their food on a campfire on the small beach beside the river.

Then Sunday morning, when Marion unlocked the front door of the church, the door bumped a box setting on the floor just inside the door (how had they gotten in through the locked door?), and a baby started crying. The baby looked to be about two days old and was a bundle of screaming, crying hunger.

It had been hard to get the minds of his congregation together to have a service. Elsie Jenkins sent their son back to the store for a glass nursing bottle, and Esther had taken the baby back to her house and fed it. A perfect, healthy little girl, it was, and not even a note of explanation came with her. Likely her people didn't know how to write.

Esther had kept the baby for the rest of the day, and Bea had kept her the next two days while Esther taught school. Then on Tuesday evening, George and Ella Marsh and Ella's parents knocked at the door.

They had chatted for a few strained minutes, then Ella Marsh began to cry. George patted her, trying to comfort her. Esther and Marion, puzzled, had just waited. Finally, Ella's mother spoke for her.

"We got a thought, Mr. and Miz Sisco, that likely you got our baby down here."

"Your baby? Did you leave that baby at the church?"

Suddenly Ella could talk. "No, sir, Brother Sisco. I wouldn't'a left my baby there. I didn't have my baby yet. But I'm thinkin' that'd be the place where God might'a left my baby. Seemed like that baby was a surprise to you, and there ain't no other body stepped up to say it was their baby." She dragged her arm across her moist eyes.

"Then I figured it must be my baby, bein' the one God sent me. I been askin' the Good Lord for a baby and been waitin' along time. Seems like that'd be my baby. You think I could have her, now, and we'd be runnin' along?"

Esther and Marion had looked at each other as a wordless question passed between them, and the soundless answer followed. Marion shrugged gently and turned to Ella.

"No way to know who left that baby, though it's likely it was the people campin' down by the river. The thing is, happen those folks change their mind and come back for her? Then it'd be right to let 'em have her. Do you understand that?"

Ella's nods of understanding were quick. "That ain't too hard to understand. If them folks come and say the baby belongs to them, then it weren't ever my baby, the one that the Good Lord sent us. I only want my baby, the one I got comin' to me."

Marion didn't like open-ended situations like this. He looked around for an answer, but there was none.

George decided to help Ella's cause. "Well, preacher, we know it'd a been a help if the Good Lord had'a left that baby at our house, 'stead'a His house. Don't know why that happened. But the same way, I don't know why He lets it rain of a Sunday, with us tryin' to get down that sticky, clay mountain, and I don't know why He lets the sun burn up my corn, the way it does some summers. Ella and me, we figure it ain't our place to call God to account of what He does. Shucks, I don't even know why the hens quit layin' eggs in the winter when we're needin' 'em the most. But we been lookin' for our baby a long time, and we been talkin' all this time, decidin' this'n got'a be for us. Wouldn't you be thinkin' that, preacher?"

It was hard to face down this faith and logic, so the Marshes took the little girl, all four of them talking at once as they left the house. They named her Mary. As the years passed, the town mostly agreed that it really was their baby, "the one that the Good Lord sent to them."

All in all, the church had been good to Esther and Marion, taking care of them in the biblical way. When a hog or calf was butchered, a goodly part of it came to the preacher. As fruits and vegetables became ripe, baskets of them arrived at Esther's doorstep. Sometimes it was a live pig, squirming around in a tow sack, or maybe it would be God's part of the honey flow.

One Sunday, Marion was handed a cheeping box containing two baby chickens. It seemed that an old hen had hid out her nest and showed up with twenty newly-hatched babies. Surely, two of them belonged to the Lord, and here they were. Both chicks had survived but never amounted to anything except as pets for the children.

The only bad memory attached to the church was the smallpox epidemic, and that was certainly not the fault of the church.

The first sign of the outbreak was at school when Eldon Carpenter didn't feel liking playing at recess. He laid his head over onto his desk, and when Esther had felt his forehead, he was fevered and flushed. Maybe it was just a cold. Maybe just measles or chickenpox, but Esther had known in her heart it was something far worse.

There had seemed to be a sweep of the disease every 10 or 15 years, and it took its toll from every age. It had hit Topeka years ago, and friends from school had been taken in a matter of days. Her parents had quarantined their well children, and they had escaped, and she was never sure if she would be naturally exempt if the epidemic should strike again.

She made a floor pallet for Eldon and sponged his face to bring down the fever, all the time fighting with her better judgment. Surely she was exposing the others, but hadn't they already been exposed? Eldon made it home but did not come back the next day. His sisters reported that he was covered with red spots. Listening, Esther felt fright bumps rise on her neck and arms.

Looking over the class of children, she made the decision.

"Daniel, son, run fast and get your father and bring him here. And listen, you will not waste time playin' on the way."

The little boy nodded and was running when he cleared the schoolroom door. Within the hour, he was back, riding a galloping horse.

"Marion, I'm certain we got smallpox in town. I'm fixin' to send the children home, tellin' 'em to stay, but some families got no youngens here. You got'a ride out and tell them."

He sighed, but his expression did not change. He was used to problems. "I'll run by the livery and get some help."

He had turned to leave when she called him back. One had to look ahead and make plans.

"Wait, Marion. You 'member how it was in Topeka? How everybody got so pulled down? I just had the thought of the church. That'd make a hospital. If you think it'd be right, tell folks to bring on their sick ones to the church. We can't have services, anyway, till this passes over."

He nodded acceptance of the plan and was gone.

Scared and sober, the children left the school, and Esther herself went to the church. She had shoved the benches around to face each other in pairs, forming long beds, three foot wide, with sides created by the backs of the benches.

Food. She'd need some help there, but soup, made on the potbelly stove, would be the staple for the sick ones. A worry nagged and pulled at her mind. Had the epidemic in Topeka actually immunized her, or had she escaped only by her parents' quarantine?

Then Bea appeared at the church, bringing her three children and little Catherine. Daniel and Ellena had been left at the house.

With tears in her eyes, Bea had confessed, "Esther, we ain't never talked about it, but I know what this is all about. My sister died last time we had smallpox. It was so awful. So awful!" She shook her head dismally. "What can I do to help what you got started? Do you reckon we got it caught at the start?"

Esther remembered her knees practically giving way from relief at hearing Bea had survived the plague. She had answered honestly. "Ain't no way to tell what's to be done next. Just to wait and see, maybe. We could pray the Good Lord to let us know the best way."

Before the day was out, Eldon Carpenter arrived at the church in the family wagon. His mother was with him, herself raging with fever, and they were put to bed.

"Bea, could you go over to the house and get something to make soup in? Tell Daniel to come and take the Carpenter's wagon over to the livery but not to come in the church. Tell Ellena I expect her to be a big girl and take care of things, and I'll not be comin' home."

Thinking back, it seemed that the town of River Bend was like a wagon rolling down hill. It took only a nudge to start it moving, then momentum took over. By nightfall, mason jars of home-canned meat and vegetables were setting on the church steps. Stacks of firewood were piled just outside the door.

Through the window, she saw her eight-year-old son untie the Carpenters' team from the post. She waved encouragement as he drove away, capable as any man. Standing at the window, she began to weep, tears streaming down, wondering how it would all turn out.

Esther and Bea had made a place for themselves in one of the tiny classroom near the front door.

There was a knock on the door, and there stood Maggie Raleigh, looking perfectly normal.

"I come to help," she announced. "My bunch can handle things at home, and I done had it." She pulled up a sleeve. "See them spots? Them's smallpox scars, so I'll be stayin' to help."

Elsie Jenkins came with an armload of clean, new bedsheets and a pan of steaming cornbread. "When you got things needin' to be washed, poke 'em in a pillowslip and set 'em on the steps. I'll get it done."

During the night, four children and two adults were added to the number. Just as light broke in the east, little Annie Gregory was joined to the number, and she lived two hours. She was only six months old, and she was just not strong enough to fight it off.

Annie's mother had a rising fever and was put to bed, and before noon, Annie's big, six-year-old brother, Alfie, was brought in.

Marion and some of the other men began making pine boxes, small and adult, and a crew of men stood by to dig graves. There was no laying out of the dead, and no funeral. It was necessary that burial be done as soon as possible.

Esther, Bea and Maggie spent endless days and nights sponging faces to give a little relief from the fever, encouraging sick children to eat, and cleaning the floor where they had been unable to keep food down. And carrying slop jars to the door to be emptied in the outhouse. The other tiny classroom had been made into a toilet, using slop jars donated by the Jenkins.

By two weeks into the siege, it seemed to the three women inside the church that it had been going on forever. The crying children, the stench, and for Esther, the concern about her own health. She found herself constantly checking her underarms for fever.

The women of the town searched their minds for something that could be of use. Eloise Forte came in with two dozen of her homemade scented candles, a very welcome contribution. Viney Peters brought a platter of frosted cupcakes, hoping to tempt the appetite of the children who were unable to eat them, but the three nurses thought they had never eaten anything so tasty, so tired they were of the soup.

Carrie Mansfield brought a pile of cleaned and pressed soft cloths to be used in cleaning children's faces and bottoms. Were they every glad to get those! A tin of coffee came from the Mathers, and Alma Benson brought a simmer kettle of potpourri of bay leaf, cinnamon bark and hawthorn berries. "This here'll change the smell in there. You got'a be awful tired of the way it smells, 'cause I remember how it was. The smell gets pukey." They had not realized quite how "pukey" the smell was until the fragrance of the bay and hawthorn filled the church.

The nurses had spent three weeks in the church without stepping a foot outside the door. There had been twenty-three deaths, but almost that many had survived and were allowed to leave. Surely, the worst was over.

Then came a knock, and Esther opened the door. There stood Harley Nelson, tears streaming down his face as he held out his youngest son. Little Frankie Nelson was flaming red and heavily marked.

Harley shook his head in denial. "Happened all of a sudden, in an hour. Others still all right."

Esther took Frankie in her arms and closed the door. Bea came to help with the new arrival, and when she looked into the face of her son, her weariness and anxiety broke to the surface. She screamed a long, keening cry, with her face turned up to the ceiling of the church. To this day, Esther could still hear that anguished cry.

Bea took her son from Esther and hugged him close, tears flowing down her cheeks and onto his clothes. Two and a half years was not long enough to have a son, but four hours later he was gone.

He was handed back through the door, Bea's tears were dried, and no other mention was made of him. Oh, the strength of Bea! The living still needed her help, and she could mourn her son later.

But at every knock on the door, to bring provisions or to take away soiled clothing, panic struck the three weary nurses, turning their hearts to water. If little Frankie Nelson could come down this late in the epidemic and go so fast, who would be next? Maggie's family of little ones? Esther's own three? Or another of Bea's children? Frankie had never been exposed that they could tell, but he was gone nevertheless.

It had been during the fourth week that the last patient had been dismissed. Maggie had been sent home a week ago, but Esther and Bea had stayed to the end.

Then came little Thelma, carried by her father and her clothing damp from his tears. And finally there came the day that the little girl sat up and stood beside her bed. Then, lowering herself to the floor, she moved on all fours because of her dizziness. She crawled to the organ and climbed weakly onto the stool.

Her weary feet pushed determinedly against the bellows, and the pale fingers hesitantly sought the right keys. Then the wavering strains of "Amazing Grace" had filled the church. Esther and Bea had laughed and cried and had clung to each other from relief. Little Thelma's song had broken the month-long bout of tension and had given them hope.

Esther had insisted that Bea leave and she, herself, spent the last two days in the church with Thelma, making sure her fever was gone and that her pox sores were no longer infected.

Struggling against her weakness, Thelma managed to sit upright on the organ stool and learn three more songs. Her father came daily to watch his daughter through the window until Esther released the little girl into his overjoyed arms.

Then Esther walked out of the church.

"Oh, Dear Good Lord, how beautiful is Your earth, and how good smelling is Your breeze!" The leafless trees waved against a sky of leaden gray, and a recent cold spell had turned the flowers into brown clumps but they were still beautiful to Esther's eyes.

Dry, brown leaves had blown against the fences, and the houses were closed against the late chill. It was a plain, little country town, but it seemed all too beautiful to imagine. The epidemic was over.

The women came to disinfect the church. Velma Doggett brought pail, mop and broom. Ella Marsh (whose baby had been delivered by God to the church instead of to her home) brought rags. Representatives from many households came to bring disinfectant and fumigating candles. Every inch of the church was liberally soaked, and the organ was put under a tent with penetrating sulphur candles.

Every bench had been carried outside and liberally drenched. The pungent smell of disinfectant inside the building was impossible to endure. All windows had been opened, and services had been held in the schoolhouse for the next three weeks. There was no Christmas program that year. A simple tree had been put up in the schoolhouse, and the children had trimmed it.

The Jenkins, possibly out of thankfulness that their only son had been spared, ordered storybooks from Jacksonville, twenty-five of them, as a gift to be left in the schoolroom. It was their present to the remaining children of the town, and those books became the start of the lending library.

Esther had slept for the next 23 hours, ate some food and slept another eight hours. *Thank you, Lord.* Her children had been spared.

She looked at the wonderful, colorful covers on the twenty-five story books (added to the five they already had), and it had spawned the dream of another auction.

It was the next summer before it had come about, and it had not been as big as the first, but now the size of the library had swelled to more than 200 books. They had been carefully guarded and watched over by the new schoolteacher that Jacksonville had finally sent them.

Esther's old eyes now closed, and a firm-lipped satisfaction formed on her face. It had been a royal struggle. But now, finally... after almost three years of begging, there was a teacher for their school.

13

The thought of that first new schoolteacher brought a smile to Esther's face. In her mind's eye, she could see her yet. She looked more like one of the students than a teacher, so tiny, with her bright eyes and her mass of almost uncombable curls.

Harley reported on the stir her arrival had made among the fellows at the livery stable.

"Did you get a eyeful o' what's come to teach our youngens?"

"Sure did, and even soakin' wet she'd not weigh more'n my hound dog. Folks in Jacksonville never did have no sense. Sendin' the likes o' her out here."

"Pretty little thing, though."

"Yeah, but it ain't pretty that learns youngens."

Harley had tried to turn the direction of the talk. "They said to us that she passed all the tests, and she knows all she's gotta know to be able to teach. Let's see how good she does."

"Reckon we'll have to."

"Ain't bad to look at, though."

"Noticed that, myself. That oldest boy'a mine, comin' on marryin' age, he ought'a come take a good look at her."

Harley had felt obliged to again jump into the conversation. "No, don't say nothin' to your son. You know if she was to marry, then we got'a have another one. The school board don't hold with married women teachin' school."

"Esther Sisco was married, and she done all right. 'Sides, she worked for free."

"If we'd paid her, 'spose she'd'a stayed?"

"No, I reckon not," Harley had told them. "She didn't take the tests, and she never wanted the job. It was her that pushed and begged and finally got this'n out here."

"She's a mighty pretty little thing. You got'a admit to that."

The new teacher's name was Daisy Stanley, and she made her presence felt very quickly. To Esther, the students had been the children of her friends. To Daisy, they were soft clay to be molded into perfection by her own efforts.

She seated them alphabetically, little ones among the bigger ones, and expected the bigger ones to help out when needed. She expected a hand to be raised for permission to speak or to leave the room. A few of the boys, Esther's own son among them, did not appreciate the education they were now getting. Miss Daisy ruled the classroom with an iron hand.

Davie Evans spent all one evening gathering frogs to populate the desk of the teacher. Then he spent an afternoon standing with his back to the classroom as punishment for his deed.

When he slipped tadpoles into the glass of drinking water that Miss Daisy drank from, Davie was kept in the classroom for two whole recesses.

Missy Evans, Davie's younger sister, was embarrassed to no end by her brother's antics, and she felt it necessary to apologize.

"It ain't all his fault, Miss Daisy."

"Why do you say that, Missy? It seems to me to be his fault."

"Well, it ain't, rightly. It's 'cause'a our daddy. He's too busy to see all the things Davie does, and it was our ma that used to whup up on 'im when he did bad things."

"Why did your mama quit whipping him?"

"It's 'cause we ain't got no ma no more."

"Oh, I'm so sorry."

"We are, too. We had a ma 'afore the smallpox came by. She died. I said to our daddy that Davie was actin' up, and he just groaned, like 'Oh, nooooo!' and looked sad, so I didn't say nothin' else to 'im. He says 'Oh, nooooo!' a lot, every since Ma died."

This was the day that Davie pitched a small rock at the wall across the classroom to make a distracting noise. His timing was not the best, and he let go of the pebble just as Josie Markham stood up to recite.

The rock struck Josie lightly on the sleeve of her snow-white shirtwaist, leaving a dirty mark. Josie surveyed the spot for a second, during which time Davie knew what was coming.

Josie resolutely marched across the aisle and, with both fists, pummeled Davie on the head until he ducked under his desk for protection. Miss Daisy did not see fit to interfere, feeling that Josie had the matter well in hand, so to speak.

However, when Davie developed a pump knot on his head from bumping it against the desk to avoid Josie's fists, Miss Daisy thought it necessary to write a note of explanation to his father.

"Yes, Missy?"

"Miss Daisy, I reckon you'd best let me take that note, if you was to want it to for sure get to our daddy. Wouldn't be countin' on it, happen you give it to Davie to take."

So Missy had taken the note home, and the next day at close of school, Dave Evans, Senior, stood outside the door of the schoolroom, hat in hand.

"Don't hardly know what to say to show how sorry I am about what my boy's been up to. It was me that done wrong all his life, leavin' the raisin' of 'im up to his ma. I just have me that weak stomach, not wantin' to hear a youngen cry, that I plum gave up on it. His ma seemed to be fair capable'a handlin' it, so I let her, knowin' sooner or later he'd get so big I'd have to take over. Seems like that time got here."

Miss Daisy invited him in to talk and had sent Davie and Missy out to play in the yard. All the other children had gone by now. It must have been that Miss Daisy had a lot to complain about, because it was a full hour later that Dave took his children home, and Miss Daisy had locked the schoolhouse.

The men at the livery noticed him as he left, because the road went right by their building. They took note that Dave was whistling as he drove along and had neglected to look toward the livery and wave as usual.

"Miss Daisy must'a had a lot to say."

"Reckon it's that boy of his actin' up again?"

"Aw, he's just bein' a boy."

"Well, I'd say she'd best do what she can. If all them boys in the schoolroom decided on bein' 'boys' at the same time, no bigger than she is, she'd be hard put to control 'em."

"Josie Markham'd help, the way I hear it."

"Always figured that teacher'd have trouble. Little as she is."

"If she had trouble, seems to me she took care of it. Sure didn't ask for no help from us."

"But Dave had to go down there, busy as he is."

"Never seen the time a man wasn't responsible for his boy. Dave went to apologize, that bein' the right thing to do."

"How do you know what was bein' said? You wasn't there, and it don't take no hour to say you was sorry your boy acted up in class."

Esther grinned at the memory. Davie must have been quite a case, because at least once a week, big Dave had felt it necessary to have a parent-teacher consultation, and then afterward he would take Miss Daisy in his wagon over to the Browns where she boarded.

Then, something must have gone wrong with the wagon, because he started coming in the buggy. Several times he left the children to play in the schoolyard when he took her home and then came back to collect them. It must have been a very bad year for Davie!

Then, about the first of April, even though nothing was wrong with the Brown's buggy, Dave dropped by to pick up Miss Daisy and bring her to church. During the service, Missy and Davie sat between Dave and Miss Daisy, and Davie was the best he had ever been in his entire life.

On the last Sunday of June, the members of the church gathered to witness the joining in matrimony of Mr. Dave Evans and Miss Daisy Stanley. As far as anyone could tell, Dave totally escaped the chore of punishing his son, but Esther herself was again begging Jacksonville for another teacher.

She had been forced to start the next school year as the teacher but was relieved in October by Vera Lee McMahan, a lovely red-head who dressed in soft blues and greens and smiled a lot.

The girls in the school adored her, but the boys had her crying more than once after the school day was done.

Then came the day when Lester Crowley, after galloping down out of the mountains to collect his five-year-old Elizabeth, heard her sobs and gallantly stayed to comfort her.

It took considerable time, due to the fact that Vera Lee was so deeply upset, but it was not a problem for Lester. No one was waiting supper at his house. Elizabeth's mother and baby brother were now in the churchyard, and any food that was served at his mountain cabin was prepared by himself and his daughter.

The next summer, the preacher joined in holy matrimony Mr. Lester Crowley and the beautiful Vera Lee McMahan, as little Elizabeth danced joyfully around her new mother.

Esther was back to begging at Jacksonville. No more beautiful girls, please. Don't you have a man? That was when Marcus Campbell had come and had done an excellent job for the next forty-five years.

He had married Maybelle Manford, a smallpox widow, and helped her raise her little Marilou and two more of theirs. It was apparently all right for a man to teach school and be married. He had someone at home to do the work.

It was through the efforts of Mr. Campbell that the storybook library was expanded to more than 500 books, and he watched over them as though they were his own personal property, making sure they were returned on time and undamaged.

All three of Esther's children were excellently taught by Mr. Campbell, who never experienced any discipline problems with the boys. A relief.

A lot of changes had been made in educating children since Esther had arrived in River Bend. Even greater than that, she had heard of a school up toward Jacksonville that taught deaf children, using a finger language. That teaching method had become necessary due to the fact that so many children were left deaf from the diphtheria epidemic. Great news. Such a challenge!

If she was just young again...?

14

There'd be no thinking about the way things were without remembering Daniel's paint pony. It was getting time for him to have a horse of his own, and when Harley's paint filly foaled, not too long after the daring river rescue, nothing would do for Harley but that he'd give the animal to Daniel.

"After all," Harley argued, "that little fellow was along for the trip, right there in his mama."

After days of thought, the boy had named the colt Rocky, after Rock Mountain, and when he was old enough, the boy himself broke him to the saddle.

And, if the truth must be known, Rocky had spent about as much time at school as Daniel had. So many of the children came down out of the mountain in saddle, cart or buggy that it was necessary to set aside a grove for the horses.

It was fenced in, and water was carried to them, and though Daniel lived close enough to walk to school, Rocky generally attended school with the rest of the animals.

The streets and roads of the little town rang with the sound of Rocky's hooves, and the sight of him picking his careful way along the edge of the river, over the peaks of the mountain, or stirring up a cloud of dust on Church Street was a common one.

Anyone with a message to be taken somewhere would just keep an eye out for young Daniel, who was glad to take anything anywhere, as long as it could be done on his paint pony.

He must have been almost thirteen when he instigated the worst scandal of his entire life at River Bend. It had been a cold, windy day, with one of those sudden freeze-ups, and the children were leaving school.

The whittlers at the livery saw the paint pony trotting along School Road, carrying double. There was the preacher's son with a girl riding on the pony in front of him. Not only that, but the lad had his arm around the little girl in a shameless manner, much too bold even for courting couples.

The identity of the girl was also well known. The long, golden hair could belong to no other than Becky Greenland, and gossip flew faster than lightning from one end of town to the other about the shameless behavior of the pair. No one was interested in the explanation from the children. What did they know? Even Mr. Campbell got his share of the blame for letting the young people leave the schoolyard in such a shameless embrace.

When Mr. Campbell heard it, he dissolved in uncontrollable laughter. He walked over to the livery with his explanation, so enough men could hear it who could possibly shut down the talk.

As it had turned out, Daniel had stepped out the schoolhouse door to go home, and Becky was behind him. Her foot slipped on the sheet of ice that had frozen at the doorway, and she went down, catching the sleeve of her coat on the door latch and ripping it almost from her coat. Becky had struggled to her feet and discovered she could not walk because of a sprained ankle.

While he, Mr. Campbell, had been trying to decide on the next move, the preacher's son had picked her up and carried her to his horse, standing her, one-legged, at its side. With the rope he always carried, he made a loop for her uninjured foot, then jumped in the saddle.

While the teacher watched from the window, Daniel looped the rope over the saddle horn and drew Becky up onto the horse. She settled comfortably into the saddle with both feet over the same side, very ladylike.

Daniel jumped on the pony behind the saddle and urged him forward, but Becky, unaccustomed to riding "side saddle" as girls and ladies must and being unable to balance herself, required support from Daniel just to stay aloft. Also, her coat sleeve hung gaping, exposing her bare arm to the elements, so it was natural that Daniel unbutton his coat to share it with her while holding her in place.

To his credit, he had restrained the pony's usual gallop to a quiet trot while he delivered the injured girl to her home, much the same way that he would have delivered a message or a package for anyone who asked.

Now, young Mr. Campbell was not a man to go looking for trouble, and actually, at that time, he had not been a great lot older than Daniel, and he had thought the problem had been admirably solved, thinking nothing more about it. Until he heard the gossip.

Daniel was all wide-eyed surprise when his father had discussed the matter with him later. Sometimes doing a simple favor was not the best thing to do when a girl was involved. There was this interesting thing a girl had which was called a reputation, and even before she knew how valuable it was, a girl must be helped to protect it.

"But, Pa," the puzzled boy objected, "she was glad to get a ride home. Her foot hurt!" The boy had argued, logically and innocently.

His father had shaken his head sadly. "It makes no difference, son. In that case, you should have gone to her house to get someone to come to collect her, or you could have gone to the livery and one of the men would have helped you."

"But, Pa...?" The ways of grownups did not make sense. Why did they always complicate matters?

"Never mind, son, that's the way it is."

Then later, by the time Daniel was eighteen, the age many fellows were courting seriously, he was restlessly straining to leave the quiet town. A few possessions on the pony one day, and he was gone. A bit of Esther had gone with him when he left, but it was a normal thing for a young man to do.

A week later, he had ridden home to tell them he had a job as animal handler at the auction. Then, months later, he got the job of registrar, listing and grouping the animals, then he became a manager of something or other, and during his life he held just about every job that was ever connected to the auction, except auctioneer.

He married a young widow with the two daughters and seemed to have a satisfactory life. Esther hoped he had. In his own matter-of-fact way, when he was through with life, he quietly left. It would be good to see him again, and she soon would....

Now, Ellena, she was a different kind of a child. Many things described Ellena. Quiet, capable, anxious, observant, one could go on and on. Mr. Campbell praised her highly because her assignments were always complete, her copy book neat and her math sums were always correct. She would not have stood for them to be any other way.

It had been hard to teach Ellena to use the spinning wheel, because one could never be perfect at first. Tears and sobbing accompanied the whirr of the spindle, and her finished product was never good enough in her own eyes.

The loom was easier for her perfectionist mind to accept. Her finished products were evenly woven and her colors well-chosen. Her knitting, also, was smooth and fast. Ellena was an excellent daughter, usually observing and correcting her own ways before another could ask her to. That was good, because criticism from others always brought on painful tears.

She was blossoming into a lovely fifteen-year-old when the Woolseys moved over from Piney. Their son, Jacob, settled his eyes on Ellena and never wavered, regardless of what she said or did.

She sat beside Oliver Field in church, and Jacob settled himself behind her. Charles Lacey came by in his fancy buggy and took her for a ride. Jacob had chosen to ride his big bay horse in the same direction at the same time.

Then Ellena was sixteen. Her turned-up nose straightened and her eyelashes curled, and Douglas Dorsett noticed her as she crossed his path. For the next weeks, Douglas had then practically taken up residence at their house, and Ellena seemed to enjoy him for a while. Jacob was around a lot, too, amusing Catherine and making himself useful to their parents.

Emmit Barker made a serious play for Ellena, and she allowed him to sit beside her in church. Douglas and Jacob sat behind her.

Then Douglas, on a sunny Sunday afternoon, took Ellena for a ride, and she was very late coming home. Sunday evening service started, and Ellena was not home. Her brother, on his pony, galloped around to all the known places of interest, trying to find her.

After the service, her father and Harley had gone out in the dark, along with several of the other men. Ellena was not one to be late, and the worst was feared.

Even today, Esther remembered the abject panic of that day and the feeling of helplessness while she waited for word. It was after midnight when a person leading a horse came walking into town from toward Jacksonville.

Daniel kicked Rocky into a flat-out gallop and met the person, who turned out to be Jacob, leading his big, bay mare with Ellena sitting in the saddle. One of her shoes was lost, and her dress was in a sad state. Her dirty face was streaked with tears and a few bruises.

Jacob calmly stated that she had needed a ride home, and he was giving her one. They both developed painfully short memories and seemed to remember nothing that had happened in the last few hours.

When Douglas appeared a few days later, he had a green and yellow ring around one eye and his right arm was in a cast. He couldn't remember anything, either, and it was a while before his fancy buggy was again usable.

Then Jacob began sitting beside Ellena in church, and he managed to get a nice courting buggy. When he took her riding, he was careful to get her home at the right hour. In due time, the preacher was happy to join his daughter to Jacob Woolsey in holy matrimony.

Two years later Jacob took her to Jacksonville. That was natural and to be expected. A man must find a way to make a living, and good jobs were scarce in the small town. Then came the three boys. Good boys, as far as she knew, and none of them ever got into serious trouble.

Then there was Catherine, two years younger than Ellena. Catherine did everything instantly. Often she did it wrong but was able to correct her mistakes and do it again, still in good time.

When Catherine learned to spin, the spindle spun like a top, and her thread had lumps and knobs. If the stocking she knitted had a lump, so be it. She put on the stocking and forgot about it.

The sound of her voice, singing merrily, was as common as that of the birds in the trees. She sang, and if she forgot the words, she made up new ones.

From the third grade onward, Jimmie Markham followed her like a trained puppy. Esther had often wondered what it might have been like if Catherine had chosen the steady, solid Jimmie, whose father set him up the first pharmacy in town. Likely she'd still be alive, but how can one know the ways of their children?

If Catherine had ever been unhappy with her eventual choice of a husband, she never let it be known. After years with no children, she finally gave birth to Jane Ann.

Catherine would bring her baby girl to her mother and leave her for a week at a time. Such a joyous week! By that time of her life, Esther had much less work to do and a lot more free time. She finally had time to enjoy a baby, to sing to her and to play with her.

It was during the summer after Jane Ann's first year of school, when she had come to spend the summer in River Bend, that her parents' house had burned to the ground for no apparent reason, orphaning the little girl. Esther would gladly have taken the child, but Ellena felt it was her right.

Esther had bargained with her for summers, and so it had gone. Jane Ann went to school in Jacksonville and took her summers in River Bend. Then the Good Lord saw fit to let her come here to live in the parsonage beside the church. *Thank you, Lord.*

Esther was feeling weary, and her eyes closed as she rocked back and forth in the chilly room. A cup of tea would be nice, but the stove was stone cold, and the water in the reservoir would have cooled as well. It was easier to just remain sitting, rocking. Stirring around had become such an effort.

The old man on the bed had periods of restlessness, turning his head from side to side, muttering words that she could not make out. The clock on the wall had said three thirty. The night seemed endless, and she longed for morning. With the daylight would come a little strength to go about the things that must be done.

Even her small duties were now so tiring, and Jane Ann kept offering to help. Perhaps she would have to rethink her granddaughter's kind offer. When making a cup of tea seemed to be an insurmountable task, she was just too old.

15

Yes, Esther thought and nodded in agreement with herself. A lot had happened in River Bend since she had watched her husband (and the Good Lord) pull her organ across the shaky swinging bridge. She had not been aware at that time that she needn't be concerned for the organ's safety. He Who could create a world from the words of His mouth and hold the stars in His hand should have no trouble protecting her (His?) pump organ from the waters of His Tuscalara River.

There were many things about the small, Arkansas town to think on. First to come to mind was the food. In Kansas she had eaten fruit, vegetables and grain, thinking her diet was as varied as anywhere in the world. There was pork, beef, chicken and fish. What else could there be?

But here, young Daniel would take his gun to the woodland for target practice and come back with a rabbit and a squirrel or, from the headwaters of Wild Turkey Creek, he bagged a few turkeys or grouse or doves. Or one or more from the skeins of geese that passed through the valley graced the table.

From the river, they pulled mossback turtles. Cut up and skinned, they produced white, succulent meat for the skillet or the soup kettle. And the river contained fish in varieties one could only imagine. It would be difficult to starve in these hills.

And vegetables. When Bea had told her that the green, finger-shaped pods, totally covered with prickles, were actually edible, she had considered it a joke. But quickly the tasty pods of okra became a staple and an eagerly looked-forward-to addition to the summer menu. The beaver tail cactus produced a startlingly sweet fruit that followed their magnificent blossoms, but the fleshy leaves themselves, when scraped of stickers, browned nicely in the skillet and made a tasty relish. They were available year round.

Another thing she had not heard of in Kansas was the Courting Candle. The nice, big, twelve-dip candles were marked off with indentations, from two to three inches apart (depending on the tolerance of the parents), to indicate the length of time the young man could occupy the parlor for courting. In this way the family members were free to retire from the room at dark, and the candle was lighted.

When it burned down to the departure line, it was time for him to go. The young man knew this in advance, and it worked fairly well. Whatever he had to say to the girl, he knew to say it while there was still time.

Marion, however, had created his own version. Instead of indentations, he hacked the candle into chunks with the hatchet. One chunk, sized two and a half inches long, was issued when the room was turned over to the courting couple.

Catherine had made no complaint. By the time the candle had burned down, she was likely to be tired of him anyway and ready for him to leave, but with Ellena it was very different.

"Don't do that, Pa. It looks funny."

"Then you got a thing to laugh about. That's a good thing."

"I don't mean funny to laugh. I mean funny strange."

"I don't know why it should seem strange. That's the same length of time he'd have if I marked it."

"But it'd look better."

"What's looks? A candle's a candle."

"It'll make folks talk about you."

"They do that as it is. They talk about me anyway. This will just give them another thing."

"But, Pa, the light goes out all at once. It don't even give him time to get his coat and find the door."

The father had smiled sweetly at his firstborn daughter. "Then we'll just have to move the settee over close to the door and let him hold onto his coat. That way, when the flame starts to gutter, he can make a dash for it."

"Oh, Pa," and with a flounce of the head, she would stalk away. Yessirree, that stub of a candle caused more aggravation to the steady, even-tempered Ellena than any other thing.

Esther herself had liked the candle stubs. They were easier to store and easier to carry. In the summer, they did not melt down and bend over in the heat. So after the girls were safely married off and gone, Marion still chopped those candles in short lengths.

Beside her rocker, at this moment, was the holder and a stubby candle chunk he had cut just last summer. He wouldn't be cutting any more candles, though, unless it was a thing they did in heaven. She sighed and allowed her eyes to follow the length of him under the quilt. When does one get their eyes filled with a loved one? How long is enough of gazing upon one who is part and parcel of oneself?

Her thoughts went on. Changes came about, and ready-made candles could be bought. They came, colored and of uniform size, in a box that was made for them. Some smelled sweet, like flowers, and that was all right, but the aroma of the candleberry, picked from the Arkansas mountainsides, remained her favorite.

There were tradeoffs, though. The picking of the berries, the boiling down and straining of the wax… it all had taken precious time from the multitude of other duties of the mountain woman.

A big change happened when Elsie Jenkins' boy, that they sent away to go to school, came back and began to make improvements to the family store. The first change was the big sign that said RIVER BEND MERCANTILE.

At first, the name seemed pretentious. There were chuckles for a few weeks, but it had been years and years now since anyone called the store anything but the "Mercantile."

That boy made the store bigger and began to stock yard goods in lots of colors to make dresses. He had stockings, shoes, hats and ribbons and lace. He ran that store all by himself for years and years, but lately he got to hiring a young lady to help him. That was a good change, too, most of the ladies thought.

It seemed that finally the state of Arkansas realized its roads were almost useless in the winter wet and began driving orange stakes along the ditches, marking where they would widen it, and in some places, straighten it. They piled gravel in the holes and graded it smooth with a horse-drawn blade.

The necessary upkeep of the road itself became a blessing to those who lived beside it. The small amount of property tax that one would pay to the state could be forgiven if one had a team and sled and could keep the road in front of their house in good repair. A few pennies were saved in this way, and there was always a use for the pennies.

In recent years, a new, high-sided silver bridge was put across the river. It quickly became a landmark and a thing of pride. It was so much safer than the swinging bridge that was always in need of repair.

The silver bridge took almost a year to complete, creating some good jobs for the River Bend men during that time. They were such good jobs that when the bridge was finally finished and the crew moved on, they took three of the town's young men along. It's bad for a small town to lose its young men, but all was not bad.

While the construction was going on, Maudie Sizemore and Delia Middleton, two of the town's more attractive young ladies, were accustomed to hitching up their buggy daily and riding down to the construction site. It was not unusual for them to take a sampling of their fresh-baked cookies or perhaps a platter of their latest divinity or fudge flavored with local nuts.

Their stated intent was to make young men, far from their homes, feel less lonely. Their caring and interest was not unrewarded.

Maudie became Mrs. Chandler, and her grandchildren are now age two and four. Delia is now Mrs. Archibald and lives on the mountain near the Chandlers. A number of other young ladies wished, later, that they had taken greater interest in the progress of the bridges builders. Delia's oldest son went to Little Rock to go to school, and he is now a doctor, practicing in Jacksonville.

Yessirree, it don't seem like much goes on in life until you get old and try to look back. Then a body notices all the changes.

16

There comes a time when it gets easier to look back than to look ahead, Esther reasoned. It was like the thing with the mirror. A young woman spends time looking in the mirror to make sure she looks as good as she can. It seems like all those times get stored up in her mind, and she starts to feel just like that person in the mirror.

For years there aren't enough changes to be concerned with or that can't be covered up. Then, around middle life, looking in the mirror don't seem so important, being that she's still got the sight in her eyes of when she was young and pretty.

Then the wrinkles set in, and her hair gets thin and gray. Her family is grown up and gone and, all of a sudden, there's time again to look in the mirror, and it makes a body draw back and look again, to figure out how she got into that wrinkled, old-woman's body.

And then there's times that a body comes up to a mirror all of a sudden, like if it's hanging in a hall, and the sight of her own face makes her wonder who that is in the mirror. It seems like all the years of her life have been no time at all, and inside her head she's still young and pretty, but the outside of her is nothing but dried wrinkles.

But then comes the time a body learns to say, *That is really me in that mirror, and I spent a lot of years doing something! What was it? Did I do what it was I was supposed to do? What I was put on earth to do? Did I do anything that made me proud to say it was me that done it?*

Esther paused in her rocking vigil and looked at the clock on the wall. It was after four o'clock, and in a couple hours daylight would be showing in the east. It seemed the old man would make the night, but still it was good to have sat and thought and enjoyed her memories.

So, looking back, what was there to be proud of? Her mind scanned over the times when she did her duty, but it paused on the time she had instigated the Tuesday Sewing Circle, one of her proudest achievements.

The ladies met to quilt their quilts, but this had nothing to do with the value of the day.

The mountains were dotted with farmhouses and cabins where lonely women took care of their duties, often shut off from everyone but their families from Sunday to Sunday. There was so much to be said and to be asked about and so much to share that the women were reluctant to leave the friendship of the church after services and often came early, hoping someone else would come early to talk with.

Then the Sewing Circle set aside a day, one day each week, for any woman who could arrange her schedule to attend. There would be someone to talk with, to laugh with, and sometimes to cry with. This way, the ladies could have an idea of what was going on with the community.

Small children could have a day to play with other children, unfettered with their Sunday clothes, and the hitching grove was always noisy with squeals and laughter while their mothers visited, drank tea and ate cookies. It was a day to be treasured by women of the town.

At first, some of the men thought it a useless habit. Did their wives not have enough to do that they had a day in which to do nothing? Most, however, were quick to see the change in their wives and strongly encouraged them to attend.

As time went on, young men whose mothers had come to the Tuesday meeting grew up knowing the Sewing Circle was a day that belonged to their wives and that it was their right to take it.

Arranging to be gone from their duties for a whole day, however, took some planning.

Cecelia Morgan, mother of seven, often brought her own mending along to do while the other women worked on the quilt. A bushel basket piled high with trousers, shirts and underdrawers was lifted from the family wagon and brought into the church by her ten-year-old son, Everett. He was the oldest of the children and took his responsibilities seriously. Nine-year-old Lizzie picked up the baby, age two months, and carried her, and Cecelia herself brought the oatmeal cookies, a water pail of them, that had been baked the previous day by Lizzie and eight-year-old Dottie.

Setting in the wagon, after the other four children between two and seven had jumped out, were three bushels of green peas, still in their hulls. These had been picked by Everett and Adam, who were five. Raymond, seven, had volunteered to do all of the barn chores to get out of the pea picking.

Everett, the oldest child in the grove that day, took charge of the entire group, totaling twenty-three children of all ages, and passed out the cups and pans and a quantity of peas, the size of the container commensurate with the age of the child.

Everyone got his share, except for Thelma, the girl with the wooden slab keyboard. Thelma was exempt, because she would be furnishing the musical diversion.

Fingering her wooden instrument, Thelma hummed the tone to match what she played, and if the fingers might have made an error, her voice did not. In this way, she "played" the songs the children had learned at school and church.

The singing spurred up the pea-shelling activity to such a pace that the three bushels were shelled in almost no time, and the succulent green pods were fed to the assembled horses.

They were now free to play, and Thelma put away her organ and the games began. Drop the Hanky, Flying Dutchman and Red Rover were played in the churchyard and around the headstones in the cemetery.

So valued was this day-out that Bernice Owens, in the last stages of her second pregnancy, could not bear to miss the outing. She had three miles to come, and a lot of it was over a rock-bottomed trail. She had a special, narrow-gauge wagon with a double tongue designed to be pulled by one horse. This was convenient due to the narrowness of the road and the height of the rock faces on both sides of it. She and her three-year-old daughter never willingly missed a meeting.

Bernice, called "Neecie" by everyone, was a bright-faced, happy girl who found life wonderfully exciting and whose presence was treasured in any group. The last couple of weeks, Neecie had opted to knit blue booties instead of working on the quilt, which was fine with everyone.

Today, Neecie had problems. It seemed that she had spent the previous day making pear honey. Her trees had dropped a windfall crop brought down by a sudden blow, and this was often a good thing. It stretched the season by bringing down the early-ripes to be taken care of before the main crop fell. It also lightened the limbs of the tree at a time when the fruit is swelling with moisture, and pear trees were very bad about bending and breaking their own limbs with their weight of fruit.

So Neecie had gathered, peeled and thickly sliced a bushel and a half of windfall pears, boiled them down, added honey and brought them to a simmer. The last hour of preparation took constant stirring, standing over the pot with the long handled spoon, or the honey would scorch. The yield had been fourteen quarts of pear-flavored honey for biscuits or pancakes.

Her pride in her achievement was offset by her discomfort. The standing and stirring had given her a backache.

"The thing I want," began Neecie, after settling herself as comfortably as possible, "is either a narrow buggy with a soft seat or a buckboard with a back on it. That bouncing all over that seat is a'wearin' me out. My back, bein' already sore after the cannin', it's fair settin' it up right now."

"You thinkin' a buggy'd be less bouncy, over the same rough road?"

"Couldn't be no worse," Neecie reasoned, "And there'd be a back to lean on."

"You get the backache real often?"

"Nah, it was just them pears. Thing is, I got the whole crop comin' on, likely in two weeks. Ain't no time now to be gettin' down in my back...."

Bessie agreed. "Ain't nothin' like that long handled spoon and the standin' up at the kettle to get me down. Seemed like it was worse when I got close... to... time..." Her voice trailed away as a thought settled into her head.

Several of the women exchanged glances. "Neecie, when're you due?"

"Not for a month more. I got time to do all the fall puttin' up. Pears, apples, muscadines, all them things. But I never had no trouble 'afore now. What I need is a lean-back on that buckboard."

"You can't use no regular buggy at all?"

"Not and come down the short cut, and that wide road is so windin', it'd take me all day and half the night, just to get here."

"How're you doin' on knittin' them bootees?"

"Got one pair. Aim to get t'other'n today," Neecie hoped, over the clicking of her needles.

It was mid fall, and the older children were in school. Fannie Lewis, a five-year-old who got a late start and didn't get to go to school that year, was the acknowledged leader of the playground.

"Follow me! I'm a leader!" she announced and ran around the wagons. Thirteen toddlers stumbled happily after her. She climbed up on a low headstone and jumped. The others followed, and those who were too small to climb on the headstone, she graciously helped.

She came wheeling around the church steps, bounding up into the building and demanded, "I want a cookie!"

From the refreshment table, Fannie grabbed a cookie and darted back out the door. The child behind her raced up and also demanded a cookie, and the next and the next.

Neecie's three-year-old was already lagging behind by now and was unhappy about it. The discouragement mounted as she saw the others come out with cookies, so she did what she did best. She stood and screamed, "MAMA!"

Neecie tossed aside the needles and the half-finished blue bootee and ran to the door. A painful stitch in her side made her stop and grab a bench for support.

"Neecie!" came a chorus of critical voices. "You hadn't ought'a be movin' like that! You in your condition!"

Neecie sat on the end of the bench and nodded. "I know that. I just jumped up 'thout thinkin'."

By now her three-year-old had managed to climb the steps and came running to her. "MAMA!"

Neecie reached down to the little girl to comfort her. "Shhh! Don't be a'hollarin'. You go get you a cookie if you want it."

The comforted little girl ran off, and Neecie tried to stand. "OUCH! I'm 'bout to be gettin' tired of that old backache!"

"Neecie, you sure it's a back…?"

With her usual merry laugh, Neecie reasoned, "Well, it's my back, and it's achin'. Reckon there'd be another name for it?"

"Yeah, could be. The name I was thinkin' on was childbirth."

Neecie's laughter rang out again. "Never! Never! Never! Not for another month, at least."

"You sure you got your dates right? You look bigger than you did last time."

"I don't think I made no mistake. But, you know, that's what Jake says. He said if I got much bigger, it'd take two wagons to get me here. I hit him for sayin' that."

She laughed merrily and struggled to her feet. By leaning on the ends of the benches, she managed to hobble back to her knitting.

Esther, at her position around the quilt, sat where she had a good view of Neecie's face. At regular intervals, the young woman's face contorted somewhat, and she chewed her lip.

Esther quilted another round, continuing to watch Neecie's face. Finally, she could stand it no longer. "Neecie, you're in labor, and you're tryin' to pretend it ain't a'happenin'. Look at you, pains comin' on, regular as clockwork. Don't you say they ain't."

Neecie's pleasant face contorted into a look of dismay. "Yeah, but I don't wanna have this baby yet. I'm 'sposed to get another month, and I got things I got'a do."

By now she had the attention of the entire circle, and she looked from one to another, begging someone to agree with her.

Esther left her needle hanging by its thread and hurried to the little classroom at the front of the church where the children's quilt pallets were kept. She shook out a few of the quilts, piling them to make a more comfortable bed.

"All right, Neecie. I'm ready for you. You're gonna have that baby before you get home, so you may as well set your mind to it."

"No, Miz Sisco. I thank you, but I got'a get on home. Right now."

That was when Bea had chimed in. "You go up that rough road, and it'll be worse'n Mary goin' to Bethlehem on that donkey. You'll be havin' that baby under a bush with only your little girl there to help."

Neecie lifted her stubborn chin and began to knit furiously, her needles clicking.

No one said a word, and all eyes were on Neecie when another pain hit her.

"OUCH!" she yelled and stood up. Those seated nearest her reached out, and she grabbed the hands closest to her. They half led, half carried her to the pallet in the classroom.

Esther tossed a light cover over Neecie and placed her hand on Neecie's abdomen.

"GIRL! You're fixin' to have that baby right now!"

The entire quilting circle crowded into the classroom around Neecie. Helpful hands stroked her brow, held her hand and tested her contracting belly. While the children played outside, Neecie gave birth to twin girls, with the quilting party fairly contesting for the right to diaper one of the babies in the tea towels they had brought with their refreshments.

The babies were snuggled into a nest made from one of the cleaner of the pallets.

The preacher showed up just at the right time and was sent home for his wagon. In a bed of quilts, Neecie and the babies were enthroned, and her older daughter was collected.

"MAMA! I wanna play," wailed the little girl, as she had to leave in the middle of a game.

Marion and Esther took Neecie home the long way, on the wide road.

"Esther, there wasn't nothin' wrong with my dates. It was on account of being' two babies!"

Well, likely she was right, partly, but Jake was one very surprised fellow. His family of two had left that morning, and it had doubled before it came home.

Later, when Neecie could come back to the quilting, she sheepishly admitted that she had known she was in labor when she left her house that day but thought she could make it until she got home. "It's just that the weeks are so long when they don't have no Tuesday in them!" she complained.

Tuesdays were important to the town. Somehow, even now, Bea found the strength to get to the Tuesday Sewing Circle. She seemed to find her own calling at those weekly meetings.

Bea would sit there quilting, listening, and the younger ladies would be talking. Then there'd be the times when the conversation took a turn that might be considered gossip, and with a word or two, Bea could bring it back to friendly chat. She would be seriously missed when she could no longer go, but, of course, the Good Lord could replace her. Maybe.

When Harley and Bea had buried their first little stillborn girl, they had placed a large slab of marble at the grave, figuring it to be big enough for the names of all family members.

After the smallpox epidemic, they had added Frankie's name, and Bea had put Harley's name there when he went on. There was still a lot of space on the large, flat-topped stone.

The very practical Bea made use of the stone every time she went to the church house. Being at the far edge of the cemetery, it made a good resting place, and she always sat for a few minutes, resting her feet, before walking the last couple hundred feet to the church door. It seemed appropriate, somehow.

The gravestones, many now leaning this way and that from time and weather, made a good place for the children to play on Tuesdays. Games were created that used certain stones as base markers, or pinnacles to leap from, or shields to crouch behind in Hide and Seek.

For the children, it was a friendly place. Tiny fingers could trace out family names. Toddlers could identify the stones of relatives, and Granny Nelson could rest briefly upon the stone before which her body would rest after death.

As she rocked quietly, Esther could vividly remember one other incident that happened on a Tuesday.

As it happened that day, the front classroom pallet contained three babies, one of them only three weeks old. The little classroom was convenient, because the sounds of the women talking and laughing were muted, allowing the babies a more quiet place to nap. Yet they were close, and the mothers were at ease, knowing they could hear the first whimper.

This particular time was in the summer. Older children came, and the play area for this day was out back of the grove where the horses were tied. The activity of the day was to build a playhouse of loose stones, and the stones were not welcome where wagons had to roll. Hence, the use of the back of the grove.

The children had spent a lot of energy building the playhouse. They carried the flat stones and shaped them in the outline of rooms and halls, with other stones designated as chairs and several stones topped by a large, flat one became a table.

Wild flowers were picked and put in a bottle to decorate the "table." Beds were made by heaping fresh grass on the ground for softness, and all the dolls were put to bed.

There had been a minimum of squabbles, and it was, all in all, a very good day. Several of the women had commented on that, looking out the window occasionally to make sure the children were still in sight.

It was when Maudie Perkins took her turn at looking out that she came back to the circle, wide-eyed and sober.

"You all know what I saw out there?"

All needles stopped, and all women were alerted. "You sayin' them youngens done run off?

"No, it ain't the youngens. They're still at the playhouse. It's Indians."

"Indians? We ain't seen Indians here in years."

"Where are they? On the street?"

"No, they ain't on the street. They're on the river."

"On the river?"

With that, most of the women crowded around the windows to see for themselves. Sure enough, a large raft was being poled slowly down the river, carefully hugging the river's edge to avoid the swift central current.

"Them the tribe that's down past Sweet Gum Hollow?"

"Likely. Never seen 'em polin' on the river, though. Mostly they come through on horses."

"I never know'd of 'em to stop in town, did you?"

"Not me."

"They never did, that I know of."

"Well, I reckon it'd be nothin' to get all heated up about. Indians never caused us no trouble."

But still they stood and watched. Several adults and a small gathering of children filled the log raft, and close behind them another raft came into view. The bright reds, blues and yellows of their clothing made a brilliant splash of color on the dullness of the river.

"Hmmmm, how many'd you say they were? Twenty-five? Thirty?"

"More likely thirty, I'd say."

"There's more'n that. Look at them youngens settin' on the edge, draggin' their feet in the water. There's fifty, easy."

"Believe you're right. They a'slowin' down?"

"Lookie! One fellow jumped ashore. Another fellow's pointin' this way."

Several of the men leaped to the riverbank and occupied themselves with something in the grove of trees. The other raft was poled alongside. The band of persons began to leave the raft, and they assembled on the riverbank a few minutes before heading out in the direction of the church.

"Look at that! They're comin' here!"

"What'll we do?"

"Ain't no time to do nothin'. We can't run; they'd see us."

"'Speck we ought'a call our youngens in?"

"Don't know why we'd do that. Indians ain't never hurt us, yet."

"Yeah, but...."

"Likely they're goin' to the store."

"Wouldn't know why. No Indian ever wanted nothin' from us in the past, so why'd it change now?"

"But here they come...."

"They ain't goin' to stop at the store. They're comin here."

"Close the door fast!"

"Does that door lock from the inside?"

"And leave the youngens out?"

"Just wait. Likely they'll go on by."

Many pairs of anxious eyes watched as the whole extended family came down Main Street and turned where Church Street angled off toward the rock face. In addition to the adults, there were children of all sizes, down to cradle-boarded babies riding their mothers' backs.

"They're still comin'. We just gonna stand here?"

"We got a choice of somethin' else to do?"

"We'd be safe in a church, don't you think?"

"Never read anything in the Good Book about that. Couldn't hurt none, though."

As the tribe neared, the women in the church fell silent, hardly daring to breathe. At the door of the church, the band stopped, and one older, white-haired man stepped forward and said something to the others. He turned and came toward the church with his group following silently behind him.

The church door was open, for better ventilation, and the old man hesitated briefly before stepping inside the building. His people followed, practically staying in step with him.

The frightened women had taken their usual positions around the quilt, seeking comfort from the familiar, but all eyes followed the invaders.

About ten feet from them, the man had stopped, and those behind him continued to gather around until the entire front of the church was full.

Esther swallowed hard and stood up. As the unofficial leader, she knew this to be her duty.

"Good morning," she told him tentatively.

The old man nodded agreeably and looked around over the others, then back at Esther.

"Man," he said.

"Man?"

"Man," he repeated, pointing to himself and several of the other men.

Puzzled, Esther had said, "Good morning, men."

The old man shook his head and pointed to Esther, struggling for words.

"Your man," he finally said emphatically.

"My man? You mean my husband?"

The man nodded and smiled, his wrinkles wreathing his face in his relief.

"Husband! Husband! I talk!"

"You want my husband?"

The man nodded vigorously. "Talk," he insisted.

Esther had told him, "My husband isn't here. Could I do something for you?"

Disappointment registered on the man's face, and he turned and said a few words to the men standing behind him. There were grunts and nods, and he turned back to Esther.

"The book," he told her.

"Book? Which book?"

He nodded and put his hands together as though he was opening and closing a book. "Book to read. I was..." and he sought for the word, then pointed to one of the children.

"Small? Little?" offered Esther.

"Little. At the church, they let me read."

"They taught you to read books?"

He nodded enthusiastically. "I have little. I teach. I want book."

"You want a book to teach these children to read?"

"Children! Yes, children. I teach."

Finally Esther had understood. "I don't know. I'll see what we have."

She knew there was nothing in the building that would be of much help to the children. Then she found the Bible Story Book she had been given as a child and had brought it to the church for use by those who taught children's Sunday School classes. She thumbed through it rapidly. The words were fairly simple, having been meant for children. There were colorful pictures to match every story.

She found a few small cards with stories and a stray hymnbook. Likely the man wanted a Bible, but clearly there was not one to spare. It cost her a pang to let the storybook go, but surely he needed it more than the children at the church.

He had been waiting patiently while she looked, and when she came bringing her offering, he smiled and nodded. He took the storybook and flipped through the pages, smiling at the pictures. He stopped at the beginning of a story.

"There... was... once... a... town... called... Ba...?"

"Bethlehem," supplied Esther, bringing more smiles and nods. He handed the books and cards to the young man standing beside him and nodded again to Esther.

"Thank... you...."

"You're welcome. If I can help you with any of the words, come back and I'll be happy to."

He nodded again and bowed his head, touching his forehead, chest, and both arms. Then, on signal, the people left the church with the old man bringing up the rear. Outside the building, the tribe rearranged itself, again following the old man respectfully. They made their way toward the river and boarded their rafts. In minutes they were out of sight.

"What do you make of that?" someone asked.

"Do you think he can really teach those children to read?"

"How come 'im to know right where to come? I'd be willing to bet he ain't been here before."

"I'd say he saw our steeple. It'd be my guess some early missionary taught him to read when he was little, and he can't remember much, but he knew the books would be at the church. Our steeple made him know where to go."

"He sure had me scared, for an absolute fact."

"Notice how he didn't want to talk to no women?"

"But he had to."

"It'd be my guess they ain't even local. I'd say they came down the river from upstate and saw the steeple, and at that minute he remembered about what he learned."

"I'd sure like to be there close to see how he goes about it. Teachin' them youngens, I mean."

Finally the talk drifted back to the usual Tuesday subjects. The day was pleasantly warm, and the children were getting along well, not running inside to the mothers to have disagreements settled every few minutes.

Suddenly Maggie, mother of one of the babies, clutched her breast in sudden concern. "I ain't heard nothin' out'a my youngen for a long time. He'd normally be screamin' to be fed. I better see what's wrong with 'im."

At the door of the classroom, she stopped suddenly, crying out in horror. "He's gone! They're all gone!"

"Who's gone?"

"The babies are gone?"

"All three of 'em!"

The entire quilting group rushed to see, led by the mothers of the other two babies. The pallet quilts were shaken and impossibly small places were searched. They had, indeed, gone. Not a trace, except for a couple of soiled diapers.

"Where could they be?"

"Mine might'a crawled. He's startin' to, but them others couldn't even turn over."

"The Indians!"

"That's what happened! The Indians stole 'em. I've heard tell of that happenin'."

"Call the men! We got'a go after 'em!"

"Call the men! We'll get 'em back! EVERETT! You come here."

Everett obediently separated himself from the contentedly playing children and came running.

"What you want, Ma?"

"You run fast down to the livery and tell the men to come quick. We got'a get 'em to follow them Indians."

"How come?"

"Don't ask questions! Run! They stoled the babies!"

Everett took off in the direction of the livery, his feet flying, kicking up little clouds of dust in the fine dirt of the wagon tracks.

About a hundred feet down the street he stopped, paused, and came running back.

"Everett!" his exasperated mother yelled at him. "Go on!"

But Everett kept coming.

"What babies was it the Indians stole?" he demanded.

"Our babies! Three of 'em, right out'a the classroom where they was asleep."

"No, ma, we got the babies."

"You what?"

"We took the babies to help us play house. The girls didn't bring enough dolls to fill up the beds so we come and got the babies."

"Without askin'?"

"Why'd we ask 'em? They can't talk. 'Sides, they like playin'."

"You could'a asked their mamas," Everett's mother pointed out.

"Come and look, Ma. They like playin'."

The women followed Everett to the group of children, now standing quietly, staring, trying to determine what the problem was.

"Can't believe that youngen ain't yellin' from bein' hungry."

"He was yellin', Ma, but then we gave him candy."

"CANDY! You'll choke 'im to death!"

"No, Ma. I tied me a string on it."

"String?"

"Yeah, see?"

Everett picked up a string, the end of which was tied to a piece of red candy.

"Watch!"

Everett lowered the candy toward the face of the chubby baby, who laughed and crowed and batted his fists toward the sweet. When the candy touched his lips, he opened his mouth greedily for it and sucked noisily.

"That's how come he ain't hungry. Jimmie brought candy, and we was all eatin', so I thought it'd be only fair to let him have some. See, I took care of 'em all."

Sure enough, there were the three babies, two of them contentedly sleeping on their grass pile beds, the stains of colored candy around their mouths.

The women looked at each other and sighed. There were a few amused and relieved smiles. The mothers of the babies retrieved them and returned to the church.

"Don't you do that no more," was Everett's mother's parting thrust.

"Sure, Ma," was his agreeable reply.

A few minor adjustments and the game continued. Mothers were so unpredictable. First they tell you to take care of the baby and keep him from crying; then, when you're taking good care of him, they tell you not to do it again. Hmmmm, who could figure out a mother?

Esther shivered to think what might have happened if the Indians had been falsely accused of stealing the babies. The town had always seemed to get along so well with the native inhabitants, but there was no knowing what could happen if they were accused of something they didn't do. It was good they didn't find out.

Those were good days, back when the children were small. Esther had so many wonderful memories in her mental file, she had only to select one and relive it any time she chose. Such a comforting library of memories!

17

There had been good times and good memories, and these were pleasant to look back upon and to sort over in the mind, fondly remembering the favorite parts. Memory could be pleasantly selective if one allowed it to be.

To be honest with one's self, however, one must also look squarely at the failures, at the work left undone, or the times when one's best efforts had not been exerted. Everyone had those times, and though it changed nothing to look back and cast blame, still, they were there.

Given time, Esther could have remembered many times when she could likely have done better, but one situation, however, always stood out in her mind. It concerned the two families who owned most of the upper region of Red Rock.

The torturous climb up the twisting, rocky road brought the traveler to the homestead of the Riggs and the McCartys. Beyond these two stops, the road faded into a trail used only by hunters and the animals they hunted until it emerged onto the treeless peak, covered with sharp-edged rocks in shades of red, rose and violet.

Centuries ago, layers of minerals had created brittle crusts of stone-like material on the floors of the ancient seas. Time and volcanic upheavals had tossed these sheets of brittle crust onto their edge and heaved them up until they became the top crust of a mountain range. They stood on edge in sheets and pillars and were locally knows as the fish fins, and the mountaintop became Fish Fin Butte.

The shallow soil at this height would support only beavertail cactus and thistles and was a haven for small animals, snakes, lizards and humans hiding from the law, and there were many places to hide.

Being isolated together on the mountain not far from the fish fins, it would seem that these two families would be obliged to hang together for companionship, but it did not happen. There was no one in the town of River Bend who did not know of the decades-old feud between the Riggs and the McCartys, though the most violent times had long since passed.

As the wife of the preacher, and the unelected leader of the women's visitation committee, Esther had, several times, made the climb to visit these mountain cabins but never without fear and apprehension.

The women, whom she would normally be visiting, were so isolated even from the tiny town on the river that conversation of any substance was very difficult. The men and boys of the families would occasionally come down from the mountain into town for supplies that could not be made at home, but women and girls were hopelessly tied to its slopes and doomed to isolation.

Lottie Riggs, near to Esther in age, had married a man named Marvin and bore him three sons to help with the farm work and to hunt in the mountains. Her fourth child, a daughter named Penelope, called Nellie, was her mother's pride and joy and possibly the only comfort she had in her whole austere life.

When she could, Lottie brought Nellie down from the mountain to be with other people and usually to be with Ellena and Catherine. Though Esther tried to be friendly to her, she knew that Lottie's only concern was for her daughter, and she thought it was Lottie's hope that her daughter not be trapped on the mountain as she herself had been. She must have known, though, that she would be powerless to stop it.

Then when Nellie was fifteen, a beauty with white skin, blushed cheeks and deep blue eyes, her father brought Hubert to the mountain cabin.

Hubert Riggs, who was the son of Marvin's third cousin over in Pixley, had been selected, it seemed, to become Nellie's husband. Lottie had sighed and had wordlessly taken to her rocker on the porch. There she rocked and stared out over the valley, drowning in a dismal pit of hopelessness.

Nellie Riggs married Hubert Riggs the next day, and Lottie refused to leave her rocker on the porch. She did not eat, sleep or speak. She stared into space and screamed when anyone attempted to move her. Ten days later, she was placed in the ground on the top of the mountain. Esther hoped Lottie's next life would be better than her first.

Several times, Esther had climbed the hill to visit with Nellie, and it seemed the girl was making the best of the situation. Her brothers had seemingly wandered off the mountain and were not heard of again, leaving the farm to their sister and brother-in-law.

Nellie dutifully produced a son, as she was obligated to do, to help tend the farm, and then she gave birth to Marianne, a beautiful porcelain doll who made Nellie's own life worth living.

In his early teens, Nellie's son left the mountain, leaving Marianne as the only child on the Riggs farm. Then, when Marianne was thirteen, both her parents were taken in an epidemic of the influenza.

Her brother came for the funeral but left the next day, glad to give to Marianne his interest in the farm in return for the freedom of a faraway place. Never, to anyone's knowledge, had he ever returned.

In due time, the "authorities" in Jacksonville learned of a thirteen-year-old girl living alone on the mountain, and they came checking. Marianne had heard of their impending arrival and had turned her livestock into the woods, and she had followed them, taking only a pillow, quilt and a change of clothing.

She was eventually hunted down and taken away to be placed in a "home". During the second night at the home, she slipped away in the dark of night. A short-range search the next morning failed to locate her, so it was assumed she fell prey, fatally, to man or beast, and they thought no more about her, their duty having been clearly done.

Within hours, however, it was known by everyone in River Bend that Marianne had returned to her home, and whose right was it to interfere? The girl had asked for nothing from anyone, and hadn't she had enough troubles without the neighbors creating more?

Marianne gathered in her cows and horses, her goats and chickens, and continued her life. She rode her pony to town to buy seed for her garden and bring duck eggs to sell.

Though Esther made several trips to the mountain to check on her, it seemed that Marianne was healthy and doing fine. She was friendly, but she didn't need any help, thank you very much!

Her garden grew prize vegetables, and she permitted no weeds to interfere. Her sow farrowed huge litters, which she butchered while they were still small enough to handle by herself. She managed wood to keep her cabin warm, and her hens hid their nests and hatched large broods of downy chicks, just as they should. She came to town for flour and sugar, trading eggs and butter and sometimes her round, pungent goat cheeses, which were in great demand.

Her dresses indicated that though sewing was not her best skill, still, they were adequate.

She had, in her teens, stopped in to see Jane Ann during the summers, and when Jane Ann married, she had continued to drop by to visit Esther on her trips into town. Often she would bring a sample of her baked goods. Occasionally she would ask to borrow a book, though when she would have time to read was a puzzle to Esther.

Marianne took care of herself well, and maybe too well, for her chunky frame filled out plumply and the dimples deepened in her round cheeks, but she still had the porcelain doll complexion, blushed cheeks and lips, and her eyes were as blue as a deep lake in October. Soft hands with tapered fingers appeared never to have milked a cow or carried out the ashes.

If Esther could claim any success from the inhabitants of Red Rock Mountain, it would be Marianne, though she felt the girl would have survived admirably no matter what life handed her.

Esther knew much less about the other family on the mountain. The McCartys were a mystery. The old man, it seemed, had brought a woman (who knew where he got her?) to the farm, and she produced eight sons. She hid when anyone approached, and when Esther tried to visit the woman, she was met at the gate by a gun-toting young man and told to go away. So that's what Esther did.

She comforted herself with the memory that when Jesus Himself sent out the 70 people as missionaries, they were not to force themselves on anyone, and if they were not accepted in a certain place, the missionaries were to "shake the dust from their feet" and go on, presumably to a place where their testimony would be accepted. Perhaps God recognized that there were futile situations, and time wasted there benefited no person.

Then the woman, pregnant with her ninth child, suddenly disappeared. Rumor had it that her remains were found in one of the many mountain caves, but certainly none of the family confirmed the rumor. Perhaps her life had finally become too much to bear, and she decided to send herself on to the next one. The man and his sons went on about their lives.

Eventually the old man died, and some of the sons were killed in scuffles with the law, and some of the others just wandered off. Then one son returned with a wife, and life in the McCarty cabin began again.

Four sons were born to the woman, but she died giving birth to the fifth son, a lad named Arthur.

Stretching back for several decades, bad blood had existed between these two mountain families, though no one was exactly clear when it had begun. Certainly no one was brave enough to ask any of the males involved, though rumors had floated about.

Some thought the feuding had begun when a particularly desirable buck was slain with two arrows, one from each family, and each claimed the animal. Others thought it was when a boy from one family "did wrong" to a daughter of the other, though no one could name names or guess what sort of "wrong" was done. Another strong rumor was that each family laid claim to a certain everlasting spring of sparkling water that lay exactly on the boundary between the properties.

The feud continued, because it had always continued, and males regularly took pot-shots in the direction of the other. There had been no deaths attributed to the feud for many years, but shots came regularly from both directions, the adult males seemingly thinking it was their duty to at least make an effort to pass down to their sons the feud that they had inherited.

It was during one of these regular routine flare-ups that Marianne's father shot his 12-gauge shotgun in the direction of the McCartys. Five-year-old Arthur was in a bramble patch at the edge of the woods, picking blackberries, when a stray shotgun blast hit him in his right calf and left wrist. The leg wound healed, but the wrist bone was crushed, and the child's hand was amputated at the McCartys' kitchen table.

The horror of it all was such that the McCarty men hung their guns on the cabin wall to be used only for hunting food. Enough was enough.

When Hubert Riggs knew what he had done, he was in mortal fear for his daughter. Maybe the McCartys had hung up their guns, and maybe they hadn't. Young Marianne was counseled never to approach, speak to or even look in the direction of any McCarty for fear of retaliation. Before Marianne could count her fingers, she was taught to fear a McCarty. Any McCarty. What a life for a little girl!

Esther rocked wearily back and forth as her thoughts returned to the present.

"Lord, did I do my best for them folks on the mountain? Or did I let fear get in my way? I think maybe I failed You there, Lord, but You know I didn't intend to. I was just weak. Maybe I could have in some way kept some of them young men from leaving for faraway places. River Bend needed all its young men.

"I'm sorry for that, Lord, and while we're on the subject of young men, I want to thank You again for letting my Jane Ann find that wonderful husband of hers. You were good to us, letting us have him." She rocked back and forth a few times and then decided it wouldn't do any harm to ask God for favor.

"Now, I wouldn't want to be demanding more than my share, but would You happen to have someone for that nice Marianne? Not wanting to tell You how to run Your business, Lord, but it'd be good if You knew some young man who likes a girl to be good and round, then he'd likely be the best for her. But she's a real good cook, Lord, and most men like that, and she's so clean You could eat off her kitchen floor. Marianne'd make a good and loving wife for some lucky man, if You could work it out. Thank You, Lord."

Esther leaned back and closed her eyes. She didn't want to think up any more of her failures. It was too exhausting. She should have done more for those folks on the mountain, but it was too late, now. *Forgive me, Lord.*

18

Then the rocker was still, and the old woman, leaning her head against the padded headrest, dreamed of hot sunshine and dusty roads. She dreamed of skipping along the path on bare feet under stalks of golden sunflowers, higher than her head. She saw meadowlarks swoop down to steal golden grain from the stalks of ripened wheat.

As she skipped, she listened, as she always did, for her mother to call. "Don't go so far that you can't hear me call if I need you, Esther."

And she always promised, "I won't, Mommy. I'll listen."

And there was a sound, but not the voice of her mother. It was the moan of an old man. Esther's pleasant dream evaporated into the past where it belonged, and she was instantly alert.

"I'm here, Marion."

"Esther, we...."

"What is it, Marion? What is it we got'a do? You thirsty, now?"

"We got'a...."

"Don't you be worryin' none, Marion. We'll get done what we got'a do. We always have, you and me."

"Late..." he muttered, "too late!"

"What was that, Marion?"

"Don't... be... late...." He forced the words from his lips.

She reached for his cool hand and caressed it with her own.

"Hush, now, Marion. We never was late. Never, ever, ever!"

She watched the rise and fall of the soft, old quilt. The fingers she held tightened slightly against her own, then relaxed. The quilt became quiet.

"Marion? You all right, Marion?"

She leaned forward and let her fingers lightly stroke his brow. Her fingers told her what her mind already knew. Her beloved husband of many years had gone on without her. His last words had warned her not to be late. That was his goodbye.

Her fingers lingered on his wrinkled brow. There were no tears. Not yet. It was not yet the time for tears. A heavy veil of sadness settled about her, closing so tightly she must force her breath in and out. She had been sure he would leave her this night, and she had been right. After so many years together, there were things she just knew.

She leaned back in the rocker and looked up toward the ceiling. Morning was coming on fast, and the room was dimly lit with daylight.

"Lord, I got things to say. I'm thankin' You again for givin' me this thing I asked You for. I always took care'a him, like I promised You, and I wanted to be the one to be by him when he left. You gave me that. I can't take care of him no longer, Lord, and he belongs to You, now."

She glanced toward the window, noting that the black squares of the pane were turning gray. There were things to be done, now. She leaned wearily forward for better balance and stood up beside the bed, pausing while the first sharp pain in her knees subsided.

Jane Ann. She must get word to Jane Ann. She moved slowly in the dim light of the room to the old chest that she had brought with her from Kansas. She lifted the lid and patted her hand around on the contents until she felt the rough fabric of the white flag. The distress flag.

Now, all she had to do was hang the flag on the mailbox, and the next person who came by would stop in to help. Whoever it was, she'd ask them to go get Jane Ann. There was no hurry, really. Jane Ann needed her morning sleep, what with that new baby and all.

The flag idea was a good one. No one could remember whose idea it had been, but it had been a help to many old folks and even to a lot of others who were not so old.

Esther opened the door and, though there was scarcely any light, she moved confidently across to the porch post near the steps. Holding to the post, she stepped down to the first step, then to the ground. In the darkness, she walked toward the front gate. She didn't need any light for that. She could have walked just as safely with her eyes closed.

She went down the short path and was about to tie the flag to the gatepost when she heard the sound of horses, the crunch of gravel and the jingle of harness. Someone was coming, so she'd just wait and save them a trip up to the door.

In a moment, she saw the horses and the lanterns hanging on the buggy corners so the horses could see the road. When the animals reached her gate, the driver yelled for them to stop.

"Whoa! Whoa up there!"

The buggy stopped, and the driver took a lantern from its hook. He came toward her, holding the lantern up.

"Miz Sisco? Is that you?"

"Yes, Patrick. It's me. I was about to tie up the flag when I heard you comin'."

He answered, "Yeah, I figured it was you. It seems right early to be up. You got somethin' you need done?"

"No, Patrick, but thank you. Everything's fine. If you would, though, when you go back by the church, will you tell my Jane Ann I'll be needin' her to come by when she can?"

"Sure thing, Miz Sisco. Are you sure I can't help? I ain't in that big of a hurry."

"Oh, no, dear. You go on. I know you got things to do, and you can tell her when you go back by."

"I can go call her now if you want me to," he insisted.

"Oh, no, I'm in no hurry. Let her sleep, and you'll be goin back 'afore noon, for sure, and that'll be time enough."

"All right, Miz Sisco. If you're sure. I won't be more'n two hours gettin' back. I got to get a package from a fellow up the mountain. Promised him I'd take it in to Jacksonville. Likely not more'n an hour and a half, and I'll be comin' back by the preacher's house. Don't you worry none. I'll tell her. You want me to help you get back to the house?"

"No, no, dear. I don't need no light to see after more'n sixty years walkin' up this path. Thank you so much."

Still he waited, holding his lantern high, until she had closed the door behind her. Lovely young man, that Patrick McGee. Making that trip back and forth to Jacksonville, bringing mail and other things folks needed. Never heard a word that was bad ever said about that young man.

Heard tell he was about to give up that mail run job to take on farming. That was good. River Bend needed young men like Patrick.

Esther sat down again in her rocker, settling into the folds and creases that had, years ago, molded themselves into her exact shape. She leaned her head back on the soft headrest and sighed a long sigh. It was always like this. You expected a thing to happen, you knew it was coming and you waited.

Then the thing you waited for happened, just like you knew it would, so what was next? It seemed she should be doing something, but her exhausted body did not move in response to her agile mind.

Later, she thought. Anything that needed to be done could be done later. Yes, that was best. Come daylight, Bea would come over to see how things were. She would sit with her, and they would drink tea and talk and cry, as they had done so many times. As they had when her Harley had passed on. They would talk about how her Marion and Bea's Harley were likely together right now. Yes, Bea would come to her when daylight came.

A serious thought flitted through Esther's mind. *Lord, did I ever thank You, proper-like, for Bea? I hope I didn't fail to do that 'cause Bea is one of the best blessings You saw fit to bring my way. Happen I didn't thank You proper, I'm doin' it now. It'd'a been a hard row for me to hoe without her alongside me.*

Gray light had filtered through the window, and familiar items took on color. The braided rugs she had made, the pink flower sprigs on her robe, and the faded colors of the quilt blocks on the old quilt, soft and comforting from the many times it had been washed.

She looked at the shape of the man under the quilt, moving her eyes from the feet up to the face of the man she knew so well. She stared at every detail, forcing its shape into her memory. Too soon that memory would be all she had left of him. Her memory would be enough. With love, she had taken care of him until the end. If it had ever been a burden to her, it was certainly a precious burden, like the pains of childbirth required of a woman to bring on a new life.

She sighed again. A chapter had been finished, and she must turn the page and begin the next. Then a sudden thought, sharp as an arrow, pierced her mind, startling her eyes wide open and her head erect.

She had cared for her husband, but who would care for her to the end? There was only one. *Oh, my poor little Jane Ann! I don't want to do this to you! I know you would love me and care for me with never a complaint, but I mustn't do that to you. Being the wife of a small town minister is three jobs already.*

She leaned back again and sighed. She was so, so tired!

Through the eastern window, a finger of yellow sunlight stabbed bravely between the tree limbs. Morning was here, and the long night was gone. There was one thing more that she must do.

"Lord, I got one more thing to say, and I'm askin' You to be patient with me as You always been. I know You gave me more than was my right to expect, and I promise You this is the last thing I'll ever ask for."

The enormity of the request she had in mind, as well as her extreme earnestness in requesting it, caused her to pause and slide forward to the edge of the old rocker. Slowly she lowered her knees to the soft fluffiness of the braided rug.

In humility before her God, she leaned her elbows against the bed and bent forward, her joints creaking painfully. Tears blurred her eyes as she reached out with her two hands and clasped them around the large, cool one beside her on the bed.

"This here thing that I want, Lord, is real important to me. When the time comes You want me to come on, could you just take me? And not leave me for Jane Ann to take care of? Would it be all right for me to ask You that, Lord? I wouldn't be askin' if it was just for me and not wantin' to go through the pain and all. There'd be no pain that I could bear that would be a whisper of what You went through for me. The reason I'm askin' is that the pain comin' to me would be pain for my Jane Ann, too.

"I know the thought of bein' with You and my Marion would take me through any pain my body could make. This here's the thing I'm askin' for my little Jane Ann, and her with so much to do. You know all about that, Lord. If You can do that for me, I promise I'll never ask for one other thing. Thank you, Lord."

Esther leaned forward, settling her face against the quilt, and she felt peace. She knew, deep within herself, that the Good Lord, her constant Friend, the Giver of good gifts, would grant her this one last, important, totally unselfish thing.

The sun climbed slowly and was now shining a bright yellow square of light on the iron bed. It shone on two people, picking silver highlights from the gray in their hair. Gray mourning doves cooed to each other from the eaves of the cabin.

Patrick McGee again passed in front of the cabin and remembered his promise to take a message to the preacher's house. He'd do that, now.

"No, your grandma didn't say nothin' about hurryin'. Just wanted you to stop by when you had the time."

Jane Ann nodded her thanks and told her husband, "Think I'll just take the baby and walk over there. Likely she needs a little cook stove wood or some potatoes from the shed. The baby always cheers her up."

Her husband started to nod agreement but hesitated. Never had there been such an early morning call for help. "I'm thinkin I might just walk over there with you. Could be something that needs liftin', and I could help."

Together they walked along the road in the bright fall sunshine, turning in at the gate leading to the worn front doorstep.

Jane Ann called out cheerily, "Gram? We're here, Gram!" Without waiting for a response, she pushed open the door and went in. Lying on the bed was her grandfather, obviously in perfect peace. Kneeling beside the bed was his life's companion, still holding his hand in both of hers.

Jane Ann knew everything instantly and threw herself on her knees beside her grandmother. "Oh, Joe! She's gone! They're both gone! I should have been here, and I wasn't. They were all alone! Why wasn't I here?"

Her mournful wail filled the otherwise silent rooms of the cabin.

Preacher Joe put the baby in her great grandmother's rocker and drew his wife to her feet. "Darling, death is very personal, and everyone dies alone, no matter how many loved ones are in the room. It is a thing that must be done alone."

Between sniffles, Jane Ann agreed. "I know! I know! But I should have been here! I wanted to be here when their time came, but I didn't know it would be now! Why didn't she call me sooner?"

Joe said softly, "She called you when she wanted you to come."

"Yes, I know that, but...."

From nowhere and from everywhere, it seemed, the women came. Neighbors and those from the church gathered to do the things they must do. They brought food and brewed gallons of coffee in the water pail on the stove. The men brought in wood, raked leaves in the yard and fed the few remaining animals, doing the things they could do. They talked in groups, here and there, and finally they came to Jane Ann.

"Miss Jane Ann," ventured one of the men, apologetic at intruding into her grief. "Askin' your pardon if we're thinkin' the wrong thing, but we was talkin', them other men and me, and we was sayin' a double casket'd be no trouble to make. 'Course, it'd be you that'd say if it was fittin'."

The man stood, hat in hand, staring at the ground just in front of Jane Ann's feet. The rest of the men stood behind him in silent respect, humbled in the face of her grief.

Jane Ann hesitated only a minute, then nodded. "Yes, I'd like that."

The men left, and Joe came to her. "Jane Ann, honey, I'm gonna preach the funeral for your grandparents."

"You? But, Joe...?"

He looked away from her, letting his eyes settle on the blossoms of the fall-blooming tea rose. "I'm going to do it, Jane Ann. They belong to me, too, and I have things I want to say. Things that need to be said."

So finally, she nodded her agreement.

19

High on Red Rock Mountain, Marianne Riggs took an apple pie and a hickory nut cake from the oven. The cake was delicately browned, and fragrant juice stained the sugared top of the pie. Perfect. But it was no surprise, or a particularly great pleasure to Marianne, because her pies and cakes were always perfect. What she thought about, though, was that it was nice to get her baking done before the day got too hot.

A restlessness passed over her. She had planned to gather nuts from the trees at the back of the house, but suddenly she did not want to do that.

Town. That was what Marianne wanted. She'd hitch up the buggy and go down to town. She'd stop in on old Miz Sisco and then go on over to Jane Ann's. She could see the baby and possibly get to rock her to sleep. Or they might put the baby in her little buggy and walk down Main Street, if Jane Ann had time, or maybe she could take the baby alone.

So what should she take to them? It was fun to take gifts to Miz Sisco, and reason told her that if she expected to have time with Jane Ann and the baby, she should take something to account for the time she would be using when Jane Ann might be doing something else.

There were the cake and pie right before her. Old Miz Sisco would like the cake, and it would last a while, just the two of them. Preacher Joe set a store by her pies, so it should go there. What else? If she expected time in Jane Ann's afternoon, she should also supply something for their supper. What? Ham, of course! She had just began to slice on a fresh one, pink and juicy, and a couple of thick slices would be just right.

She could cut three slices and nibble on one during the long trip downhill. It would be bad manners to arrive at someone's house hungry. Certainly not Jane Ann's. Skinny as she and the preacher both were, likely she had not had time yet today to do any cooking, and it would be best to play it safe.

The horse needed no direction, as there was only one way down the hill, so Marianne held the slice of ham in her soft, delicate white hand and tore away pinches of it to pop in her mouth. Life was good, and she was content. Sometimes it would be nice to have neighbors closer, though most of the time she was glad they weren't.

In due time, the road leveled out at the foot of the mountain and the horse went, without direction, to the Siscos' house.

As she neared the cabin, Marianne sat up straight and stared ahead, puzzled. Why were all of the wagons clustered around the house? Had the old preacher taken worse? Hmmmmm. Jane Ann must be here if everyone else was.

Balancing the cake and pie in either hand, Marianne approached the house. Carrie Raleigh met her at the door. "Just put them on the table, honey, and thanks for bringing them. Lookin' for Jane Ann, she'd be in the back bedroom."

Adjusting her eyes to the indoor light, Marianne glanced about the room. There on the bed lay the old couple, carefully covered with a quilt, pulled smooth of wrinkles. Sadness clutched at her heart as she saw the quiet, peaceful face of the woman who had been a friend to her family. She breathed deeply and sighed. There was no time to mourn. There were things to do.

Taking her baked goods to the kitchen table, she turned to the back room just as one of the gathering of women handed the fussing baby Sally over to another. Marianne now knew, beyond the shadow of a doubt, why she had not gone to gather nuts from the hillside.

Without a word, she tapped a shoulder and smilingly eased the baby into her own arms. Pressing the tiny head against her pillowy bosom, she patted the blanketed backside, noting a moistness against her arm. No wonder the little thing was fussy... no one had taken the time to keep her dry.

She found a soft cloth, though not a diaper, and was able to make the baby more comfortable. Now what? Find Jane Ann. Go to the back room and find Jane Ann. Yes.

Jane Ann, with eyes red and tear-stained, met her at the door and leaned against her, sobbing. Oh, glorious moment for Marianne! Someone needed her, and joy was almost too much to contain as she extended her embrace to include her bereaved friend.

"Jane Ann? Not meanin' to be a bother, but I had a thought. You got all you can carry, and I can't help much here, but I'd purely like to care for the baby. I could go to your place and get diapers and bottles. I know where everything is. That'a'way you'd be free to talk without worryin' none about her bein' took care of."

The offer of help with the baby brought on a new flood of tears from Jane Ann, which made Marianne brave enough to state the last of her offer.

"I know you'd be wantin' to talk with the preacher first, 'afore you give me an answer, but I'd like to say this. Happen the time I got'a go back up the mountain to take care of my livestock, and you not havin' a body down here to help, I could take her with me in her basket and keep her through the night. It'd be something I'd like to do, if you could spare being away from her. I'll go now, and let you think on it."

"Wait! Marianne, I don't need to think on it. If you feel you can, I would be so grateful, and I'd know she was as safe as if I had her myself. You are such a good friend."

Marianne took the baby to her buggy and urged the horse up the road to the parsonage. Fed and rocked, the little one was soon asleep in her basket. Marianne looked around. A few things could be done while the baby napped.

There were a few dishes dirty from breakfast, and there were always soiled diapers when there was a baby. The kitchen could use a bit of mopping, but first she must sweep. A peek under the bedspread revealed a few dust bunnies beyond the reach of the broom. It would be best to get them out of there, to save Jane Ann the embarrassment of realizing they had been there and someone else had been in the house.

It would be a shame to waste the heat from the stove after the wash water was hot, so she stirred up a double batch of oatmeal cookies. Maybe they would help the preacher to put on a bit of weight. By that time, little Sally was awake and cooing in her basket.

Marianne's heart pounded with anticipation as she gathered the essentials needed by the baby for an overnight stay. As the horse started the climb into the mountain, she gazed at the baby in the basket at her feet. Goosebumps arose on her arms from awe of the gift that had been given her. She would have a whole night with the baby! She would feed her and sing to her, and when she was asleep in her basket, Marianne would put the basket on the bed beside her so she would not fail to hear any nighttime restlessness.

Then there would be the night feeding, and that would provide another opportunity to rock her back to sleep. She shook her head with disbelief over the wonder of it all. And the knowing horse pulled the buggy up to the tidy mountain cabin.

"All right, cats," she told the animals lapping from their milk bowl. "You eat up, then you go back outside. No laying around the kitchen tonight. We have a baby here."

As she began to prepare her own food, she felt the excitement of the day deserved a little extra touch, so she broke a dozen eggs into a quart of top milk and made a baked custard, spicy with cinnamon and nutmeg. She baked a small amount without spice in a tiny custard cup.

Thrills of excitement raced up and down her back as she fed tiny bites into Sally's willing mouth. Such a wonderful evening lay ahead, one to be savored and committed to memory so each detail could be remembered later. Babies were such a wonderful gift from God.

And from Jane Ann.

20

As the day came to a close, the people of the town filtered away to attend to families and chores. The double pine box had been installed in the parlor, and candles were lit for the night vigil. They were not the short, chopped off stubs but were tall, white, store-bought taper candles furnished by the Markhams. Perfume of roses filled the room.

Preacher Joe and Jane Ann were finally alone in the house when the kitchen door opened without a knock. The old woman held her arms wide for the granddaughter of her best friend.

"Oh, Aunt Bea! I wasn't here! They left, and I was at home. Gram didn't call me! Oh, I can't stand it! What can I do?"

Tears soaked the shoulder of the housedress and warmed her skin as Beatrice Nelson patted the girl's back.

"Of course you were here with them, Jane Ann, honey. Don't you never think you were not. Your gram did not leave without you, because you were with her every minute. All your life you were a pure pleasure to her, and your love was always with her. Many things brought your gram heartache, and some things brought her peace, but when she needed love, she expected to get it from your grandpa and you.

"Both of you were with her when she left, and if you don't believe me, you just see how you will feel in the next weeks and months. You will know that a piece of you went with her, and it is a part of yourself that you will never get back." She paused to blink back the moisture in her own eyes. She must not give way to her grief with Jane Ann here.

When she could, she continued, "That's the way it is. She took a piece of me, too, and I have lost so much of myself, from the buryin's I've seen, there seems to be more on the other side than on this side. Don't you never think you weren't with her when she left."

Jane Ann refused to be comforted. "But, Aunt Bea, she should have called me. I wanted to be here when her time came."

"I know that, but that is not what she wanted. If she had wanted you sooner, she would have had young McGee come to fetch you. She did this for you, wantin' to make losin' her easier for you... and that's what she did. She was asleep when you got here, and you will always remember that, not that she suffered or had hard decisions to make. It was her last gift to you, and you must treasure and cherish it."

Jane Ann dried her tears and was finally able to speak. For the next hours, good times were remembered. Happy summers were lived again with one who cherished the memory with her. Aunt Bea Nelson was able to give her best friend, Esther, one last gift, as she comforted the granddaughter she had left behind.

Then it was morning. The pine box was taken to the churchyard, where it waited in the bright fall sunshine as final words were spoken.

Preacher Joe McCrey began. "These two people were my family." Here he paused, took a deep breath and squared his shoulders, as any brave soldier would when preparing to step in the battle.

He continued, "When my parents gave me birth, they loved me because I was theirs, and they had no other choice. These two people we have come to honor, they owed me nothing, and yet they loved me anyway. They seemed to consider me capable of filling the shoes of the pastor of this church, though I was so young and inexperienced. Even more so than I knew at the time. They were many things to me.

"I have thought of them as shepherds, caring for the sheep of this town. I have thought of them as a tower of help in time of trouble, for they gave their strength to anyone in need. They were a strong pillar in the time of storm, a guiding lighthouse in a dark night and an anchor against a rough sea. They were many things, but my best thought of these two people is of Psalms, chapter one.

"'Blessed is the man that walketh not the way the sinner tells him to, nor spends time with the ungodly. His delight is in the law of God,' and it was this law that Preacher Marion studied, day and night. But here is the best part.

"'He shall be like a tree, planted by the river of water, bringing forth his fruit in its season and his leaf also shall not wither and whatsoever he doeth shall prosper.'"

He paused and wiped his knuckles across his eyes. "I have not known Preacher Marion as long as many of you here, but I saw him as a tree firmly planted by our river, far from his family and friends. There he was planted to bring forth his fruit, as so many of you know. His leaf has never withered, and without him, my Jane Ann would not have been mine. What he began in River Bend will prosper, because he rooted it in obedience to the God Who called him here.

"It is right and proper than they should leave together, because they are one... in every sense of the word.

"Marion and Esther Sisco are a tree... one tree. Preacher Marion's roots went deep, and his branches spread wide as he grew here among us, but Esther was his heart. Without her, he would never have had the strength to go on, and without him, she would have had nowhere to go."

The young Reverend Joe McCrey looked at the tall trees towering over the cemetery and continued, "Yes, he was as the tall, strong, spreading cedar that keeps its strength and color from summer sun to winter storm, but she was the heart of the cedar, for that is where the strength of the tree is produced, and it is entirely fitting that God did not leave one of them to try to exist without the other."

His words ceased as he gazed around at his assembled flock. He took the snow-white handkerchief from his pocket and dabbed at his eyes. Finally his trembling chin was steadied, and he could continue.

"I will miss them sorely, and it is impossible for me to keep back the tears. I cry, but my tears are selfish ones. I weep not for these two people who have gone from us, but for myself, because I will no longer have their strength and wisdom to draw from. I can no longer depend on their experience. I and my Jane Ann will be alone here, with only God and you, our earthly family, and only your prayers will enable us to go on. We stand here and humbly ask you to stand with us as you have stood with them, realizing we are as children beside these two people." Another pause and a dab with the handkerchief before he could go on.

"This is not a funeral sermon. It would be foolish for me to stand here and tell you about these two people when their life has been an open book before you for more than half a century. I can only say he was a tree among us, a mighty cedar, and we will sorely miss the shade of that tree."

Preacher Joe dabbed his eyes again and stepped away from the box. The men of the church came forward and released the restraining bands, bowing their heads as they waited for what must come next. There must be an acceptance of the passing and permission to commit the box to the ground. Who was there to do this except Jane Ann?

Jane Ann knew her terrible duty, and she breathed deeply, raised her head and squared her chin. She moved toward Granny Nelson and took her arm, leading her toward the open grave. Together they bent to grasp the handful of fresh clay. Jane Ann extended her arm, releasing the soil onto lid of the box, but Beatrice Nelson did not quickly drop the dirt from her hand.

She held it high and looked up into the cloudless blue of the sky. "Esther Sisco, you went on and left me here alone. I know why. You was always faster with your doing than I was, me being so easy to sidetrack.

But I kept up with you, and you know I did; it just took me a little longer. Now you went on, and I know that was what you wanted to do, but don't you get yourself so busy you can't be watchin' out for me. Seems I still got things to be doin' down here, and I ain't surprised about all that. I can look around and see what ain't been done yet, but I'll be tendin' to it, much as I can, and then I'll be on along. After that, things is gonna be done by your little Jane Ann, and she's gonna be up to it just like you was. You gave her strong hands and a willin' heart, so she'll know what to do. Just you wait and see, Miss Esther."

With that, Beatrice shook her wrinkled fist into the air, still clutching the red Arkansas soil. Then she lowered her hand and let the dirt filter slowly through her fingers, as though to prolong the final farewell.

The members of the assembled crowd were silent as they waited. The only sound was the rise and fall of the soft voice of a contented baby, cooing at the birds in the trees as she was being patted lovingly against a soft bosom.

When the last grain of dust fell from the gnarled old fingers, Bea Nelson turned and leaned onto her cane as she allowed herself to be led away by Jane Ann.

The crowd parted before them like the Red Sea parted before Moses, and the two walked away toward the large stone with her Harley's name carved on it.

"I can't be restin' here like usual, Miss Jane Ann. Things got'a be done. One thing is, from now on, you gonna call me Granny, 'long with other youngens your age. I can't take the place of your Gran, but I got my own place in your life. Best you get used to it."

Jane Ann looked at the wrinkled old face and the faded eyes swimming with moisture. "I know things got'a be done, but we'll do 'em, you and me, Granny. You can't be thinkin' on leavin' me anytime soon."

Old Granny Nelson looked down at the carved headstone and nodded. "Reckon I can rest a minute. Gonna need my strength."

Jane Ann's arm around her tightened and steadied her as she sat down beside her on the wide, cool stone. Rest was for today. The tomorrows would come.

Together, they would be strong enough for whatever must be done.

A FRIEND LOVETH
AT ALL TIMES

1

F rom the top of her chest of drawers, Marybeth Maisone took her comb and a handful of hairpins. She stood at the window as she combed her waist-length, midnight-black, wavy hair. As she brushed, she watched the squirrels outside her window. Chittering and scurrying, going about their fall business. Her mother stood nearby, watching her, and Marybeth knew, as she always knew, that her mother was preparing for a lecture on an old subject.

"It's time and past time," her mother began. "Seems there'd be some appreciation for what I want to do for you and how I want you to take thought for your future. It'd be a good thing for you, helpin' me with birthin', me teachin' you what you need to know to go on your own. Makes a good livin', it does, payin' a five dollar bill for every trip."

Marybeth put down the comb and began to twist her shining hair around and around her hand, then she pushed the loop of hair against her head. She secured the twist of hair with hairpins, then returned the comb and the leftover pins to the drawer. She said nothing.

Martha Maisone continued, "These here hills is gettin' so full'a folks movin' in from everywhere, and the town keeps spreadin', goin' in all directions. You been out with me enough to know already what you'd need to know to be goin' to take on the carin' for a woman, one not havin' a first baby."

Marybeth took her sweater down from its peg on the wall and stood by the door. She knew from memory how the rest of the lecture would go.

Her mother continued, "A body could only imagine what'd'a happened to me and to you two girls, if I hadn't had me the little trainin' I had in that line'a work. Precious little I knew then, but I had to use it fast when your pa skipped out on us. Be a sight easier for you, me bein' here to help. You now, comin' on twenty years old, that'd be a good time to start."

"Mama, I got'a go now," and Marybeth reached for the knob of the door.

Her mother kept talking. "Can't nobody say it ain't a good, honest business, and folks'll keep on havin' babies till the end'a time. You wouldn't never have to depend on nobody, 'specially a man. I wish't I'd'a know'd as much as you know, back when your pa took off."

At this point, she always paused significantly, then added, "Not that I ever heard one word'a gratefulness out'a you."

Marybeth paused, "Thank you, Mama. I'll go with you when you need me, but right now I got'a go."

Her mother was not to be put off. "Don't you understand nothin'? It ain't me needin' you. It's you needin' me and needin' what I can tell you. Where do you think you're goin', now? Down there to see that Irena again?"

"Goodbye, Mama." Marybeth eased out the door and closed it softly behind her. It was impossible to wait for the end of one of her mother's tirades, because they never ended. Her mother could talk on the same subject forever.

Her mother was, of course, without doubt the best midwife in the town of River Bend and was constantly in demand. It was true that the pay was very good, and it was also true that her mother could use some help. The real fact was, however, that Marybeth did not want to be a midwife. The worst part of the job was having to traipse all over the hills in all kinds of weather, at all times of the day and night.

Not so with her mother. Her mother never refused to go when called and was always prepared. She had her basket of soothing tea to help with the labor, reduce the pain and produce more milk, or whatever she thought would be best.

By now, she knew all the back rubs that eased the pain and the belly massages that worked with contractions to speed labor. Mama was very good at what she did.

Marybeth didn't mind going along, really, but just now she felt she should be with her pregnant friend who seemed to be having all kinds of trouble. Irena Boudreau lived a half a mile down the hill and a quarter of a mile up Rock Creek Road. Just a good stroll.

Back in the house on the hill, Martha Maisone stood, after her half-finished sentence, staring at the closed door. She sighed a long sigh and once more checked her midwife basket. It had to be kept ready because she was subject to call at any time.

The basket was complete, so Martha took the comb from the drawer and proceeded to comb her own hair, once blond, now gray streaked. She sat down heavily in the rocker and moved back and forth, unmindful of its squeaking.

It could work well if her daughters would only listen. Here she was with eighty acres of land, mostly timber and paid for mostly with money that she herself had earned, and it was all hers now. It was a very good place. She would divide it between the girls when they married.

Having land of their own would assure that her daughters would attract a good catch. If there was such a thing. Men were men. Some were dependable, and some weren't. Just ask her, Martha Maisone, and she could tell you all about that.

The midwife pinned up her hair, replaced the comb, and made herself a cup of tea. Peppermint, it was, made from the wild peppermint plants from her own eighty acres.

Seventeen-year-old Laura, her second daughter, was very good at gathering the herbal plants she needed in the midwifery business. The girl prepared and packaged them, and they were always ready when they were needed.

It would be very simple, Martha had decided. When she divided the land, Laura would get the upper forty acres, that being the place where most of her plants grew. Marybeth would have the lower forty acres and would carry on the midwife business when she, Martha, became too old.

It would work if Marybeth would only cooperate.

At this moment, Laura sat in the room with her mother, and her ears heard the words her mother said, but her thoughts were her own. On the table in front of her were several Kerr fruit jars with tight lids.

Scattered about were various dried plants, heaped in their own segregated piles.

Some plants were to be snipped into pieces, using the entire plant. Others required that each leaf be removed and the tough center vein of each leaf be stripped out. The thin papery part of the leaf was dried and then crushed fine as dust. Some of the plants were valued only for their roots, which were cleaned of dirt, carefully dried and chopped. The finished product was protected in the airtight jars, stored carefully away from damaging light.

Today, Laura had something to say to her mother. While she worked, she was carefully considering if this was the best time to say it. The problem with her mother was that there were not many good times, so she might as well plunge in. The words were burning a hole into her thoughts, and she felt she might explode if they were not uttered.

She sat down at the table, chin in hand, staring through the window at the jays energetically shrieking and flapping about in the trees.

She chewed her lip, thoughtfully… trying to gain strength for the words. As though it mattered what was said. What would it hurt? Mama was mad anyway. Yes, she'd just say what she wanted to say.

"I been thinkin', Mama. 'Stead'a trampin' around on the whole eighty acres, lookin' for special plants for you to do doctorin' with, I could pick out a good place down here close to the house. Then I'd take a shovel and lift the plants in the fall and set 'em down here. That way we could water 'em and take care of 'em right along with the other garden things. Likely that'd make 'em have bigger leaves and roots. It'd save time, I been thinkin'."

Not a moment was wasted between the suggestion and the proclamation that it was unworkable, unnecessary and impossible. It was not that Laura did not expect exactly what happened. Mama was totally predictable.

"Waste'a time, waste'a time," pronounced her mother without taking a moment to consider the merit of the suggestion. "The movin' of 'em would take a sight'a time, and if you got the plant in your hand, the place to go with it is to the dryin' shed. Your way'd make double work. Best to leave them wild plants out where they grow. They know where they want to be, and it'd likely mess up the strength in the plant, movin' it. Ain't natural. Seems like you got time enough to find what's needed. 'Course, we'd all have more time if your sister'd listen and do her part, 'stead'a runnin' to the neighbors all the time."

Laura resisted pointing out that if Marybeth was also doctoring, she, Laura, would need even more herbs. That was not the point. Mainly, she wished to head off the old tirade.

"Mama, I got'a tell you this. Talkin' to Marybeth, you're workin' on the wrong girl. I'm the one that wants to know doctorin'. I want to know everything you can tell me and even more. Marybeth ain't happy runnin' around the countryside. I'd go anywhere I was needed."

She paused for breath and to see how her mother was taking it. Not well, it seemed, but Laura continued. "I told you I was the one to learn birthin' and that you keepin' after Marybeth was a waste'a time."

The midwife picked up her favorite complaint. "So now you know more'n your ma? And you just a shirttail youngen, barely out'a Mr. Campbell's school? And here you are, thinkin' you're gonna tell me how to raise my girls? What do you think I got… no brains? Seems I had enough brain to take care of me and the both of you good enough."

Then she added, "With no help from no man, neither."

Laura stared out the window. A squirrel slithered around the tree trunk into her line of sight. The tiny animal skillfully took a nut from its swollen cheek with tiny feet, artfully turning the nut around, nibbling rapidly, then tossing the empty shell to the ground. It was a sight how fast a squirrel could empty the kernel out of a nut whose shell seemed hard as a rock.

She continued to chew her lip. Something more had to be said. It was clear Mama was in a bad mood, not ready to listen, but when was she ever in a good, agreeable mood? Laura had given a lot of thought to what she was going to say and had practiced it many times. Now, all those well-thought-out words vanished from her mind, but she must not let that stop her. She took a deep breath, licked her lips and once more plunged in.

"I got'a say somethin' more, Mama, and you got'a listen to me. I done decided I'm gonna learn what it is I want to know. I ain't aimin' to spend every day up here by myself, thinkin'a what I'm missin' and what I'd like to know. And thoughts and more thoughts goin' round and round in my head. If you ain't gonna see me bein' a real person, one to talk to and tell what you know, then I'll do what I got'a do. I'll be leavin' here."

She paused. At least she now had her mother's attention, so she continued.

"Maybe not today and maybe not tomorrow, but soon. I'm far past sixteen years old, and girls get married and have babies at sixteen. That ain't what I want, but I decided I'm a'gonna get what I want." She had the grace not to say, "In spite of you and what you say."

After a moment of silence, Laura sighed loudly. "And that's what I wanted to say."

The midwife of River Bend knew when it was time to stage a retreat. Even she knew there came a time to quit pushing.

"Noticed we was about out of Solomon's Seal, and we don't never have too much peppermint," she began, continuing in a softer voice. "Better run up to the high pasture and see what you can find. Happen the frost'll come in here in a month or so, killin' the leaves. Better we get 'em than the frost, and you might see what else there is to find."

She had refrained from adding, "and likely the walk'll make you forget your fool notion of runnin' off." The unsaid finality was fully understood by the girl, however.

Without a word, Laura left the house. From the drying shed, she picked up her wooden bucket and a dirt scoop she had made from a plow point.

Mama just didn't stop to think that year after year of gathering had made the plants hard to find. In a garden, they could be tended and carefully harvested so they would multiply into a continuous source.

Laura already had an idea where the new garden would be. If she could put it by the house, it would be handier, but the spot she had located hidden in the woods would also be all right, and the best part was that Mama would never see it.

The midwife sat for a minute in the quiet house, then rinsed her teacup and put it away.

Outside the window, the squirrels barked and chattered noisily, skittering about for the best positions on the limb. One of the blue jays, considering the limb to be his, zoomed between the squirrels, snatched a nut from small, brown and furry paws, then sent them scampering to the treetop.

The midwife returned to her thought. Marybeth had refused to stay continuously at home ever since Irena had married that stranger. Seemed she liked Irena's house better than her own, helping her with her gardening, housekeeping and canning. Irena was never one to be able to do anything by herself. If there was a mistake anywhere to be made,

Irena would find it and make it, expecting Marybeth to get her out of it. Whatever did Marybeth see in her, anyway?

Seemed to her that when Irena married that good-looking, dark-haired fellow that had wandered into town, Marybeth would leave them alone and get on with her own life. But, no… and now that Irena was pregnant, it was even worse.

Irena was a good enough girl, for that matter, and the girls had been friends since school, but then Irena had met that stranger. Well, we'd all see how long that fellow stayed with her after she saddled him with a baby. They could just ask her, Martha, what happened with handsome strangers who came into town, with no family around to settle them down. They didn't stay, that's what!

Stubborn and pigheaded, that was Marybeth! From what just went on, it seemed Laura wasn't much better. Imagine the like of her, stewing about learning things she had no earthly use for! How did she get ideas like that in her head?

2

Marybeth walked down the hillside lane toward Rock Creek Road. Now that she had left the house, it seemed safe to think her own thoughts. Mama's constant nagging made life miserable at home.

She didn't mind doing the cooking and the housekeeping. In fact, she liked it most of the time, but it did no good to tell Mama over and over that she really didn't want to go traipsing over the mountains on call to any house and cabin, alone, with her birthing basket and herbs and her scant knowledge of ways to make a delivery more comfortable.

Cleaning the babies and dressing them was all right. Nice, in fact. And she'd go willingly on occasions when Mama asked her to, it being only fair that she should do her share, but it was not something she would ever want to do alone.

She wouldn't mind keeping the house running smoothly while Mama was away, except that Mama was unbearably particular. Curtains must be ironed one certain way, food cooked exactly the same way, the broom must be propped against the same spot on the wall or Mama got mad. It was no wonder to her why her papa left.

When she was little, she used to tell herself that Papa would be back. Or that he would come to her when it was dark, sneak her out of the house and take her away somewhere. Maybe he wouldn't even tell Mama where she was.

But that was a long time ago, and now she felt sure he was dead. Otherwise, he would let her and Laura know where he was. Oh, well. He was gone, and if Mama didn't curb her tongue a bit better, Laura would be gone, too. Her younger sister would never be as patient as she, Marybeth, had been.

She reached Rock Creek Road and turned south away from the river. Alongside the road babbled the brook called Rock Creek. Clear and sparkling it was, in its rock-bottomed bed. The water was as clear as plate glass, and the tiny minnows and crawfish of all sizes darted about.

The water in Rock Creek had a taste all its own. Marybeth stopped beside the stream and cupped her hands for a drink, savoring the sparkly, peppery, almost crisp taste of it. Maybe it got some of its peppery taste from the crisp green watercress growing thickly along the banks.

She pulled a sprig of the cress to chew as she walked along, humming to herself. It was a good day. The weather was still warm, but winter was just around the corner. Enjoy the sun while she could; that was best.

Surely Irena would be better today. When Marybeth was away from Irena's house, it was easy to think she was surely better, but her mind soon changed each time she saw her. Being pregnant had made such a terrible change in her. Seemed some women could be pregnant most of the time and hardly notice it, but Irena had been nothing but sick.

Strange, too, that all that being sick didn't keep her from getting big. Very big. She had always been such a narrow, skinny little thing all the years they had known each other, and now she was so big she could hardly get out of the chair by herself, and she had two whole months to go. Almost looked like she was big enough for two babies, or maybe she had her months mixed up. Anyway, Marybeth just hated to leave her friend alone very long.

She sighed with frustration. It was so different with friends. She couldn't just say, "Lie down here, Irena, and let me check your belly to see if maybe you're carryin' two babies. I just want to make sure everything's all right."

She couldn't say that. She couldn't even suggest that Irena let Mama check her. Poor Irena was scared enough as it was. Here she was, alone, with her family gone on to the west more than a year ago.

But then, how would I know if there was trouble? I ain't no midwife, she told herself sternly. *We're just gonna take one day at a time, and when we got that'n gone, we'll take the next 'un. That's what we'll do.* But her words did not ease her mind.

Some men could be a help to a woman, but not Irena's husband. Poor Cal, he was good as he could be, but he didn't know nothin', neither. Not that there was anything much that anyone could do for Irena now… but wait.

Cal was not brought up to be a farmer, and he had such a hard time with his farm. Any fool could see that he was never meant to be one, but he kept on trying. Plum stubborn-headed, he was.

Even she, Marybeth, could have told him before he bought it that his farm of low, flat clay would never grow crops. It was either too sticky and wet, or it was dry, hard-baked and cracked open. Weeds grew in it faster than crops, and they couldn't be gotten out. Rock-hard ground messed up the crop plants.

But there was one thing about Cal Boudreau, though: he was not a quitter. He stayed with it and kept on trying.

Irena's fuzzy little dog, Yoyo, heard Marybeth coming and came bounding down the road to meet her, barking and whirling in circles of joy. At the front gate, she waved to Cal, who was working in the shade of a tree by the shed. He seemed to be trying to remove the horns from a bull calf, amid much bawling from the calf and struggling by the man.

Another mistake. Likely no one bothered to tell him that small farmers didn't keep bull calves. They sold them or ate them because, even without horns, they became too unruly to put up with. Oh, well.

Marybeth crossed the yard to the back door of the cabin and, not bothering to knock, she went in. Irena sat in the big rocker by the window. Balanced on her huge belly was a skein of bright blue yarn and a half-finished baby bootee. She greeted her friend happily.

"I sure am glad you come by. I'm dyin' for a cup'a tea and was dreadin' gettin' up to go fix it."

Marybeth grinned. "You're gonna have a cup of tea, all right, but not the tea you was fixin' to make." From the pocket of her sweater she produced a packet of crushed leaves and stems she had taken from Laura's supply.

"This tea's gonna be good for both of us, Laura thinks." The aroma of the tea had begun to fill the air even before the boiling water was poured over it. The room smelled of woodland flowers, cedar trees after a rain and mountain spearmint, gathered mid-morning on a sunshiny day.

"Laura thinks this tea is good for babies, those on the way and those that ain't started yet. Says she made it up from things Mama had wrote down, blendin' in the best-tastin' plants. She named it 'Mother's Mix'."

Irena put aside her knitting and picked up the steaming cup. Blowing away the curls of steam, she took a tiny sip, sighing contentedly. Her fingers clasp the thick cup as if to gain warmth from it.

"Tell Laura for me that it tastes good, like it'll make me feel better, and I could use some'a that."

"How've you been?"

"Still hurts, some. Still makin' spots."

Marybeth was thoughtful. Pain and spots were both bad at this time in the pregnancy. Even her limited knowledge told her this. What could she say to her friend to comfort her without making her even more scared than she was? Of course, there was one thing.

"I don't think you ought'a be up out'a bed. Be best for you if you'd just lay down, don't you think? Might ought to not be usin' up strength."

Irena chuckled dryly. "With me not up, there's not much gets done," she pointed out. "Then again, there's not much gets done when I do get up. Mostly, I get up on account of Cal. If I don't, he gets more worried about me, and when he worries about me, it bears on his mind, and then he can't get nothin' done, neither."

Marybeth nodded and glanced around the room. "I'm here now and got nothin' else to do today, so I could pick up a bit. What you got'a do is finish that tea and lay down a spell. Likely you'd wake up feelin' better. We got us a good clothes-dryin' day outside, and I could rub out a few things while you rest. Would it be all right to tell Cal to light a fire under the wash kettle?"

Marybeth would rather have lit the fire herself, but in this way, her friend might feel less bad about having to accept help from her. She held a hand toward Irena to help her up from the rocker.

While the water in the wash kettle heated, Marybeth gathered the dirty clothes and sorted them on the kitchen floor. The warm tea seemed to relax Irena, who was now asleep, so Marybeth spread a warm quilt over her. Then she washed up a small accumulation of dirty dishes. She rubbed out the clothes on the scrub board, rinsed them and hung them on the line to let them whip themselves dry in the wind.

From the shed she gathered an apron full of potatoes, carrots, turnips and onions to start a stew for their supper. Also a quart jar of home-canned tomatoes.

Let's see, what should she fix with the vegetable stew? Irena needed meat to gain strength. Maybe she should ask Cal to catch and kill a chicken. No, fish would be better. A big mudcat with its white, succulent meat, fried crisp and brown. That would tempt any appetite. Should she ask Cal to quit what he was doing and go get a fish? It would take him no time at all, really. Why not?

The shed was piled full of wood for the kitchen, so Marybeth filled the wood box behind the cookstove. One thing about Cal: he always kept a shed full of cookstove wood where it would always be dry and ready. While the clothes dried on the line, she scrubbed the kitchen sparkling clean, and while she had soapy water, she washed the kitchen windows. It might be a long time before Irena would be strong enough to do these necessary things.

She brought in the dry clothes and put them away. There'd be no use to heat the flatiron and press Sunday clothes, because no one from this house would be able to attend church until after the baby came. A trip to the church in the jiggly wagon would bring on the baby in no time at all… but too soon.

The jiggly wagon and the rocky road would be a worse trip than Mary had on the way to Bethlehem, and everyone could see what that did, bringing on Baby Jesus before they could even get settled in a hotel room.

The delicious aroma of cooking onions reminded Marybeth that it was time to add the jar of canned tomatoes and a pinch of several good stew herbs that she had helped Irena gather last summer.

Cal stamped his feet noisily on the doorstep to remove loose mud, then entered carrying three catfish, each one so large it would make more than enough for three people. Good! That would mean leftovers, and if any place could ever make good use of leftovers, it was this place!

With an experienced hand, Cal gutted and beheaded the fish, carrying the waste to the chicken pen while Marybeth stirred up a batter for hush puppies.

From the bed in the front room of the cabin came sighs of appreciation. "Something smells wonderful. I'll be in there to help if someone will come and help me up from the bed."

Cal looked at Marybeth with worried eyes. Marybeth held her finger to her lips and shook her head.

"I was countin' on us having a picnic," she called in reply.

"Picnic? Well, I don't know if...."

"Just sit tight," she was instructed. "We're fixin' to bring the picnic in there. Too windy to be outside."

She pulled the wooden breadboard from its slot in the kitchen cabinet and set the bowl of crisp, fried fish and the platter of steaming hush puppies on it. Beside them, she set three bowls of the colorful stew.

"Cal, would you pull that little round table over here to the bed close enough for Irena to reach it?" Then she handed him the breadboard. "And I'll just run out to the well house and bring in some buttermilk."

With pillows behind her back, Irena was able to sit up and reach the food on the table beside her.

"Wonderful," she pronounced, biting into the crisp batter of the fish. "Gettin' a meal like this ought'a get a body feelin' good in no time."

Between bites, Cal commented, "Sure is a big run'a mudcat down in the river today. Just thinkin', while I was pullin' these out, about somethin' I could do. I could seine out a good wagonload'a fish in no time, and if I was to run them over to Jacksonville, they'd sell good. Could bring cash enough to buy diapers and such for the baby. I was thinkin' I could do that, but I was knowin' I'd be gone seven, maybe eight hours, all told. Said to myself that Reenie hadn't ought'a be left alone for that long a time." His eyes pled with Marybeth.

Irena looked helplessly from one to the other, flinching and biting her lip as the baby moved against a sore spot.

"No problem to that," Marybeth assured them. "I got me some things to do at my house tomorrow, but the day after that'd be good for me to come and stay till you got back. If you was wantin' to have them fish all seined up and ready, I'd come real early. It'd be no problem to me, 'cause likely I'd be down here sometime during the day, anyway."

Irena made no reply. Problems seemed to melt away when Marybeth was around. It had been like this since they had been little girls together. Marybeth always knew what to do.

Cal set his empty bowl on the breadboard. "Could'a done that today with all the luck I been havin' with that calf." With that summation, he was gone.

Irena was put back to bed. At least she had been able to eat a good supper. She would be better now, maybe. It was so easy to get one's hopes up.

Marybeth cleaned the dishes, then skimmed the sour milk and put the cream in the churn to make butter while heating the milk curds for cottage cheese. The cheese would be good for Irena, and she could easily fix it for herself tomorrow.

Occasionally, she stepped to the door to check on Irena, resting pale and motionless against the white pillowcase. The great mountain of her belly lifted the quilts gently as she breathed. She was resting, and that was good. Marybeth paused to stare, unobserved, at the belly. *There just has to be two babies in there,* she decided, shaking her head. *Please, Lord, make it be just one!*

Returning to the kitchen, she mulled over in her mind about the diaper trip. Maybe she should try to determine how many babies there were before he bought them. Could need more than they figured on.

No, she once more decided. Irena was a friend, and there were things you just did not do to a friend. If Irena was well and healthy, it would be nothing to say, "Just let me check, and likely you ought'a think up two baby names," making a game of it, but not the way Irena was feeling.

And the pain? What could be causing that? Could be that feeling around down there in an examination would only make it worse. Better let things alone. Cal could always get more diapers if they were needed.

She began to turn the churn handle again. The dasher in the sour cream roiled the liquid around, sticking the particles of butter together and making the wheel hard to crank. Time to turn it out in a bowl and press the butter globules together with the backside of a large wooden spoon.

She packed the butter into the mold and took it to the wellhouse. She'd make up a pan of cornbread before she left, and Cal could have it with cold buttermilk for tomorrow's lunch. Maybe Irena would feel like eating some. If Irena didn't want the cornbread, Cal could open up a jar of peaches to put on the cottage cheese. Irena just had to get some strength somehow.

Milk custard; that would be good. She'd make one before she went home.

When she finished in the kitchen, she picked up the knitting needles and worked on the bright blue bootees while Irena dozed restlessly. She quickly finished the bootee and started on another pair. Even if there were not two babies, it would be nice to have extra bootees, with winter coming on. If it was two babies... well, it was better not to think about that.

Everything was quiet outside. The calf quit bawling, so Cal must have been successful with the horns, or maybe he gave up, though that didn't sound like Cal. Or he could be down at the river.

When she had four tiny bootees finished, she put on her sweater and slipped quietly out the door. Irena did not stir. Outside, she was met by the bouncing Yoyo, leaping against her leg and nibbling at her knuckles, yipping and bouncing. She picked up the little dog, cuddling her.

"You want in that house, don't you? Would you promise not to wake Irena if I take you inside? 'Course, if I don't take you in, you're probably gonna bark and scratch at the door till she gets up and lets you in, aren't you?" The little dog squirmed and wriggled in her arms, trying to lick her face and neck.

Marybeth quietly opened the door and took the dog to the bed where Irena still slept. She set her down on the quilt, patting her into silence. The dog responded with a happy wagging of her tail.

Back outside, she hurried her steps to be home before darkness fell. There was a strong east wind and black, lowering clouds, warning of fall weather to come. It had been a good thing to get the washing done while she could get it dry, and if the weather held, she'd wash out a few things at home tomorrow.

She followed Rock Creek for a quarter of a mile as it flowed toward the Tuscalara River, then she turned east to climb the half-mile of hill to the house where she had been born. Close to home, she saw Laura step out of the trees into the path ahead of her.

3

Laura had a good day. She had found Solomon's Seal and bone-knit, both very important plants. She had selected a protected place beside a dense grove of trees and had begun her secret garden by transplanting them both.

So she wouldn't be bringing home an empty bucket, she had filled it with mountain spearmint. She always had a need for a lot of it. The herb made a refreshing tea, all by itself, and it had a way of making the bad-tasting herbs not so bitter.

While gathering the plants, she had done a lot of thinking. She really was going to do what she told her mother she would do. All she had to do now was figure out how and when.

As she reached the lane that led to the mountain cabin, she joined her sister.

"Have much luck today?" asked Marybeth companionably.

"Some," was the reply, as she presented her bucket for inspection. "Is Irena doin' any better?"

"No. I can't see that she's a bit better. It's going to be a long two months. I think she needs to stay in bed."

"Do you think Mama ought to go see her?"

Marybeth shook her head. "I think Irena may know she ain't doing well. If Mama saw her, Mama'd say what she thought, and it might scare Irena even worse. She's already a jittery case of nerves. I'm just going to have to be down there a lot."

Laura nodded. "Likely you're right. Sorry."

Together they entered the empty house. The birthing basket was gone, and so was Mama, so it could be a pleasant evening. It would be quiet. The girls might be able to talk a little.

The younger girl spent most of the next day tramping about in the woods, leaving Marybeth alone in the house with the laundry. She even managed to get the towels and sheets dry before the rain started. She heated the flatiron on the woodstove and pressed everything in the ironing basket and cooked beans with ham for their supper.

The rain outside was damp and chilly, but the hot stove and the bubbling bean soup made the house seem cozy. If Mama came in wet and tired, likely she'd appreciate the heat. But Mama didn't come in.

Laura, however, did come in, and was totally soaked and absolutely appreciative of the heat and the food.

"Hmmmm, them beans smell better'n anything I ever smelled in my life. You makin' cornbread?"

"Thought I would."

The sisters went about their activities in silence for an hour or more. Laura was first to speak.

"You're bein' more'n worried about Irena, ain't you?"

Marybeth nodded. "Wish't I knew what it was I could do to help. Cal, he'd do anything for her, but he don't know what to do neither. I can go down there and do things to help her out, but she ain't gettin' no better. She don't want no doctor brought out and Mama don't seem to care for nothin' 'cept actual birthin'. I don't know what to do that I ain't already done."

Laura sighed and continued to eat her beans and cornbread, sopping the bread into the thick, rich, ham-flavored broth. Her sister's words just pushed her farther in the direction she had already decided to go.

When she finally spoke, it was with firm determination. "Marybeth, it ain't always gonna be that a'way. Nothin's gonna happen soon enough for Irena, but it just ain't right, havin' things go wrong and not knowin' what it is. And most times a body's just scared what they do is wrong. Things is gonna hafta get better for women havin' babies."

4

It was long before daylight when Marybeth awoke to the sound of rain on the roof and aroused herself to put on the kettle for breakfast tea.

Then she dealt with the same old thought. What would be best for Irena's pain? It would help to know the cause of the pain. Mama might know if she dared to ask; however, Mama was not here. In the end, she just took a supply of the Mother's Mix and headed down the hill. It might not help, but it couldn't hurt, and Irena liked the taste of it.

Fall weather was indeed settling in, and the sky looked threatening, so she changed from her sweater to her winter coat. The upper part of Rock Mountain was hidden with dark clouds. Lightning crackled, and forks of fire shot out of the clouds. Some bad kind of a storm must be brewing up there on the mountain!

In a couple of hours of this, River Bend would also be in the rain. Rock Creek would swell up out of its bank and flow through the yard around Cal and Irena's house. The lower field would be flooded again, and slick, black mud would be everywhere.

By the time she got to Rock Creek Road, the water was rising fast. Off came her shoes and stockings, and she slogged barefoot through the icy, cold puddles. Better to be cold for a little while than to have wet shoes all day. What a day for Cal to be going to town!

Closer to the house, the road was completely underwater. If Cal was not already on the road, it was too late now. Even two strong horses could not pull the wagon through this mud.

But he was gone. The shed was empty. Water was knee-deep in the lower yard. The little cabin stood proudly on its island, but the fields Cal had tried to farm were totally underwater… yet again.

Marybeth waded to the house and scraped the mud from her bare feet; then she stepped inside the cold, damp, quiet house. A quick glance toward the woodbox told her she could have the cabin warm before long. Cal had left it full.

There was no sound from the bed, so she began to build up a fire in the kitchen stove. The blaze crackled merrily, and she dared to look in on Irena. If it was not for the faint movement of breathing, one could not be certain there was any life in her. Marybeth felt the limp wrist. Pulse very faint. Irena opened her eyes.

"Better?" asked Marybeth foolishly. Anyone with an eye in their head could see she wasn't.

Irena smiled. "Maybe. I'm sure glad you're here, Marybeth. Cal was gettin' on my nerves, lookin' like a little boy about to cry. He always wants to do somethin' and don't know what. I'm glad he'll be gone today and doin' things, so he don't be worryin' about me for a while. Is it still raining?"

"Sure is."

"I hope you didn't go and get your feet wet comin' in here. That yard gets so soggy in the rain."

"My feet are perfectly dry," Marybeth assured her truthfully. "How are your sore spots this morning?"

"Same," Irena told her. "No, that ain't the truth. I was lyin' to you the way I lie to Cal. The sore spots are worse. Hardly got no sleep, between the sore spots and knowin' Cal was a'layin' there awake and worryin'."

Marybeth smoothed the quilts over Irena. "I'll make breakfast, and you will eat two eggs."

Irena cut in, "And that tea? Did you bring any more? And then I want to say something to you, and you'll have to bring a chair over here to the bed to listen."

Marybeth scrambled the eggs and buttered the biscuits. The tea steamed fragrantly as the breadboard tray of food was brought to the bed.

"All right, let's talk."

Irena sighed. "Promise you won't stop me till I've had my say."

Marybeth nodded agreeably, sipping her tea.

Irena began. "I love Cal. He's a good man, and I know there's things he don't know, but he always wants to learn. Now listen. If you was me and said to me what I'm fixin' to say to you, I'd say, 'Yes, Marybeth, I'll do it'. Now promise me."

Marybeth chuckled at the obvious trap. "I'm thinkin' I ain't gonna like what you're fixin' to say."

"Promise!" Irena demanded.

"All right, I promise." Anything to keep her from getting excited.

Irena continued. "Sometimes I think my baby won't make it, but more times than that, I think it'll be me that won't make it."

"Hush your mouth, Irena. I didn't come down here to listen to that rot."

"No, wait, I got'a say this. If nothin' don't happen, then you ain't to be held to no promise. But if I ain't here, and he's got no baby to show for my passin', or even if he has, my Cal gonna need help. You bein' my closest friend, you'd be the one who's gonna give it to him."

"Oh, Irena! Please!"

"Wait, I got to say this. I ain't meanin' anything but for you to be just a friend. He'll need someone with words to hold him together till he can do it for hisself. He wasn't never taught to stand alone at death trouble, without family like folks here. Now look at me, and tell me you'll promise."

"Now, Irena, I can't...."

"Course you can. You just say, 'Sure thing, Irena. I'll do what you say, and you don't need to worry'. Now do it quick, because my eggs are gettin' cold."

"All right, Irena. I'll promise, but it won't mean nothin'. I'll be here to help with the baby till you're up and about. That'll be all I'll be needin' to do. Now eat your eggs. No, wait, don't sit up. I'll feed 'em to you."

Marybeth's experienced eye judged the mound under the quilt. Two babies, for sure. How in the name of the Dear Lord is she going to manage to birth two babies? And even worse, take care of them afterward?

Irena ate her eggs and slept, and the rain kept pelting down. Marybeth waded to the shed for more wood. She needed to keep the cabin extra warm and dry. Couldn't risk Irena catching cold on top of everything else. Coughs might just do her in. Wouldn't help the baby (babies?) none, neither.

Icy mud oozed between her toes as she struggled to stay upright on the slippery ground. The water was a lot deeper now. Should have looked around for some boots or something.

What about Cal out in this? He'd be plenty miserable, but the fish were bound to be in good shape after being pelted with cold rain for three hours. Even in the old oilskin coat and gum boots, Cal must be wet to the bone and freezing cold.

Nothing he ever does seems to work out to be easy. But that Cal, he keeps on going.

She brought more vegetables to the kitchen and checked the hen house for fresh eggs. Then she opened the oven door to thaw out her own frozen feet.

Idleness left her time to think, and she didn't want to do that right now, so she picked up the knitting needles and began to work on more bootees. Couldn't have too many bootees. She wished she could find the pink yarn. She was getting tired of blue.

Rain beat steadily on the windows and streamed down, blotting out the little bit of available light, so she lit another lamp. She sang softly to herself to steady her nerves. She'd just as well settle in, as she'd never be able to leave here in this rain. Why, if it didn't stop soon, water would be on the doorstep.

Late in the afternoon, she braved the lake of water in the yard to get to the barn to milk the cow. While she was out, she fed the chickens and brought in another armload of wood for the stove.

It was getting late, and where was Cal? One look at the road told her he wouldn't be traveling on it today. Well, he'd do something. She had enough to worry about. Irena was definitely not better.

In the back of her mind, she sincerely wished for her mother… someone who could tell her what to do. *Do something, Marybeth,* she commanded herself. *Anything!*

She opened a jar of blackberries she had helped Irena pick and can. When they were boiling, she added honey and spoonfuls of dumpling batter. The dumplings swelled in the hot oven and floated lightly on the bubbling purple juice like violet clouds in a summer evening sky. She added a lot of butter, and it melted in yellow puddles among the violet clouds of the puffed dumplings. Then she slipped the dumplings back into the oven to brown on top.

That, together with milk and fresh eggs, took care of supper. Cal would be freezing cold and starving hungry when he came in. That is, if he made it home at all. Sometimes in the high water, the swinging bridge got washed away. Maybe that happened again. She hummed softly, so she would quit thinking.

Darkness fell. Where was Cal? She set the lamp in the window just in case he was fool enough to wade through the mile of water. Surely he stayed in Jacksonville. Why, a man wouldn't throw his dog out in weather like this.

Dog! Where was Irena's dog? This minute was the first she had thought of her. Surely she didn't follow after Cal! Oh well, nothing could be done about that now.

"Irena," she said softly. "You have to wake up again and eat."

A groan came from the bed. "No, I have to sleep."

"First you eat. If you don't eat, I will take back my promise. You think I want to take care of some runty little old baby because his mama starved herself to death?"

Irena, awake now, smiled faintly. "Smells good. Blackberry dumplings? I think I can eat some. Where's Cal? He back yet?"

What should she tell her? A glance at the door showed a puddle of water just inside the door and wet rivulets followed the groove of the floor boards, making their way toward the bed.

She decided. "Weather got worse. Cal likely stayed in Jacksonville. He'd know he couldn't make it home in weather like this, and he won't worry 'cause he knows I'm here."

"Maybe," was all Irena found the strength to say. She seems hardly to have the ability to lift the spoon to her mouth when given the hot rich dumplings topped with fresh cream.

Marybeth forced herself to only think positively. She's still eating. Maybe there's a chance.

The puddle by the door had enlarged itself, so after supper Marybeth picked up slippers and other things from the floor and put them on the kitchen table. Who could know how high the water would get. Then she stretched out on the bed beside Irena and began talking about things that had happened and things they did when they were girls (so many hundreds of years ago!).

Occasionally Irena would say something, but mostly she just drifted in and out of sleep.

Marybeth kept thinking, *If only Mama was here.* She strained her mind to remember what her mother might have said at some time, but she herself could remember no similar situation. All she knew for sure was that Irena was not doing well.

But the rain had stopped finally, and Irena seemed to be sleeping. Things would be better now, and Marybeth dozed.

Then suddenly she and Irena were both little girls, walking down to the Mercantile to buy a piece of candy. It was a Saturday, and Irena had spent the night with her. They had played "dress up" for a while, even pretending Laura was a baby. Laura got tired of staying in the bed, as a "baby" should, so they had gone on to other games.

So now the girls crossed the swinging bridge and stopped to look over at the swift running water. Irena leaned far over the cable railing, dropping leaves and pebbles in the water.

Marybeth watched her, thinking. Things always happen to Irena. If there were kittens, she got scratched. If it rained, she got muddy. If they ran, she fell down. Here she was leaning far out over the safety cable, looking down at the fast-moving water. What should she do? Or say? Should she pull her back?

"Marybeth?" a voice called. Marybeth startled out of a sound sleep to respond. The voice came to her again. "Wake up, Marybeth."

The urgency of the voice had a paralyzing effect on Marybeth. Her arms and legs seemed to be made of lead, and her mind tried to block out the sound. Struggling against the inertia of sleep, she sat up in the bed.

It was past midnight, and the room had become clammy and cold. Her eyes darted to the door where the puddle had formed, and the glance registered that the spot of water was no larger. She forced herself to look at Irena, lying beside her.

Irena's eyes were wide and frightened, and her face was white in the lamplight.

"What's wrong?" Marybeth asked.

"I don't know. Everything, I think. I can't wait any longer."

"Can't wait? What are you talking about? I'll stir up the fire and get you something hot to drink." Her words tumbled meaninglessly from her mouth as she tried to clear her mind. *What am I going to do?*

"No, Marybeth, I don't need nothin'. I got awful pains everywhere. I'm really glad you're here, 'stead'a Cal. He gets so scared, and then he can't do nothin' at all. I know you know what to do 'cause your mama taught you."

Sweat stood out in beads on Irena's face, and she groaned, clutching her belly with shaking hands.

Marybeth drew in a deep breath and slipped her feet into her shoes. She had just stood up when Irena screamed with pain.

The agonized sound brought Marybeth into action, and she frantically searched her mind for all she could remember from being with her mother on midwife calls. But this was different. Everything about it was different, and besides, never had she ever been entirely alone at a difficult birth.

Cold sweat broke out on her face. Merciful Heaven! What could she do now? Her feet finally moved across floor and flew to the kitchen. She crammed sticks of dry wood into the stove and lit a stick of kindling, enveloping the wood with flames. Fortunately the water in the stove reservoir was still almost hot.

She shook tea into a cup but the water was not quite hot enough for it to steep the tea leaves properly. She'd have to wait on that. What now?

Oh, clean cloths. This couldn't mean the baby was coming, but… *Dear Lord, help me know what to do.* She pulled the cloths from the drawer of the dresser and put them on the little table.

This is a false alarm, she told herself hopefully. First babies always gave a lot of warning. Likely she was hurrying around all for nothing. What next? But the obvious thing was, Irena's screams seemed like a warning!

Towels. She set them where they would be handy. Now what?

Oh, of course! The cradle box! She set it high on the top of the warming oven of the cook stove. It would be warm and toasty if it was needed, which, of course, it would not be. This was not happening, surely. Now what?

The patient, of course! Oh, poor Irena. Why wasn't she saying something? Anything!

She hurried to the bed and lifted aside the quilts. Even in the dim lamp light she saw too much blood. She rested her hand lightly on the bulging belly and felt the weak muscle action. Good! Maybe! Baby still alive, but labor had started. Now what?

Oh, Mama, where are you? Then there was more blood. How much could Irena afford to lose? This was not right.

Irena screamed and clutched her belly with white-knuckled fingers. Marybeth massaged as she had seen her mother do in difficult cases and large babies, and this was definitely one large baby! And worse, it was not even full term. *Oh, Mama! Where are you…?*

Irena screamed again, startling Marybeth out of her thoughts, but she recovered quickly enough to catch a scrawny, squalling baby, its purple face wrinkled with angry yelling.

Marybeth stared with unbelieving amazement at the squirming bundle in her hands. Such a tiny girl! Such a loud noise! Then memory kicked in.

She shook out a towel with one hand, holding the slippery infant in the other, and wrapped the baby carefully against the chill of the room. There was no response from Irena, but she was still breathing. Marybeth settled the screaming infant on her mother's bulging stomach.

The scissors. Oh, she had forgotten them! Where were they? She knew where there was a sharp knife. She released the towel-wrapped squalling baby from her shaking hands and dashed to the kitchen. The teakettle was now bubbling, but who had time for tea!

Grabbing the knife in one hand and the cradle box in the other, she dashed back. Still no response from Irena.

The terrified Marybeth unwrapped the baby and made a quick tie then slashed with the sharp knife, and the baby was on her own. Then she sat on the edge of the bed to finish cleaning the little thing and in horror saw that, there on the bed beside her, lay another scrawny baby, perfectly motionless.

Quickly putting the complaining, towel-wrapped baby into the cradle box, she shook out a fresh towel and covered the second baby girl, patting gently on the tiny back. There was no sound and no breath. The little thing was as tiny and motionless as a toy doll and just as silent.

Dear Lord, she breathed, *what do I do now?* Irena must have been in labor for at least two days, and she had not known it. Some midwife she would make! Spots and all? She should have known! She felt her heart beat violently against her chest in her terror.

She had to do something quickly! This baby was as blue as the violets in the woodland. She looked at the tiny face, then slipped her finger in the baby's mouth and could feel nothing wrong. It occurred to her to wonder if she had washed her hand, and Mama would be furious, but if something did not happen immediately, it wouldn't matter anyway.

She knelt beside the bed with her knees on the cold, damp floor and put her mouth over the baby's tiny mouth, blowing gently. The baby's chest expanded. She blew again and again. While she blew, she searched her mind for something else she could do.

With her free hand, she gently scratched the soles of the baby's feet and produced a faint jerk in the tiny leg. *Oh, thank you, Lord!*

At last, the little thing was breathing! Finally the tiny, wrinkled face puckered, then a whimper, and at last the voice of the tiny girl joined her sister's wails.

Marybeth breathed a sigh and glanced at the clock. Surely more than six minutes had passed, but that is what the clock said. With a quick tie and a knife slit, the second little girl was placed in the warm cradle box. They were so tiny, there was plenty of room.

Now she felt more confident. When she had gone working with her mother, the babies had been her special charge. They were never as small as these, but she knew about babies and wrung a soft cloth out of the warm water, gently cleaning the ears, eyes and nostrils and the soft folds of their arms and legs. She could again breathe normally, grateful for the strength of their yells.

Fear for Irena nagged at her. Irena had lost so much blood, she must surely be very weak, but at least there was no pain at the moment. Seemingly. Fainted…? Sometimes a faint could give blessed relief. Mama always took care of this part of the birthing.

True, passing out had its blessings, seemingly, but now something must be done for her. But what? The tea would be good for her if she would wake up.

Together now in the cradle box, the first baby had managed to get a fist in her mouth and became silent. A soothing pat hushed the other one. The sudden silence in the cabin almost hurt her ears, but she smiled to herself with satisfaction. Just wait till Irena saw these two darling little girls.

Irena! She suddenly remembered her again.

With a cloth and a pan of water, she went back to the bed. There was still breath. She felt the weak pulse. At least the heartbeat was still there, and the worst was over. Wasn't it? Now Irena could have a long res,t but she really should have some strengthening tea first.

With the warm cloth, she stroked Irena's forehead, cheeks and neck. Massaging and encouraging blood circulation. It's what Mama would have done. Maybe….

She went to the kitchen and poured the cup full from the bubbling kettle. If she couldn't wake Irena, she would drink it herself. She started to leave the kitchen, and the crying began again. Marybeth put down the tea to pat the baby back to sleep, but both babies in the cradle box were quiet. What was going on here?

She hurriedly put the cradle box back on the warming oven and dashed to the bed. *Lord, help me,* she pled. She had forgotten to finish the job and had missed a third baby. What else could it be?

She threw back the quilt, and there it lay, even scrawnier than the other two, but at least it was crying. Like a frightened baby kitten. With horror she realized that if the middle one had been the last one, it would have been left to die while the dumb midwife did other things.

She cleaned and wrapped the third tiny little girl in a towel and fitted her in the cradle box with her sisters. Three little girls! Imagine the wonder of it all, and the birthing had been a success. The huge baby that was the mound in its mama's stomach had become three manageable infants and had practically birthed themselves. *Thank you, Lord!*

What now? Should she try to remake the bed or let Irena rest? The room was still cold, and that helped her decision. She pulled the quilt over her patient and patted her snugly. At least, there were no more babies, and Irena seemed to be breathing better. Then she remembered the tea. Now was the time. Her patient really must have some liquid after such a great blood loss. The patient must not be permitted to be dried out inside. Mama had said.

"Irena?" No answer.

Again. "Irena?" Still no answer so she patted the pale face. "Irena? Wake up! Open your eyes."

Slowly the blue eyes opened, and she looked hazily at Marybeth.

"It's over," Marybeth told her joyfully. "You're all through with everything, and you have a beautiful little girl." Time enough later to tell her about the other two.

Irena sighed and smiled faintly… uncomprehendingly. "Am I alive?" she wondered.

"You bet you're alive, and right now you're going to drink this tea. I'm gonna feed it to you with a spoon, and you're gonna drink all of it."

After half the tea had been spooned into her mouth, Irena drifted into sleep. She was breathing better now, and the tea did seem to help. Maybe. Marybeth decided she herself really did need a cup of it.

First I have to do something about that bed. Oh, I know. I'll just gently slide her over to the other side and… But suddenly another realization struck her.

Milk! There were three babies in the kitchen who were going to be howling hungry any minute and who had no mother to feed them. She left Irena and hurried to the kitchen.

There were no bottles, of course. Who would think they would be needed? Also no diapers. All they were wearing was the towels. But first the food.

Her eyes scanned the kitchen. What could she feed them with? A teaspoon would be too big for their tiny mouths. She filled a tin cup with milk she had collected a few hours before. A minute on the warm stove, and the milk was ready. She washed her hands thoroughly and dipped her finger in the milk. Two drops fell back into the cup. It would have to work until she had another idea.

One of the babies whimpered softly, sounding almost like a baby kitten calling its mother. Marybeth reached into the cradle box and gently lifted her away from her sisters. The large towel totally enveloped the tiny, doll-sized baby. She worked the edge of the towel away to reveal the miniature face, whimpering and scowling impatiently. Then she lifted the cradle box back to the top of the warming oven.

Holding the tiny bundle easily in one hand, she dipped her finger in the tepid milk and held it over the baby's mouth. Two drops of the liquid slid off her fingertips. Maybe the baby swallowed. She couldn't tell for sure, but she dipped her fingers again, and there were two more drops.

Marybeth searched her mind for answers. These babies were clearly only about half the size of a normal baby. How much milk was enough? Babies normally sucked until they were full, and then they quit sucking.

What if she made them sick? The tiny mouth puckered and twisted, dealing somehow with the milk. How could anything this tiny be alive? This one seemed to weigh no more than the wadded towel that was around her.

Another one should be hungry soon… if they were still alive. How much to feed them? She decided on ten finger dips… twenty drops. That would be enough for a start.

Oops! She had forgotten something else. The hand that held the towel wrapped baby felt moisture. The bundle had developed a small, warm, damp spot. The babies were still naked, without diapers. How could she put a diaper on a doll? Even more important, what could she use for a diaper?

Carrying the baby with her, she searched the dresser drawers. Handkerchiefs? No. They were the right size, but they were too flimsy. She kept searching. Ah, there it was! Cal's socks! She experimented with the folding and found they had just the right stretchiness and bulk. Hmmmm, how many socks did he have? Not enough, for sure.

She found four pairs of socks that would make eight diapers. Well, it was a start.

She diapered the girl's tiny bottom and re-wrapped her in a dry warm towel. The squinty eyes were drooping sleepily, so Marybeth returned her to the cradle box, continuing to pat her until she was quiet with tight-shut eyes.

The other two babies were not fussing yet, but she thought she should start the feeding. Lifting the next baby from the box, she tapped her finger against the tiny cheek to arouse the sucking instinct. The baby turned slightly toward the finger, working her miniature mouth. Good!

The milk was beginning to cool, so she pushed the cup nearer the hot part of the stove, and discovered there was no longer a hot part. The fire was going out.

Holding the baby in one hand, she opened the firebox and poked at the coals, stirring them into a blaze, adding two sticks of wood and closing the door. Now she had to wash her hands again.

She slid a chair over to the washbasin and sat down, holding the towel-wrapped bundle in her lap while she carefully washed her hands. Mama had been firm on that. Wash your hands good so you don't have sick babies.

Marybeth dried her hands on the towel that was wrapped around the baby and dipped her finger into the milk. By now the baby was squirming restlessly but quieted as the warm milk touched her lips. Having no nipple to suck, she began to suck her tiny tongue. That helped a lot. Ten dips, twenty drops and she patted the baby against her shoulder. The tiny eyes closed, and she was quiet, so Marybeth returned her and picked up the third one.

No response. The baby's head lolled to one side. Frantically, Marybeth slid her fingers under the towel to rest against the tiny chest. Faint movement. At least it was still alive, so should she let the baby sleep or feed it? Then she felt the warm, wet spot on her lap.

Put on a diaper, that was what she'd do. Then she remembered she had not diapered the second baby. Oh, well.

Carefully she began to peel back the edges of the towel. The baby's body lay limply across her lap, but her little chest heaved slightly as she breathed. This one seemed even smaller than the other two.

She looked at the tiny girl and shook her head. How could anything this small be alive? The legs seemed no bigger around than her own thumb, and the stubbed nose was no bigger than a huckleberry.

Dear God in heaven, you got'a help me now, 'cause I'm scared witless bein' here alone. But You know that, don't You? What am I gonna do about this baby 'afore it dies? You got'a help me, 'cause You're the only one here but me.

Spreading a clean towel over the warming oven to heat, she took one of Cal's socks and folded it, pinning it on each side of the baby as it lay limply in her lap. She began to massage the tiny feet between her thumb and forefinger. The feet seemed no bigger than the speckled butterbeans from the garden. The red skin of the baby's foot felt thin and fragile, but it was still warm. Blood was still moving.

Working her hands up the legs, she continued to massage. Up to the tiny chest she moved her hands and stroked her fingers up each arm and around the miniature fingers.

By now the dry towel was toasty warm, so she spread it on her lap and transferred the baby, pulling the soft, warm folds about her, close and tight. She lifted the warm bundle and placed her cheek against the baby's cheek, scraping her brain for what to do next.

Then it came! A hiccup! A real, actual, wonderful hiccup! *Thank you, Lord!* That hiccup was a wonderful, welcoming sign! Every midwife was happy to welcome a hiccup. It meant the tiny insides were alive and trying to do their job.

She patted the tiny back, and after two more hiccups, the baby began to whimper softly. Marybeth looked toward the ceiling and smiled her thanks and relief.

Touching the baby's cheek with her finger, she watched with satisfaction as the little mouth began to work. Dipping her finger in the milk, she fed the baby two drops. They slid out of the tiny mouth. Marybeth touched her pinkie finger to the baby's lips, and the cheeks contracted slightly.

The miniature tongue curled around her finger, sucking slightly. Marybeth tried the milk again, and it went down somehow. By the fifth dip, this one was also sucking her tongue instead of Marybeth's finger.

In the midst of her relief, Marybeth's heart stopped. She hadn't washed her hands after the second baby. Oh, how could she have forgotten, as many times as she had helped her mother? How many times had she heard the instructions?

I'm sorry, God. I was worried and I forgot.

Irena! Oh, my! In her fear and concern for the babies, she had once more forgotten the mother. Carefully, so as not to wake the others, she tucked the baby in the box with her sisters.

Putting the tin cup of milk in the warming oven, she slipped another stick of wood into the stove. She took a step toward the front room but stepped back to slide the teakettle closer to the heat. Somebody was going to need some tea very soon. Probably herself.

So now it was time to force herself to go through the door to Irena. Dread filled her heart and seeped all the way down to her feet. She had tried to save the babies, and what had she done to Irena? *Oh, Mama, I wish you were here.*

She forced her feet to go through the door, and she turned her attention to Irena and the bed. Flexing her shoulders to relieve the tension cramp, she studied her patient. Breathing seemed to be better. Color was terrible, but what else could it be after such a blood loss? If she moved her, would that start the bleeding again? Maybe if she just eased her over a little... actually, Irena was so small it should be easy, and then she could remake the soiled bed.

A weak groan but no resistance met her efforts, and Irena sighed and drifted away again. Well, that wasn't so bad. She even managed to finish with the bed before the babies woke up, so she laid herself down beside Irena, carefully, so as not to jiggle the bed. She needed a closer look at her condition... clearly, something had to be done for her.

Irena turned to her with a smile. In a soft voice, she said, "Marybeth, let's go on up there and gather them blackberries. If we don't, they gonna be so ripe, they'll be fallin' on the ground. Turtles'll get 'em."

"What?" was Marybeth's startled reply.

"See the dog? She wants you to hurry. She's just about to jump herself silly."

Dear Lord! I thought it was good she was just breathing, and she's done gone out of her head! What am I gonna do, her talkin' no sense at all? Reaching across the bed, she patted the pale face gently. "Hush, honey." She spoke as she would have to a child. "You're dreaming. Go back to sleep."

But Irena didn't hush. "There's a spider. I don't like spiders. Cal, can you kill that spider?"

Marybeth clapped her hands together sharply. "Got it!" she said. "Killed that old spider dead."

"Thanks," came the faint reply. Then she was quiet, drifting back into sleep or wherever she had been.

Marybeth closed her tired, burning eyes and stretched herself out on the bed once more. She was instantly asleep but fell into a dream of fighting a sudden brush fire that had threatened her home as a small child. She dug her fists into her burning eyes to remove the flying cinders from the brush fire, and the force of her fingers woke her up. Just as well, she decided, when she heard a chorus of whimpers from the kitchen.

The rain had stopped, and the frogs outside were croaking and singing, adding their voices to the chorus of the babies. Mama used to say that a storm brought babies. Well, it likely brought these babies, and them a month and a half early. To the best of Irena's reckoning.

The morning sun broke through the clouds, creating a square of weak sunshine on the cold, damp floor. The fire had died down, and the babies still whimpered, so Marybeth thrust her feet onto the icy floor, shivering from head to foot.

When the tin cup of milk was ready, Marybeth carefully washed both hands. By bracing the cup into the corner of the cradle box, and by careful coordination, she could dip the forefinger of both hands into the milk, that way doubling the speed of the feeding. The only problem was the fists that kept popping back into their mouths or waving about. She tucked the tiny arms into their towel wrapping and temporarily solved that problem.

As she fed the babies, her mind began to race ahead, trying to anticipate further needs. Bottles. She would need at least three, maybe a spare in case one broke. Would the rubber nipples be too big for the babies' mouths? She'd have to see. And more socks. Until the babies got a little bigger, the socks fit better than diapers, and Cal could always use them later. That would be better than having to cut up a bed sheet or cut down the diapers Cal would be bringing.

Again, she wondered briefly where Cal was. She could use a little help. Of course, Mama would send Laura down soon when she didn't show up at home.

One drop, another drop. Sucking their tongues softly. The soft whimpering and fussing had been tempered down to gurgles and hiccups. How much milk was enough? She sure didn't want any upchucking, hard as it was to get the milk into them.

A voice came from the other room. "Marybeth, are you in there?"

"I'm right here. You're awake, huh?"

"I'm awake. You know what? I hear baby kittens. Did that old cat have another litter behind the woodbox.… again?"

Thank You, Lord! Irena was talking sense. Marybeth chuckled to herself. Kittens, indeed! If Irena only knew! Should she tell her the whole story now? Could she stand the shock? *Well, they're her babies, and she has a right to know, so here goes.*

"No kittens, Irena. The sound you hear is your own little girls."

"Girls? I done had twins? What foolishness are you talkin' about?"

"I'll show you." Marybeth lifted the cradle box down from the warming oven and carried it to the bed.

"Girls," she said to the babies. "Here's your mama."

Irena looked into the box, then looked way, rubbing her eyes. "My eyes feel funny. It looked for a minute like there were three babies in that box."

"It's not your eyes," assured Marybeth. "The birthin's all over and you have three little girls. Now you're gonna rest and get well, and you don't have to worry no more."

Irena sank back on the pillow and sighed. She certainly didn't look as if she would be fine. "Marybeth, tell me what happened. I don't remember nothin' after we went to bed. I thought when women had babies, it was gonna hurt awfully. How come it didn't hurt? I don't feel no different'n I felt yesterday. Something's wrong, and you got'a tell me what it is. I wake up, and you say I got three babies. You say it's over, and I still hurt. It's scary."

Marybeth searched her mind for something comforting to say. There was nothing. "Don't think about it, Irena. You had plenty of pain, all right. You been havin' so much pain ever since these babies were on the way, you just didn't know it when it came on at the last. We got lots of time to talk about everything after you rest. I'm gonna go to the kitchen and make up a fresh egg custard. That'll make you feel a lot better. Shut your eyes, now." With that, Marybeth left the room.

The babies were still sleeping. Marybeth removed a large baking dish from the cupboard, poured in top milk and broke ten eggs. Adding vanilla and a pinch of salt, she whipped it carefully with the whisk, trying to make no noise at all.

In trying to be quiet, she realized there was a lot of noise coming in from outside. The cows were mooing, and the roosters were fairly setting it up. Chores! She had forgotten all about the animals. How could she leave the babies and Irena now and go take care of them? But she must.

She slid the custard into the oven and quietly looked out the door. The standing water in the yard had gone down somewhat, but thick mud was everywhere. She found an old pair of Cal's work shoes and put them on and took an old coat from its peg by the door and put it around her shoulders.

Opening the door, she found herself face-to-face with Cal, carrying a dripping dog at arm's length. Cal was covered with mud to the knees, and his clothing was totally soaked. Tiredness looked out of his eyes, and his black hair was plastered wetly against his forehead. A quarter-inch of dark beard covered his exhausted face.

He thrust the dog toward Marybeth. "Take her, will you? She was covered with mud, and I washed her off under the pump. I'll go now and clean the mud off myself."

Marybeth took the squirming, whimpering, dripping dog. She was shivering from head to tail from the cold water, so Marybeth took the old blanket from the dog's bed and wrapped her in it. Then she tucked the shivering creature behind the woodbox where it was warm. At least that settled the question of where the dog had been.

Later, Cal came into the kitchen, barefoot and carrying his soaked shoes. He had rinsed them under the pump, and they were most certainly ruined, but he put them on the warming oven anyway, not noticing the cradle box.

"Sort'a got caught in the storm," he explained. "Came back in town late yesterday, and the river was so high I couldn't get the horses to step out on the swinging bridge. Water was up over it. Took 'em back to the livery stable and left 'em, plannin' to come on in by foot. By then the river was so high and the current was so strong, I was afraid it'd take out the bridge again while I was on it, so I went back down to the silver bridge. Had to come up through the fields on the old road south of the river, and mud was up to my knees in places."

He sighed, and his eyes drooped. He forced himself to continue.

"Wouldn't'a been so bad, but the fool dog hid herself out in the wagon. Should'a thought to look, 'cause she likes to do that, and I didn't see her back there with the fish till I was halfway to Jacksonville. Nothin' to do then but put up with her. Kept her tied to the buckboard seat. And then she couldn't walk in the muddy fields, bein' so little, and I had to carry her all the way home from the livery. Bad mess."

Then he seemed to remember his wife. He nodded toward the door to the other room.

"She all right? She didn't get scared, me not gettin' home, did she? I was worried, fit to be tied. Been walkin' all night, seems like."

Marybeth nodded assurance. "She's all right. Gone back to sleep now. You got'a sit down and let me get some warm water out'a the stove for your feet. This ain't no time for you or me neither one to be gettin' sick. We got things to do. Be lucky if you don't catch cold, bein' wet and out in this wind."

Marybeth handed him dry clothes and left the kitchen while he dressed. She sank into the big rocker and tried to plan. Cal, dressing in the kitchen, made small noises as he moved about, but fortunately he did not wake up the babies.

Irena had thrown back her quilts, and her skin felt hot. Not good. Gonna have to wake her up and make her drink somethin' for fever. Can't be lettin' her get dried out inside. Gonna have to sponge her down to hold back the heat before it goes too high. She can't be getting' sicker, now. She has to get well.

But when Marybeth stood up to go to her for a closer look, she was forced to grab the foot of the bed to keep from falling forward. Dizzy! Of course, she was! She had had no breakfast and had been worrying herself sick. Likely Cal was no better. Gonna have to cook some food the very first thing. Her feet felt heavy, and her mind seemed thick and dull.

What could she fix? Something quick and easy. *Pancakes with butter and honey. That would be right. I need somethin' quick and Cal'd need something to give him a lot of energy.* He was going to need it! The mooing from the barn was becoming insistent and impatient.

"Cal," she called. "Did you get diapers?"

"Sure did," he called back. "Left 'em in the wagon, though. Figured to go get 'em when the mud let up. Allowed there was time enough for that."

Marybeth grinned to herself. If he only knew!

"You can come in now," Cal called to her.

He was hanging his wet clothing on a nail behind the warm stove. Without a word, Marybeth went to the stove and lifted down the cradle box. She held it out toward Cal, and he leaned forward to peer into it. It was then he came face to face with the three pink miniatures.

Cal stared wordlessly into the cradle box, then turned to Marybeth. "What's that?"

Marybeth burst into laughter at the stupidity of the question. "That, Cal, is your three baby daughters. They came last night."

"Daughters? Three? And you were alone? They are the baby? And Irena, I mean, is she...?"

Marybeth nodded. "She's asleep. She had a really bad time, and she won't be up for days. Maybe weeks. And, Cal, we need three baby bottles."

"You mean she...?"

Marybeth shook her head sadly. "She'll never feed them. She couldn't feed three, even if she was well."

The cows were mooing even louder, but Cal stood motionless, still in a daze.

"First thing now," Marybeth began, "is for you to go milk and I'll cook. Then one of us goes after bottles and diapers 'cause four miles walkin' two ways is gonna take some time, and we ain't got much." She'd tell him later about the socks.

Still in a daze, Cal turned wordlessly and went to the barn with the milk pail and Marybeth began to stir up the batter.

A knock on the front door.

"Marybeth? You still here? Mama got to worryin' and sent me. Hey, Marybeth?" Laura eased open the front door and stood just inside with mud squishing between her toes, shoes in hand.

"Wait, Laura," her sister warned, "and I'll bring the wash pan for your feet."

"Should'a wore my gum boots that I wear in the woods. Didn't look for the mud to be so deep. Likely the water kept you from comin' home. But you know Mama!"

Marybeth nodded. She knew Mama. "Yeah, the mud and other things kept me from comin' home."

"Irena worse?"

Marybeth shook her head. "It's over."

"Baby...?"

Marybeth held up three fingers.

"Three? You mean three babies? Triplets? I never saw triplets before!"

"Me, neither."

Then Laura stared open-mouthed at her sister. "Oh, my! You and Cal had to deliver 'em! By yourselves!"

"No Cal. Just me."

"No Cal? Stuck in the storm, for sure. Whee-ow, I'd be scared spitless, all alone!"

"Think I wasn't? I'm sure glad you came. You got'a help me. Cal came in dead on his feet. Been tramping the mud all night to get home. Left the horses in the livery with the diapers in the wagon. I need bottles and nipples and men's socks."

"Men's socks?"

"I'll show you."

Laura followed her to the stove and watched her peel back the towel, revealing the sock diaper. The girls chuckled at the sight. "But I need to get them other diapers from the wagon to use for wrappin' blankets."

"I'll go right now," offered Laura.

"No, pancakes are cookin', and it'll be a tough walk in the mud. You need to eat first. I got some old shoes here for you to put on."

"No, I'll just take this and go. I'll tell 'em at the store to charge it to Cal." With that, Laura picked up two fragrant, steaming pancakes, rolled them into a fluffy tube, slipped her feet into the old shoes and left.

Dear Laura, thought Marybeth gratefully. Nobody had to slap her up the side of the head to get her to see what was needed.

Cal came in with the pail of foaming milk, strained and ready to pour into the crock. Setting the pail on the floor, he took the cradle box down from the warming oven. While he ate, he sat with the box on his lap and stared at his daughters, pink and quiet, their eyes squeezed shut and the tips of their tongues showing between their lips.

"So tiny," was his truthful but abysmally inadequate comment.

Marybeth watched as Cal put the box back on the warming oven and went to see his wife. She was white and motionless beneath the quilt. He looked up at Marybeth.

"Reckon I'd be needin' to try to find 'er a doctor?"

Marybeth reminded him, "Don't know where you'd find one that'd come here in this weather. I sponged her down, and it backed up her fever some. While she's sleepin', think you ought'a try and get some rest? Likely, I'll be needin' you to spell me with the babies later on. Laura's gone for the bottles, gonna charge 'em at the Mercantile till you get time to go in. She'll be gettin' the diapers out'a the wagon at the livery, too. I fixed you a pallet in the sleepin' loft, thinkin' it'd be quieter for you up there."

Cal nodded and came back to the kitchen to climb the ladder to the loft, relieved to have a decision made for him regarding the babies and his own bone-weariness. Things like this made him feel so helpless. In moments he was asleep from sheer and total exhaustion.

Laura came with the bottles, socks and diapers, then left to report Marybeth's situation to Mama.

It would be feeding time soon, so she had better get ready. She put a little milk in one of the bottles and turned it upside down. Nothing. The babies would never get the milk from that huge nipple if they had to suck it out. With a sharp knife, she jabbed into the rubber nipple, slitting it into an X-shaped hole. Now the milk dripped out, several drops at a time. Maybe it would work.

One baby whimpered restlessly... time to try the bottle. The hungry little mouth seemed willing, but in less than a minute of sucking, it stopped, and the baby dozed off to sleep. The little thing needed more milk than she had consumed, so Marybeth tapped the tiny cheek but got no response. The eyes remained squenched tight in sleep. She lifted her and patted her gently with her fingers on the miniature backside to bring up a barely audible burp.

The other two were still quiet, but she must work out some sort of a system in order to survive. She tapped another cheek and was able to get a few drops down another tiny infant.

Within minutes, the babies began a restless fussing. They were not really crying, but they whimpered and flailed their arms about. Then they upchucked. For no more than the tiny things ate, the cradle box was a soured mess of caked and soggy clabber. It must be changed out completely. Then they'd have to be fed again.

Marybeth was so tired!

A few more drops into the tiny mouths, and she'd wait to see if they could keep it down. She felt her head nodding forward. So tired! Just to close her eyes a few seconds was so tempting... and then the big black bear charged into her life!

She knew that bear. It had been there before. It had once charged out of the timber beside her as she walked along the road.

She ran from the bear, forcing her stiff, wooden legs to move toward the only tree she thought she could reach, even though it was a very small one and she knew that black bears can climb trees easily as a person can.

She clung tenaciously to the limb, just out of reach, though she was forced to dangle her legs down just low enough to be in reach of the bear.

Then the bear began to lick her leg. She screamed and kicked furiously at it, and fuzzy, little Yoyo was scooted across the floor, yelping in pain.

Marybeth awoke to find herself sitting at the kitchen table with her head resting on one arm while the other arm dangled over the edge of the cradle box. Milk had leaked from the bottle and had soaked one side of the cradle bed.

The bear's tongue was nothing more than the warm tongue of little Yoyo, asking to be put outside.

She rubbed her tired, sandy-grained eyes. Yoyo was cowering behind the woodbox, and the babies were screaming. The sounds in the sleeping loft above her must be Cal scrambling to get downstairs to answer her scream.

She let the dog out and cleaned the babies, then, at Cal's insistence, gave him the baby bottle and lay down on the bed beside Irena. She was instantly asleep. She slept three wonderful hours before she was wakened by sounds of distress in the kitchen. Her eyes popped open to see Irena propped up on one elbow looking at her in surprise, as though wondering why she was there.

Scratching noises sounded at the door and a shuffling sound came from the kitchen. The babies!

Her bare feet hit the floor and she ran to the sound of the babies' cries. Cal stood in the kitchen beside the table. One towel-wrapped baby was being held against his shoulder, and a stream of sour milk spots trailed down his back. His other hand was jiggling the cradle box, trying, ineffectively, to quiet the distress of the other two of his daughters.

From the bed, she heard Irena's voice. "Marybeth, bring a pan! I'm gonna..." But speed was not necessary any longer, and the bedding would have to be completely changed.

Of all the sounds of distress, the dog was the closest. One hand opened the door, and Yoyo shot in, muddy feet and all, and leaped, landing in the bed with Irena. Oh, well....

She took the crying baby from Cal. She was the smallest one, the one born last, and she quickly realized the tiny thing needed attention of another kind.

The two dozen pairs of new socks lay on the table where Laura had left them. While Cal continued to jiggle the cradle box, Marybeth dampened a cloth and cleaned the messy baby, making herself ignore the chorus of whining cries beside her. She wished she had asked Laura to get more towels. She handed the clean baby back to her father while she changed the other two.

The tin cup was again filled and heated on the stove. Somehow they had to keep something in the babies' stomachs… and whatever could be causing the upchucking?

While Cal patted his babies and tried to sing to them, Marybeth tackled Irena's bed. She stripped it down to the mattress after helping (practically carrying) Irena to the big rocker. She was horrified at how little she now weighed.

Got to make her eat more, Marybeth decided, as she located a change of bedding. *Have to get Laura to bring the sheets from my bed at home,* she told herself. At this rate, they were sure to be needed.

With Yoyo under the stove and Irena back in bed, she rubbed her tired eyes with her hands, deciding what to do next.

Food. Easy food. That was beans. While they were cooking, it would be eggs. A skillet of scrambled eggs with cubed ham. If she and Cal didn't get some food soon, they would be of no use to the babies, and if Irena didn't eat a lot, very soon, the babies could even lose… *No! Don't think that way.* Well, it wouldn't take long to make the eggs.

Practiced hands rinsed the bowl of brown beans and tossed them in the bean kettle with a liberal dollop of bacon grease for flavor, then she filled the bottle with milk and sent Cal to the shed for a thick slice of ham.

Each of the babies managed to take a few drops, so she set out the biscuit pan and the batter bowl. Drop biscuits, it would have to be. No time to roll them out and cut them. By the time Cal returned, the biscuits were in the oven.

Tea for Irena. Heat the water in the tea kettle. *Keep doing things, Marybeth,* she told herself, *and don't get behind.* The whimpering of the babies caused tension pains in her neck and a strange jerking in the muscles in her arms. She must be awfully tired to let that be such a bother.

But what if she dropped a baby? *Don't think of it! Keep moving and it'll go away. Won't it?*

With a sharp knife, she cubed the ham and tossed it into a smoking skillet. Cal had gone to sit beside Irena. She could hear murmured voices.

Then Irena's voice called out, "Can I help with anything?"

"No, don't get up," Marybeth called back, "but Cal can bring you tea." She shook the herbal tea into a teacup and poured in water. Cal picked up the teacup and a spoon and left.

Babies. Another few drops each. Could it be she was feeding them too much too fast? Didn't sound reasonable, but maybe that was why they couldn't keep anything down. Should she back off a bit? Worth a try.

One hand turned the pan of biscuits so they would brown evenly, while the other hand stirred the ham cubes. Meanwhile, her eyes noted the size of the pile of wet and dirty clothing collecting on the kitchen floor. How could she get diapers (socks) dry? Cal would have to string a line over the stove until the sun came out.

Eggs. "Cal, would you see if there's more eggs? I don't think we gathered them at all yesterday." She moved the sizzling ham to the edge of the stove where it was not so hot and moved the browned biscuits to the warming oven just before they began to burn.

The babies. She looked in the box at the red faces, twisted with whimpering. A touch on the cheek produced no response except more crying. She set the cradle box back on the top of the warming oven, trying not to hear their cries. She couldn't tend to everything at once. Food for herself and Cal was the current priority.

Then Cal was at the door with the eggs. With relief, she took them from him. Eggs were something she knew what to do with, and she cracked an even dozen of them into the skillet smoking with the ham and fragrant bacon grease.

Plates, cups, butter and honey on the table. Then the biscuits, still in the pan, and the mound of fluffy, scrambled eggs, still in the skillet, were setting on the quilted potholder to protect the table.

"Cal, can you help Irena to the table?"

So Cal pushed the big rocker to the kitchen and went back for Irena. Finally the adults were seated around the food.

Eggs. They were wonderful things. They were magic. Fluffy, yellow and tasty, they eased the stomach and made the mind think that anything might be possible. A true gift from God, these wonderful eggs!

EGGS! She jumped up from the table, knocking her chair over backward in the process. The startled Cal also jumped up and reached for her, likely expecting a faint, but Marybeth was not on the floor, so he retrieved the tossed chair… which was lying backward on the floor… and stared at her.

From the cupboard, Marybeth snatched up a bowl and put it on the table. From the basket of fresh eggs Cal had just brought in from the henhouse, she took two. She skillfully separated them, setting the whites aside. The yolks she beat into a golden froth, and added a cup of warm water, then she beat the eggs again. The resulting liquid was the color of April buttercups.

In the speed of her excitement, she flipped the nipple off the bottle and poured the remaining milk into Yoyo's dish, filling the bottle with the egg mixture.

By now, Cal had pushed back his chair and sat down, mainly to get out of her way. Marybeth took down the cradle box and set it in Cal's lap. With one hand, she scooped up one towel-wrapped bundle of howling baby while its parents stared at her, open-mouthed.

She looked toward the parents. "Feedin' 'em milk, we was fixin' to lose 'em. Little'ens like this got nothin' in 'em to live on while we figure on what to do for 'em. God made eggs, and God made babies. Both of 'em good, and I'm just puttin' the two of 'em together. If cow milk don't work we'll try chicken eggs. I'm trustin' these eggs."

Into the crying mouth, Marybeth put the nipple. The tiny tongue curled around it, sucking greedily, and Marybeth began to count. "One, two, three, four, five, six, seven, eight, nine, ten."

And with that, she pulled the bottle from the baby's mouth, which made it start crying again. She repeated the counting as she fed the other babies.

"Gonna wait, now," she told the parents. "Fifteen minutes'd be about right, I'm thinkin'. Don't be lookin' at me scared. You both eat all them eggs. Eat biscuits and honey. You got'a get strength, 'cause we're gonna need it 'afore we get through here."

They ate. When commanded in this way, what else could they do?

In fifteen minutes on the dot, she repeated the feeding-counting process, burping them carefully before returning them to the box. One baby began to suck her tongue contentedly, her eyes drooping. Then the eyelids closed, and the sucking stopped.

One was asleep, and one of the others had stopped crying. Little middle baby still whimpered, so Marybeth picked her up. The others were being jounced gently in their box on their father's knees.

Middle baby whined, squirmed and whimpered, then burped loudly. As Marybeth patted the tiny backside with her fingers, the crying ceased, and the eyes drooped. All the babies finally slept.

By now Irena was drooped tiredly over the arm of the chair, so Cal returned her to the bed. Marybeth followed him.

"I hate to be bringin' this up and all. I know we got enough on us and Irena feelin' poorly, but I got'a say this. These babies got'a have a name. I got'a know what to call 'em. You two be thinkin' on it, will you?"

With that admonition, she left them and dipped warm water into a small wash bucket. Socks first. They could be dried inside over the stove. The soiled bedding would have to be dealt with later.

Cal came into the kitchen and Marybeth asked, "You got names?"

He shook his head, and she demanded, "How come?"

"She went to sleep. Said she was too tired to think."

Marybeth nodded with understanding. "Sleep'll be good, now. She ate some. Not enough, of course, but some. Cal, I got'a have a line strung over the stove where it's warm. Got'a dry these socks. 'Nother thing. I've been thinkin' about the milk. I've heard tell of babies that couldn't be nursed and havin' to be on the bottle and not bein' able to keep down milk. Seems like they found out that goat's milk was better for 'em. Not tellin' you what to do, but that's what I heard. Shame you got no milkin' goat so we'd have a chance to try."

"I'll get goat milk," Cal stated firmly as he walked away. He returned with a length of cord for the line, but the babies were still asleep, and he couldn't hammer in the nail. "Give me a jar and I'll get milk."

It was three hours later when he returned with the jar full.

"Made me a deal. Family over by Piney got a lot of nanny goats and a lot'a youngens. Can't sell me milk regular, but they'd swap a gallon a day for a gallon and a half of cow's milk. Told 'em we'd see if this worked, and I'd bring it over in the mornin'."

One thing about Cal: when a problem was explained, he took care of it. Most times.

The beans bubbled aromatically on the stove. The kitchen was warm and cozy and smelled only slightly of drying socks. Marybeth sat down and laid her head on her arms on the table.

An hour later, a soft sound woke her up. Baby kittens! No, it was a soft mewing, cooing, tongue-sucking sound from above the stove. Could it be? It was! The babies were making normal baby sounds, not the painful screams and irritated whimpers.

She added warm water to the yellow bottle and offered it to the first baby. This time she counted to fifteen before she removed the bottle. Soft little burps told her the liquid was going down. The second round was another count to fifteen.

171

What else for supper? Cornbread, of course, with the beans. Some canned greens? Fresh ones would be nice, but the garden was long since past. Watercress, crisp and peppery wilted with bacon grease. That's what they needed, and it grew in Rock Creek, right in front of the house.

Dessert? Apple Brown Betty? Yes, the smell of sugar and cinnamon was cheerful in rainy weather. And so was a skillet of fresh onions, fried brown, soft and savory. That'd do it.

From the cradle box she heard whimpering, so she lifted down the box to get at the fussy baby before she woke her sisters and as she set it on the table, a rumbling burp sounded. Yellow fluid flowed from the mouth of the middle one. Oops! Should'a been burped!

Cleaned, re-fed and carefully burped, middle baby drifted into sleep again. Have to remember that one. Middle baby got'a be burped really good. Every time!

Irena didn't want to wake up, and she certainly didn't want to eat. Marybeth opened a quart jar of canned peaches and cut up several into cottage cheese, feeding it her a tiny bite at a time. Urging... insisting... encouraging... demanding!

She tried talking. "Gonna have you up and around in no time. You're gonna want to take care of them little girls. They're doin' fine now. Liked that goat milk."

Irena seemed to listen but did not respond.

"You thought about three little girls' names?"

"Cal gonna have to do it. I'm too tired," and she flatly refused to eat anything more. Firm lips. Not another bite.

Cal instructed Marybeth, "You sleep. I'll feed the babies."

The offer was too tempting to turn down. "Till midnight," she told him. "Wake me up then, so's you can sleep. Don't go to thinkin' it'd be doin' good for you to stay up all night to let me sleep. We both gonna be needed."

At midnight, Marybeth fed the little girls and took the box to the big rocker. Setting it on the rocker arms, she rocked gently, the motion putting herself and the babies quietly back to sleep. They slept for an hour and a half, the longest time ever.

A noise on the floor beside her made her look down. There was Yoyo, lapping the milk and egg yolk mixture up from off the floor. The little dog had chewed the top off the nipple and knocked over the bottle. Poor little Yoyo, she had forgotten to feed her. She gave her a piece of cornbread and washed and filled another bottle.

Then it was morning of the fourth day since the babies were born, and Laura had brought the requested bedding.

"What's Mama sayin' about me bein' gone?"

"Plenty."

Marybeth had no courage to ask what Mama actually said, and Laura slipped out and returned home. Everyone had things to do.

As she rubbed her tired eyes and fed the babies, Marybeth made up her mind that one certain thing was going to happen on this day. The babies had no names, but today would be the day they got them. Names were needed for the midwife paper. Such a small but important thing, and it would be done before night.

The aroma of fried ham, cottage-browned potatoes and ham gravy brought Cal down from the sleeping loft.

"Cal, somethin' got'a happen today. These babies gonna have names. Papers got'a be filled out on 'em to go to Jacksonville. Someone's gonna think up their names."

Cal nodded agreeably. Mothers named their babies, so he'd ask Irena again what she wanted to name them. What did he know about girls' names? She'd be the one to know.

But Irena refused to listen, and she refused to eat. She sipped her tea and lay back down. "Cal, I don't know no names. Had it in my mind it'd be a boy, me bein' so big. Gonna name him after you, and right now my mind don't go no farther'n that."

"But we got three little girls needin' names."

"I'm too tired. I got'a sleep."

Marybeth looked at Cal. "Can't you think up names? I can't keep callin' 'em this'n and that'n and t'other'n. They're persons and they got'a get names."

Cal nodded and looked back at Irena, who made no response. She lay back on the pillow with closed eyes. He turned dull eyes back to Marybeth.

But Marybeth was determined. "Lookie here, you two. You gonna name these babies, so I can make out the proper papers, or I'm gonna name 'em. I'm takin' care of these babies, and they're humans, so I got'a call 'em somethin'!" She looked impatiently from one to the other.

Irena nodded. "You name 'em."

"Really? You mean that?" She looked at Cal, who nodded with a shrug of his shoulders. This was just another of his problems that must somehow be made to go away.

Marybeth reached into the cradle box and gently took out one baby. "This'n here, she's gonna be named Charlotte. She was born first, bein' the very first baby that I was the first one to touch. Gonna call her 'Lottie', her bein' too little to be called by her whole name."

She tucked the baby into Irena's limp arms. "You got'a 'member, now, we're gonna call her Lottie." She picked up another bundle, peeling the folds away from the tiny red face.

"This here's Margaret. She was born last, but she could yell the loudest. I wasn't expecting' her, and she yelled at me so's I'd know she was here and for me to come and get her. Gonna call her 'Maggie'. Time she's growed up and wantin' a big name, then she can say her real name's Margaret." Marybeth handed Margaret to her father.

"Now this'n here, she was the one that scared me bad, havin' trouble startin' to breathe. She was blue-colored and still, and I blowed in her mouth and rubbed her feet. I asked the Good Lord to show me what I ought'a do, and I did it. Then she started to breathe. Been callin' her 'Middle One', but I ain't gonna do that no more. She's got her a good name. She's Lucinda. Read a book, one time, had a girl named Lucinda, and I thought it was a pretty name. But that's her big name. Right now we gonna call her 'Lucy'."

With that pronouncement, she lifted baby Lucy to her face and pressed her tiny head against her own cheek. Gently warm, with a soft fuzz of hair and sweet-smelling the way a healthy baby should be.

"Now if you don't like any of them names, you tell me now and give me a better one, 'cause Laura's gonna bring us the sheets we got'afill out and mail to the court house. They always want to know right away, after babies are born, what their names are."

Cal spoke first. "Sound like good names." He looked at Irena, who nodded wearily.

Marybeth took Lottie from her mother's side. It was all a little disappointing. The babies had names, and she had wanted that, but she hoped the naming ceremony would spark more interest in their mother. Maybe she wouldn't like the names and demand the babies be named something else. That's what the old Irena would do. She wasn't ever a pushover. Clearly, this was not the old Irena.

Marybeth was now forced to face the fact that all was not right with her friend. In fact, it seemed that perhaps nothing was all right.

Indeed, something was bad wrong. New mothers were often tired, and Irena certainly had a right to be tired after the three of them. This

174

was something else. She seemed to have no interest in the babies, acting as though they maybe belonged to someone else.

She had no interest in food, or even in her little dog, who begged for attention. It just seemed as though all the strength and life within her had just drained away. What was left still looked like Irena, but there was nothing inside.

All Marybeth could think of to do for her was food. Good food cured everything. Fish would be good for today. She'd tell Cal. And baked custard? Irena liked that. And she liked peach cobbler. Which? And baked sweet potatoes. They'd give her strength.

And the babies could now regularly sleep an hour at a time. Sometimes as long as an hour and a half. The goat milk worked out well, but the daily swap to get the milk seriously cut in on Cal's morning. Time he couldn't well afford to lose.

The babies were a week old when Marybeth left for a while to go home and get some more of her things, as it seemed she would probably be staying the winter. Unless Irena got a lot better in a hurry.

Three hours later, Marybeth returned to find Cal in the kitchen, holding the cradle box in his lap. His eyes were red, and his face was flushed. Was he sick? No, she guessed, but it did look as though he had been crying. Maybe not. He looked at her and smiled and set the box back on the warming oven.

Then, in a flash of knowledge, she knew. Cal had thought she might not come back, and the whole of the problem must have seemed more than he could handle. But why wouldn't she come back? She was Irena's friend, and friends helped out when they were needed.

Not only that, Marybeth was glad to be back. Her mother had been more than usually irritating with many cutting remarks. The appreciation she saw in Cal's eyes helped to soothe her.

"Brought back some things," she mentioned brightly. "You and Irena gonna need help right now, so you got'a put up with me. Babies are sleepin' better, and you got things to do outside, like always on a farm. With me here, Irena's gonna rest better."

Call nodded, relief written on his face.

The verbal battle with her mother had left her depressed, and when she was depressed, she wanted to cook. Something sweet. Cake? No, something sweeter than that. Peanut candy. That was it.

She checked the supply of sugar. Plenty. Peanuts? She'd have to go to the hayloft and pick them off the peanut vines stored there for hay.

She put on her coat and climbed the ladder into the hay barn. The many kinds of grasses making up the hay gave off a pleasant "walk in the woods" kind of smell. A smell like she could just lie back and go to sleep. Yep, taking care of babies was one wearying job, and it made a body quick to grab a minute's rest.

Resisting the impulse, she began to pull the peanuts from the vines. With her pan full, she climbed down from the hayloft and washed the dirt off them at the pump.

The oven was quite warm, but she added a stick of wood anyway so the peanuts would roast quickly. One thing about Cal was that he kept enough wood cut. That was a thing a woman appreciated.

The smell of roasting peanuts filled the cabin. Maybe it would tempt Irena's appetite. Into the heavy iron skillet she poured the sugar, stirring it while it caramelized, then she dumped in the roasted nuts. In minutes, the candy was hard. With a knife handle she tapped the golden platter of sweets, cracking the whole mass into sharp-edged squares and triangles of a manageable size for snacking.

Cal came in the house for something. "Want some candy?" she suggested.

Cal nodded, picking up three pieces. One thing about Cal was that he didn't talk a body's ear off. Didn't go around wastin' no words, Cal didn't.

After he left, Marybeth began to think about her mother's anger. It had been question after question. When would she come home? Why couldn't the babies' daddy do for them? What, exactly, was wrong with Irena besides being the puny little thing like she always was? What would the neighbors think, her living there with Irena an invalid, if she really was?

The last question made Marybeth smile. Not that they had been overwhelmed with neighbors, nor would they be, at least until the road and yard dried out from the slick layer of sticky, gummy mud.

Then Mama wanted to know why it should be Marybeth who did everything. Marybeth had answered, "Friends take care of friends, Mama. You remember I'm her friend, don't you? Who you think's gonna do what I can do if I don't?"

Mama couldn't name anyone, and Marybeth took advantage of the rare moment of silence and left.

On the way down the hill she had told herself that if any neighbors happened to come up Rock Creek Road and see her there, they would likely be glad she was there, so they wouldn't be feeling guilty for not being there themselves. Folks knew what they had to do, and what she had to do was right in front of her, plain as the nose on her face.

Why did she let Mama egg her on like that? Of course, a girl twenty years old like she was, usually she had her own home and was not still under Mama's nose.

Well, it was a month until Christmas, and she'd not be home before then, for certain. Irena couldn't even take care of herself, let alone the cooking and washing and all. Then there were the babies, being a handful all by themselves. Marybeth grinned. Irena had always had a way of getting into scrapes and needing help to get out. It was never her fault, and certainly never on purpose… it just happened. Always it had been that way, and Mama ought to be used to it by now. And here she was in another "scrape" and needed Marybeth's help, as usual.

But Marybeth felt utterly helpless this time. *How come it is I can't do what I need to do for Irena? I keep thinkin' and workin' and ain't gettin' nowhere. I thought a mama always wanted her babies, but I don't understand Irena. She seemed like she wanted one till these got here. She must be awfully tired. Hmmm.* She sighed and shook her head with dismay.

Marybeth continued to mull over her problems. Likely, when Irena got better, it would be the time for her, Marybeth, to find another place to live. A place other than Mama's house. Maybe she should get married. Maybe Mama would be happier if she did. Maybe not.

Then she shook her head. Maybe not marriage, at least not yet. Daddy tried it and couldn't take it and went back south (at least that was where they guessed he had gone, but they didn't know for sure). Not that it mattered; Mama was mad at him all the time, anyway. If she, Marybeth, married, would she turn out to be the way Mama was? Loud and cranky?

Most of her friends, like Irena, were already married with babies. Even the ones who weren't considered pretty, they were married, and she knew, as a girl always knows, that she, herself, was considered pretty. Tawny skin and the black eyes she inherited from her father. She was tall but not skinny, the way a lot of tall girls are.

Her heavy black hair hung down to her waist when it was not twisted up on her head. She even had a dimple in her chin, but what good were all these things if she was not in love with someone? Would love come later?

But enough about that; here was a sick woman and three little red-faced babies. She was here now, and she had things to do, so she put her belongings in one of the dresser drawers and put her comb and hairbrush on top.

Cal slept in the loft under the sloping roof that would be the girls' room when they were bigger. A routine began to form out of the chaos. She and Cal did what had to be done, working as a team and expecting nothing from Irena, who most often seemed unaware of either of them.

5

The babies were two weeks old before the people of the town felt they could brave the mud to stop by. The good ladies tried to talk with Irena, to encourage her, to swap birthing experiences, and to congratulate her on the triplets. They tried, but they were disturbed by her unresponsiveness, her lack of interest and her general lassitude and did not know how to react to her.

In their forgiving manner, though, they went away saying that it was likely brought on by the fact that she had been unable to nurse the babies and therefore felt inadequate. Glass bottles were unnatural-like, weren't they?

And who were they to talk about how she should feel? None of them had ever birthed three babies at one time. Horrible thought!

That could do it, couldn't it, they asked each other hopefully That could be the whole problem, couldn't it? If so, she should be well soon. Shouldn't she…? Unspoken among them was the guilty relief that Marybeth was there, and there was no need for someone else to be there.

The visitors brought food, every lady bringing her own specialty, and that was a welcome gesture. They brought whatever hand-me-down clothing they thought they could spare, and everything was appreciated… though the thanks was proffered by Irena's friend, Marybeth. Irena couldn't seem to grasp the fact that she was being given a gift. She hardly seemed to recognize ladies she had known for years.

Granny Nelson, always quick to size up need, brought a whole bolt of soft outing flannel she got from the Mercantile. She would have made up the flannel into soft gowns and diapers, but her age and rheumatism prevented it. However, Jane Ann McCrey, the young preacher's wife, happily took the flannel home with her and made up the gowns, all eighteen of them!

The rest of the bolt of flannel turned into absorbent diapers. And there was Jane Ann, herself as big as a barn with her own baby!

Now that most of the women from the town had made their visit to Rock Creek Road, there was a fresh topic of conversation for the Tuesday Sewing Circle down at the church.

"Did you ever see the like of them babies of Irena Boudreau's? Look like tiny little dolls. Must be a trick to gettin' 'em fed."

"Yeah. I figure puttin' 'em all together, they wouldn't weigh what my Billy weighed. Seems a miracle somethin' that little could even breathe on its own."

"Lucky to have a friend like Marybeth, that Irena was, her learnin' what to do from her mama. Irena'd been up against it without one of her people here to help."

"Reckon how Marybeth's mama is gettin' on without her, her bein' tied up there?"

"With a lot'a loud words, I'd guess."

"Imagine! Three babies at once! Think of all of them diapers! I thought my Billy was hard on diapers, but just think, three of them!"

"Way I see it, if them babies had any sense, they'd'a come to a daddy with a good farm, not one with that crawfish land he's got that'll never be able to grow food for 'em."

"Well, he don't lack for tryin', that Cal don't. He don't seem to be lazy, neither. Thought for a while Irena might be makin' herself a mistake, but she seemed happy enough. Or she did till all this happened."

"Likely she'll pull out of it, Marybeth bein' there."

"Puzzle about Marybeth still bein' not married and free to go help like that. A body'd'a thought she'd be married a long time ago, anybody that looks like she does. Always a right pretty girl, she was, and even more so now that she's got some size on her."

"Yeah, I'd'a thought so myself. Thought her to be a lot better-lookin' than Irena, her bein' so little and pale like she always was."

"For my money, I'd bet that Cal ain't never goin' to be a farmer. Seems good at fishin', though."

"If it weren't for the fish in that river, he'd likely have a skinny dinner table."

"Oh, I don't know. Takes good care'a his livestock and garden vegetables. Things always neat and clean. 'Cept for that mud every time it rains, and that wasn't no fault'a his."

"I can't get over them three babies. Bet they kept that girl awake all night that last month, them'a kickin', turnin' and rollin' like babies do."

"Irena didn't have no last month. Them babies come more'n a month early, Marybeth said. I could believe it, lookin' at 'em. Look like they was picked 'afore they was quite ripe."

"Three babies! How'd a body nurse three babies? Women just ain't set up for three babies."

"Seems like there'd be nothin' but nursin' and diaper changin' with three. Glad mine all come one at a time, proper-like."

The Tuesday Sewing Circle was not the only place buzzing with curiosity and amazement. The men, those there on business and those just loafing, gathered at the River Bend Livery Stable where there was sure to be the latest news.

"Hear about that southlander gettin' hisself them three babies? Girls, they all were. Who'd have thought it?"

"He'd have done better to have boys, considerin' that clay farm'a his. Three girls! Likely he'll be mortally afraid to try again, fearin' he'd get three more!"

Loud laughter filled the stable.

"How they managin' up there? Anyone hear?"

"I hear that oldest girl'a Martha Maisone's, she's been down there to help out. You single fellows eyed at that girl lately? Sure gettin' to be a looker. You'd think she'd have picked out a fellow to marry."

"She gettin' nigh onto twenty years old 'bout now? Should be birthin' her own youngens, you'd think."

"Wonder what she's lookin' for in a man?"

There was a short silence as the men deliberated on this.

"That man of Irena's, Cal Boudreau, sure ain't one for words. Don't no one know much about him 'cept he came from down south."

"Sure looks like a foreigner. That dark beard'a his."

"Three babies. Scrawny little things, I heard. Would'a lost 'em if Marybeth Maisone hadn't been there, knowin' what to do."

"Notice how that other Maisone girl is takin' after her sister? Both of 'em lookers. Good thing they had a handsome pa to take after."

"Seems like looks was about all he left them girls."

"Reckon where he went to?"

"Long way away from Martha's mouth, I'd wager."

"Well, they sure are good-lookin' girls. Marybeth gonna be a midwife like her mama, do you suppose?"

"Likely. Leastways till she gets married."

"Three babies at once. Hmmmm."

"Hope their daddy figures out how to make that old clay farm pay off. Gonna need to get a crop off of it to feed them babies."

And back on Rock Creek Road, they took the days one at a time. When the eighteen warm, flannel gowns were delivered, things seemed a lot brighter. This gave Marybeth a break from the daily washing.

When the babies were a month old, Marybeth could use the regular diapers, and that was a help.

But Irena was no better. She lay listlessly inert on the bed, dozing and staring at the ceiling, taking no interest in anything. When forced to, she ate a few bites, and when spoken to, she gave the shortest response possible. Or drifted off into a dozing sleep.

Then there was the day Irena asked Marybeth, "Did you ever talk with an angel?"

Surprised, Marybeth had laughed. "Time comes I start talkin' with the angels, that'd be the time I'd worry about myself."

Irena had not laughed. "I did, and the angel told me the babies would be going away."

"Not with me here, they ain't! Them babies are stayin' right here, and anyone that says they ain't got'a go through me first." Then, in a lighter tone, "'Sides, who'd want 'em, cryin' all night, keepin' folks awake?"

But Irena was not to be jollied away from her subject. "I mean they was to be really leavin', like not comin' back."

"Dyin', you mean? Not these healthy little rascals."

Irena sighed and continued as though Marybeth had not spoken. "I told the angel, don't take the babies. They ain't had no life yet. If someone was to have to go, it'd ought'a be me."

"You didn't do no such of a thing," Marybeth told her sternly. "You just tryin' to scare me, tellin' me a dream you had or somethin'. Who you think'd be takin' care of these babies, you bein' gone like that?"

Irena gazed out the window. "Same person as takes care of 'em now," she answered practically. And Irena wasn't through with the angel.

There was the day she saw the angel through the window, where Marybeth could only see where a dirt dobber wasp had built its mud house against the window frame. She stared, amazed, while Irena chatted with the heavenly being she thought she saw.

Irena told the angel all about the babies. "Middle one, that's Lucy. She's always got'a burp. Every little bit, she got'a burp or she gets the bellyache."

Irena smiled at the angel as they chatted. "Yeah, they're all pretty like their daddy. See them dark eyes? They got dark eyes like my friend, Marybeth. You know Marybeth?"

Listening, Marybeth felt the goosebumps form on her arms. What now? Maybe Laura had some kind of tea that would help bring her back to the living. But how could she get strength if she would not eat enough?

Cal was never one to talk much, but he tried to talk to his wife. Even his words seemed not to be able to reach her.

The preacher from the church came and said a prayer for her, but that did not make the angel cease its regular visits at the window.

Neighbors who dropped in did not stay long. The Tuesday Sewing Circle tried to make sense of it all.

"What's the latest about Irena Boudreau?"

There was silence as they glanced at each other. Needles flew across the bright-colored quilt blocks, and more tea was sipped. It was a hard subject to get a hold onto.

Old Granny Nelson was first to take it on. "Came by up there three days ago. Have to say that Irena looked like death warmed over. But then, Marybeth, she didn't look that much better."

"She still stayin' down there? I didn't know."

"Yeah, she's there. That's how things get done."

"That Irena, she's been down too long. Do her good to get up and stir around a little. What's it been now, a month? Or more? That's too long to stay a'bed."

"I wouldn't know. How many women do you know that had three babies at a tick?"

"But they was so tiny. Couldn't'a been too hard to do, gettin' 'em birthed."

"Still and all, there was three of 'em."

"So little they wore folded socks for diapers. Got 'em in regular diapers, though, now."

"Marybeth got her hands full. That's for sure."

"'Spect Cal helps her a lot."

"You kiddin'? You must've forgot what farm he's got. Remember the fellow that built that cabin up there? He starved out, and him a farmer by trade. Cal likely gonna do the same."

"Don't know about starvin'. That other fellow likely couldn't fish as good as Cal."

"Hear Marybeth is havin' trouble with her mama wantin' her to come home."

"She'll not go, though. She wouldn't leave them three babies. Leastwise, I hope she won't." It was clear to all of them that some help had to be there, and it could be up to them to take a turn. If Marybeth wasn't there… wicked thought.

"Her mama just wants to keep them girls under her nose is all."

"Nobody ever heard what happened to those girls' daddy?"

"Likely dead by now."

"Or got 'im a woman that don't yell at 'im."

"Think them babies is puttin' on any weight?"

"Haven't been there myself. Been thinkin' to go. Just haven't. Seems like it'd be hard to find a thing to talk on."

"Yeah, there don't seem to be time for nothin' no more."

"Beats me how Cal's gonna feed that family. Can't even grow corn. Everything that gets planted there, the sun comes out and dries up the land, squeezin' the life out'a the roots. Happens nigh onto every year."

"He'll have to be doin' somethin'."

"Likely move."

The days went by. Marybeth spent Christmas at the cabin on Rock Creek Road, just as she had expected to. Some days were not so bad; others were worse.

Irena had to be coaxed to eat every bite. Marybeth fed her with a spoon as she would have fed a child. Without the bulging belly, Irena hardly made a mound under the quilt, and she seemed to be withdrawing more each day.

Sometimes Marybeth felt so tired, she would like to just like walk out the front door and keep walking. She wanted to be far away from the weariness and the sadness, but she did not go. Irena was her friend, her best friend, the one who had always understood her.

It was a few days after Christmas that Irena called to her. Her voice sounded stronger, just like old times. Marybeth's heart leaped with happiness. She had been lying on the bed beside her, hoping for a nap to make up for her nightly lost sleep, but Irena's new voice had her instantly awake.

"Marybeth," she demanded. "You got'a wake up and talk to me."

Excited, Marybeth sat up in bed. "You're better! Why, Irena, you look so much better! Shall I call Cal?"

"No, I want to talk to you. Listen to me now. Do you remember your promise? The one about Cal, I mean?" Irena's voice was insistent.

"Sure, I remember. But that was a long time ago, and nothin' happened to you. You're just fine, see?"

Irena ignored her. "Listen to me. Cal, he's a good man, but he don't think'a things sometimes. I ain't meanin' you got'a take care of 'im or nothin'. He can do that. It's just that you got'a be a friend to him, like you are right now, till he can get a grasp and go on. He'll be fine, come summer. You'll see."

"Sure. All right." What was the harm in a promise, and what in the world was Irena trying to say? Her skin tingled with apprehension.

But Irena was not through. "I know you been a friend to me like I had no right to have with these here babies, and I been a burden heavy on you. Cal, he knows that too, but he can't come right out and say it. Time'll come he'll need help with these girls, and you'd be the natural right one to ask, you bein' here at the birthin'." She sighed and drooped wearily on the pillow but forced herself to continue.

"I wouldn't fear to leave 'em with him, like I got'a do, if I was to be sure you'd always be watchin' as long as was needed. You could say a word or two to him, and likely that'd be all he'd need, and that wouldn't take a lot'a your time. You gonna promise me?"

"Sure, Irena. I promise. I keep on promisin', but it don't matter, 'cause you're better now, and if you go back to sleep, likely you'll wake up good as new."

Marybeth patted Irena's pale arm to sooth her.

Irena's eyes closed, and then she opened them suddenly. "You remember, you promised." Then she closed her eyes again.

Marybeth settled back down, but that last look of Irena's was burned into her mind. She knew that look. It was Irena's "You'd better believe me, because I'm not kidding" look. Maybe she should have insisted Irena stay awake a while and have a cup of tea. Maybe it was better to let her nap.

Which? Sleep had to be the best, and maybe now the worst was over. But if so, why that last look? What had the angel told her that only she could hear?

Weariness took over, and Marybeth dozed again. If the babies woke up, they must have put themselves back to sleep, because she certainly did not hear them. Nothing was said that evening, and Irena seemed no worse, so Marybeth put the incident from her mind.

Then it was morning. She lay looking at the early morning sunshine streaming through the window, noticing that the corner of the window had a cobweb. She'd get that thing down first thing, before Irena noticed it. Nasty things, cobwebs were.

She had a strange, light feeling this morning. Maybe because she had slept so soundly? Probably not. But maybe something good had happened. What was it? Then she remembered: Irena was better!

She reached out to pat Irena's arm companionably and recoiled as though she had touched a snake. Tears instantly choked her breath away, because she knew... she knew instantly and for certain, without looking again, that indeed Irena had gone.

The invitation from the angel must have seemed too tempting to ignore. It must have been even more inviting to her than the tug of her family and her best friend. It was evident that Irena had decided to go with the angel.

Marybeth sat up cross-legged on the bed and bowed her head between her knees, sobbing disconsolately. Her weariness and frustration poured forth in raging, gaging fury, and her tears soaked her arms.

Her breath came in ragged sobs. Her friend was gone. Her best friend had betrayed her. Her best friend just gave up and wouldn't even try to stay on the earth when the going got hard. Why? Why? WHY? Marybeth had done everything she could... hadn't she?

Irena was gone. She couldn't be, but she was. There she lay on the white pillowcase, a faint smile on her pale face. *What happened, Lord? I prayed so long and so hard, and I did the best I could. Why did You have to take her? We needed her. Cal and me and the babies. Why, Lord?*

She leaned forward again, racking sobs building up within her, tearing at her throat, tears burning her eyes. She wept for the babies, who would never know their mother, and for Cal, who was losing a wife who was much too young to die.

But mostly, Marybeth wept for herself and the loss of the one true friend who had loved her without reserve. The one friend to whom she could tell everything. Her one close friend in her whole life. *Oh, Irena, why did you have to go?*

She heard Cal coming down the steep loft ladder, his footsteps slow and careful, as though dreading what he knew he would find when he reached the floor.

Then he stood there at the foot of the bed and looked at Irena. He had not even the comfort of tears... only an unspoken, unrelieved agony that gazed out from his dark eyes. Tense throat, swallowing with difficulty. Hands that gripped the railing at the foot of the bed, showing white knuckles through the dark, work-worn skin.

Cal sighed and turned away to look toward the window where Irena had seen the angel, and then, without a word, he turned away and went to the kitchen, shoulders hunched in despair.

Marybeth wiped her eyes and followed him. She watched as he went to the cradle box that held his sleeping daughters. Placing the box on the table, he lifted them, one by one, patting them gently and waking them up to their morning hunger.

Tiny things. They began to cry, and he stood watching them, their healthy hunger making them demand attention. They cried with the self-centered drive that kept a baby alive... demanding care and comfort from the world.

He watched them and smiled. A tired smile. At least he had them, Irena's last gift.

Then he turned away and began to build up the fire in the kitchen stove. By the time the blaze was curling around the sticks, the babies were sucking their fists, smacking loudly. Whimpering and restless.

When the milk in the cup was warm, Marybeth filled the bottle and picked up Lottie, who seemed to be fussing the loudest. Cal took another bottle and fed Maggie, leaving Lucy to fuss until it was her turn. Neither Cal nor Marybeth said a word until the girls were fed and changed.

Then words had to be said.

"Cal," Marybeth began, "I been thinkin'. I reckon it ought'a be me that goes down to the church to tell the preacher. I'll be gettin' ready to go, and you be thinkin' on somethin' special you'd want him to say at the service. He'll want to know that. Preacher McCrey always wants to say at a funeral anything the family wants said."

Marybeth put on her coat, and she was gone. She knew Cal would need time alone before anyone else knew. She'd do the best she could for him and give him that. Before the day was out, the house would be crawlin' alive with town folks.

That was the way it was done, and the folks of River Bend were very good about that. They would always ignore their own pressing duties to come and help at the time of a passing.

All she had to do was go tell the preacher, and then the town would know. The preacher would handle everything. And they would come.

When Marybeth closed the door behind her, Cal returned to the bedside and pulled up a chair. He took Irena's cold hand in both of his, as though he could restore her life's heat by giving her some of his own. His eyes finally filled.

"Reenie, we had us a good life. Only thing is, it wasn't long enough. Wish't you hadn't felt you had a good reason to go away. Wish't you hadn't seen no angel. I did my best for you, little Reenie. Wish't I could'a done better...."

He tucked the cold hand carefully under the warm quilt, though its warmth meant nothing to her now.

One little girl whimpered in her sleep. Cal went to the box and lifted the tiny, warm body, holding her close to his face. She hiccupped softly and that small, natural sound broke the spell and loosed his tears. Unchecked, they flowed, soaking the baby's flannel gown. He wept, groaning in his unrelieved agony of loss. Lucy's flailing arms and tiny fists beat against his face, tiny, aimless feathery touches, and the empty corners of the house absorbed the sound of her father's sobs.

He returned the baby to her bed and cried until his tears were spent. Then he went to the window that faced the river and stared at the flooded fields of his frustration until he heard the sound of Marybeth's return.

Together, they bathed the girls and put them in clean gowns. Marybeth stirred up a pan of biscuits for breakfast, feeling they had not the appetite for more, and then the people came.

The ladies from the church came first, bringing bowls of food as they always did. They brought crispy fried chicken, spicy potato salad, fresh-baked bread and jars of their special jellies. They brought cobblers and cakes and metal cans of ground coffee to be boiled in a bucket on the cookstove. They brought butter and cream and light, delicate sugar cookies.

They stood around in groups and pairs, chatting about ordinary things, as though everything was normal and they had just come for a visit. As they talked, they skillfully did essential things. The ladies of the church knew how to perform this necessary kindness, and they knew they were appreciated.

And they knew how to prepare for the funeral. The dressing and the other arrangements must be done by someone. They went about their work without asking needless questions and causing those in loss to unduly remember their sadness. They gave the bereaved a day of protection against the rawness of their loss. There would be time later for them to face it, when their senses were a bit more dulled by time.

Marybeth, who had many times seen this ministration of the church ladies and who had occasionally been a part of it, had never realized what comfort it brought to the bereaved to see this effort expended on their behalf and this time so freely given. It was generously given as though there were no other duties demanding their time, as though they had no family to care for, and as though it was nothing to give up a whole day.

They cared for Marybeth as though she had been a blood sister to Irena, knowing the loss to her was just as heavy. They arranged among themselves that she would never be alone during this terrible day. She was encouraged to talk about last moments, and the babies were admired in her presence, as though they might be her nieces.

The men gathered around Cal to talk of crops and animals, of the weather and of a new strain of pasture grass they had heard about. Cal did not join in the conversation, nor was he expected to, but they were there doing the thing that was required of them. It was the thing that they could do, and they willingly did it.

They sat with him under the tree in the weak, winter sunshine or stood with him in the shed where he did most of his work. They offered help, knowing full well that the only help he needed was the help they could never give. But they were there, and they offered, because it was the thing to do.

Granny Nelson had not come to the laying out or to the sociability of the day. She knew that hers was a special duty, something she always did and could always be counted upon to do.

When the good ladies left, it was her time.

There were people to laugh with and people to work with. The joy of a wedding, bringing together the community to create a new household, that was a joy anyone could share.

There were people to cry with, but that person must be someone who had done much crying. So it was, when the day was done and the good ladies left to go home to take care of their families, and when the men finally dispersed to attend to their chores, that was when Granny Nelson came.

She came to spare the family from the indecency of spending the first night alone with their deceased loved one. When the day, with its normal conversation and its necessary activity was over, she came.

Granny Nelson had no pleasant, comforting words and no loving pats for those bereft. What she had was tears, and they would be shed together in genuine sorrow over this loss. She had words to say, and she said them. The loss of a loved one was a terrible thing, and great suffering was theirs to be endured.

Granny Nelson had lost many people during her lifetime, and she knew the agony of it all. She talked of her own losses, and she explained her agony, and everyone was glad she was there. Yes, she knew what she did best, and she did not bother with food, friendliness or other activities. Those things were left to others.

So it was Granny Nelson who sat in the big rocking chair, as was her due, and talked while Cal and Marybeth bore their grief. It was Granny who talked about the loss of a mother to the babies, the loss of a dear friend, and mostly, the loss of a loved wife.

It was Granny who, in spite of her old weariness, sat up the night through with the family gathered around, and they were glad she did.

With the daylight, Granny Nelson was gone, walking slowly with the help of her two walking sticks. She had refused the offer of the wagon. Cal had other things to do. She knew she had done what was hers to do, and now she would rest until the funeral.

The funeral. The pale sun arose over the crest of the mountain and shone on the little house on Rock Creek Road, creating a false sense of warmth. The breeze coming down from its peak knew it was still winter. A gust of wind rushed past Cal as he stepped inside the kitchen to bring in a pail of warm milk.

"Cal," began Marybeth, "I been thinkin'. This'd be no kind of a day to take the babies out."

"Been thinkin' that myself."

"So what I'll do is stay here with the babies, so you can go on and not worry."

"But, Marybeth, Irena was your best friend. You been friends for a lot longer than I knew her. I wouldn't want you not to go."

"No," Marybeth told him firmly. "A husband, that'd be closer than a friend, no matter for how many years. You'll be goin', that bein' the only fittin' way."

But Laura came in through the front door. "I come to stay," she announced. "I know I can't be to them babies what you'd be, but they can just make do with me till you get back."

She looked from Cal to Marybeth and smiled her bright, dimpled smile that told them the problem was solved, and she'd hear no more words about it.

Cal nodded his thanks. He still had to go to the neighbor's to swap out the milk, and he still must drive the team and wagon down to the church to deliver the pine box for the funeral. Finally, that accomplished, the team plodded back up the road with the empty wagon and went into the shelter of the barn. The family would go to the funeral in Martha Maisone's buggy, which Laura had just brought down the mountain.

6

The little church building was full. A colorful shawl, crocheted with many kinds of flowers, covered the pine box. Songs from the church hymnal were played on the pump organ as people talked together in quiet tones.

Cal and Marybeth sat like statues, willing the day to be over... to be gone and to take their grief with it. That's all they wanted. For the grinding agony of loss to pass over and leave them free. But they knew that it could not happen, and it would take a lot of time to soften even just a little.

Ina Mae McCann sang, her beautiful voice drowning out, for a moment, their thoughts. Jane Ann McCrey said words about Irena and her pleasant ways. The preacher read about another life in a better place, and everyone sang again. Time went by.

Then they stood at the graveside in the churchyard. The sun had gone behind a cloudbank, and a strong east wind had sprung up. It flapped at coattails and tweaked at hats. It chilled cheeks, still wet with tears.

Cal and Marybeth stood beside the grave as final words were said. Then came the pause. It was time for a loved one to step forward. Permission must be given for the grave to be closed.

Cal looked at Marybeth, and she shook her head, so he walked the few steps alone but hesitated and returned. With a light but insistent touch at her elbow, he brought her forward.

Together they picked up a handful of the cold, wet dirt. It made a vulgar, indecent sound as it echoed against the wooden box. Cal flinched at the sound of it, and they stepped back to the waiting mourners.

There was nothing more to be done, so Marybeth climbed into the buggy with Cal, and they made their way back to the little house, the babies and Laura. The little girls had been fed and were asleep. Laura reached for her coat to leave but turned to her sister.

"I got'a talk to you, Marybeth. If you want me to, I can wait a while about it but not for very long. Two things got'a be said right away."

Cal slipped on his heavy work coat and eased out the door. Likely the ladies would want privacy for their talk.

"Let's have the bad news now," Marybeth invited. "I'll make some tea, and we can talk."

Laura patted the now-fussing Lottie, and the baby closed her eyes again.

The distraught seventeen-year-old couldn't wait for the tea. "Marybeth, I'm gonna run away. What I want from you is to tell Mama after I'm gone. Won't change nothin' but still, she's Mama and deserves to be told and not left wonderin' what happened to me. If I tell her, she'd likely do something like lock me up. Or somethin'."

Marybeth stared. "What are you talkin' about, girl? Runnin' away? From what? Where you think you're goin', runnin' away?"

Laura's dimpled chin firmed, and her eyes glistened. "I'm goin' all right. There ain't no way to go on livin' alone up on that mountain with Mama, and I know you got'a stay down here. Mama fixes it in her mind how everything is, and if it don't go that a'way, she don't leave no stone unturned. You know that."

Marybeth nodded. She knew, all right. "But what good will runnin' away get you?"

"It's like this. I told Mama I'd go with her, takin' your place, kind of, till you came back. She don't want me with her. No one is gonna take your place in her mind, and she's determined for you do what she says, with no mind to what you want. I told her you didn't want none of what she did, and she told me to shut up."

Laura sniffed and turned toward the window, then looked back and continued. "Thing is, I stay shut up all the time. She means me to stay up on that hill, seein' no one from one month's end to the next. She thinks I ought'a be content to do housework and get her medicine plants and not have an idea of my own. I'm goin' to Jacksonville to get me a job doin' somethin'. I got things to learn. I want to talk with someone who knows doctorin'. Someone who knows more'n Mama."

The teakettle was bubbling, and Marybeth measured tea into the cups and added the boiling water. The spoon clinking against the cups was the only sound. Then she sighed.

"Not wantin' to change your mind none, but I'd like to say this. If you could think of waitin' a few days till I get somethin' figured out about these babies, I'd like to run over to Jacksonville with you. We could take the wagon from here and look around a bit while we were over there. That way, I'd know where you were if we was to need one another."

"You'd not tell Mama?"

"Promise. I'd say nothin' to Mama you didn't want said. Now what else is wrong? You said two things needed to be said."

"Yeah, the other thing is about you. Mama's been madder'n a hornet over you bein' still down here. She was bad enough before, but now there ain't no sick wife 'tween you and Cal and all the talk that'll be comin' down on us."

"What talk?"

"Talk about you two livin' here together in the same house. She says the whole town gonna be lookin' down on us on account'a you."

"Well, little sister, you tell her she's got no cause for worry there. It's plain as a nose on her face these babies got'a be took care of. Irena got no folks, and Cal got no folks. Who'd there be left but me?"

Laura nodded. "I can tell her that, but it won't mean nothin'."

"Well, you can say to her that quick as someone who wants to talk shuts up their mouth and comes out here to help, that'd be the day I'd leave. Folks with lots to say generally don't do much. If Mama wants to come down here and take care of these babies, then I'll go. Tell her that."

Laura grinned. "Yeah, she probably gonna do that, and probably trees gonna grow upside-down. Just don't hold your breath!"

Marybeth took a sip of the tea. "Enough about that. Let's talk about you. Tuesday of next week ought'a give me about enough time. Between now and then, you bring down what you mean to take with you. Won't need much. I'll be knowin' where you are, and I can bring you what you need. While you're comin', you might bring me more of my things. Stockings and stuff. Then, come Tuesday, you'll be here early, and we'll head out. Provided it don't rain, that is. That suit you?"

Laura nodded and smiled. "I can wait. I'll try to make Mama settle down, and thanks." Then she was gone.

Marybeth sighed and finished the tea. There was more of Mama than one person could absorb at times, and Laura was up there all alone. She had a point.

7

Cal came into the kitchen from the shed.

"Marybeth, I got'a talk."

So after days of silence, everyone had to talk. She motioned him to a chair and poured tea.

He added cream, clinking his spoon on the cup, dreading to say what he must. "Marybeth, there'd be no way I could thank you for all the things you done for me and these babies. But I been thinkin' about everything, and I know this. You need to be goin' away from here. I got the wagon hitched up out there, ready to take you."

Marybeth set her cup sharply on the table, causing Cal to look at her, startled. "Now, Cal Boudreau, you know as well as I do there ain't no way you can take care of these babies by yourself. Nobody could. I'm here, and I'll not be leavin'."

Cal turned away from her gaze and stared at the floor. "Marybeth, I got eyes as well as a nose. There'd be talk, and it wouldn't do you no good."

"Aw, shucks, Cal. Folks got'a talk about somethin', and it might just as well be me. Time comes for me to leave, then I'll go, but it won't be today, and it won't be tomorrow. I got'a ask one thing, though. Next Tuesday, Laura and me, we got business in Jacksonville that's gonna take us all day. Got reasons why we can't take Mama's buggy, so we need you to hitch up your team for us. Just need it for the day."

So it came about that Cal moved his bed from the warm loft of his cabin to the openness of the hayloft. It was up to Marybeth to keep the night stove stirred up warm enough for the babies. And it was up to Cal to make the hayloft livable in the damp, winter weather.

8

Then it was two days after the funeral. Marybeth had cooked the ham and eggs and biscuits, and Cal was out of the house. She took warm water from the stove reservoir and set out a pile of soft towels. Bath time.

One by one, the little girls were stripped, bathed and dried, then dressed in fresh flannel gowns. They were fed and rocked (the cradle box just fit the arms of the big rocker, so they could be rocked all together) and they were now getting dopey with sleep. That was when a loud banging sounded at the front door.

The babies screamed in fright at the noise and Marybeth set the box on the bed and hurried to the door. There, she came face to face with her mother.

"Got the buggy out here, Marybeth. Get your things together, and get yourself on out there."

Marybeth lifted one of the howling babies to her shoulder, gently patting her into silence.

"I can't go, Mama. I got'a stay here."

"What're you sayin'? Sure you can go, one foot after the other. This ain't your kettle'a fish no more, Irena being gone now."

"But the babies...."

"Ain't your babies, neither. Takin' care of babies belongs to them as makes the babies. Put it down, and get movin'."

Martha Maisone looked around the room as if to help her gather up her things. "It's sinful and wicked, you stayin' here alone with that man. Ain't nobody in this town ain't had their say about the goin's on in this house. You made me the laughin' stock'a the whole neighborhood."

"Not you, Mama... me. What's said ain't gonna be said about you. I'm twenty years old, and it's gonna be said about me. You just go on home now."

"Well, I never! You think what's said about you don't reflect on me, no matter how old you get? Here I try to raise decent girls, and all I get is sass. You got no man of your own as it is, and now no decent man'll ever have you, livin' here in front of everyone."

"Nobody'll know where I am less'n they come snoopin'."

"They'll be snoopin', and you can count on that. You done your part here and then some. Time for someone else to do somethin'."

"Tell you what, Mama. Quick as someone else comes up here to do their turn, that'll be the time I feel I can leave. You think someone'll be here today?"

"Don't sass me, girl. What I say is for your good."

"Mama, I got to get these babies to sleep. I'll try to think of somethin'. You go on now, so I can get at it."

"I'll go and be glad to, but you better hurry up and get yourself out of this wickedness." Then she left, slamming the door so hard the house shook, causing the babies to scream louder.

Marybeth pulled the rocker close to the bed, where the babies lay screaming in the box. Putting a pillow in her lap, she lifted the tiny girls onto it, side by side by side with their little bottoms up. She rocked gently, patting all backsides and humming softly.

Gradually they quieted, and Marybeth's own mind began to settle. Things had to be thought out. Mama had a point. She hummed and rocked and patted, and they drifted into sleep. Gently she transferred the pillow from her lap to the cradle box, and the babies slept on. Marybeth continued to rock and think. She was still there when she heard the door open. Cal came in and stood in the doorway.

"Your mama come for a visit?"

Marybeth nodded.

"Didn't stay too long. I should'a come on in and made you and her some tea. Or something."

"She had to go back."

"Oh."

"Cal, I been thinkin'. Would it be a worry to you if I was to take these babies up to my house? If I was to do that, there'd be three of us most times, and we'd be able to take good care of 'em till you could do better."

Cal stood looking down at his feet, then he looked at the sleeping babies. "Reckon I couldn't be lettin' the babies go. My Reenie died givin' me these babies, and now I got nothin' else'a her left, 'cept them."

Marybeth began to rock the rocker and stare out the window. She was afraid this would happen.

Cal continued. "I know you got'a go. It's natural this would be a worry to your mama. I thank you for your help, and folks'll talk if you don't go. But these babies, well, I just got'a keep 'em here. They're mine."

Marybeth nodded. "That's what I thought you'd say. It's what I'd say, bein' in your place. Cal, you rememberin' I need the wagon for the trip to Jacksonville?"

Then it was three days after the funeral. Marybeth had lain awake for hours the night before, though exhaustion had pulled her to the bed early. Words that were burning to be said continued to flood her mind.

Irena, you could'a got well, she kept saying to herself... saying it as though her friend was alive and as though she had not said these things to her many times. Still the strict admonition flowed insistently through Marybeth's mind.

Her eyes burned, and her head ached. After breakfast, and after Cal had left the house to go for the milk, Marybeth took the cradle box to the bed and lay down beside it. Maybe the headache would go away. Jiggling the box soothed the babies into sleep, and her own eyes began to droop. The wind round the corners of the cabin and the sound of a shower of rain lulled her into sleep with their familiar sound.

It was while the windows were dark from the weather that she noticed one window was light, like maybe the morning sun was shining through. She remembered that was the window with the nasty cobweb, but she didn't see it now, though she didn't remember cleaning it down. It was strange that only one window was light.

While she watched the window, a flock of bluebirds flew by. It was unusual for the shy bluebirds to fly up to a window that way. For a minute, Marybeth felt honored by their appearance.

Then she saw a smiling face, but it was no one she knew. The features of the face became plainer and closer. The angel! It must be the angel. Irena had seen the angel, and it had called her away. It could only mean one thing.

"NO! GO AWAY! You can't take the babies!" The face did not go away, and she kept on screaming. She heard other screaming sounds and knew it was her own voice echoing inside her head. She forced herself awake as the kitchen door opened, and Cal came running.

Her eyes opened, and she was sitting up in the bed holding the box with the yelling babies in it. "It's all right, Cal. I just had a bad dream."

Cal nodded knowingly. "You're too tired. I'm gonna sit in the kitchen with the babies, and you're gonna get some sleep." And she did, for the next fourteen hours. Somehow, Cal managed.

9

Early on Tuesday morning, the winter sun shone on the Maisone sisters heading west in Cal Boudreau's wagon. A picnic basket of lunch was between them, and warm quilts were tucked around their legs and feet. They were set for the three-hour trip to Jacksonville. A box containing a few of Laura's necessities rode in the rear of the wagon.

Later that daym the ladies of the church gathered in the church building for their Tuesday Sewing Circle. Tea was brewed, and cookies were set out. The frame on which was stretched the current quilting project was let down from the church ceiling by means of a pulley. The ladies gathered around it with needles and thread and open ears for whatever could be learned.

"Anybody heard how Cal Boudreau's gettin' on with his babies?"

"Marybeth's still there, helpin 'im."

"Not today. Earlier, I saw her and Laura headin' toward Jacksonville in Cal's wagon."

"What'd they be goin' there for?"

"Didn't ask 'em."

"You say Marybeth's still there? With Irena gone?"

"Yep. Sure is."

"Wonder what's goin' on?"

"A lot'a work, I'd say."

"Cal can't get along by hisself?"

Granny Nelson broke off her thread and sipped a bit of tea. "Think on it. Cal, he's got two arms. Divide that into three babies and you got one baby left over. That means one more person. 'Spose you ladies all been up there and offered to take your turn?"

A long silence fell over the sewing circle. Needles punched in and out of the quilt, and thread was pulled tight. Glances were exchanged.

"Well, all I can say is the whole thing looks shameful to me."

"Shameful? How?"

"Well, you know what I mean."

Granny Nelson motioned to the preacher's wife. "Jane Ann, honey, will you fill my teacup? Needs warmin' up." Then she turned back to the circle. "I know what you mean about bein' shameful. All I can say is it's too late now. Something should'a been done 'afore this."

"Too late? Too late for what, Granny Nelson?"

"Why, I'd say it was far too late. They're too big now, and it would be shameful."

"What's too big? What're you sayin'?"

"Why, them babies, a'course. Anybody could'a told him what to do about them. Been doin' it to extra kittens all along. 'Afore they got too big, he should'a got 'im a sack and put 'em in it. Tied a rock to the top so it wouldn't float."

"Granny Nelson!"

"Why shore, and if he done that, there'd be no problem now. There wouldn't be no call for Marybeth to be there, helpin' out."

"Aw, now, Granny Nelson, that ain't what we meant!"

"I know that. But it ain't too late for somethin' else. He could put 'em in a box and left 'em here on the doorstep'a the church. It's been done before. Likely, anyone of you ladies'd be glad to take them babies in, all of you with two grown people in the house to care for 'em."

No one felt brave enough to come up with an answer. Jane Ann, the preacher's wife, felt the sudden urge to stir up the coals in the big, pot-bellied stove. That way she could hide her effort to keep from laughing out loud. She poked at the coals until she had a reasonably straight face.

Granny Nelson wasn't through. "Jane Ann, honey, you see any more of them molasses cookies over there? Yeah, I been thinkin' there'd be another way that problem could be took care of. We could cut strips of paper, same as the number of all of us, and write the names of the babies on three of 'em. That way would be fair, and it would spread 'em out, even-like. Be easier on us that'a'way. Or another thing, we could take turns, say a week at a time, havin' 'em in our house."

Silence. The only sound was the clicking of needle against thimble.

Granny just couldn't leave it alone, once she got started. "They's an orphanage over in Jacksonville that takes in babies. Grows 'em up big enough to work and then lets 'em out to those as wants 'em. Or needs 'em. Could do that. There's always a place for extra girls."

No response.

"Or there's one other thing we could do, and it'd maybe be the best thing. We could let Marybeth alone to do her Christian duty for them babies left by her best friend."

The big hand on the church clock made at least five complete turns in silence. Its tick-tock and the crackle of the flames in the stove were the only sounds.

Hattie McClendon remarked, "Sure was glad to see that strong breeze this morning. Them clothes I put on the line, they'll be dry enough to iron, quick as I get home."

Ella Draper said, "Nothin' like a whippin' wind to give clothes a good smell, I always say."

Carrie Ellen Cook put in, "I saw a recipe in the Gazette I sure want to try."

Maisie Jones responded, "What was in it?"

Carrie Ellen tried to remember, "Well, it called for chicken, potatoes and tomatoes. And something else. I'll bring it next week."

"Sure."

Cal Boudreau's team and wagon had crossed the silver bridge and headed on west. It was bumpy and jiggly, and their mother's buggy would have been much more comfortable, but there had been no possibility of using it without making known the purpose of the trip. And besides, Mama could get a call.

The first full strong rays of the sun shone on Laura as she reached for the picnic basket. A fruit jar of cold tea was set on the bench between them. Four large, fluffy biscuits were unwrapped from the huge towel. They were still slightly warm. She skillfully split the bread and spread on blackberry jelly and, handing one to her sister, began to eat one herself.

Marybeth held the reins in one experienced hand and ate with the other. Between bites, she ventured, "What sort of job was you thinkin' you might get?"

"Anything," answered her sister.

Half a jelly biscuit later, Marybeth continued, "Girl of seventeen like you are, you'd likely be only able to get a job helpin' in the kitchen somewhere for folks that has a lot of money."

"I'll do it."

Marybeth changed her tactics. "Mama really on you all the time?"

"All the time."

"Me bein' gone don't help none. That leaves you takin' the whole load."

"Yeah, but that ain't your fault. You only do what's got'a be done."

"If Mama couldn't get at you so much, that'd be better, don't you think?"

"Anything'd be better."

The wagon rolled along. Breakfast was over, and the basket was put away. Marybeth began again.

"Rich folks bein' able to hire help as good as you, they'd likely be the kind to yell at their help. I'd hate to see you yelled at by strangers."

"Think that'd be worse'n bein' yelled at by my mama?"

Marybeth chuckled at her inconsistency. "Reckon not. Then again, I never thought you to be one to take on a kitchen work job."

"Ain't wantin' one, especially."

The horses plodded along. Winter crows darted like sleek, black arrows among the trees. A startled rabbit ran in front of the horses but they did not miss a step. Rythmatic hoof steps on the gravels of the road.

"Laura," Marybeth began again, "if you was to get what you want, flat out, what would that be?"

Laura was silent a full minute. "My real want would be to do maybe what Mama does, but that ain't enough. She only wants me to deal with plants. I want to know more. I want to know everything, like a real doctor."

Marybeth sighed. "But Laura, they's schools you got'a go to for bein' a doctor. There ain't no way they'd let a woman go to that kind of school, even if there was enough money. And you ain't even a woman. You, bein' a seventeen-year-old girl, you got no chance'a doin' that."

"You asked."

"Yeah, I did."

The far horse pulled to the edge of the road for a mouthful of dry grass, but Marybeth's skillful hand brought him back.

"The way I put it together," Marybeth continued, "is that you gonna change kitchen work and yellin' at in River Bend for kitchen work and yellin' at in Jacksonville. That the way you see it?"

Laura had no answer.

Marybeth added. "Top'a that, there'd be no walks in the woods like you like, lookin' for plants. Another thing, there'd be no one to bring me peppermint tea to cheer me up, takin' care of them babies."

That brought a weak smile to Laura's face. "I'd be missin' that, all right."

The wagon rolled on. The road twisted and turned to avoid the hills, and there were many small bridges over tiny streams coming down from the mountains.

"Seems to me what you want is learning, not runnin' away. That about right?"

"Yeah, but Mama don't want me doin' anything but just what she says. She don't listen to nothin' I say."

"Does she make you hurry back when you go out walkin'?"

"No."

"You was always a good reader, back in school. 'Member them ribbons you won for bein' the best speller?"

"Yeah, why?"

"Well, if we was to find a book with what you want to know, that would make sense, wouldn't it? You'd be able to understand everything you read and take your time a'readin', wouldn't you?"

"Mama wouldn't put up with it."

"She would if she didn't know about it."

"What you thinkin'?"

"I was just thinkin', and maybe nothin' could come of it. Doctors have books that tell what you want to know. If we was to figure out how you could get a'hold'a one of them books, maybe even buy one, I got a little money, if they don't cost too much."

Laura asked tentatively, "You think that could happen?"

"Don't know till we try," came her sister's reply.

The winter sun was brighter now and shone down on the roofs of the first buildings of Jacksonville. The sight of it brought its own warmth.

"The first thing to do is find out where the doctor's offices are and then wait till they open up."

Laura leaned back, gripping the backside of the buckboard seat with apprehensive knuckles. Then she jumped up and squealed, startling the horses and causing them to break into a trot.

"Whoa, there," commanded Marybeth to the horses, then to her sister, "What got into you? A bumblebee sting you?"

"No," and she squealed again. "It was a doggie lick! Lookie who came along!"

The small, fuzzy Yoyo, now liberated from the need to hide, came bounding up onto the buckboard seat, nose and tail wriggling with happiness.

Marybeth groaned. "Now we got trouble. I thought she was locked inside. She thinks she goes wherever this wagon goes. Been tryin' to keep her shut in till she gets out'a heat. Should'a thought to check on her."

The exuberant, liberated dog flounced about, licking up biscuit crumbs and panting happily.

"Laura, better scrounge around back there and see if you can find a piece of rope for this dog. Likely gonna need it before the day's gone."

Laura was successful, and she tied the rope around the little dog's neck, then held her on her lap cuddled within the warm quilt.

"You were talkin' about gettin' a book," she reminded Marybeth.

"Yeah, and there'd be no way to know if we could buy a book till we try. Seems like today'd be the time to find out."

They had reached the beginning of Main Street, a wide brick thoroughfare presenting an even bumpier ride for the girls.

"You watch that side'a the street for doctor's office signs, and I'll watch this side. And maybe you better tie that dog to the bench; no knowin' when she might decide to jump out."

It was still early, and Jacksonville was just waking up. Shop owners were unlocking doors, and deliverymen were lining the street with their wagons, waiting for a chance to deliver their wares.

The horse pulling the milk wagon clomped past to the musical jingle of glass milk bottles. It stopped in front of the door of a shop that proclaimed ice cream at three dips for five cents.

"There's one. It's a Dr. Midland," Laura noted.

"And there's another one. Two doctors work there. That looks good," added Marybeth.

Laura chuckled. "Look behind us. Got two dogs a'followin'."

"Oh, shucks! I could'a bet on that!"

"There's another doctor. Funny-spellin' name. Must be a foreigner."

They passed three more signs. Jacksonville must be a very healthy town, or maybe a very sick one to need so many medical men.

"If we was to turn around and go back up the street, we'd see if we missed any. We still got lots'a time, and we could start with Mr. Midland. You thought on what you'll say to him?"

"Me? You got'a go in with me. You were the one to tell me what I wanted, so you got'a go in. You will, won't you?"

"Only one thing I see against that. No doctor gonna want that dog in his office."

"Yeah, that's right. I'll just leave her tied to the wagon seat. Won't hurt her none."

"Now, you got it in your head that I go in to talk about what you want. That right?"

"Why not? You knew 'afore I did. I left River Bend thinkin' I was runnin' off. Hey, look, Marybeth. We got five dogs after us now. I can't go in. I got'a stay out here and keep them dogs off Yoyo."

Marybeth could see the logic of that. "Well, see you hang onto her," and she stepped out of the wagon and disappeared through the door.

Hardly a minute passed before Marybeth returned, chuckling. "That doctor's a horse doctor. He got him a big laugh, though. I liked him. Seemed like a real nice man."

The office with the two doctors sent Marybeth away before she had a chance to state her case.

Now seven dogs were following them.

She tried the next doctor. It was hard to explain to the busy doctor what she wanted, even though she was willing to pay for the visit. The doctor had people waiting, and she would have to take her turn, so she left.

By the time they reached the end of the street, they had had absolutely no luck except in attracting dogs. They now had eight dogs with none of them showing any sign of leaving.

"Got me an idea," announced Marybeth as she turned the team and wagon around once more. "We're goin' back to that nice horse doctor. I didn't fair give him a chance to say anything. Doctorin' is doctorin', and likely he'd know where to get books."

The horses clomped back up the brick street, collecting only one more dog at the tailgate. The street was crowded now, nearing the time for the shops to open.

Laura waited with the dog while Marybeth went back into Mr. Midland's office. In a short time, she reappeared with the doctor behind her. The sight that greeted them in front of his office sent them both into hysterics.

In the wagon, which was pulled up to the curb in front of the doctor's office, there were the beginnings of a full-fledged circus. Laura stood on the buckboard seat holding the fuzzy little dog as high in the air as she could reach… the dog herself was fiercely struggling to get down.

Standing on the seat with Laura was a red-bone hound and a liver and white setter, jockeying for the best position. The hound had swiped a muddy paw against the skirt of Laura's light blue coat.

Two beagles were in the wagon, trying without success to gain a position on the seat with the larger dogs. A rawboned, mixed-breed animal leaped lightly over the tailgate and was advancing on the beagles.

On the street around the wagon, several smaller dogs leaped and bounded against the wheels and wagon bed, and others milled about under the wagon and round the legs of the horses. A mixed grayhound calmly lifted his leg and anointed the nearest wheel.

People on the street had stopped to watch the show. Even busy deliverymen slowed to better appreciate the scene.

From the doorway, Marybeth and the doctor rolled in laughter, encouraging many in the audience to join them. Laura was not amused.

"You got ideas of what to do now, I'd be ready to listen. My arms ain't gonna hold out too much longer, and that setter keeps tryin' to lift his leg on me."

Marybeth went to the wagon and reached for the dog. "We can take her inside. Dr. Midland says dogs are allowed to come in the office of a horse doctor. On top'a that, he wants to talk to you."

The doctor led the girls back to the office, chuckling as he went. "I got what you need for that little dog. Cost you a nickel, but without it, chances are you ain't gonna be able to get back in the wagon for the dogs crowdin' in on you."

Once inside the office, he handed Laura a bar of evil-smelling soap, reeking heavily of medicinal herbs.

"All you got'a do is dip that bar in water to get up a lather. You'll find it to lather up good, and you rub it all over her. Ain't meant to be used for that, but I found it works well. What I made it for was to rub on scrapes and scratches farm animals get, like from briers and barbed wire. Cleans 'em out and makes good use of the healing benefits of the herbal plants. That soap is one of the best things I ever made."

"You made this soap?" Laura was impressed.

The doctor settled his large body into his chair, long since pressed into an exact reverse duplicate of his own bulky shape. The springs of the chair squealed in protest as he turned, on ancient casters, to face the girls.

"Yep, I made that soap, and I made a lot of other things. Got a lot more ideas in my mind of things to make, come the time I get the chance." He motioned the girls to sit in the two straight chairs facing him. "Now, would you two young ladies tell me just exactly what it was you had in mind?"

But Laura was examining the soap. "Would you talk more about this soap? You got aloe in here. What makes the lather? Dagger plant?"

The doctor turned surprised eyes toward her. "You're right both times. How could you tell?"

Marybeth smiled with pride and butted in. "My sister is real good with all kind of plants. She learned a lot from our mama and taught herself a lot more. She knows all kinds of plants, just to look at 'em."

Dr. Midland nodded and cleared his throat loudly.

"You ladies like to drink coffee?" he offered. "Or is it tea you like? Tea is quick to make and is good for warming up the insides. Let's have tea."

Without waiting for an answer, the doctor lit a match to his gas hot-plate burner and set on the teakettle. The tongues of blue flame licked around the edge of the pot, adding more blackened soot to that already there. He measured tea directly into the kettle and watched for the first sign of a simmer. At the chosen moment, he turned off the flame and went to his icebox for a jug of milk.

"Top milk," he explained. "That's the secret of this kind of tea. Got to have cream in the milk to bring out the best flavor of it."

The girls watched, intrigued by the sight of a man making tea for them instead of the other way around. They were also intrigued by his running explanation, as though they had been fancy tea drinkers all their lives and this was just a tasting session. They were silent, though, because to comment would seem impolite.

While allowing the tea to steep in the hot water, the doctor handed a thick book to Laura. "Young lady, turn a few pages in that book and tell me if you see anything you know about."

Laura took the book eagerly, and the doctor set three teacups on the edge of his desk. He poured the cups full of tea and added a liberal amount of the top milk. The aroma of the tea instantly filled the room.

The doctor handed a cup of tea to Marybeth and took one for himself. Laura did not look up from the book.

"Real good flavor to that tea," commented Marybeth appreciatively.

Laura's drink cooled as she turned the pages. "I know about this and this. We have it on our land. And this one grows down over the edge of the bluff where it's hard to get at. I saw this, too, and had no idea what it'd be good for. And here it is, right in your book. Are all these good for medicine?"

"Some are, some aren't, but they're all in the book. You take this tea and drink it and listen to what I have in mind. You and me, we might be able to make a deal."

Laura reluctantly set as the book aside and took the tea.

The doctor continued, "Now tell me, Miss Laura, are you very sure that it's people you want to doctor? That can be done, but it's a sight easier and quicker to doctor animals. Chances are, there'd be more money in it for you, too."

"Money?"

"Sure enough, money. Farmers take care of their animals and manage to pay good money to make them well. It's an interesting thing how a sick youngen is put to bed with chicken soup or castor oil, but if his heifer is sick, he calls for the doctor."

Laura listened with interest.

"Now you see here," he continued, "I make that soap right here in my back room. The only hard thing I have to do is to find the right plants to put in it. Sometimes, bein' out on a farm to treat a sick animal, I find plants along the road and such, but it all takes time. And again, I got no big place to store all the plants here. You see what I'm gettin' at?"

Laura waited with respectful silence, permitting herself a small nod, but she leaned forward in her chair in her eagerness for him to continue.

"Yes, Miss Laura, I feel sure I can give you something you want, and you can give me something I need very much. You may take any of my books, one at a time, and read them. In return, you bring me the plants I need when you can find them."

A sip of tea and he continued, "Tuesday was a very good day for you to come in here, because that's the day I always stay in the office. Much of the other time, I'm gone out on calls. A horse doctor mostly has to go out to where the animals are, and a people doctor mostly has his patients brought in. That's one big difference, but I never considered it a bad thing, bein' that I like drivin' out along the road. Lucky for us we caught up with one another today. So, Miss Laura, you like anything you're hearin'?"

Laura sipped the tea and nodded eagerly. "I like everything I hear, and I really like the taste of this tea. I put things together sometimes to make different flavors, but I never made anything that tastes good as this. You gonna tell me what's in it?"

The doctor chuckled, amiably. "Not today, young lady. Gonna let you think about it a little while. You take that book, there, and read it, and come back here in two weeks on a Tuesday. I know its wintertime now, but if you was to find any roots that you remembered where they were, you bring them on in. We'll make us some time to talk about what we can do next."

Laura set aside her empty teacup and hugged the book. "I can do that, Dr. Midland. I can bring some roots back with me."

"Wonderful. Now, I need to get a nickel for that soap, and you need to use it before you leave here. That herd'a dogs is still outside the door."

Marybeth handed him a nickel, and the doctor took the coin and held it up.

"See here, Miss Laura, this soap sold for a nickel, but, for the things I have to buy to go into it, it costs me less than a penny. I now have four cents that I didn't have. That's the kind of things you can learn to do by reading that book. Now bring that little dog, and come in the back room. We'll fix her up good."

The dog wiggled and whined but was eventually covered with the cream-colored, high-smelling lather.

"Now just let it dry," advised the doctor. "Won't take but a few minutes for the foam to melt away so it don't show, but the good will still be there and will last a couple of days. Might have to use it again to get her through her heat. Now, ladies, you take care of yourselves and come back."

Once again in the wagon, Marybeth wrapped the damp dog in a piece of old quilt to keep her from chilling and tied the dog's neck rope to the buckboard seat. Now they were free to do a little looking around.

"We could go down to the Five and Dime," Marybeth suggested.

Laura heard her and nodded but did not lift her eyes from the herb book as the horses plodded down the short distance toward the Five and Dime and the ice cream store.

"What flavor are you going to get?" Marybeth asked. "I think I'll take one just like the picture with chocolate and vanilla on the bottom and the pink one on the top."

"Me, too."

But when they entered the shop, they saw the other flavors.

Laura changed her mind. "Look at that flavor. It says honeydew. What's a honeydew? I never heard of one. And there's peppermint. What I want is chocolate and honeydew with peppermint on top."

"I still want the one in the picture."

"Let's sit in here at these wire chairs and eat it. It's too cold to sit in the wagon and eat ice cream. Yoyo, she'll be all right, now. No dogs hanging around. Likely she's gone to sleep."

Laura glanced into her lap. "I guess I can't look at the book. I might get ice cream on it."

"Might. How did you like them things the doctor said?"

Laura quit eating and stared out the window, biting her lower lip. "Marybeth, you think it'd be all right to believe what he said? Seemed a mite too good to be true and all."

"He's a doctor. Reckon he wouldn't tell you what wasn't true."

"Yeah, but you know what Mama always said about listenin' to what a man says."

Marybeth sighed. "Mama has her problems. Happen they're just hers, though, and not ours, and everything she says maybe don't actually pertain to us. Could be that she's wrong sometimes. See, you got that book in your lap, and it must'a cost a sight'a money. That man just let you take it off with nothin' more'n your promise. Seems that'd count for a lot."

"Yeah."

"Laura, do you see that ice cream a'meltin'? Runnin' right down over your fingers. Reckon you ought'a eat it, maybe?"

Laura grinned and attended to the eating of her ice cream.

"Marybeth, this here honeydew ice cream tastes like muskmelon. Sort'a. You want a bite?"

Her sister took a small taste of the gold colored ice cream. "Hmmm, does, sort'a."

"I like it. Do you?"

Marybeth nodded. "But not as good as vanilla."

From the ice cream store, they walked a few doors down to the Five and Dime.

The little store was crowded with merchandise from front to back and top to bottom. It stocked no farm supplies or seed or feed, like the Mercantile at River Bend. This store had fancy lace and scarves. It had rings and combs, fancy buttons and every kind of yard goods, and every sewing need a body could ever imagine. It had toys and baby clothes, and dolls and balls and jump ropes.

It was a place of wonder, and Marybeth would have been glad to spend a little time just looking at what was for sale.

Laura followed her around and answered when spoken to and gave an opinion when asked. Her eyes, however, were on the book. When encouraged to look at this or that, she did so, but her finger held her place in the book.

With a small sigh, Marybeth paid for the scarf she had picked out. Ten cents, it was, and then she suggested it might be time to head back to River Bend.

After all, Marybeth thought, she had been successful beyond all hope in diverting her sister from what had seemed to her to be a disastrous plan. And, as that had been the purpose of the trip, they could now go home. No mention was made of the small package of personal possessions waiting in the wagon. So they climbed onto the buckboard seat with Yoyo and headed east.

It was still fairly early, just barely past noon, when Cal Boudreau's team and wagon left the brick streets of Jacksonville for the gravel road that followed the river. The little dog slept contentedly on the quilt, lulled by the jiggle and roll of the wagon. Winter crows still busily flapped about in the trees on either side of the road, and cows cropped dried grass from the fencerows. An occasional rabbit dashed across the road, and the blue jays quarreled with the squirrels.

Laura struggled to hold the book still enough to read, and Marybeth sighed with relief to see her sister seemingly content after the state she had been in.

In truth, Marybeth thought, she herself should take a share of blame for Laura's predicament. The thought of it made her sad, but she had thought and thought, and there seemed to be no other way for her to have gone, other than to help Irena when she was needed. Most of the blame, she knew, belonged to their mother, but that was an old story. So now it seemed, the trouble she had caused her sister had seemingly been corrected with her luck on this trip.

With Laura's mind far away, Marybeth rode along in her aloneness, relaxing comfortably, her body responding to the motion of the wagon. This left her free to think.

An old thought settled itself down over her. Her best friend was gone, and it might have even been her fault. When Irena needed help, Marybeth was busy with the babies, that being what she knew best. Should she have left the babies to tend to Irena? If she had, one or more of the babies would likely have died. It had been a terrible decision.

There, at the very bottom of the decision, lay the fact that she did, at least, know more about newborn babies than about their mothers. Mama always took care of the mothers, and Mama had never lost a mother.

On the other hand, Irena had not died for another month, so should the death be held at her doorstep? True, she never seemed normal after the delivery. It seemed almost as though the babies took all of the life out of her, and her body was not able to make more. Having no life left, there was nothing to do but listen to the angel.

During this past week, in the darkness of the night, she would startle awake, thinking Irena was calling for help. Then she would lie there and think, just as she was thinking now, being angry with herself. Following that, she became angry with Irena for letting her life slip away seemingly without a struggle.

Then she was angry with herself for being angry. Getting mad was such a waste of energy when she seemed to be tired all the time.

And Cal. If he would just let her take the babies home with her for a few days, Laura and her mother would help, and she could get a little rest. At least Laura would help. Her mother seemed to hate Irena and might hate the babies, as well.

Now, as the wagon rolled along, she decided she was too tired just now to get angry with herself. Looking back did no good, so she'd have to remember to look ahead. What would be good to fix for supper?

They were leaving town earlier than she had expected, and there would likely be time to cook beans after she got home. It would need to be butterbeans; they cooked faster. And, of course, cornbread always went with beans. There were still a few jars of poke greens left from the spring canning.

A skillet of fried turnips and onions would be good, or she could leave off the turnips and onions and fry up some apples studded with chunks of ham and sprinkled with brown sugar. That sounded good.

Planning a meal was a pleasant task, especially when there were so many choices of food and such a good supply of dry kindling wood for the stove. One thing about Cal was that he kept dry wood for her, and there was never a shortage. A lot of women, herself included, set a great store by having a good, big woodpile.

And the food, too. As much trouble as Cal had with cash crops like cotton and corn, it was interesting that his garden vegetables were excellent. It was true, of course, that the kitchen garden was grown on the best land he had, the land that did not get soggy or brick hard.

Then the babies. She really needed to get some weight on them. If they should get really sick and not want to eat, it would go very bad for them. They'd done well for the first six weeks, but they needed to weigh more. If they could just hold out until they were big enough to eat table food (that would be likely be the fall), could be they'd be all right.

Then, after the babies, she began to think of Irena again. When you lose your best friend, what do you do then? Indeed, what...? How does one go about filling the gaping hole left by the loss of a friend? Indeed, how...?

After three hours of riding, the girls reached River Bend. They crossed the silver bridge and turned down Main Street, passing the livery stable and on to the Mercantile with its shoppers and loafers milling about.

Next came the church, where the Tuesday Sewing Circle had met earlier in the day. They turned south and crossed the swinging bridge, held up by stout cables attached to massive rocks on either side of the river. Then they started up Rock Creek Road.

Laura finally came to life. "Marybeth, just let me out at our road here, and I'll get my things later. Mama'll be wonderin' what in the world happened to me. Bye now." She jumped off the still-moving wagon and started up the road, reading as she went.

Marybeth was again alone with her thoughts.

When the girls had passed the livery stable a few minutes ago, they had not gone unnoticed.

"Ain't that them two Maisone girls in Cal Boudreau's wagon? Looks like 'em. Reckon where they been?"

"Come from the direction of Jacksonville, seems like."

"What'd they be doin' over there?"

"How come they ain't usin' their ma's buggy? Heap more comfortable for ladies."

"Notice how them girls both took after their daddy in looks? You'd go a long way to find a better pair of lookers than them two."

"That Marybeth, she's a mite tall for a girl. What'd you say, five-eight?"

"Likely that, for sure. That least'n, she's not far behind. And they ain't skinny, like you'd expect for a tall girl. Appear to look like twins, almost."

"You'd think they'd be out sparkin' more. Don't hear nothin' about them seein' nobody."

"Boys maybe all afraid of their mama."

"Yeah, that'd be a thing to consider. Reckon that Cal's missin' havin' that Marybeth down at his house takin' care of his youngens?"

"He ain't missin' her yet. She ain't left."

"Ain't left? She still down there alone with him?"

"Seems to be."

"He's a lucky man, that Cal. Hear tell that girl's a real good cook."

"Yeah, he's lucky, all right! You fellows forget he just buried a wife, hardly a week past? Leavin' 'im with three babies? Would you be thinkin' that was lucky?"

"Yeah. That's right."

"What's gonna happen to him when she finally leaves? Him with all them youngens?"

As she neared the house, Yoyo aroused from her long nap and jumped up onto the seat beside Marybeth. The foam from the lather had dried and disappeared, but, as the doctor had promised, the smell remained.

Marybeth held her nose. "Phewww! You smell bad." She ruffled the hair around the little dog's ears. "Saved your life, though, didn't we? I ain't sure you're worth a nickel, but them big dogs, they'd'a had you for lunch. Didn't want that, did we?"

Cal met her in the yard to take care of the horse and wagon, so she went on to the house. He followed a short time later and sat at the table, watching her.

"Your mama came while you were gone, thinkin' to find Laura and maybe talk with you."

"Hmmm, that all she wanted? Didn't say nothin' to you about sendin' me home?"

"She did say somethin'. I told her that for you to leave was likely the best thing to do for everybody. I told her if you was to go, then I'd be able to move my bed back into the house where it was warm. Told 'er that hayloft where I been sleepin' gets a mite drafty on a windy night."

"Then what did she say?"

"Nothin'. Just stood and looked at me."

"Were you tellin' the truth? Do you want me to go?"

"That ain't for me to say."

"It is, too, for you to say, and you're gonna say it."

"I can say it. Marybeth, you got'a go. I can't have folks sayin' and thinkin' things I caused and your mama was hoppin' mad."

"It don't take too much to make Mama hoppin' mad. But I can say this, you don't have to bring it up again, 'cause I'll go."

She tilted her face and stared him, boring into him with her black eyes. "Then come time you got'a go chop some wood to keep this house warm and cook food, you gonna take these three undersized babies along with you. You can lay 'em right there on the ground and take care of 'em while you're swingin' the ax.

"You can't stay in here while they have their nap, so you can take 'em to the shed with you. It won't matter if the wind's blowin', 'cause they'll be there with you. It won't matter that they don't weigh no more'n a settin'a eggs, all told.

"And you'll figure how to warm their bottles on a campfire while you're down at the river gettin' fish. You take them fish over to Jacksonville 'cause you need cash money, and them babies can ride along on the buckboard. Maybe it's rainin' or snowin', but that won't be no surprise. Remember, it's still wintertime.

"You go swap out the milk, and they'll go jouncin' along. Take you twice as long in the wagon as on the saddle, but you can't leave 'em alone. Won't matter to the babies if it's rainin' pitchforks at the time.

"Think about if you have to go down to the Mercantile for somethin' or other, and plannin' to bring it back, how you gonna do it? You with two arms and three babies? You gonna hitch up the wagon every time? Maybe you could get you a big bucket, and you could pitch them babies in it and carry 'em that'a'way."

By now, Marybeth's anger had begun to cool, having delivered the result of her thinking during the trip home, and her senseless words were beginning to sound funny.

She smiled but continued, "Now, if what I said don't paint a picture you can put on the wall'a your mind, I can keep goin'. Come spring, you'll think you got'a tackle that clay field down toward the river. Be no trick to carry these babies piggy-back, goin' up and down them rows. Sun beatin' down on 'em right through their sunbonnets. Reckon that's what you'd want to do?"

By now, even Cal was grinning. It seemed ridiculous, the way she said it. He began to laugh and Marybeth laughed with him. They laughed until they had tears. There sometimes comes a time when things get so painful and mixed up you got no more tears to cry... then you laugh. That's all that's left to do.

Finally, the laughter subsided.

"Now, Cal Boudreau, I know this is your house, and these are your babies, but you can listen to me for a minute. Until you get someone to move in here and take care'a these babies, you just get used to me, 'cause I'm stayin'. Ain't humanly possible for you to do everything that's got'a be done, and you know it. If you got a sister somewhere that you could send for, then I'll be goin'. Till I hear different from you, I'm stayin'.

"Now, tomorrow I got'a go and bring back more of my things. Sorry you got'a stay in the barn where it's cold, but I don't see no other way."

Anger gave her strength, and in no time at all, the stove was blazing and the bean pot was bubbling. She brought a slab of ham from the smoke house and an apron full of apples from the shed. After all the goings on, she was bound to be starving hungry very soon. She would cook a good supper, and then she would feel better. Perhaps then, she could make a bit of sense somewhere in all of this.

Later that evening, she sat at the kitchen table, staring out the window at the blackness of the night. She heard "tap-tap" on the roof and saw rivulets of water stream down the windowpane. More drops. Then the window was a solid stream of water, reflecting back the light of the oil lamp in moving sparkles.

"Cal," she called to the other room, where he was rocking the babies in the big rocker. "I hear rain on the roof. Comin' in from town, it felt like it was blowin' in colder. You gonna have to think on bringin' your bed back into the attic till this cold spell blows over. You can't be stayin' out there in this."

"Got to," he called back. "There ain't no more room in the attic. I went up there and nailed up some dryin' line for hangin' wet diapers. With the weather comin' into spring rains, figured it'd be needed. Managed to get a lot of line strung out, and heat from the cookstove goin' up, we could be gettin' them diapers dry. Other things, too."

"Don't reckon you'll be sick? Sleepin' out, like that?"

"Naw. I done some boardin' up to block the wind. I'll do good out there."

"Cal, I thought you told my mama you'd bring your bed back inside." She chuckled. "You know'd all along I'd be stayin' here, didn't you?"

After a moment of silence, "Thought it wouldn't hurt to wait and see."

One thing about Cal was that he didn't get in a hurry about changes. He gave things time to work out on their own, if they were a'mind to.

Cal went on, "I got a mess'a fish in the big bucket outside. Offered 'em to your mama, but she told me she don't like fish."

Marybeth broke into laughter. "Mama was just bein' stubborn. Fish'd be the food she'd most like, but she couldn't think'a takin' a present from you."

Cal set the cradle box on the warming oven and left for the shed, and Marybeth moved to the big rocker. She still had thinking to do, and it was difficult to halt the thoughts circling in her head. Thinking was extra hard to do in the wintertime. It was all such a puzzle. Come spring, there would be an answer to all of this. And the fact was, if she didn't get to bed and get some sleep, she would still be awake for the midnight bottle.

At midnight, when Cal woke her, the rain was coming down in sheets and buckets, and by dawn, Rock Creek was running full. A rushing waterfall spilled over the rock ledge and began to flow across the yard.

Cal stomped mud from his gumboots as he brought in the fresh milk from the barn. It would be a sloggy trip to go after the goat's milk, but it had to be done.

With breakfast over, Cal lingered over his coffee at the table, and Marybeth carried her mug of dark brew to the window. A solid flow of water covered the windowpanes, creating a chilly, dismal feeling inside the house. Between the streams flowing down the window, she could see the water collecting in pools on last year's cotton field. If the rain kept up all day, the field would be solid water over a layer of slick mud, and it would be forever drying out. The discouragement of it all matched her dismal mood.

"North forty's goin' under water," she commented.

There was no response from Cal. He just took another sip of the comforting hot drink. Her words were not news to him.

"Looks dark over in the northwest, like it's settin' in for a week or more," she continued, pronouncing further gloom over the day.

Still no comment.

"You know what, Cal, it's a cryin' shame it ain't catfish you been tryin' to raise down in that cotton field. Seems to me like they'd grow better'n anything you raised down there yet. Could be worth more money, too."

"Likely," was Cal's typical one-word reply.

After filling the woodbox, Cal disappeared into the shed, and Marybeth went about the housework. Later, when she went to the shed for turnips, he was so intent at the grinding wheel that she came and went unnoticed. Sparks flew from the wheel as he sharpened the teeth of his long-toothed harrow. Keeping tools in condition was a needed winter job for a farmer. Sharp tools made the hard work a little easier. Cal stayed with the job all the rest of the day.

And this was the day Preacher McCrey chose to make a pastoral call. He tied his horse to the gatepost and slogged up to the door in gumboots. At Marybeth's invitation, he stepped inside and removed the boots. In sock feet, he admired the babies and sat with Marybeth to have a cup of tea. Marybeth was so glad to see someone to talk with other than her own face in the mirror, she drew a chair to the table and listened while Cal and the preacher talked about the weather and the animals, the weather and the crops, and the weather. And when the preacher asked Cal if there was anything he could do for him while he was here, Cal took him up on it.

"Be obliged, Preacher, if you'd come out to the barn and help me with a little job I need done." So they donned their gumboots and splashed their way through the rain to the barn.

Leaning against the corncrib, there stood three long boards. Cal indicated the ladder to the loft, "Now, Preacher, if you was to climb up that ladder, I'd be liftin' these boards up to you. If you'd guide the end of 'em over to the north and lay 'em down on the hay, it'd be a big help to me."

The preacher complied, carefully negotiating the ladder in his clumsy boots, slippery with mud. At the top of the ladder, he stepped gingerly onto the board floor of the loft. To his left, the hay was piled to the roof of the loft, while on the right, a wooden bed had been built against the wall. The bed was complete with a cotton-stuffed mattress, goose down pillow and hand-pieced quilts. Lots of quilts.

"Ready, Preacher? Here they come."

Preacher McCrey leaned over the top of the ladder and caught the end of each board, one by one, and guided them back until there was room to lay them on the floor. It only took a minute, then he carefully descended the ladder.

"Thanks a lot to you, Preacher. Needed to get them boards up there. Fixin' to close off that little window up high. Wind gets to comin' in there, come time it shifts around to the north."

Joe McCrey nodded. "Tell me, Cal, are you making it all right, now?"

"Sure, Preacher. Gonna be a lot better now. Likely to have eight, maybe ten, weeks'a winter, yet. Then there's always that cold snap right 'afore Easter. Gonna be good and warm up there."

He paused and then nodded agreeably, adding, "Summers are right pleasant up here. Most always get a breeze."

The men naturally gravitated toward the shed, the logical center of male endeavor in River Bend. The sharpened long-teeth had been partly re-attached to the harrow, but a pile of the teeth remained on the workbench. Cal resumed his work as they talked.

"Got you a job'a deep scratchin' comin up, huh? Notice you settin' them teeth on there mighty high."

"Yeah. Come time this rain ever lets up, I got a lot to do. Have to hurry to get into them fields between the slick mud and the sun-dried brick, if I'm aimin' to get anything done. Mean to have these teeth sharpened up and ready to go."

"Gonna put somethin' new in that field? Givin' up on cotton this year?"

"Could be. Still thinkin'."

The preacher allowed it was time to get on down the road, so he splashed out to his drenched and dripping horse. As he mulled the conversation through his mind, something became clear. That Cal was sure tight with his words. Getting a bit of information out of him was akin to pulling hen's teeth. Come to think of it, though, it really wasn't any of his business what Cal did with his lower fields, and that's what Cal had told him, in a very polite way.

That night at supper, he passed along to Jane Ann the news of the babies and of Marybeth. He told his wife, "Cal said he had need of a little help and had me climb up to the loft and guide up some boards for him."

"Good timin', then, wasn't it? You decidin' to go up there today, in spite of the rain?"

"Nah, that wasn't the way it was at all. Cal didn't need no help. Judgin' from the things he does for himself all the time, he could'a got them boards up there without any help from me, and maybe quicker. He just wanted me to see he had made himself a bed up in the loft and that he was stayin' out there. He was sayin', without words, that he was leavin' the house to the babies and Marybeth, to keep down the talk. Wouldn't hurt none if the word was passed around at the Sewing Circle."

Jane Ann was wide-eyed. "He's stayin' the night in the barn loft? In the dead'a winter? He's gonna freeze to death!"

"Not likely. Had 'im a dozen or more quilts and a goosedown comforter on that bed. No way he could get cold."

Two days later, the rain stopped. Cal's heavy, long-toothed harrow was ready for his next dirt project.

10

The baby girls were now three months old. The balance scales said they were about 6 pounds each. At times, now, they could sleep as long as two hours and a half (a big improvement). They waved their fists and smiled and kept the loft clothesline filled with diapers.

Cal left one afternoon and returned with a young goat tethered to the saddle horn. The animal waddled along with ungainly steps.

"Swapped out for her," Cal said, by way of explanation. "Folks over toward Piney didn't need her, and she's comin' fresh from a good sire in a day or two. Arranged to take 'em over a mess'a mudcat once a week for the next ten weeks. Expect to save a little time, me havin' the goat here."

One thing about Cal was that he knew how to bargain. Three girls on goat milk only made it sensible to have his own goat.

The very pregnant goat was tied, protesting, in the barn while Cal headed for the river. Half an hour later he was back with a half a pail of crawfish. Tails skillfully removed, de-shelled and de-veined, they were delivered to the kitchen, ready for the pot. Crawfish soup!

Marybeth cubed the potatoes, onions, carrots and mushrooms. Added to the crawfish, now browning in the skillet, were the seasonings and spice. Into the pot went the vegetables to simmer, and at the last moment, top milk was added to round out the flavor. Wonderful winter soup to be served with biscuits and fruit cobbler.

The new goat bleated half the night, but she had a good reason. By morning, she had produced two snow-white, tail-flipping babies, a billy and a nanny. One to make sausage, and one to make future milk. Good combination. Or the sausage goat, if he had inherited enough good traits, could possibly see a better, more pleasurable future. Time would tell. Then again, he might get a trip to the auction barn and be swapped for one of a different bloodline than his ma.

The next day the sun came out. Weak and lacking in warmth, it was welcome, nevertheless. Cal hitched the team to his harrow and headed down to the north forty cotton field alongside the river. Marybeth saw him go and wondered curiously why the push to drag the field in the middle of February, but what he did was his business. She had plenty to do inside the four walls.

Cal marked off a square of ground thirty by fifty feet and dragged the heavy, long-toothed harrow across it, back and forth. The freshly sharpened teeth of the harrow dug into the soft ground, stirring it to a depth of more than 6 inches deep and a swath four feet wide. He keenly examined his work, nodding with satisfaction. Then he hitched a cart to one of the horses and began to shovel the fresh dirt into the cart. The February wind was brisk, but in no time, Cal had removed his coat and rolled up his sleeves.

The full cart was drawn up into the yard near the front door. He began to off load, making an eight-inch deep layer of wet dirt, packing it down firmly, building it level with the doorstep. Another load of dirt followed it, and before the day was over, eight loads had been deposited. The front yard looked as though he was making a dirt porch from the material taken from the low cotton field, which made it lay even lower. Cal surveyed the results of his labor with satisfaction, mopping the sweat from his face.

The next morning, he disappeared for a couple of hours, returning with a metal dirt slip in his wagon. It was a loan from Johnny Scott, dating back to the time Johnny had such trouble with the river eating away at his own property. The dirt slip could move a lot of dirt much faster than a shovel and cart. Trouble was, the dirt slip had a broken handle that took an hour and a half to replace.

Then he was back with the harrow, scratching dirt from the marked area and then gathering it into the slip. Horsepower was easier than manpower as the heavy, wet dirt filled the shovel-like slip. Still, guiding the animals and operating the slip made a man feel he had done a man's day's work.

Another glance out the window made Marybeth even more curious, but it was none of her business. One thing, though, was that he was bound and certain to be extra hungry, so she opened a jar of home-canned beef and browned it in the kettle. Adding water and wide, homemade egg noodles made a meal to fill the emptiest stomach. Maybe she needed to make a supper cake from sweetened, spicy batter drizzled with butter and honey. Good to top off a winter supper and if any happened to be left over, it was good the next day.

In the River Bend Livery Stable, the customers and loafer were puzzled.

"Heard Cal Boudreau took the loan of that dirt slip of Johnny Scott's... the one he used when he fought the river off cuttin' into his land."

"What'd he be needin' with a dirt slip?"

"I can tell you one thing. Appears like he's been diggin' a grave for a giant. Maybe diggin' his own grave, from the look of it."

"What'd ya mean?"

"That low forty by the river, you know? Well, he's scratchin' up the dirt with the long-toothed harrow and haulin' it away."

"Hmmm, a body'd think he'd be tryin' to haul in, 'stead'a haulin' out."

"That'd be what anybody else'd do. I'd be tryin' to build that field up to get it out'a the wet."

"He better have himself a good idea, him with them three girls comin' on all at once."

"I still say, he'll never raise a family there. Don't get a cotton crop more'n once in five years. Takes all the high ground for corn and garden crops. Nothin' for cash. 'Course he's got all that blackjack timber."

"Yeah, could clear that out. Mighty hard to get rid of all them roots, though."

"Man, you ain't thinkin' proper. He's got'a keep that timber; else what'd he use for firewood?"

"Say, how's he takin' care of them babies?"

"Don't you know? That oldest Maisone girl, she's still there."

"Still there? Wonder that her mama lets her stay there."

"Don't reckon her ma can do anything. Girl's over eighteen, time to be havin a man'a her own."

"Got her cap set for Cal?"

"Likely not. She was around while her friend was courtin' with Cal. If Marybeth'd wanted Cal, she could'a had 'im then, like as not."

"You'd be right, there. No fellow would'a took to Irena if he had a chance at Marybeth. Cal, bein' an outsider, would'a took what he could get."

"Yeah. What chance would a foreigner like Cal have, knowin' she turned down all them local boys? He'd be smart enough to know that."

"Maybe he'll get a chance at her, yet?"

"Could be. She seems to be fair attached to them babies of his."

"You'd think so, but some woman are just foolish over babies, no matter who they belong to, and don't even see the man."

"Ain't many women foolish enough over babies to bottle feed three of 'em at once, night and day, like she has to. Way I hear it, them babies wouldn't have made it without her knowin' what to do when they came."

"What'll he do when she leaves?"

"Best he can, I reckon."

"He'll be hard put to find a ma for 'em, scarce as girls are in this town. If he'd go to Jacksonville, might have better luck."

"Don't reckon he's thinkin' on that right now, being' he just buried a wife less'n three months back."

"One thing about it, you'd never hear it from Cal if he had plans. He don't talk to nobody about nothin', that man don't."

"You're sayin' right on that. He come in here a few days ago, postin' a notice of a cow for sale. He's goin' over to goats on account'a them babies bein' bottle fed. Hard to think a goat'd be better'n a cow, but I 'spect he knows."

"Still wonder what he'd be diggin' that pit for. The one in his low north forty."

"We'll know when he's done, and I wager it'll be no sooner than that, knowin' Cal."

The weather held, and the gloomy winter skies retained their load of rain. With plenty of food available and the woodshed stacked deep with dry wood, Cal had time to work on his project uninterrupted. Methodically he hitched the team to the long-toothed harrow and scraped away at the heavy clay, often riding on the harrow to force the teeth deeper. When a layer of dirt was scratched loose, he changed the horses to the dirt slip and began to haul it out. The thirty by fifty foot rectangle sunk deeper and deeper.

Not the least of his accomplishment was what happened to the yard. From the house to the road, a layer of clay, from eight inches up to one foot thick, had been carefully patted smooth and raked level. At the edge of Rock Creek, between the road and the house, he had built up a berm of dirt, protecting the creek side of the berm with a layer of flat stones to prevent washing out in high water.

In addition, the flat rocks were taken from the basin of Rock Creek, deepening the channel and reducing the chance of spillover into the yard. As he contemplated his handiwork, Cal stroked his chin thoughtfully. Next time into Jacksonville, he'd stop over at the feed store and get a pound of grass seed. The seed would bury up in that mud and be just right to sprout come April sunshine.

At noon on Monday, however, he cleaned his equipment and put it away as he did on all Mondays lately. Tuesday was fish day.

Four or five dozen large mudcat caught on Monday afternoon were taken to Jacksonville on Tuesday morning. Sometimes he sold them to the meat market, and other times he merely parked his wagon in the town square, and customers found him. It was a totally reliable source of cash, as the people in town seemed to have an insatiable desire for the large, succulent fish and wouldn't, or couldn't, catch them for themselves.

Cash coins would be dumped in the jar in the cupboard, handy for a sudden need.

Tomorrow he would have a passenger on his trip. As she had every other week for the past two months, Marybeth's sister went along. It was good that Cal didn't particularly need company, because Laura was no company at all. Her nose was buried in the book from the time the horses took their first step until they stopped at their destination. He dropped her off at the office of the horse doctor and collected her when he had sold the fish.

This Tuesday, however, he had a little stop of his own. At the Five and Dime, he bought a shiny blue and red rubber ball and three tiny dresses made from white dimity and trimmed in dainty lace.

Wednesday, however, found Cal back in the clay pit, anxious to accomplish what he could before the next rain. That hole, being where it was, would fill up in no time, and that would set him back on his plan. It was now four feet deep, and the haul-out dirt was being used to build up the area around the shed and out toward the barn. There were plenty of places to put it, and one load followed the other. The large stones found in the clay were strung along the edge of the pit, and by now they made the appearance of a low stone wall.

A new bit of town talk occurred because of a decision made by Laura and Marybeth. When it seemed the trips to Jacksonville would become a regular thing, and in concession to the lively imagination of the town people, it was decided that Laura would wear overalls, a man's coat and a cap with the capacity to conceal her long, heavy, black hair. This gave the appearance of two men riding along in their wagon, one driving the horses and the other intent on something held in his lap.

The ladies gathering at the church for their usual Tuesday Sewing Circle were first to take notice.

"Saw Cal Boudreau's wagon headin' into Jacksonville. Wonder what got him out so early? Had another fellow with him, too."

"I know why he'a goin' early. It'd be to get the best price on them mudcats he takes in every week. Don't know about a fellow with him, though."

"'Spose he's got folks up from the south country visitin' him?"

"Could be. Maybe his ma or a sister or someone come to help with them babies."

"More likely to help 'im move down there."

"He ain't showin' no sign'a movin'."

"No, but that'd let Marybeth off from takin' care of the little 'ens. Bet them three babies are 'bout to run her ragged."

"Been nigh onto six months since she's been down here to the sewin'. Must be dull havin' no more company than she's likely to have."

"Yeah, cooped up in that little old house with Cal and them little girls."

"Cal ain't there."

"Huh?"

"Cal, he ain't stayin' in the house. He took to the barn and made hisself a place in on the loft."

"The barn loft? He'll catch his death out there in the weather!"

"Reckon he hasn't yet. Seen 'im just this mornin', headed west out'a town."

"Wonder who that was with 'im."

At the other end of town, a number of men were gathered in the livery stable.

"Saw Cal Boudreau go by toward Jacksonville. Had a fellow with him."

"Who was it?"

"Couldn't tell. Had his face down. Maybe a brother or someone."

"Could be someone over from Piney to help him with the fishin' he does every week. Must take him right smart'a time to catch that load he had on."

"Naw, them folks from down south, they're good at fishin', having so much water about all the time."

"But who was it?"

"How big a fellow was it?"

"Seemed littler'n Cal, was all I could tell."

"Anybody see that hole lately, the one he's put in the low cotton patch? That's one sight of a hole! Sides squared off and everything."

"Find out what he'd got in mind?"

"Not for the hole. Plain to see what he's usin' the dirt for. Got his yard all filled in, now. Last winter with a lake in his yard likely gave 'im ideas. If he was to get a sod'a grass on that mud, a body'd be able to get to the house without havin' to swim or wade black gumbo clay. Right good-lookin' rock work he done on the west bank'a the creek. Ain't likely to wash over into his yard anytime soon. Sure took a hole out'a the cotton patch to do it, though."

"That'd not be much of a loss. Didn't have a crop more'n one year out'a five."

"Reckon who that was that went into town with him?"

And Cal kept scratching up the dirt and hauling it out. When he reached five feet deep at the edge and six feet deep in the center, he stepped back to look it over. Just about right. Don't need to get it too deep, just enough so the sun don't get it too hot in the summer. Willow sprouts at the edge would help keep the water cooler. Maybe get some pond lilies. They'd help a bunch.

Now for the next step. From south of the barn, he pitched last year's spoiled hay into the wagon and hauled it to the site of the hole, spreading it over the bottom of the pit. Then for the water.

He pieced together all his hoses and strung the resulting long tube from his freshly-dug pit to the clear running water of Rock Creek. Siphoning the water through the hose, he trained the flow down into the square pit.

Now to wait. He stood for a long moment surveying with satisfaction the tiny stream of water spreading out under the straw.

Then Cal stepped off fifty feet to the west of the pit and marked off another rectangle, thirty feet wide and fifty feet long. First thing in the morning, he'd hitch up that long-tooth harrow and hope the weather held.

11

It was mid-February, and the babies were now four months old. Their wrinkled, red skin had changed to a creamy tan, and their smoky blue eyes had turned into dark chocolate drops. The spikes of fine baby hair could now be combed into curls.

The after-bath powder and comb session had become routine, the babies chuckling, grinning and waving their arms with pleasure. *Irena, you ought'a be here to see these babies! You done good! That Lucy, she got eyes like Cal, but the way she looks out of 'em, that's just like you.*

And they were becoming themselves, each tiny girl developing her own ways. Maggie always reached for the powder can and fussed when she couldn't have it. But the powder always made Lucy sneeze, no matter how careful Marybeth was.

When she picked up little Lottie, the baby always reached her hand toward Marybeth's nose. Often, she managed a lopsided grin... Irena's grin. *Lookie at that, Irena! Time she gets good at that grin, she'll likely look like you did when you were jokin' me.*

It was strange, somehow. The babies were no longer three little creatures, like three puppies in a litter. Their eyes were alike, yet different. A twinkle, a sideways look, or a crinkle at the corners.

They were beginning to look like little girls. It seemed strange and surprising, as though she had expected them to remain miniature dolls forever.

The cradle box became too small. Cal eased Lottie's arms aside to make room for Maggie. Then Lucy's waving arms whacked Maggie in the face, and Maggie whimpered.

The next day, Cal made two more boxes. The three boxes would no longer fit on the warming oven, nor did they need the heat. The boxes now occupied half the kitchen table.

Cal put the babies on the big bed on their tummies and put the new blue and red ball in front of them. Lottie turned her head sideways to squint at the ball. Maggie reached a tiny arm tentatively in the direction of the toy. Lucy just stared, the pupils of her chocolate-drop eyes pulling together in their intensity. A stream of saliva drooled down her chin as she struggled to lift her head higher for a better look.

They stayed awake more, now, gurgling and playing with the toes of their upraised feet, or the toes of each other. They demanded more time. Marybeth watched them and sighed long sighs of frustration. Irena shouldn't have gone and left these babies, but maybe it had been her fault and not Irena's. She should have known more of what to do for her.

Then, on the third week of February, a large skein of geese flew over, honking their spring chorus, heading north. The wavering "V" of the skein forged ahead, the sound of their conversation drifting down to earth with a promise of the coming spring.

The lonesome sound of the geese pulled at Marybeth's heart, stirring its heaviness with their cries. She stepped out into the yard and looked up, watching them as they passed overhead. When they were gone, tears from deep within her filled her eyes. She continued to look up into the empty sky.

As the first tear spilled from her eye and trickled down her cheek, she lifted her hands to her face, rubbing furiously. *Marybeth, what's going on with you? Standing here with tears, and you with things needing to be done!*

But still she stood, staring out in the direction of the river... staring toward the tinges of green that showed on the tops of the willows and cottonwoods. Staring toward the pale, blue peak of Five Mile Hill, raising its rocky slopes beyond the town. Staring toward the bell tower of the church, extending above the still-leafless trees of the city.

Down on the streets of River Bend, there were people. They would say to her, "Good morning, Marybeth. Nice day, ain't it?" She would agree that it was a nice day, and she would be comforted. She would stop in at the Mercantile to look at the ribbons or buttons. She would hum to herself as she climbed the hill to go back home.

She sighed again. She didn't want to cook any food. The diapers, now whipped dry in the wind, called to her to be taken down, but she refused to answer. They were dry and ready to be folded, but she turned away. Marybeth was tired of talking to diapers.

She walked out to the road and began to climb up Rock Mountain. The chill of the spring air nibbled at her nose, ears and fingers.

A male cardinal was poised on a wild plum bush and did not move as she passed by. His mate was in a nearby blackjack oak, searching for the perfect nest site.

A flash of blue caught her eyes. In a nearby cedar, a pair of bluebirds tweeted and twittered, fluttering their wings. The feelings of spring stirred in their blood, their wings and their voices. Spring meant a nest. It meant eggs... and babies... and a summer of work.

Green sprigs of growth popping up through the dead winter weeds caught her attention. Fresh, green tips of poke sallet. A true sign of spring. There was not enough yet to make a meal, but poke sallet grew fast, and there soon would be. Maybe three days.

Marybeth sighed and turned around. Time to go back. The nest... the babies... the work. Diapers had to be folded, and food must be cooked.

She gathered watercress from the edges of Rock Creek and carried it, dripping, with both hands extended before her to keep her dress dry. From the shed, she picked up a slab of bacon and a quart jar of plums.

She sliced three strips of bacon into the iron skillet, browning them to crispness. In another skillet, she diced onions and potatoes, and then cubed the ham. She stirred up a pan of drop biscuit batter, filling the seasoned pan. With the remaining batter, she created a topping for a plum cobbler by adding butter, sugar and cinnamon. The biscuits and the plum cobbler were popped into the oven. The potatoes and onions were tender and brown, so she tossed in the ham cubes.

Into the crumbled bacon and grease, she broke the tender, crisp, peppery watercress, tossing it lightly to coat every sprig with flavor. At that exact moment, the biscuits were browned, the bubbling plum juice had thickened, and the ham cubes were juicy and lightly browned. The meal had taken thirty minutes, during which time she had folded the diapers and added a pail of water to the stove reservoir to heat.

The aroma of food brought Cal from whatever he was doing to wash up for supper.

The food was tasty and perfectly done, but then, it always was. Marybeth gave the food no thought as she ate. She had more important things on her mind.

"Cal, it's gettin' to be feelin' like I need to get out some. I was thinkin' to go down to the Tuesday Sewing Circle next Tuesday. Seems like it'd do me good."

"Reckon so."

"Only thing is, that's the day you go to Jacksonville with the fish. I wonder, could you go on another day, one time?"

"Be no problem," Cal agreed. "Likely be a good thing for you, gettin' out and all. Didn't ever mean for you to be tied here. Helpin' out the way you do. Laura won't be goin' in next time, and that'd be a good thing to do."

Marybeth sighed. "Just feelin' a little spring restlessness, likely. Makes a person want to do whatever it is he ain't been doin'."

Cal nodded. "Natural feelin', wantin' to be there with other ladies. Be no problem with the fish. Folks in Jacksonville gonna want fish whatever time they can get 'em. One day'd be good as the next."

So Cal seined up the fish into a holding net and set out for the city early on Monday morning. Loafers were already gathered at the livery stable.

"Hey, I was thinkin' it was Monday, but there I see Cal Boudreau goin' by with his fish, headed for the city."

"But it is Monday. It ain't Tuesday."

"Then what's he doin', goin' today?"

"Beats me."

"I reckon nothin' was ever said that he had to go on any one particular day."

"That Cal sure knows how to get the most out'a a team and wagon. Got them horses on the go all the time."

"Keeps 'em in good shape, though, you'd have to say."

"Got 'em haulin' dirt when they ain't haulin' fish. Most horses get the winter to rest up."

"The wife dropped by to see them babies t'other day. Says they're growin' like persimmon sprouts. 'Course, they got a way to go, startin' out so little."

"Marybeth still there, helpin' out?"

"I 'speck so. Leastwise, I didn't see no babies in the wagon with him."

"Anybody ever figure what them square holes he's makin' is for?"

"Nope. Ain't seen 'im around to ask."

"Likely wouldn't get a straight, flat-out answer if you did ask."

Marybeth was standing before the kitchen window with her coffee cup in her hand when one of the babies whimpered. It was Lottie. Marybeth lifted her from the bed. "Well, Miss Lottie, what was it you wanted to say to me? You're sayin' you're wet? Well, I should say you are!"

The baby squealed and lunged toward Marybeth's face, patting her wet, drooled-on hands against Marybeth's cheeks. Her happy squeal alerted the others, eager to join in the fun.

"I only got two hands," she told the noisy trio as she transferred them, one at a time, to the big bed for diaper changes.

Oh, Irena, you should see your babies! A body'd need six hands to take care of 'em proper! Gonna be a sight to see when they start a'crawlin'. Likely, they'll be goin' three ways.

Then she forced herself to remember Irena would not be seeing them crawl. She sighed deeply and held back the tears that she had no time to shed.

She put the red and blue ball on the bed in front of Lucy. The baby waved a hand at the ball, her tiny fist bumping it against Maggie. Surprised at her accomplishment, she momentarily pulled her pupils into their cross-eyed eagerness. Maggie crowed with pleasure as the ball bumped against her nose. Lottie squealed, and Lucy looked up at Marybeth, her eyes looking straight forward again.

The sound of the babies aroused her loneliness, and her eyes began to blur. *Oh, Irena, I can't do this for you. I shared my lunch with you, and I held up the fence wire so you could get through. I helped you bandage your cuts and bruises, and I helped can your tomatoes. But, Irena, I can't take care of these babies for you. You had no right to ask me to.*

She lay across the bed, her head in her arms, and sobbed. Her tears soaked the quilt, and her sobs shook the bed.

Why did you go? I know it's my fault not knowin' what to do for you, but you might'a helped me. You listened to the angel and wouldn't eat and get well. Oh, Irena, I'm so sorry for you, and I'm even sorrier for me!

The sound of her heartbroken sobs alarmed the babies on the bed beside her, and they began to howl.

No, Irena, I can't be lookin' after your babies. They ain't my babies, and it ain't gonna bring you back. It ain't fair to hold me to a promise I made not knowin' what you was fixin' to let happen.

She paused between sobs, but the babies cried on.

"Oh, you poor little things! Got nobody but a big bawl-baby here to take care of you. We got'a find us somethin' fun to do."

At the sight of her smile, they began to be quiet, hiccupping and staring at her with quivering chins. Marybeth grabbed up one of the cradle boxes and placed Lottie in a sitting position in one corner and the other two in other corners. In their laps she plopped a pillow, adjusting it around them, to hold them up in a sitting position. She tossed the ball lightly onto the pillow. Maggie squealed. Tiny fists reached out to pat the ball.

Picking up the box, she carried it out to the yard, setting it down on the hard clay of the newly built-up yard. A crisp breeze blew, but the babies were snug in their box. She sat on the ground beside them, and the little dog came bouncing over to sniff at the babies. She sat there with the sun on her back, warm for late February. Signs of spring were everywhere. She circled her knees with her arms and leaned forward, and Yoyo's tongue was warm against her arm.

Lottie squealed. Marybeth knew without looking that it was Lottie. She didn't know how she knew; she just did. She looked up and saw Maggie was leaning forward, sleepily, and Lucy was pressing her face against the ball, trying to suck.

"You ladies must be tired and hungry. Let's go eat."

Fed and put down for their naps, the babies drowsed, and Marybeth eased away and out the door. Baked sweet potatoes would be good for supper. And green beans. Two large catfish circled each other in the big wooden tub. Cal had brought up two of his catch. She stood by the kitchen door, admiring the grace of the swimming fish. Perfect specimens. It was no wonder the ladies of Jacksonville were happy to get them.

Then a piercing scream of pain sounded from the kitchen. In a second, Marybeth was back inside the house. Lucy! An open diaper pin? She grabbed the baby from her box and hugged her to her own shoulder. Rumbling up from the tiny stomach came a resounding burp, bringing up a large portion of what she had just eaten. Marybeth felt the warmth and moisture on her shoulder and down her back.

She wiped Lucy's tiny face clean, and the black eyes drooped sleepily as Marybeth replaced her into her box and went to change her dress.

She washed diapers and a few other things, and the day passed. The winter sun had set, and there was no Cal returning from Jacksonville. She ate and fed the babies, setting Cal's food inside the warming oven so she could clean the kitchen. He had still not come when she finally went to bed.

The babies woke her at midnight, whimpering hungrily. As she fed them, she saw, there on the table, three tiny lace sunbonnets and a box of candy. Store-bought candy. The picture on the box showed chocolate with creamy white filling. A red cherry was tucked into the white center.

Holding the bottle with one hand, she opened the box. The sweetness of the creamy center and the strong chocolate flavor blended with the sharpness of the cherry, causing a warmth to flow into her feet and legs. She ate another.

With the babies fed and asleep, she went back to bed, lying there with wide open eyes, thinking of the candy. With a sigh of having lost a mental battle, she got up and got the candy box, putting it beside her on the bed in the dark room. Before finally getting to sleep, she had eaten half the candy.

She ate most of the rest of the candy while cooking eggs, ham and biscuits for Cal's breakfast. Cal did not mention the candy. "You needin' to have the wagon to go down to the church?"

"Reckon not, Cal. Been thinkin' the walk in the air'd do me good. Seems there ain't much wind."

Cal nodded.

The sun was shining when she left the house. Thoughts crowded in on her, but she pushed them away. Thinking was too hard. She'd do it later. She crossed the swinging bridge and walked on to Main Street. As Rock Creek Road crossed Main Street and angled east, it became

Church Street. A quarter mile past the crossroad stood the church… the whiteness of its steeple sparkling in the sun.

Clustered around the building were wagons and buggies and horses of all sizes and colors, waiting patiently. Children, old enough to be outside alone and too young for school, played together on the church steps. Wisps of smoke arose from the chimney and joined themselves to the drifts of fine clouds. More geese went honking overhead. They were in a straight line, instead of a "V", as they prepared to settle on the river to feed. Likely come down the valley from past Jacksonville.

She climbed the steps and went in.

"Oh, lookie! There's Marybeth!"

"Wonderful! Come on in here, girl."

"Sit over here. There you go. Maisie ain't gonna make it today, so you can take her place."

"It's been such a long time!"

"How've you been?"

"How're the babies?"

Marybeth smiled at the circle of warm friendliness, not bothering to answer individual questions. There would be time enough for talk as the morning wore on. Love and friendliness flowed around her, wrapping her as warmly as a goose down quilt.

Jane Ann McCrey brought her a cup of steaming tea. Ina Mae McCann moved over a little to give her more elbowroom to quilt her block. Friends and warmth and something to do… that was what she had needed. Conversation began to weave its web around the ladies, drawing them together.

"Glad to see that sun. I was a'gettin' tired of wet overalls and diapers all over the kitchen."

"Me, too. See them geese a'goin' over?"

"Sure did. Spring's just around the corner."

"For sure."

"Be time to break the garden and get the spinach and peas in."

"I'm feelin' hungry for the first mess'a poke sallet."

Marybeth remembered the sprigs of green along the garden fence. "Noticed poke was up in Cal's fence row."

"Up at your house? On Rock Creek?"

"No, it was by Cal's fence. Seems to be later comin' up at my house, up on the hill. Maybe the chill wind holds it back."

"Marybeth, I 'speck you could tell us somethin' we been wonderin'."

"What's that?"

"Them square holes Cal's diggin' down towards the river. Two of 'em, side by side. Drivin' the men folks crazy, wonderin' what they'd be for."

"Oh."

"Don't you know?"

Marybeth shook her head. "Wouldn't know why I'd know. Wasn't none of my business. The fellows wantin' to know, they could ask Cal. That's what I'd have to do to find out," Marybeth looked up to see a circle of somewhat puzzled faces watching her. She sought to soften her reply, "Just never thought to ask, bein' busy as I am, most days."

"You'd be busy, all right."

Jane Ann asked, "How are the babies? Haven't had trouble with colds gettin' at 'em?"

Marybeth shook her head. "Been keepin' 'em in, mostly. Bein' so little, I'd be afraid'a colds."

Someone else had a question. "How do you tell 'em apart? I'd never know which was which."

"Sure you would. They're all different, like the way their smile is or the look out'a their eyes. Or the way they move their hands."

The ladies thought about the answer. Since they had never had triplets, it was all very interesting.

Then Eleanor Crocker thought of something. "Marybeth, I cut somethin' out'a the paper you might like. I'd like it myself if I had a baby girl. Maybe next time. But I can bring it. It's a pattern to the prettiest little crocheted bonnet a body ever saw. It'd be pretty as a picture on your little girls."

Marybeth looked at Eleanor in surprise. "I'd thank you, Eleanor. If I ever have me a little girl, I'd likely try to make it up."

"But you got those three girls, now!"

Marybeth stared in disbelief. "Those babies I take care of ain't my babies. I thought you all knew that. They're Irena and Cal's babies. I been puzzled at the things you say, talkin' like Cal and them babies was mine. I'm takin' care of 'em till Cal can get some help."

Silence settled on circle of ladies.

"But, Marybeth, we didn't mean nothin'...."

Marybeth pushed back her chair. "Sorry, but I ain't feelin' too good. Think I need to be gettin' on..." With that, she secured her needle into the block she was quilting and arose with dignity, leaving the circle.

"Marybeth...?"

"I got'a go," she told them firmly. And she did.

Outside the church she turned and went over toward the cemetery. Headstones in ancient shades of gray and cream, many were so old they leaned over in various directions. Some were small, simple and square, and others were ornate with carvings.

The newest grave had no headstone, as yet. Only a metal marker proclaimed the name of Irena Boudreau. The rough, cloddy clay had weathered through the winter to a smooth finish. A few tentative blades of early grass had bravely sprouted on the mound.

Marybeth picked her way among the graves, stooping down beside the newest one. She lowered herself to the damp ground. *Oh, Irena, why did you have to go?*

She heard a sound beside her and looked up to see Granny Nelson settle herself on a solid-looking headstone deeply carved with lilies. The old woman steadied herself with her two walking sticks and sighed loudly.

"Phewww, times I think I ain't gonna make it up to this headstone to rest and get the strength to go on. Always like to sit here a minute or two. You been all right, Marybeth?"

Marybeth smiled a reply. She didn't trust her voice.

Granny Nelson continued, "Lookin' at you makes me think you could make use of a mite'a rest yourself. You gettin' any sleep from them babies?"

"Some. They sleep two hours at a time, right along, now."

Granny nodded. "Them little 'ens, takes 'em a mite longer to sleep of a night."

They sat in silence for a while. "Marybeth, I been meanin' to ask you somethin' and just hadn't been up to gettin' over there. What I wanted to know was, what are you doin' up at Cal's house?"

"Huh?"

"Just wondered what you was doin' up there."

Marybeth stared in puzzlement. Did Granny Nelson forget about Irena? Did she forget the night she spent talking with herself and Cal before the funeral? And the babies, did she forget about them? Well, she was old, and likely it slipped her mind.

"Well, Granny," she began kindly, "I been takin' care of the babies. You know, the three little girls."

"Whose babies are they?"

"Why, they're Irena's babies."

"When's Irena gonna take over and let you get some rest?"

"Huh? Don't you remember, Granny? Irena died most five months back."

"Oh, then she won't be comin' back. Whose babies are they, now?"

Marybeth hesitated. "Well, they're Cal's...."

"Right you are. He been after you to stay and take care of them babies for him, huh?"

"No, I reckon not."

"Then how come you to be there?"

"Well, Granny, the babies need someone."

"You gonna stay forever?"

"Course not. I'm just stayin' till he gets someone to take care of 'em. He's just one man. Can't do it all by himself."

"He got someone in mind right now?" Granny demanded mercilessly.

"Ain't said nothin' about it," Marybeth admitted.

Granny shifted her back into a more comfortable position. "Marybeth, you cook good meals for Cal, don't you?"

"No, Granny. I cook for me the things I like. Cal eats it 'cause that's what's there."

Another pause, then, "Man like Cal, he don't say too much about things, does he?"

Marybeth thought a minute, then nodded. "Cal don't waste no words."

Squirrels raced around overhead in the tall oak trees. It was time for spring mating and nest-making. And babies. And a lot of work, feeding the babies... after all, it was spring.

Granny continued. "Marybeth, I want to ask you to put yourself in Cal's place. Here he is, not likin' trouble but finds he got himself a lot of it. 'Afore he has a chance to decide how to tackle it, along comes an answer. Would he be one to throw away that answer and go lookin' for another one?"

"Well, I...."

"Put it like this. You think you'd ever hear Cal say, 'Marybeth, you got'a leave the babies now, 'cause I got someone else to take over, lookin' after 'em for me.' Think Cal might say that?"

"No, Granny, I don't reckon he would."

"Then it'd be up to you, wouldn't it? You'd need to say, 'Cal, it's time for me to be goin' on, now. I got another month, though, 'afore I have to go. That'd give you a chance to get things worked out and get you some help.' That'd be the fair way, not just walkin' out."

"But Granny, where at would he find help like he'd need?"

Granny paused to consider her reply. "You told me them babies was Cal's babies. That'd make the problem of takin' care of 'em to be Cal's, too, wouldn't you be sayin'?"

"Reckon so, but...."

"Marybeth, honey, I ain't here a'tryin' to say what you been doin' wasn't a wonderful thing, you workin' yourself to a nub doin' your Christian duty. For sure now, the Good Lord got Himself a plan, and you usin' up your strength on babies that ain't your babies, that ain't part'a His permanent plan.

"Happen, at times, folks find themselves all wound up inside a problem so tight they can't get loose to see the answer comin' at 'em. Need to stand aside to get a better look."

"But, Granny, there's another thing you don't know."

"What'd that be?"

"It's all my fault. I got'a do what I can, it bein' my fault."

"Your fault?"

Marybeth unsuccessfully fought against the tears. They filled her eyes, and she brushed them aside impatiently.

"I ain't told nobody else. Not even Cal, bein' so ashamed. When them babies was born, bein' so tiny and born early, I got scared. That middle'n didn't breathe till I breathed in her mouth. Cal wasn't there to help, and I did my best for the babies, but I didn't have no time to see to Irena. There could'a been somethin' I could'a done."

Granny nodded. "I can see how you likely thought you was strong as the Good Lord Himself."

"Huh? But, Granny, I...."

"The Good Lord, child, He'd be the one to decide if someone was to live or not. He let that girl live long enough for her to say last words to you. Wasn't you tellin' me that she was talkin' with an angel? Well, don't you reckon she'd be happy there with the angel and thinkin' her Cal had ought'a be free to find a mama for his little girls? Ain't no way he can do that with you there."

Marybeth sniffed and wiped the tears away.

"You see, you thinkin' it was up to you if Irena lived or died, that'd mean you was thinkin' you was in the Good Lord's place... that bein' what He does. A body that does the best she can, like you done, got no fault on her at all. Irena was such a little thing, the babies must'a just fair took all the life out'a her, wouldn't you say?"

"But, Granny, she made me promise...."

"Marybeth, honey, there ain't no promise lasts t'other side of the grave. The person that goes don't know how it is for those left behind. Decisions affectin' the life of the livin', they got'a be made by those still alive." Granny Nelson leaned forward and placed her walking sticks solidly on the ground. Leaning forward, she was able to get to her feet.

"Reckon I'd best get on in there 'afore they get that old quilt done without me. Now, honey, you go on home now and think about my words."

Marybeth watched as Granny hobbled off in the direction of the church, then she left the cemetery and walked down Main Street to the Mercantile. Outside the door she stopped, not being able to remember anything that she wanted to see inside the store. She turned and came back to the swinging bridge and Rock Creek Road.

Cal registered no surprise that she was back so early. He sat at the kitchen table with the parts of a rope pulley spread out on a towel. Oil can in hand, he commented, "Needed to get this pulley oiled up. Got'a butcher that hog 'afore the weather gets too hot." But as he spoke, he gathered the pulley parts and the array of other tools, preparing to return to the shed.

Marybeth picked up the candy box and ate the remaining four pieces. "Cal, you need to kill a chicken, if you can. Thought I would cook up a mess of dumpling."

"Could do that," he agreed, and he was gone.

On Wednesday, Cal was up before daylight, standing before the second square hole. Another foot and it would be deep enough.

The first hole was brimming full of water, so he cut off the siphon, leaving the hose in place.

He opened the burlap bag of clover seed he had bought in Jacksonville and poured a bucket full. By criss-crossing the former cotton field, he was able to broadcast the seed thickly and evenly over the damp soil. With the walling up of Rock Creek, the next rain would likely stay in the creek bed and not overflow the field, washing his seed down to the river.

Clover plants were good for restoring nitrogen to the soil, but even better, their blooms attracted bees and grasshoppers as well as other insects. It was necessary to his plan to have many insects.

Carl Morgan, from three farms to the west, had a good crop of pecan seedling on his calf pasture. Told Cal he could have all he wanted before they had to be rooted out, so as not to disturb the grass. Cal had dug a bundle of them. All around the square pond, he set the little two-foot-high trees. Also around the second pond he put trees, as well as the marked-off squares for two more ponds. Shade along the edge of the bank would help the success of his plan for the ponds.

Also, don't little girls like pecan nuts to put in candy and cookies? Didn't it take five to seven years for trees to start bearing? In truth, very good timing!

With the clover planted and the nut trees set in the ground, Cal again hitched his horses to the long-toothed harrow. Back and forth, this way and that, and the hole became deeper. He was beginning to feel a pressure of time.

Here it was, late February, and none of next year's stove wood had been cut. And there was the table garden. March was late for the first breaking. Spinach and peas should be already in the ground. Needed to get at it.

One big thing was in his favor, and it was a very big thing. There would be no cotton planted down on the low north forty. No cotton to plow, to chop or pick, or to watch dry up. That would help on the time he needed for his plan.

Another thing was that there'd be only half as much corn this year. Only enough for the table and the animals, and maybe a little for the pond. It'd be a help in the winter for the pond to have extra grain to toss in, and the success of the pond was of utmost importance.

But then, he'd need more peanuts. Roasted, ground peanuts mixed with honey was good on biscuits. The little girls would like that and, being a year old and more by then, they'd likely be big enough to eat some.

He'd need to make cuttings from the plum and huckleberry bushes. He could make use of a lot of them as the girls got older. And goats. Maybe he'd keep one cow to provide beef calves, but mostly he'd have goats. He'd need to get a billy at the auction so as not to confuse the bloodline when he raised his own. The little billy he had now, it could be the start of a swap. Little girls needed milk to grow strong. Maybe four or five nannies would be right for a continuous supply.

Eggs. Already the girls ate eggs, thanks to Marybeth's good idea. Likely, eggs was the saving of them, truth be told. And there'd be ducks for the ponds. And more eggs.

As he hauled the dirt from the hole, he searched his mind. What else was required to raise three little girls?

The second pond was now deep enough and ready for the spoiled hay to start the breeding of insects, and he could stretch the hose now to fill it up. It would take at least four days to fill, but that was all right.

While the second pond was filling, Cal took the fine-meshed seine to the river. Minnows, crawfish and small turtles were dredged up and put in the washtubs of water to be poured into the first pond. Four trips, eight tubs full, and that was all the time he could spare for the ponds just now. Two more weeks, and the catfish could be added.

If only the days were longer, then he might be able to catch up on what he had to do. The sense of urgency oppressed him.

Marybeth set a platter of crisply fried catfish on the table beside the hush puppies and potato salad, thick with eggs. From the warming oven she took the whipped turnips, yellow with puddles of melted butter. The gingerbread muffins were left in the oven to stay warm.

Cal was washing up. He always sensed when the food was ready.

Marybeth began bravely. "Cal, I got'a say somethin'. Gettin' on into spring and warm weather now, and I got'a get on with what I'm gonna do. I wanted to tell you so's you could get to makin' plans. I won't be leavin' till the first of April. Figured that'd give you time... for the wood cuttin' and all."

Cal nodded. "That'd be for the best. You done gave more'n a body'd expect to get. I know I got you to thank for them little girls bein' alive, and there ain't no words to fit the importance'a that. Come April, I'll be ready to handle it on my own."

Marybeth was doubtful. She wanted to say, "Cal, pay me no mind. I didn't mean what I just said." But she didn't say it. She was brave. She would no longer be hiding in the middle of someone else's problem. She buttered a muffin and fed it to Yoyo.

Cal continued as he ate. "Reckon I'll need to make two trips a week to Jacksonville. Got to bring in things I'll need for the summer."

Marybeth did not respond. He'd do whatever he had to do. It was no bother of hers.

She'd tell Mama she was ready now to learn what she could and to help her with the birthing of the community. She could clean up and care for the babies and still ride away without the leaving of the babies pulling a hole in her heart. She could do that.

Mama was right, and she'd tell her so. She'd look at the books of Dr. Midland's, the ones that Laura borrowed, and likely learn a little more. Could be that Laura had learned things she could tell her.

Then she'd need some new dresses, maybe about three. She'd need a horse and buggy if she was going to work on her own, like mama said. Then she'd need a basket. No, she didn't want a basket. She'd get that tiny suitcase she saw in the Five and Dime over in Jacksonville. That's what she'd do. By the first of April, she'd be ready to get started.

After supper, Cal lit the lantern and picked up his chopping ax. Marybeth saw the wavering path of light the lantern created as Cal made his way up into the woodlot. She could still hear the sound of the chopping as she drifted into sleep.

The woodlot was quiet at one o'clock when the babies woke her up for their feeding. At daybreak, however, the sound of the ax could again be heard.

After breakfast, Cal stepped off the dimension of the new room he planned at the north side of the house. He'd add a twelve-foot wide addition to the length of the house, part of it being for his own bedroom, but most of it would be for the girls. The sleeping loft above the kitchen would make a warm place for them to play in cold weather. He'd make the new addition with logs, and he had them a'plenty, just for the cutting.

Taking the shovel to the persimmon grove above the garden, he lifted two dozen small trees that he set in the ground below the pond. The dried persimmons made very good candy and could be used to sweeten pumpkin for pies and apples for cakes. Seeds and any leftover persimmon fruit were good for fattening out pigs.

He marked off the extension of the strawberry patch, and lifted rooted runners to set in the new site. Next year's strawberries were now assured.

He measured the wagon and decided he could fit six metal washtubs in it. The three hours from the river in River Bend to Jacksonville would be impossible to make in the summer without keeping the fish in water. In addition, fish so fresh they were alive and swimming, they would bring more money and likely sell faster.

The first trip to Jacksonville, he brought back the metal tubs, also 200 baby chicks and 100 baby ducks. The next trip produced a thirty-foot-wide mesh dredging seine and a toy wagon, one big enough to carry a cradle box. Likely he'd want to take the girls outside on a sunny afternoon.

By now the old cotton patch was covered with a fine, green haze of tiny clover plants, and the second pond was filled to the brim.

With the wide seine, Cal dredged up more than fifty large, breeding-size catfish and loosed them in the first pond. Then he brought up twelve tubs of minnows and crawfish for the second pond. Needed to let it get started.

In the shed, Cal built a small wooden platform the size of a kitchen table. To each corner, he attached a long rope. The platform was hauled down to the first pond and set afloat in the water, and the four ropes were attached to the four corners of the bank so the platform would float in the center of the pond and not drift to the edge. On the platform he had secured a kerosene lantern. The sun was sinking and dusk was settling in, so this might be a good time to see how well the lantern idea worked out, so he lit it.

The lantern on the platform reflected off the water in golden streams. Two moths were attracted by the light and circled the lantern. They were joined by several other insects of unidentifiable origin…. circling, dipping and fluttering as they surrounded the lantern.

One of the moths, exhausted at last, dipped too far and landed in the water, its fluttering wings making a circle of ripples. In an instant, the moth was gone, destined to become part of a big catfish.

Marybeth, watching from the yard, was suddenly consumed with curiosity, so she walked down to the pond.

"What you got in the pond? How come the lantern on the water?"

"Got catfish in there."

"From the river?"

"Yep. Got more'n fifty of 'em in there right now. Expect to have maybe 500. Come spawnin' season, gonna have baby catfish in there thicker'n flies at a picnic. Then I'll seine out the big fish and sell 'em."

"Hmmmm. What they gonna get to eat, all penned up in there?"

"Watch!"

Another of the moths fluttered too close to the water and a spiral of ripples told them a catfish broke surface and snatched the insect from the air.

Cal continued, "Think about the grasshoppers in the summer daytime. Then a lantern settin' out here, lighted all night, attractin' who knows what all from the air. Be pretty good for feedin' them fish, wouldn't you think? Clover comin' up all over, that'll attract bees, and some of them'll find their way to the water."

"Think that'll feed 500 fish?"

"It'll help a sight. 'Course, winter'll call for some grain, like leftover corn, kafir and sorghum."

"These fish gonna taste as good as fish from the river?"

"Better. Usin' Rock Creek water and the lanterns, these fish don't have to do nothin' to stay alive, just lay on the bottom and wait for food. Gonna be fat and sassy in no time. I'm thinkin' up a way to have the horses pull the seine full of fish to the bank; it'll be so heavy."

"Hmmmm."

Then it was the second week of March. Marybeth turned out the house completely, as any River Bend woman would do in their spring house-cleaning. She washed and ironed the curtains and scrubbed the windows inside and out.

She cleaned and polished the cookstove and the wash kettle. Some of Irena's dresses still hung in the closet, so she put them in a box and took it to the loft. They would be good for the time the girls wanted to play "dress up".

Then it was the third week of March. Cal made three trips to Jacksonville that week, and the only things he brought home were a pink comb and brush set and a small rubber doll with its clothes molded on, and painted in bright colors. The girls took turns chewing on the doll's fingers and toes.

Marybeth clipped Yoyo's hair for summer cooling and filled the little dog's bed mattress with fresh, young walnut leaves to keep down the fleas and ticks.

She sorted among the winter vegetables still in the shed, throwing out those past use and cleaning up the remainder. It would be time for fresh ones soon. Already, the green shoots of turnips showed in the garden. Another week and she could cook a mess of greens.

Then it got to be the last week of March.

Marybeth washed all the quilts, putting away the heaviest of them for the summer. She sprinkled mothballs liberally among the folds to keep out insects and packed them in a trunk in the hayloft. She inventoried all the fruit jars she had emptied during the winter and rinsed them out, grouping them by size and possible use for whoever it was that would be canning the summer produce.

Then Cal made the last trip to Jacksonville. It was a trip that Laura rode along, and hours before he was expected back, Laura came driving into the yard in a two-seated buggy behind a black pony with white blaze and socks.

"It's Cal's," Laura explained. "Said he'd need somethin' to keep the girls in out'a the weather. He's coming' on behind. Said whenever you or me needed to make the trip into town or anywhere, we could take this."

The sisters circled the buggy, admiring its shiny silver trim and bright red wheels. Cal was right; he was going to need it sooner or later.

All too soon, it was the first day of April. Laura had taken a lot of Marybeth's things home during the last visits, and now that it was time to leave, she was surprised at the small size made by her last bag of possessions.

She took one last look at the babies, sleeping soundly. Lottie with little squench marks on her cheek where she lay against her own tiny hand and Maggie with the tip of her tongue showing between pink lips. Lucy's thumb had slid from her mouth, but her lips were still parted, drool still shiny on her rosy cheek.

Cal stood awkwardly by the door. "Wish't you'd let me take you home in the buggy."

"No, thanks. It's a nice day to walk."

"I want to say better words to thank you, but I'm not good with them."

"That's all right. I know." She turned quickly away and shut the door softly behind her.

She walked down Rock Creek Road as if in a dream. The river and the town were just ahead, but she turned to climb the hill to her mother's house, now her own house again. *This was truly the right thing to do,* she argued with herself. *I got the right to live my own life.*

Her mother was at home. "So you come back, huh? Finally come to your senses and through wastin' your life on other folks' problems. Well, you're lucky to have a place you can come home to."

Mama was right. She was lucky.

Laura watched in silence.

Marybeth went to her bedroom. It seemed unfamiliar, as though she had been away for many years. She put away the few things she carried and lay down across the bed. Nobody called to her. Nobody needed her, so she stayed there on the bed and looked at the ceiling and then at nothing. Tomorrow, she would look at Laura's book, whichever one she now had borrowed.

But what would she do today? There were the dresses she'd need, and she just as well get started on them.

"Laura, I'm thinkin' on walkin' down to the Mercantile. You goin' along?"

"Sure thing."

The sisters walked down the hill in silence for a while, then Laura spoke.

"Gettin' you a new dress for Easter Sunday?"

"Easter? Yeah, sure. It's for Easter. Been needin' me a new summer dress."

They reached Rock Creek Road and turned toward the river. Marybeth did not look toward the left where she would have seen the two square ponds and the tiny pecan trees recently planted around them. The sisters did not hurry. Why hurry? No one was waiting for them anywhere, and no one needed them. Particularly.

Marybeth looked at all the dress fabric and finally settled on a pink, dotted swiss with double dots, a good summer color. White buttons would be placed close together down the front. That was a lot of buttonholes to make, but she would have plenty of time. Now.

She chose a ball of white crochet thread for the collar. She'd make it extra wide and lacy to look summery and cool.

A hat? No, she really didn't like the feel of hats. She'd just get combs with shiny sets. No, the ones with the tiny pearls would look better with the double dots. She took two of the decorated combs.

Laura was busy across the store, examining a small grinder with different grinding plates to make the finished product larger or smaller. She tested the gears, watching them with fascination as they meshed. Marybeth could hear the grind of the handle as her sister turned it.

They climbed the hill again.

Marybeth spread the pink fabric across her bed and pinned her pattern to it. There was no need to hurry. This was all she had to do.

12

Easter Sunday dawned a picture book of a day. Early yellow daffodils dotted every yard, and the spires of golden forsythia reached up toward a sky of forget-me-not blue. Tiny leaves, shiny in their newness, fringed the tops of the trees. New grass covered the ground.

As was the Easter custom, the church bells had been rung at the first ray of sunrise, heralding the celebration of the risen Christ.

The Maisone ladies in their buggy came jiggling down the half-mile of wagon trail to Rock Creek Road. They turned right, crossing the swinging bridge, and proceeded across Main Street. Past the crossroads, they rode a quarter of a mile up Church Street.

Many buggies and wagons were clustered around the church, horses snorting, switching flies and shaking their harnesses in boredom. The Maisone buggy was inserted among them.

Martha Maisone, in her best Sunday dress, was first to enter the church. The building was almost full, but seeing a space near the front, she led her daughters down the aisle.

Laura came behind her, her light blue taffeta skirt whispering as it moved with her walk. Her snowwhite shirtwaist had many pleats down the front, each of them edged in delicate sky blue lace. Her shiny, black hair had been french braided, starting at the crown of her head, and was set off with a blue taffeta bow at the neck. Below the bow, black waves of hair cascaded down over the white shirtwaist, all the way down to the belt of her blue skirt. She sat down beside her mother.

Behind her came Marybeth in her pink, double-dotted swiss dress with its tiny, white buttons. The dress molded itself to her back and arms, the fitted sleeves gathering lightly at the shoulder and the wrist. Front pleats fell softly from the shoulder to the very low waist. A wide belt circled the hips below the pleats, cinching the fullness of the skirt, itself edged with white, hand-crocheted lace.

Tiny buttons, hardly an inch apart, marched down the front between the center pleats, snug in their perfectly-made button holes.

The white crocheted collar was wide, spreading to the edge of her shoulders and bordered with roses, their white lace petals starched crisply to stand out realistically. A tiny bow of shiny white ribbon was tied just under her chin.

Marybeth's black hair was arranged with three large sausage curls pinned securely across the top of her head. A braid wound around the curls holding them together like a crown of ebony. The pearl combs brought up the back, holding stray wisps of hair in place.

Every eye watched with an appreciation of beauty as Marybeth and Laura walked by. Hardly more than two inches difference in their height, they walked behind their mother but were no more like her than a pair of goldfish resemble a trout.

The church filled quickly, and the last stragglers were forced to search for a place to sit. Among the last of the worshipers was a tall, dark man carrying what looked to be a dresser drawer with handles.

The man looked for a place to sit, and out of sympathy, room was made for him and his box on the rear deacon's bench.

Only those nearby were able to peer into the box at the three tiny girls dressed in soft white dimity, embroidered at the neck and fancy lace caps tied under their pink chins. Like three baby dolls, they slept side by side. Three filled baby bottles stood upright at three corners of the box.

Traditional songs were sung to the music of the pump organ. Preacher McCrey read the story of the first Easter in his musical voice, then he set the Bible aside and began his talk.

Baby Lucy whimpered and sucked her thumb, smacking loudly. Her father gently eased the thumb from her mouth and offered the bottle, which was greedily accepted. Her pleasure with the bottle of milk produced such an abundance of noise that her sisters began to arouse, squirming and waving their arms.

When Lucy had enough, she pushed the bottle from her mouth with her tiny tongue. Her eyes drooped, and she turned her head away, drifting into sleep.

Lottie and Maggie now demanded to be fed. Every person within noticing distance tried to get a better look at the activity on the deacon's bench. The little girls sucked noisily as their father held the bottles, one in each hand. They sucked and watched their nearby admirers with unblinking, chocolate eyes. Baby Lucy slept on.

Preacher McCrey told of the angel and of the empty tomb. He paused, and at that moment, a piercing scream filled the church. So startling it was that no one breathed for an instant then turned their heads to locate the source of what must certainly be a massacre.

Marybeth, sitting on the end of her bench, did not need to guess the origin of the sound. She knew. Jumping up, she ran down the aisle, and grabbed the tiny girl from her bed. She held her against her shoulder, patting the small back as the entire church body remained pin-drop quiet, watching.

The rumbling burp found its way up to the tiny girl's throat and was loudly released, bringing with it the contents of the bottle she had just consumed. Curdled milk sprayed over the crocheted roses of the lace collar and down the back of the pink, dotted swiss dress.

Now greatly relieved, Baby Lucy crowed happily, dimpling as she recognized her beloved Marybeth. A tiny hand patted Marybeth on the nose. Cal stood and picked up the box as Marybeth, carrying the baby, started for the door. Cal fell in behind, following closely.

First one, then two, and finally the whole church joined in, clapping their hands with appreciation over the whole performance.

Cal walked silently to the new buggy and Marybeth followed. He set the box on the seat and held Lucy until Marybeth maneuvered the fancy skirt aside and climbed in. Then he took the reins and urged the black pony toward Rock Creek Road.

Marybeth smiled. "I never even seen you come in, or I could'a come back and helped." Lucy still gurgled with pleasure as she was held against Marybeth's shoulder. The clean shoulder.

Back at the house on Rock Creek Road, Cal produced a robe Marybeth had forgotten to take away. She put on the robe and rinsed the curdled milk from her dress, then made tea.

Cal set his cup of tea on the table.

"Marybeth, I got somethin' to say. I aimed to wait a mite longer, and I still can, but you got'a right to know how things stand with me.

"I know all them things you done up here all winter was not done for me, and they was not even done for these here babies. I know that everything you done here was for Irena. It was plain you thought you had to pay a debt'a friendship, likely even guilt, 'cause you was the one to stay when she had to go. I know'd how things was, so I didn't say nothin'.

"But now I got'a say it. It'd be good for me to have fancy words right now, but I ain't got none. Marybeth, I want to marry you. I'll court you as long as you want me to and be happy to do it, but I just want you to know what's on my mind and where I'm headed, so as not to have any surprises."

Marybeth looked at the teacup in her hands. "Cal, likely you'll find this nigh onto impossible to believe, but I can tell you that today was the first time I ever noticed you bein' a man. It was back there in the church. 'Course, I knew you were you, but you were always Irena's boyfriend and then Irena's husband. Then all this happened and you were the babies' daddy, and I didn't see nothin' outside'a that."

She smiled shyly, "It seems sort'a like we might'a just met."

Cal nodded. "I know you didn't see me, but I saw you. It'd'a been hard not to. I seen you comin' and goin', and here and there, doin' things for your mama and helpin' Irena out when she had trouble. I saw you doin' things, not needin' the help of no man. Then I saw Irena, always needin' help."

"Irena was a good wife, and I wish't she didn't have to go."

Here he paused significantly, then continued. "Marybeth, Irena wasn't like you. She was a girl that men naturally reached out to, wantin' help, makin' 'em feel needed and important. She never had much to give, but she was willin' to give what she had. Reckon when them babies was born, she gave everything she had left. Then, when everything's gone, it's gone. Nothin' left to do but listen to the angel.

"You was never that'a'way. You always been a girl that makes men naturally stand back and admire you, seein' you know who you are and what you want and them not knowin' where they might fit in. You, havin' so much in you, likely you'll be givin' all your life and still have everything you need, right there inside you. That's a lot to consider when a man is lookin' at a girl. Seems like a fellow needs to be needed. At least, that's how a lotta fellows'd feel."

A long silence. "Not me, though. Never felt that'a'way, myself."

As though the lengthy, unaccustomed speech had drained him, Cal placed his hands on the table, palms up. Marybeth put hers in his, feeling that this was the first time she had ever touched him.

"Cal, it wasn't you or nothin' you did, keepin' me from seein' you. It was me and the troubles I had inside me. I had to step outside the trouble. I had to leave it and look back, then you were there. Now that I done that, I know all I need to know. We been here for more'n four months, workin' together and helpin' out on what had to be done. I already thought out how long you got'a court me. I reckon it'd be about one day, this being that day. Then we can get married, soon as you want to."

Cal smiled and lifted her hands to his lips. "Fair enough. I'll court you till we get to the preacher's house."

"Cal, there's one thing to think on. How you gonna feel when you think'a Irena bein' gone only four months?"

Cal's sober face stared toward the north window overlooking the square ponds. "Marybeth, Irena's gone, and waitin' a certain time ain't gonna bring her back. Folks gonna say things if they want to, and it'd likely be the same things they said already. We can get married now, or we can wait if you'd d'rather. Either way it goes, I aim to have you, even if it takes the rest of my life. I want you, and the girls want you. They don't know no one else."

He tugged gently at the hands he held, and Marybeth stood and took a step toward his open arms. At that moment, Maggie aroused from sleep and flung her arms away from her face, thumping the sleeping Lucy on the nose. Startled awake, Lucy yelled in anger, directing most of her voice into Lottie's ear. The irritated Lottie began to cry, and Maggie added her voice, as it seemed the thing to do. Marybeth hesitated, shrugged, smiled and turned her attention to the clamor in the bed box.

It was not yet daylight on Monday, April 7, when Cal hitched the black pony to the buggy with the red wheels. The church-going baby bed just fit the floorboard of the buggy, and a light blanket was spread across the top of the box to keep out the damp morning air.

A quart of goat milk was packed in the bag of extra diapers. It was really a daring plan to take such young babies on such a long trip, but it seemed right, somehow, that they should be along on this important day. The red and blue ball and the rubber doll lay in the bed with the babies.

They crossed the swinging bridge and turned west on the dark street, passing the Mercantile and the livery stable. They proceeded to the silver bridge at the end of Main Street and again crossed the river. The first rays of light caught them just beyond the silver bridge. The reporting eyes of the livery stable loafers were denied the sight of Cal Boudreau and Marybeth Maisone, with three tiny girls, heading west to Jacksonville to obtain a marriage license.

Breakfast was eaten on the road. Biscuits, surrounding a slab of ham, still a little bit warm. Molasses cookies and a jar of cold tea.

The April air was warming quickly, and a symphony of birds chittered and tweeted overhead. Cardinals, robins and thrushes all joined in the spring chorus that led to aerial courtship displays. Today was a day of singing.

Next would come the nests. Then eggs... and babies. Lots of work for the birds to do. Spring was wonderfully full of things to do!

The pony broke into a trot of joyful excitement in the cool, morning air. Marybeth the capable became suddenly shy, leaning against the corner of the buggy. Cal, the man of few words, suddenly had a lot of them.

"Them little ducks sure took to that pond. Likely have to make 'em a shelter down there to protect 'em from the varmits. They'll not be wantin' to leave the water. Gonna be a lot'a good eatin' when they get some size on 'em."

He held the reins high, giving the pony his head as he trotted along, the light buggy bouncing softly on its new springs "That new room I got stepped off, you think it'll be big enough for later when the girls get big? Easy to make it bigger if you think so. Was thinkin' you'd need me to put up a summer kitchen for the cannin' and summer bread bakin'. Keeps the house a sight cooler.

"Them little fruit and nut trees gonna be good when they start to bear. Thinkin' on addin' a few apple trees. Can't have too many fruit trees.

"Marybeth, a lot of what I been doin' is on account'a what you said that rainy day a while back."

Marybeth was puzzled. "What I said? What did I say?"

"It was a day the rain was comin' down good, and you was standin' there at the window, lookin' toward the river. The water was overflowin' out'a Rock Creek, and you said it was a shame I wasn't in the business of raisin' catfish 'stead'a cotton. It put me to thinkin'. Old timers said the cotton on that field only made a crop every four or five years. Catfish'd make a crop every week if I worked it out that'a'way. They'd keep comin' on and not have to be planted, chopped or picked. I got you to thank for that, well as a lot of other things."

Early spring wild flowers grew in colorful clumps along the road. All the newly-hatched turtles wanted to be on the other side of the road today, and tomorrow they'd cross back. Rabbits jumped and ran alongside the buggy, then disappeared into the trees.

Marybeth commented, "Them girls are sleepin' good. Seems like they might like ridin'."

Cal chuckled. "That Lucy. Seems strange about her burpin' the way she does. Back there in the church, I thought about it and figured trouble was a'comin' at me, but I just didn't have me enough hands to stave it off."

The morning sun shone warmly on the back of the buggy and the chirp of the birds sounded above the crunch of the gravel under the pony's feet.

"Marybeth, it wouldn't surprise me none if we had jars'a honey to take into Jacksonville along with the fish. I caught me two swarms'a bees and got 'em to take to the hives. Figure there'll be more swarms come by to fill them other four hives. That cotton field full'a clover, that'll make a sight'a honey when it gets goin'."

After a breath, he continued, "Be a lot'a good things happen by gettin' rid of that cotton field. I'd been thinkin' on where to get clay to build up the yard, and the ponds took care'a that, too. The cotton fields, if they make, they bring in money all at once. Fishin, though, that'd spread the money along, week to week, and be a sight easier than choppin' cotton."

They were nearing the city and the April sun sparkled off the new green of the plants. Lottie, lying in the center position, began to fuss, whacking her arms against her sisters. Marybeth lifted Lottie and Maggie to her lap. Lucy whimpered, so she made room for her. What a lapful of squirming and twisting.

"Cal, can you reach that box to set it up here on the seat with us? These babies got'a be fed."

Lottie and Maggie were nestled into the box, and Cal held the bottle for the closest one. There was only one way for the pony to go, and he went without direction. Lucy lounged in Marybeth's lap while she fed a baby with each hand. "Easier to get 'em fed when they wake up one at a time." she commented.

Lucy was burped thoroughly and carefully. Couldn't afford a messed up dress today.

They left the gravel road and turned right. Main Street of Jacksonville was crowded with delivery wagons, shop attendants and early shoppers.

"Marybeth, I want you to think on gettin' somethin' new that you want. You could get a white dress to be married in, if you wanted to."

Marybeth thought about it. She looked down at the pink dotted swiss. It was a little crumpled. Actually, it was very crumpled. Cal wanted her to wear a better dress, and she could understand that. "All right."

At the store, they looked at the dresses. The white ones were nice.

"See one you like?" they were asked by the bored male clerk.

Cal looked at Marybeth, and she looked back at the dresses. "I could like that one," and she pointed to a ruffled and lace creation.

"Would you like to try it on?" was the invitation.

Marybeth hesitated. "Cal, you wantin' me to get this dress, I can do it. I know this'n I got on to be kind of a mess, with the babies and all. But I got'a say this. For the price you'd be payin' for this dress, I could have six new ones if I made 'em. That'd be dresses to last this summer and next."

Cal looked at the clerk, then at Marybeth. The young man came to the rescue. "Perhaps the lady would like to look at our fabric department." With that, he led the way to another part of the store.

Bolts of every color and type of fabric were lined up across the counter like a rainbow after the rain. Cal stood holding the box with its light blanket covering while Marybeth surveyed the choices. The clerk waited, impatiently, to be sure, for her to make her selection or turn down everything. Who knew what made a woman decide on anything?

But she picked up the blue and white stripes, and the pink and yellow flowers, then hesitated in indecision. Finally, she said to Cal, "Only thing is, if you was wantin' me to be married in white, there'd be no time to make it up. The weddin'd have to be some other day."

Now the young male clerk was impatient no longer. This lady customer had his full attention. What young lady was ever negotiable about the date of her wedding? And who was this fellow with the odd shaped box that he was the one to make the decision?

The tall, dark fellow responded. "I wasn't wantin' white, especially. Just wanted you to have somethin' new to remember the day by. If you like them both, take 'em and get some others, too."

"You partial to white?"

"White'd look good on you, your hair bein' so dark."

The clerk watched Marybeth examine the choices of white fabric, settling on an all-over lace eyelet. She looked at the fellow with a question in her eyes, and he nodded. She added it to the pile.

Something stirred in the odd box the man carried. The light cloth that covered it began to dimple and jiggle, as if whatever it covered was alive. The man looked at the quivering blanket with concern.

The lady kept looking at the bolts of fabric and selected a dark blue with tiny white dots.

A faint, whimpery sound came from under the covering of the box.

The young lady pronounced, "That'd be Maggie. I better take her 'afore she wakes up the rest." With that decision voiced, she eased the covering aside and lifted out a tiny baby girl in a lace bonnet. It took no great powers of deduction to know the baby was hers. The skin and hair were exactly the same color as the lady's, and with the baby over her shoulder, she continued to shop.

A bolt of green and black plaid was added to the pile, and the baby pounded her tiny hands against the lady's shoulder, squealing loudly and grinning with the pleasure of life itself, in addition to the good view of the goings on in the store.

The squeals of the baby caused the covering of the box to erupt with noise and fury. The man calmly put the box on the carpeted floor of the store and lifted out two more babies, identical to the first one. It was amazing that the man was able to slip his large hands, one under each baby, into the box and lift them to his shoulders in one swift and gentle movement. He held them there, whispering softly in their ears while they drooled on his shoulder.

Then he said to the girl, "Marybeth, you don't have to do this today, you know. I ain't wantin' to put pressure on you. The preacher'll still be there next week or next month."

The woman shook her head. "No, we planned on today," she pointed out, "and I got no fault with that if you was not set on marryin' me in white. You think this'n I got on'd be all right? Likely gonna have more wrinkles in it, time we get there."

"Wrinkles ain't no problem to me, long as you get what you want."

Satisfied, the girl turned back to the shopping, still patting the baby on her shoulder. The clerk was intrigued. His eyes were glued to the scenerio before him. In fact, wild horses themselves would have trouble dragging him away from the scene.

So the man was the boyfriend, and the girl with three babies was stalling, though he had invited her to marry in white. Hmmmm.

A bolt of bright red cloth joined the pile. That made the six she had referred to. Would she stop there? Apparently so.

"Well, I was thinkin', was you wantin' to get dresses for the girls?"

The clerk's head jerked around. Huh? What woman ever asked any man's opinion of what to do about her daughters, whether she was married to him or not?

"Might as well," was his reply.

Pale blue dimity and white voile with tiny yellow flowers topped off the pile.

"You got any white lawn?"

"Huh?" The young clerk finally realized she was speaking to him.

She repeated, "White lawn cloth. You know, for makin' pettislips for babies. You got any?"

"Sure. I'll get it for you."

While the young man measured and cut the fabric, the couple chatted.

"You say anything to the preacher about us comin' by?"

"Ain't had the chance."

"'Spect he'll be there? Where'd he be goin' of a Monday?"

"Don't know. Would'a told him, but I didn't know till last night, 'member? License gonna still be good for three days, anyway."

The fabric made a sizeable pile when cut and stacked. Some buttons and lengths of lace and braid were added. It also came to a sizeable amount of money, and the man counted out the bills. The clerk was now free to go, but he made no move to do so.

It would truly be worth missing a sale to the next customer to see how this couple got out of the store with the box, the three babies, now actively awake, and the massive pile of cloth.

He was a little disappointed. The girl reached out her arm without a word and received another baby. The man leaned down, still holding the third baby, and picked up the box. He set it on the counter and divided the fabric into two piles, setting them in the box. The baby he held was nestled between the two piles.

He picked up the box, and the girl led the way, skillfully bending slightly to negotiate the door handle around the strap of her handbag. The man caught the bottom of the door with one foot and held it for her to go through. He followed, steadying the door with his shoulder so it wouldn't slam.

The clerk continued to gaze at the closed door for several minutes in total admiration. There'd be nothing that life could throw at that couple that could stop them, the way they worked together. Even if they were actually a trifle late with the wedding.

Cal and Marybeth took the fabric to the buggy and left it, going on down the street to the Five and Dime.

"Could get the girls a store-bought teething ring," Marybeth suggested.

"Do they work good?" Cal wondered.

Marybeth replied, "Don't know. I never had a baby."

They selected a pair of rubber rings, one blue and one yellow.

"Marybeth, I sort'a liked them combs you got in your hair. You could get some other kinds, maybe, to go with the new dresses." So she picked a pair that sparkled like diamonds and another pair of pink ones, molded to look like a row of tiny flowers.

"You ready for ice cream?"

"Anytime you are."

Marybeth elected to stay in the buggy with the babies, now back in their box playing with their toys. "Make mine all three dips vanilla," she instructed.

Cal returned with the full cones, and they ate them, watching the babies play. Then the black pony was happy to be moving again and stepped daintily onto the brick street, turning without direction onto the gravel road toward River Bend. It was past noon, and the April sun was becoming very warm. The jiggling of the buggy lowered the eyelids of the babies, and they were fast asleep.

Butterflies tended the flower clumps beside the road, and bees droned by. Birds were carrying sticks and twigs for their nests.

"Cal, I been thinkin' of somethin' we forgot and likely ought'a go back and get it."

"What'd that be?"

"I'm thinkin' it's usual to have a ring to get married."

"Didn't forget."

"Didn't aim to get one yet?"

Cal shook his head. "Got it already. Right here in my pocket. Wouldn't'a come off away from the house without it. Was aimin' to carry it till I put it on your finger."

Marybeth looked at him with surprise. "I didn't see you get it. Did you get it when you went after the ice cream?"

"You didn't see me get it 'cause you wasn't along when I got it. Got it last week. It was the license I got when I went after the ice cream."

"But we wasn't about to get married last week."

"Sure, we was. You just didn't know it yet."

"But you didn't know I'd say yes."

"Didn't matter. Said I was gonna court you till you married me if it took the rest of my life. If I died still courtin' you and carryin' this ring, I'd still be doin' what I said I'd do."

"Oh." Marybeth nodded. That was what he had said, all right.

The babies shifted their positions occasionally but continued to sleep contentedly. Cal and Marybeth snacked on the remaining biscuits and ham. She peeled the boiled eggs, and they ate them as the buggy rolled along.

"Right up the road there's a spring with good, fresh water. We can get a drink."

They rode on in silence for a couple of miles.

"Marybeth, you're bein' uncommonly quiet. You still thinkin' we don't need to wait a while?"

Marybeth thought a bit before answering. "It ain't that, fer a fact. It's just that I keep lookin' over at you, thinkin' about what I told you. Funny thing to me how I never thought to look at you or think anything about you. Seein' you now tells me I might should'a looked around me a little better. Seems like a puzzle, don't it?"

But Cal answered, "Don't seem like no puzzle to me. You bein' the kind of a girl with a lot to give, and you been givin' to Irena and helpin' her out for a long time. Bein' like that, there just wasn't no way you could'a stopped, sudden-like, just because she wasn't there no more. You needed to sort'a taper off, so to speak, and there was them babies, bein' hers, and they took that need off'a you."

Then he added, "Many's the time I would'a liked to say something, like how good you were to the babies, but I knew it wouldn't be right. You was doin' somethin' you had to do. But I wasn't gonna let you get away from me, though. I was watchin', and come time you thought you could let Irena go, I was aimin' to be there to help. And that didn't mean no disrespect or lack'a love to Irena, 'cause my lovin' her ain't gonna bring her back.

"I thought to myself, though, that when the time come, likely you would think I wasn't quite up to what you'd be lookin' for in a man, and I was countin' on them three girls to make up the difference."

Marybeth grinned shyly. "Looks like you might'a figured things out wrong, but it took actual lookin' at you for me to see that. Them babies, they'll just be the little extra, like maybe the frosting on the cake. Cakes is good plain but maybe better frosted."

The black pony rounded the bend in the road known as McDuff's Corner. They were now two miles from River Bend.

Marybeth lifted the corner of the blanket and patted Maggie, the closest to her.

"Wake up, little Maggie. Time to eat. We can't have three little girls gettin' hungry all at the same time."

Then Lottie was fed. Lucy was last, Marybeth holding her against her shoulder and patting her to keep her awake long enough to burp.

Cal was thinking. "Was you wantin' to go get Laura and your Mama to have 'em there for the marryin'?"

Marybeth thought. "No, I reckon not. Laura's gonna be happy about whatever makes me happy, and Mama, well, she'd gonna be whatever she thinks about bein' at that moment."

The preacher was standing on the roof of the church with a can of tar in his hand, searching for the source of a leak. Cal stepped down from the buggy and walked over to the house.

"Preacher, we got need'a your help. Marybeth and me, we need your name on a marriage license."

Preacher McCrey answered with a wide grin. "Reckon I could help you out there." Leaving the tar on the roof, he descended the ladder.

In the parlor of parsonage, Cal stood in his somewhat rumpled Sunday suit. The collar of the white shirt was completely wilted, and his shoes were covered with a liberal layer of dust. Marybeth stood beside him in her pink, dotted swiss dress. Gone were the soft pleats and the smooth skirt of yesterday. Six hours in the buggy had taken a heavy toll. The crocheted collar was pulled lopsided by Lucy's tugging fingers. Maggie had much earlier removed the shiny white bow, and it now lay in the bed box, soggy with drool. Wisps of hair now straggled down from the teeth of the pearl trimmed combs. Together the man and woman stood before the preacher as he opened his book.

Cal stopped him. "Wait, I got'a wake up the girls and get them in on this. Marybeth said she'd marry me, even without them, but I ain't ready to take no chances."

Lottie and Maggie peered over his left shoulder and Lucy occupied the right one as they were pressed between their parents in the first bridal kiss.

A few minutes later, the pony was trotting up Church Street, turning toward Rock Creek Road.

"Them three babies sure are good travelers," their father commented. "Gonna be a good thing, too, lettin' us make a trip into the city any time we're a mind to."

Little Yoyo, waiting by the front gate, saw them coming and tore down the road to meet them, bouncing like an animated fur ball. She leaped toward the buggy seat, missed and fell, rolling in the dirt. She righted herself and leaped again, this time successfully landing in Marybeth's lap.

Nearer to the front gate, the bleating of the goats and the mooing of the cows met them with noisy insistence.

"Ain't surprisin'. Milked 'em so early this mornin', they're bound to be in a bad way."

He stopped the pony beside the kitchen door.

"Wait," he told Marybeth, as he wound the pony's reins around the holder. Yoyo jumped to the ground, and Cal stepped down and walked around to Marybeth's side. Reaching into the buggy, he gathered her into his arms.

He crossed the threshold and set her down in the kitchen. In a moment, he was back with the box of sleeping babies. He set them on the kitchen table.

"Mrs. Boudreau, here are your three daughters, and you may never see 'em this good again."

He made a step toward Marybeth, but the noisy outcry from the barnyard called to him. He turned away from his bride with a sigh and with a firm set of the chin. "Reckon I got'a get them animals took care of," he shrugged, and then he was gone. There would be time later....

Marybeth stirred the coals in the cookstove, coaxing them into a blaze. The teakettle seemed to be full, so she pulled it over the flame. On the table, she set two cups. What tea would be right for this special day? Peppermint and chamomile, maybe. Always a good combination. Her hands did the familiar things, freeing her mind to think.

She sat down at the table, waiting for the water to heat. Excitement stirred in the depth of her stomach as she looked around the kitchen at the well-used things, once Irena's and now hers. The heavy iron stove she had so often cleaned and on which she had cooked so many meals. She looked out the window to where the stakes driven into the ground indicated the new rooms which had never been Irena's..... the ones Cal had started as part of his courtship of her.

She smiled, thinking of the ring he had carried in his pocket with total confidence that he would win her some day, no matter how long it took.

Past the fence and down toward the river were the two square ponds brimming with water and fish and the two marked out places for two more ponds, evidence that he looked ahead, possibly with the idea of someday having sons to help. The ponds had not been Irena's but were a result of her own timely suggestion.

The bleating of the goats was because of her remembering something she had heard about goat milk. In truth, the girls were almost hers from the beginning, owing their lives and their names to her. They now slept soundly, side by side by side in the wide, wooden bed with handles.

Her babies. They looked a lot different than they had even yesterday. They were hers now, and how did she feel about Cal? He was a stranger who came to town yesterday, who was exactly like a man she had known, admired for many things, and had worked with in a very difficult and trying situation. He was like the man who had been her partner with a shared problem.

He was also like that man who had patience, endurance and foresight, and, so importantly, a man who could stand adversity without falling apart. His world could be swept away in a moment, and, instead of despair, he gathered together what was his and moved into the future.

In addition, he had known what she, Marybeth, was going through and had sympathy for her, though his own loss was so much greater. He was willing to wait and watch and never question her decision on what was best for herself. To him, she was a complete and capable person. He had always treated her as a respected equal.

If she could ever love a man, it would have to be a man like Irena's husband, and she was so fortunate to have met a man just like him. He had walked suddenly into her life, and she knew instantly that he was the one. It didn't matter that she had actually known him only one day. It had seemed a lifetime.

The water in the teakettle was hot and bubbling with the steam whistling through the spout, so she measured the tea into the cups and sat down to wait for the man she just met.

In a half an hour, Cal returned, a pail of foaming milk in one hand and the pillow from his loft bed under the other arm. He entered the kitchen, quietly easing the door closed with his heel.

He saw the teacups, but he reached past them toward Marybeth, and she came to him.

"Mrs. Boudreau," he said, "remember what I said about you bein' behind on the courtin' you got a right to expect? We got'a work on that, startin' now, and we won't be caught up no time soon."

And the weary babies slept a long time.

- BONUS EXCERPT -

TAMING THE WILDERNESS
HISTORICAL FICTION SERIES FOR ADULTS

VOLUME 2

GUIDING WINDOW
&
SUNLIGHT THROUGH
THE CLOUDS
An Anthology of Historical Fiction

GUIDING WINDOW

One

G od told you to WHAT?"
Kathleen Palmer stood with her soapy hands spread apart in amazement as she stared at her new husband of six months. Her rosy red-gold curls had been pushed back with her sudsy hand, leaving a glob of white foam on her forehead. The clump of foam was sliding, unnoticed, down toward her lovely pink ear.

Hapgood Palmer, new husband, sighed and began again. He had known it would be this way. He had tried every way to get out of it, but he had no better luck than many before him, when they had tried to get out of a direct command from above. No amount of ducking away or attempts to move sideways removed him from the direct command that came down on his head and resounded around within himself, like the water wheel that drew water for the cattle.

He had repeatedly explained to God that He was talking to the wrong person.... as had Moses and Gideon before him. He explained to His maker that it was surely a case of mistaken identity, but God had not been successfully convinced and remained stubbornly adamant, succinct, and well centered with His wishes. Just as He was with Gideon and Moses. His attention was absolutely not to be drawn aside by a mere mortal.

The young man knew, however, that his wife deserved the best explanation he could give her. He began, "There don't seem to be no way to git around it. I got'a be a preacher."

Kathleen expertly stripped the foamy suds from her hands, flinging it into the tub containing her embroidered unmentionables, still bright and pretty from her bridal trousseau. She wheeled around on her shapely barefoot heel and led the way from the washtubs of wet clothes to the door of the mountain cabin. This news was clearly something that should be taken sitting down and with full attention.

Hapgood, usually called "Hap," brushed back his coal black hair with a nervous hand and followed her.

Plopping herself onto the handmade wicker settee, she demanded, "Now, tell me again. Just exactly what was it that went on 'tween you and God?"

Hapgood, not feeling that he deserved to sit on the settee beside her, at least until this new directive from above had been absorbed, settled for a low stool at her feet and planted himself tentatively upon it.

"Lena, honey, don't think I ain't been a'tryin' to get away from it. I know what it's like bein' a preacher… livin' with one in the family I did. I know what it's like on the preacher's wife, and her bein' the innocent party to it all. Learned it all watchin' my ma. I talked to God, and I talked to God, and Him not seemin' to care how I feel about it all. Didn't notice that he took much notice's you, either."

Kathleen bent her lovely head forward and studied her toes, slightly muddy from the slopped over wash water and the rich, black dirt of the mountain farm. "You sayin' to me that this ain't a new thing to you? That you been hidin' all this from me? Now, Hap, you know we promised to not do that." The rebuke was gentle, but firm.

Hap had remembered. It had been easy to promise anything to the beautiful Kathleen O'Keen. The best day of his life was when he had stood in the parlor of his parent's house and promised to love, honor and protect her… and that was all he wanted to do, but there was no way to protect her from this. They were clearly in it together.

"Lena, honey, I wasn't in no hurry to talk to you, thinkin' it could be that I misunderstood what God was a'sayin' to me. I kept hopin' and hopin' I misunderstood."

She studied him for a moment. "How could a body misunderstand God?" Kathleen studied his pleading, open face, with a puzzled frown on her own.

Hap sighed, long and knowingly. "Ain't hard to misunderstand what God says if He's a'tellin' you to do somethin' you don't feel capable'a doin'. Wasn't hard at all."

Kathleen still struggled to understand. "Why'd you not be feelin' capable'a doin' what you was told to do?"

With a sigh, he began. "Well, I ain't studied, and I…"

Kathleen interrupted, "I 'spect they was a time your pa hadn't studied, neither. Wouldn't that be right?"

"Yeah. That was one'a them things I thought of."

Kathleen pressed unmercifully forward. "What was the other thing?"

"Huh?"

"The other thing you thought of? What was it?"

He sighed. "Gideon, in the Bible. About him bein' a farmer and God told him he was gonna have to be a general in the army. He didn't believe God, neither, and wanted a sign. 'Member, how he put the wool fleece in the bowl and asked God to make the fleece wet with dew and the grass dry? God did, and Gideon still wasn't sure, so he asked God to make the grass wet and the fleece dry and God did that."

"You sayin' you put out a fleece to God?"

"Yeah, you might say."

"What was it?" she demanded.

Hap hesitated. "Aw, Lena…"

"Tell me!" his wife demanded more sternly.

"I said to God if'n you didn't start in a'cryin' when I told you, I'd take it for a sign, for sure, that I hadn't been hearin' wrong. You bein' in the middle'a makin' baby things, like you are, I figgered cryin' was a cinch. Figured that'd give me the perfect out."

"You was expectin' me to cry? About words you was hearin' from God?"

"I thought it might be an even chance."

The girl nodded with understanding. "You wanted me to cry, to let you out'a doin' God's will."

"Well…" he hesitated, painfully. "I wouldn't put it like that, exactly. But they was another thing I thought of."

"Let's have it."

He summoned his courage and began, "You know, Gideon, he put out two fleeces to God. I only gave God one chance to back out'a callin' me. God ought'a be given another chance, wouldn't you think? Could be He's changed his mind."

Kathleen nodded, slightly, and turned her gaze out of the cabin door. Her white teeth caught her lower lip, as they often did when she was thoughtful. The color of her eyes turned from the pale blue of the summer sky to the deep swirling slate blue of a Kentucky mountain lake.

Hap waited. Ever since they were children in school, this color change had often brought on an idea. Some good, some not so good, but a thoughtful idea, just the same. It seemed to be worth the time, waiting to see what came forth.

263

"Now, Hap, I know the Bible didn't say nothin' about no Mrs. Gideon, but since this here thing affects me, too, I'd think it was fair if I was to get to put out the second fleece."

After a slight hesitation, Hap nodded. Why not? Seemed only fair, all right, and that'd put some of the responsibility on her.

Kathleen nodded and continued, "I want God to give us a sign so powerful that we know we didn't make no mistake. That'd seem fair to ask, don't you think? And I want it to happen tomorrow, before noon."

"Before noon?"

"Yeah. Gideon asked for his fleece to be wet over night. Seems like it'd be fair for me to put a time on it?"

"And what'd that sign be?"

"What it can be is for God to decide. He'd know how to make it big enough that we didn't make no mistake about it. We'd just have to trust 'im on that."

Hapgood Palmer watched the tiny smile creep into the edges of his wife's lovely mouth, and he saw the sparkles dance in her eyes. Once more he was thankful for the gift of this lovely creature. As soon as she understood the problem, she shifted the responsibility of it neatly back onto the shoulders of God... where it belonged.

What was it that could possibly happen that would be so big, as to be unmistakable, and occur before noon tomorrow? Especially in the tiny log cabin perched on the Kentucky mountainside so far from any main road to anywhere?

Hap breathed a sigh of relief. He would never have thought of anything so wonderfully hard for God to do. Nothing of such great importance and no surprises ever happened on this mountaintop.

He reached out from the stool where he sat and clutched the two bare feet before him, still slightly muddy and pulled them toward him.

"Now, Hap, you be careful!"

"I am! You notice I didn't grab a handful'a that hair. I'm bein' careful on account'a there being two a'you." He did, however, tug gently on the feet until she was removed from the settee and onto his lap.

Two

Kathleen's wash water had cooled considerably before she returned to it and rinsed her unmentionables, hanging them on the line to dry. But she spent some very thoughtful time beside the washtub, before her dresses, and Hap's overalls had spent their time on the rub board and were on the line beside the underwear.

Hapgood went back to his fence mending. If a fellow aimed to keep his hogs from wandering the mountains and getting long legged and skinny, he must be diligent with the fences and plug up the holes they rooted along the edges. Fence mending was good for thinking and he had some of it to do.

He had his plans. Good plans. He and Kathleen'd likely need to spend two, maybe three years here on the mountain, and then he'd sell out and be able to get something larger closer in to town.

This cabin was a nice place for two people. Nice, until they decided to go somewhere in rainy weather. The mountain roads, and especially the one leading up to his house turned slick as glass and ran red rivulets as the rainwater washed potholes into the clay. That was good, in a way, because it had made the cabin affordable. But, he reasoned, pigs weren't going anywhere, anyway, except to market. Humans would just have to deal with it.

Wintertime meant there wouldn't be much going, anywhere. There'd come a time when coming and going would be more important, like when their children would need to be educated.

He whistled a lighthearted tune as he drove stakes into the ground at the site of the latest hog wallow. He occasionally glanced over the fence at the noisy rooters. They were looking good, this batch of hogs. If he could just keep them penned up, and not out running off all their meat, he'd make a nice profit when they were sold.

With that, and the money from the sale of the wicker chairs and settees he made, he should be able to afford a nice place in town in a couple of years, three at the most. His plans were firmly set.

He circled the hog pen, checking for other rooted-out escape holes and moved on to another enclosure, also filled with grunting Hampshire sows. Their white hair was now dyed red with the mud from the wallow, but their characteristically patterned white "jackets" over the black body were still evident. He liked Hampshires. They put on weight very well, the boars were fairly even tempered... for a male hog, that is... and the little white jacket pattern made them look like they were dressed up. When they weren't covered with mountain mud, that is.

He had done all the right things, hadn't he? God had said in His book that the man who did not provide for his family was worse than an infidel. Well, he was not one of them. He was as prepared for marriage as any 21 year old, maybe better than most, and Kathleen's pa had been first to say as much.

As he headed back to the cabin, he walked through the patch of corn that he grew to feed the hogs. The shiny, flowing leaves on the cornstalks reached his armpits, just as they should this time of the year. Ears were beginning to head up all along the stalk. There would be corn kernels for weight gain in the hogs and plant stalks for roughage.

This spring's litters of baby squealers were beginning to put on weight, and his highly-bred sows were still young. Clearly, everything was working out, and it had seemed that God approved and was on his side.

Next spring…? Well, anyway, things were looking very good.

Now this…

Three

The pitch of the Kentucky mountain, leaning toward the south, as it did, created a lovely, cool night breeze blowing up the mountainside. The white starched curtains at the wide cabin window moved with the force of it.

It would be so pleasant to lie in the bed in the mornings, now that Kathleen was over the worst of her sickness, but they had already heard the flap of the rooster's wings, preparatory to the morning serenade. What with the crowing of the Barred Rock roosters, the mooing of the jersey cow, and the scratching of the dog at the door, it seemed time to get out of bed. They were clearly outvoted.

Besides, it was almost light in the east. Sunrise came early on the hilltop.

Another thing. God had until noon to do or not do what He wanted to get done. After that, they could settle into their planned routine without any upsetting problems to concern them. Their baby would be born, the farm would be in better shape than when they bought it, and they would get a good price for it. Then they would move down closer to the valley and their parents and friends.

But now it was time to get up. The corn could use another plowing before it got so tall the horse couldn't get through it. That should probably be the duty for today.

Hap pulled on his clothes and followed Kathleen to the kitchen. It was a pleasure to watch her cook. In addition to the knowledge that good food would be served, watching it being prepared was akin to watching a pair of orioles in flight, dipping and spinning in their courtship dance. Or a doe running through the trees, her fawn at her side. Or maybe a squirrel bounding about on the tree limbs, so nimble its feet hardly seeming to touch the limb. The whole thing made him feel poetic.

She stood there at the stove, his Lena, stirring the oatmeal with one hand, while dumping biscuit ingredients in the pan with the other. Sliding the oatmeal aside, she moved the skillet over the flame and plopped in a dollop of bacon grease, followed by four thin-cut pork chops. Then, both hands joined over the biscuit mixing bowl, and in seconds, the doughy globs were formed, popped in their pan and shoved into the oven.

The pork chops, crisp and brown, were fished from the skillet with the long-handled fork and put into the overhead warming oven to stay the right temperature while the eggs were cooked. One hand skillfully broke the eggs into the skillet, while the other hand set the jelly and honey down from the cupboard above the stove.

Milk, honey, jelly, and butter came to the table. The eggs got turned. Silverware arrived, followed by bowls of oatmeal and plates of meat and eggs. Lastly, on came the pan of biscuits, the tops as evenly tanned as a jar of bee tree honey. Hap could have gone on to the barn and already had the milking done, but then he would have missed watching the breakfast preparation. That surely would have been a pure waste of lovely viewing… maybe even a sin of wastefulness.

With a flourish and a swirl of her apron, Kathleen seated herself in the sturdy cane-bottom chair, made by her husband, and bowed her head.

Hap's voice intoned, "Dear Lord, we thank you…"

He had just picked up a biscuit and opened it for the butter when a light rapping sounded at the door. He and Kathleen looked at each other with surprise. How did anyone get past the dog without it setting up a racket?

Kathleen whirled from her chair and went to the door. The old man on the porch tipped his hat and smiled a snaggle-toothed smile.

"Mornin' Miss…"

"Mornin' to you, Mister. You come to see my hu…"

"You're fine, Miss. I come a'askin'."

"Askin'?" She was apprehensive.

By this time, Hap had managed to put down his biscuit and join his wife at the door. If someone needed directions, then they were certainly and hopelessly lost because the mountain cabin was not on the way to anywhere.

"Help you, Mister?" Hap asked, politely.

"Yes, Son, you can. Me and my missus, here, we come about as far as we can go. She's ailin' and we're two days short'a our destination. She was sayin' if there'd be a body close by that'd let her rest on their porch, maybe stretch out a bit without the swayin' of the wagon, it'd be a comfort to 'er. Maybe an hour... or two. Then, if there was a bite to eat that could be spared, that'd get us on our way."

Hap looked quickly at Kathleen's worried expression. She had only cooked the usual amount for the two of them, but they had two pork chops each in their plates, untouched. There were always biscuits...

"You folks come on in. We was just fixin' to sit. Your missus in the...?"

"There in the buggy," he supplied.

"You needin' help..."

"Yes, Son. A little help with 'er, if you will. My old arms, they ain't so strong nomore."

Hap followed the old man to the buggy in the yard, and Kathleen surveyed the table. Sliding two of the pork chops onto fresh plates, she opened four more eggs in the skillet. Two more oatmeal bowls... there was plenty of it. She always made extra for the dog. Biscuits? ...enough. Jelly? ....honey? ...enough. Yes!

She peeped through the curtain and saw the old woman being guided toward the porch steps. So thin, she was, that she was practically skin and bones, and her claw-like hands shook with palsy. Oops! Better fry them eggs a mite longer. Them old hands would never manage runny yolks.

Then they helped her through the front door, and the old woman was even worse off than she had appeared to be through the curtain. Her skin was darkened with age, her teeth, nonexistent. Her sparse gray hair was wadded into an inept knot on her head.

She smiled her toothless smile and settled into the chair designated for her. Kathleen slid the hard-fried eggs onto the plates and set them in front of the old couple.

Hap, the comfortable host, instructed them. "Dig right in, folks. It's done been prayed over."

Even eating as slowly as they could, Hap and Kathleen finished before the old woman, and finally Hap had to excuse himself to take care of the bawling cow. After the milking, he carried grain and water to the buggy horse.

Kathleen tried to keep from staring, and wanted, more than anything, to offer to feed the old woman with her own steady hand, but she kept silent until the food was gone. Finally, the toothless mouth was gumming its last bite of biscuit.

"Honey," the old woman said, smiling at Kathleen. "You been so good, I hate to ask one more thing, but I ain't got use'a my hands like when I was young, and getting' my hair combed, it's right much of a chore. If you could comb…?"

"Sure. I can comb your hair for you." Whereupon Kathleen picked up her comb and stood behind the old woman's chair, relieved to have something to do to keep her eyes off the pain in the old face.

Drawing the comb through the strands of oily hair disturbed her sensibilities. "Ma'am, you want I should wash out your hair? Bein' on the road like you was…"

"Honey, if you'd do that, it'd be a blessin'."

Draping the thin old shoulders with a thick wedding-present towel, she dipped water from the reservoir and moistened the gray strands. Massaging gently with her fingers, she brought out the dirt and oil, rinsing it off by holding the old head with one hand, and pouring water through her hair with the other, catching it in the dishpan. She blotted off the moisture and swished the comb through the soapy water.

Gently pulling through the snarls, she combed the hair until it was silky dry, and then skillfully twisted it into a stylish figure-eight knot, securing it using a few of her own pins. It helped the old lady's appearance quite a lot.

The old woman again gave her a toothless smile. "Now, Honey, if I could rest a mite. Your nice front porch'd be good. Just a little rest to get away from the swayin'a the buggy."

"Oh, no, Ma'am, you got'a lay on the bed. It's a good bed. My ma and me, we stuffed that mattress ourselves. My ma, she keeps geese just for the feathers. Says, otherwise, she'd not bother with the worrisome, noisy things. Here, you come on in here." Kathleen grinned, conspiratorially, "Them geese do make right smart of a tasty Sunday dinner, though."

Insistently, she guided the old woman into her bedroom. "Your Mister, he could come, too. He could likely use rest the same time as you."

She helped the old legs to straighten out, then covered them with a wool afghan knitted for her by her grandmother when she was a little girl. It had rested for years in her bridal chest. She stretched it to cover the feet of the old man, too.

"Now, you just rest and I'll be quiet as I can. Maybe them old roosters'll shut up."

Slipping back to the kitchen, she dipped water from the reservoir but it wasn't very hot. She had used most of it for the hair wash. Stirring up the firebox, she poked in several sticks of wood. She brought a pail of water from the well and dumped it into the stove reservoir. While it heated, maybe she'd stir up a little cake. Yes, an apple cake. If the old couple could rest until dinner, it would be a good desert to send them on with.

When the cake was ready for the oven, the water in the reservoir was hot again, so she could wash the dishes. Thoughts bubbled in her head. How did these people get to the porch without the dog barking, and how did they get so far off the main trail? If they were two days from their destination, would the old woman even make it? They must not have any food with them, so when they left her house, she'd need to put in enough to get them where they were going. Disturbing thoughts niggled themselves in the back of her mind, but she shoved them aside.

So what would two days worth of food be? Boiled eggs, cornbread, biscuits, cake, butter, canned peaches (did they have a jar opener?), a baked sweet potato… they were good even served cold, and… Well, what else?

She found the right size basket and packed the food inside so it would be ready. She even took it out to the buggy and set it on the floorboard, so there would be no argument about taking it. She felt a tinge of regret that she would loose that particular basket, but Hap could make her another one.

Glancing around in the buggy, she was amazed that they had so little in the way of comfort. Actually, they had nothing. But they'd get where they were going in two days, and for certain, they'd have plenty to eat.

By then, it was ten thirty. What for dinner? Fried potatoes, ham, green beans, spiced apples, and the cake? Good enough.

By eleven, the old couple was stirring, and Hap came in wearing dirty overalls.

His wife held her nose. "Been wrestlin' them pigs agin?"

Hap grinned as he changed. "I like them Hampshires, but they're the stubbornist critters for rootin' under the fence, that was ever made by God. Or whoever it was that made 'em."

By eleven twenty, the four of them were at the table, once more. "Where ya headed?"

"Uh, down Louieville way," was the noncommittal answer.

A slight hesitation. "Well, ya ought'a make it. Good weather."

Four

At ten to twelve, the old woman was settled onto the buggy seat, exclaiming over the wealth of food in the beautiful basket. At five to twelve, they waved goodbye and the buggy moved toward the gate.

Hap and Kathleen stood on the porch as a good host and hostess would, waiting until they were out of sight before going back into the cabin, but instead of pulling through the gate, the horse was reined in and turned around to come back to the house.

"Young man," came a call from the saggled-toothed mouth.

Hap walked out to the buggy.

"All I got to give you for the help is my thanks, bein' I got no money. But I got this other thing, been savin' it for the right person. Figger that person must be you. Reach around here back'a me, and get that box."

"Mister, you don't…"

"I know that, but you're the right person to have it. I'm sure of it. Lift it on up there. I'd help, but my old arms… There, Son, slide it on over. I figger you and your bride might like lookin' at that, and time might come it'd mean somethin' to you. Be careful and keep it from bumps till it's opened. Wouldn't want it to break."

"Well, thanks… Mister."

"Don't mention it. God bless you."

Kathleen left the porch and joined her stunned husband who stood holding a box made of rough wood, about 3 1/2 feet by 4 1/2 feet, and only 8 inches thick. It was a bit heavy, as well.

"What ya got?"

"I don't know. Right now I'm tryin to figure where this was. There weren't enough room in the back'a that buggy for it. You can look at and see, it's too big for the space that was in that little old buggy."

Kathleen nodded, soberly. She, herself, had looked around, nosily, when she had loaded the lunch basket, and if the box had been there, she would surely have seen it. It was now twelve o'clock.

Taking the box to his workshed, Hap carefully lifted the shiny new nails and pulled the boards apart. Inside was a window... heavy glass... made of several glowing colors. He carefully lifted it from the box and held it up to the light. The Kentucky sun shone its light through the prisms of colored glass and created a picture of a baby lying in a manger. Each new color of glass was piped in a thin casing of lead. A lot of work went into making this picture.

Splinters of golden glass created the hay in the manger, and a silver halo crowned the baby. Far away into the blue sky, tiny angels of white glass filled the heaven. A slight movement of the window, and the angels seemed to move. The rough stones of the stable were each a different shade of brown or gray, and the white covering over the baby seemed to have sparkles captured within the glass.

It was just too beautiful for words, and they stared at it, until seven minutes after twelve.

Hap tilted his head to view the picture from a different angle. "This here's purty enough to go in the parlor... when we get one."

Kathleen was silent.

"Don't you think so, Lena?"

"Hap, don't you think this here picture's big enough?"

"About three feet by four feet, I'd say. How big ought it to be?"

"You ain't thinkin', Hap. It come to us before twelve o'clock, and it didn't come from nowhere in that buggy."

"But..."

"I know. You ain't a'wantin' to think on it, but that don't keep it from bein' right there in front'a you. It'd seem to me, we're fixin' to change our plans."

Hapgood Palmer gently placed the beautiful picture back into the box that was obviously made for it and pressed the boards back in place. Twitchy itches played along his arms and neck. Turning, he scooped his arm around his wife's somewhat expanded waist and led her to the kitchen of their two-roomed cabin.

Without a word, she pulled the kettle over the fire to brew a batch of tea. It would be ginger and hibiscus flowers in a background of raspberry leaves and a pinch of oregano. Zinger Tea. They would certainly need its slight bracing effect.

Kathleen was first to speak. "What now?"

"I haven't settled on a thought, but the first thing'd be to go down and get pa's study books. Seems I'll be puttin' in the winter a'studyin'."

"And practicin'."

"Now, honey, you know we can't get down that mountain in bad weather."

"Don't have to. Me'n the baby'll be your congregation. I've listened to sermons all my life, chances are I could even be a help to you, here and there. Leastwise I'd be interested. You'll not do much better'n that."

The colored tea flakes steeped in the hot water, releasing their flavor. The steaming liquid swirled around in the cups, pink from the flowers and spicy from the ginger. Kathleen added a spoonful of sugar to each cup, stirred briskly, and slid one across the table to her husband. It was time for serious thought.

She began. "I just thought on somethin' bout that picture."

"What was that?"

"It ain't no picture. It's a window. It ain't made for havin' the wallpaper showin' through it. It's got'a have outside light to show up the colors. As many pictures of church buildings as I've looked at, I should'a knowd it from the start."

"It's a window...?"

"Yeah, it's a stained glass window. Next thing is, what do we do with it?"

Dimpled chin in hand and elbows on the table, Kathleen stared into the dregs and leaves of her tea.

Beside his wife, the young Kentucky farmer slouched in dejection in the solid and attractive chair he had made with his own hand and tools. His arms hung from his sides, and his eyes drooped, staring at nothing. It seemed there would be a turn in the road where he had mapped... and the Zinger tea was sipped in thoughtful silence.

- END OF EXCERPT -

ADDITIONAL BOOK SERIES BY JOANN KLUSMEYER

The Great I Am Bible Story Series for Kids
6 books

The Young Pioneers Adventure Series for Kids
5 books

The Wentworth Triplets Mystery Series for Young Teens
3 books

Footsteps in the Canyon Adventure Series for Young Teens
4 books

Burnt Tree Junction Historical Fiction Series for Adults
6 books

Ozark Mountains Historical Fiction Series for Adults
7 books

Taming the Wilderness Historical Fiction Series for Adults
4 books

The Sheltering Stones Historical Fiction Series for Adults
5 books

The Trilogy of Wishbone Hollow Historicial Fiction Series for Adults
3 books